COME TO GRIEF

Dick Francis was one of the most successful post-war National hunt jockeys. The winner of over 350 races, he was champion jockey in 1953/1954 and rode for HM Queen Elizabeth, the Queen Mother, most famously on Devon Loch in the 1956 Grand National. On his retirement from the saddle, he published his autobiography, *The Sport of Queens*, before going on to write forty-three bestselling novels, a volume of short stories (*Field of 13*), and the biography of Lester Piggott.

During his lifetime Dick Francis received many awards, amongst them the prestigious Crime Writers' Association's Cartier Diamond Dagger for his outstanding contribution to the genre, and three 'best novel' Edgar Allan Poe awards from The Mystery Writers of America. In 1996 he was named by them as Grand Master for a lifetime's achievement. In 1998 he was elected a fellow of the Royal Society of Literature, and was awarded a CBE in the Queen's Birthday Honours List of 2000.

Dick Francis died in February 2010, at the age of eighty-nine, but he remains one of the greatest thriller writers of all time.

Books by Dick Francis

THE SPORT OF QUEENS
(autobiography)

DEAD CERT
NERVE
FOR KICKS
ODDS AGAINST
FLYING FINISH
BLOOD SPORT
FORFEIT
ENQUIRY
RAT RACE
BONECRACK
SMOKESCREEN
SLAY-RIDE
KNOCK DOWN
HIGH STAKES
IN THE FRAME
RISK
TRIAL RUN
WHIP HAND
REFLEX
TWICE SHY
BANKER
THE DANGER
PROOF
BREAK IN

LESTER:
The Official Biography

BOLT
HOT MONEY
THE EDGE
STRAIGHT
LONGSHOT
COMEBACK
DRIVING FORCE
DECIDER
WILD HORSES
COME TO GRIEF
TO THE HILT
10-lb PENALTY
FIELD OF 13
SECOND WIND
SHATTERED
UNDER ORDERS

Books by Dick Francis
and Felix Francis

DEAD HEAT
SILKS
EVEN MONEY
CROSSFIRE

Dick Francis Novels
by Felix Francis

GAMBLE
BLOODLINE
REFUSAL

COME TO GRIEF

Dick Francis

PENGUIN BOOKS

PENGUIN BOOKS

Published by the Penguin Group
Penguin Books Ltd, 80 Strand, London WC2R 0RL, England
Penguin Group (USA) Inc., 375 Hudson Street, New York, New York 10014, USA
Penguin Group (Canada), 90 Eglinton Avenue East, Suite 700, Toronto, Ontario, Canada M4P 2Y3
(a division of Pearson Penguin Canada Inc.)
Penguin Ireland, 25 St Stephen's Green, Dublin 2, Ireland (a division of Penguin Books Ltd)
Penguin Group (Australia), 707 Collins Street, Melbourne, Victoria 3008, Australia
(a division of Pearson Australia Group Pty Ltd)
Penguin Books India Pvt Ltd, 11 Community Centre, Panchsheel Park, New Delhi – 110 017, India
Penguin Group (NZ), 67 Apollo Drive, Rosedale, Auckland 0632, New Zealand
(a division of Pearson New Zealand Ltd)
Penguin Books (South Africa) (Pty) Ltd, Block D, Rosebank Office Park,
181 Jan Smuts Avenue, Parktown North, Gauteng 2193, South Africa

Penguin Books Ltd, Registered Offices: 80 Strand, London WC2R 0RL, England

www.penguin.com

First published by Michael Joseph Ltd 1995
Reissued in Penguin Books 2013
002

ISBN: 978–1–405–93843–3

www.greenpenguin.co.uk

Penguin Books is committed to a sustainable
future for our business, our readers and our planet.
This book is made from Forest Stewardship
Council™ certified paper.

In November 1994, as part of the BBC's Children in Need Appeal, Radio 2 gave an auction of opportunities 'that money can't buy'. One of the lots was 'To have one's name used as a character in Dick Francis's next book'.

The lot was secured by Mrs Patricia Huxford. It has given Dick Francis great pleasure to include her in *Come to Grief*.

CHAPTER ONE

I had this friend, you see, that everyone loved.

(My name is Sid Halley.)

I had this friend that everyone loved, and I put him in the dock.

The trouble with working as an investigator, as I had been doing for approaching five years, was that occasionally one turned up facts that surprised and appalled and smashed peaceful lives for ever.

It had taken days of inner distress for me to decide to act on what I'd learned. Miserably, by then, I'd suffered through disbelief, through denial, through anger and at length through acceptance; all the stages of grief. I grieved for the man I'd known. For the man I *thought* I'd known, who had all along been a façade. I grieved for the loss of a friendship, for a man who still looked the same but was different, alien . . . despicable. I could much more easily have grieved for him dead.

The turmoil I'd felt in private had on public disclosure become universal. The press, jumping instinctively and strongly to his defence, had given me, as his accuser, a severely rough time. On racecourses, where I chiefly worked, long-time acquaintances had turned their backs. Love, support and comfort poured out towards my friend. Disbelief and denial and anger prevailed: acceptance lay a long way ahead. Meanwhile I, not he, was seen as the target for hatred. It would pass, I knew. One had simply to endure it, and wait.

On the morning set for the opening of his trial, my friend's mother killed herself.

The news was brought to the law courts in Reading, in Berkshire, where the presiding judge, gowned, had already heard the opening statements and where I, a witness for the prosecution, waited alone in a soulless side-room to be called. One of the court officials came to give me the suicide information and to say that the judge had adjourned the proceedings for the day, and I could go home.

'Poor woman,' I exclaimed, truly horrified.

Even though he was supposed to be impartial, the official's own sympathies were still with the accused. He eyed me without favour and said I should return the following morning, ten o'clock sharp.

I left the room and walked slowly along the corridor towards the exit, fielded on the way by a senior lawyer who took me by the elbow and drew me aside.

'His mother took a room in a hotel and jumped from the sixteenth floor,' he said without preamble. 'She left a note saying she couldn't bear the future. What are your thoughts?'

I looked at the dark, intelligent, eyes of Davis Tatum, a clumsy fat man with a lean agile brain.

'You know better than I do,' I said.

'*Sid!*' A touch of exasperation. 'Tell me your thoughts.'

'Perhaps he'll change his plea.'

He relaxed and half smiled. 'You're in the wrong job.'

I wryly shook my head. 'I catch the fish. You guys gut them.'

He amiably let go of my arm and I continued to the outside world to catch a train for the thirty-minute ride to the terminus in London, flagging down a taxi for the last mile or so home.

Ginnie Quint, I thought, travelling through London. Poor, poor Ginnie Quint, choosing death in preference to the everlasting agony of her son's disgrace. A lonely slamming exit. An end to tears. An end to grief.

The taxi stopped outside the house in Pont Square (off Cadogan Square), where I currently lived on the first floor, with a balcony overlooking the central leafy railed garden. As usual, the small secluded square was quiet, with little passing traffic and only a few people on foot. A thin early October wind shook the dying leaves on the lime trees, floating a few of them sporadically to the ground like soft yellow snowflakes.

I climbed out of the cab and paid the driver through his open window, and, as I turned to cross the pavement and go up the few steps to the front door, a man who

3

was apparently quietly walking past suddenly sprang at me in fury, raising a long black metal rod with which he tried to brain me.

I sensed rather than saw the first wicked slash and moved enough to catch the weight of it on my shoulder, not my head. He was screaming at me, half demented, and I fielded a second brutal blow on a raised defensive forearm. After that I seized his wrist in a pincer grip and rolled the bulk of his body backward over the leg I pushed out rigidly behind his knees, and felled him, sprawling, iron bar and all, onto the hard ground. He yelled bitter words; cursing, half incoherent, threatening to kill.

The taxi still stood there, diesel engine running, the driver staring wide-mouthed and speechless, a state of affairs that continued while I yanked open the black rear door and stumbled in again onto the seat. My heart thudded. Well, it would.

'*Drive*,' I said urgently. 'Drive on.'

'But . . .'

'Just drive. Go *on*. Before he finds his feet and breaks your windows.'

The driver closed his mouth fast and meshed his gears, and wavered at something above running pace along the road.

'Look,' he said, protesting, half turning his head back to me, 'I didn't see nothing. You're my last fare today, I've been on the go eight hours and I'm on my way home.'

'Just drive,' I said. Too little breath. Too many jumbled feelings.

'Well . . . but, drive where *to*?'

Good question. Think.

'He didn't look like no mugger,' the taxi driver observed aggrievedly. 'But you never can tell these days. D'you want me to drop you off at the police? He hit you something shocking. You could *hear* it. Like he broke your arm.'

'Just drive, would you?'

The driver was large, fiftyish and a Londoner, but no John Bull, and I could see from his head movements and his repeated spiky glances at me in his rear-view mirror that he didn't want to get involved in my problems and couldn't wait for me to leave his cab.

Pulse eventually steadying, I could think of only one place to go. My only haven, in many past troubles.

'Paddington,' I said. 'Please.'

'St Mary's, d'you mean? The hospital?'

'No. The trains.'

'But you've just come from there!' he protested.

'Yes, but please go back.'

Cheering a little he rocked round in a U-turn and set off for the return to Paddington Station where he assured me again that he hadn't seen nothing, nor heard nothing neither, and he wasn't going to get involved, did I see?

I simply paid him and let him go, and if I memorised

5

his cab-licensing number it was out of habit, not expectation.

As part of normal equipment I wore a mobile phone on my belt and, walking slowly into the high airy terminus, I pressed the buttons to reach the man I trusted most in the world, my ex-wife's father, Rear Admiral Charles Roland, Royal Navy, retired, and to my distinct relief he answered at the second ring.

'Charles,' I said. My voice cracked a bit, which I hadn't meant.

A pause, then, 'Is that you, Sid?'

'May I . . . visit?'

'Of course. Where are you?'

'Paddington. I'll come by train and taxi.'

He said calmly, 'Use the side-door. It's not locked,' and put down his receiver.

I smiled, reassured as ever by his steadiness and his brevity with words. An unemotional, undemonstrative man, not paternal towards me and very far from indulgent, he gave me nevertheless a consciousness that he cared considerably about what happened to me and would proffer rocklike support if I needed it. Like I needed it at that moment, for several variously dire reasons.

Trains to Oxford being less frequent in the middle of the day, it was four in the afternoon by the time the country taxi, leaving Oxford well behind, arrived at Charles's vast old house at Aynsford and decanted me at the side-door. I paid the driver clumsily owing to stiffening bruises, and walked with relief into the pile I really thought of as home, the one unchanging constant in a life that had tossed me about, rather, now and then.

Charles sat, as often, in the large leather armchair that I found too hard for comfort but that he, in his uncompromising way, felt appropriate to accommodate his narrow rump. I had sometime in the past moved one of the softer but still fairly formal old gold brocade armchairs from the drawing-room into the smaller room, his 'wardroom', as it was there we always sat when the two of us were alone. It was there that he kept his desk, his collection of flies for fishing, his nautical books, his racks of priceless old orchestral recordings and the gleaming marble and steel wonder of a custom-built, frictionless turntable on which he played them. It was there on the dark green walls that he'd hung large photographs of the ships he'd commanded, and smaller photos of shipmates, and there, also, that he'd lately positioned a painting of me as a jockey riding over a fence at Cheltenham racecourse, a picture that summed up every ounce of vigour needed for race-riding, and which had hung for years less conspicuously in the dining-room.

He had had a strip of lighting positioned along the top of the heavy gold frame, and when I got there that evening, it was lit.

He was reading. He put his book face down on his lap when I walked in, and gave me a bland noncommittal

7

inspection. There was nothing, as usual, to be read in his eyes: I could often see quite clearly into other people's minds, but seldom his.

'Hullo,' I said.

I could hear him take a breath and trickle it out through his nose. He spent all of five seconds looking me over, then pointed to the tray of bottles and glasses which stood on the table below my picture.

'Drink,' he said briefly. An order, not invitation.

'It's only four o'clock.'

'Immaterial. What have you eaten today?'

I didn't say anything, which he took to be answer enough.

'Nothing,' he said, nodding. 'I thought so. You look thin. It's this *bloody* case. I thought you were supposed to be in court today.'

'It was adjourned until tomorrow.'

'Get a drink.'

I walked obediently over to the table and looked assessingly at the bottles. In his old-fashioned way he kept brandy and sherry in decanters. Scotch – Famous Grouse, his favourite – remained in the screw-topped bottle. I would have to have Scotch, I thought, and doubted if I could pour even that.

I glanced upwards at my picture. In those days, six years ago, I'd had two hands. In those days I'd been British steeplechasing's champion jockey: whole, healthy and, I dared say, fanatical. A nightmare fall had resulted in a horse's sharp hoof half ripping off my

8

left hand: the end of one career and the birth, if you could call it that, of another. Slow lingering birth of a detective, while I spent two years pining for what I'd lost and drifted rudderless like a wreck that didn't quite sink but was unseaworthy, all the same. I was ashamed of those two years. At the end of them a ruthless villain had smashed beyond mending the remains of the useless hand and had galvanised me into a resurrection of the spirit and the impetus to seek what I'd had since, a myoelectric false hand that worked on nerve impulses from my truncated forearm and looked and behaved so realistically that people often didn't notice its existence.

My present problem was that I couldn't move its thumb far enough from its fingers to grasp the large heavy cut-glass brandy decanter, and my right hand wasn't working too well either. Rather than drop alcohol all over Charles's Persian rug, I gave up and sat in the gold armchair.

'What's the matter?' Charles asked abruptly. 'Why did you come? Why don't you pour a drink?'

After a moment I said dully, knowing it would hurt him, 'Ginnie Quint killed herself.'

'*What?*'

'This morning,' I said. 'She jumped from sixteen floors up.'

His fine-boned face went stiff and immediately looked much older. The bland eyes darkened, as if retreating into their sockets. Charles had known Ginnie

Quint for thirty or more years, and had been fond of her and had been a guest in her house often.

Powerful memories lived in my mind also. Memories of a friendly, rounded, motherly woman happy in her role as a big-house wife, inoffensively rich, working genuinely and generously for several charities and laughingly glowing in reflected glory from her famous, good-looking successful only child, the one that everyone loved.

Her son, Ellis, that I had put in the dock.

The last time I'd seen Ginnie she'd glared at me with incredulous contempt, demanding to know how I could *possibly* seek to destroy the golden Ellis, who counted me his friend, who liked me, who'd done me favours, who would have trusted me with his life.

I'd let her molten rage pour over me, offering no defence. I knew exactly how she felt. Disbelief and denial and anger ... The idea of what he'd done was so sickening to her that she rejected the guilt possibility absolutely, as almost everyone else had done, though in her case with anguish.

Most people believed I had got it all wrong, and had ruined *myself*, not Ellis. Even Charles, at first, had said doubtfully, 'Sid, are you *sure*?'

I'd said I was certain. I'd hoped desperately for a way out ... for *any* way out ... as I knew what I'd be pulling down on myself if I went ahead. And it had been at least as bad as I'd feared, and in many ways worse. After the first bombshell solution – a proposed solution – to a crime that had had half the country baying for blood (but not *Ellis*'s blood, no *no*, it was *unthinkable*), there had been the first court appearance, the remand into custody (a *scandal*, he should of *course* be let out immediately on bail), and after that there had fallen a sudden press silence, while the *sub judice* law came into effect.

Under British *sub judice* law, no evidence might be publicly discussed between the remand and the trial. Much investigation and strategic trial planning could go on behind the scenes, but neither potential jurors nor John Smith in the street was allowed to know details. Uninformed, public opinion had consequently stuck at the 'Ellis is innocent' stage, and I'd had nearly three months, now, of obloquy.

Ellis, you see, was a Young Lochinvar, in spades. Ellis Quint, once champion amateur jump jockey, had flashed onto television screens like a comet, a brilliant, laughing, able, funny performer, the draw for millions on sports quiz programmes, the ultimate chat-show host, the model held up to children, the glittering star that regularly raised the nation's happiness level, to whom everyone, from tiara to baseball cap worn backwards, responded.

Manufacturers fell over themselves to tempt him to endorse their products, and half the kids in England strode about with machismo in glamorised jockey-type riding boots over their jeans. And it was this man, this *paragon* that I sought to eradicate.

11

No one seemed to blame the tabloid columnist who'd written, 'The once-revered Sid Halley, green with envy, tries to tear down a talent he hasn't a prayer of matching . . .' There had been inches about 'A spiteful little man trying to compensate for his own inadequacies.' I hadn't shown any of it to Charles, but others had.

The telephone at my waist buzzed suddenly, and I answered its summons.

'Sid . . . Sid . . .'

The woman on the other end was crying. I'd heard her crying often.

'Are you at home?' I asked.

'No . . . In the hospital.'

'Tell me the number and I'll phone straight back.'

I heard murmuring in the background; then another voice came on, efficient, controlled, reading out a number, repeating it slowly. I tapped the digits onto my mobile so that they appeared on the small display screen.

'Right,' I said, reading the number back. 'Put down your receiver.' To Charles I said, 'May I use your phone?'

He waved a hand permissively towards his desk, and I pressed the buttons on his phone to get back to where I'd been.

The efficient voice answered immediately.

'Is Mrs Ferns still there?' I said. 'It's Sid Halley.'

'Hang on.'

Linda Ferns was trying not to cry. 'Sid . . . Rachel's worse. She's asking for you. Can you come? Please.'

'How bad is she?'

'Her temperature keeps going up.' A sob stopped her. 'Talk to Sister Grant.'

I talked to the efficient voice, Sister Grant. 'How bad is Rachel?'

'She's asking for you all the time,' she said. 'How soon can you come?'

'Tomorrow.'

'Can you come this evening?'

I said, 'Is it that bad?'

I listened to a moment of silence, in which she couldn't say what she meant because Linda was beside her.

'Come this evening,' she repeated.

This evening. Dear God. Nine-year-old Rachel Ferns lay in a hospital in Kent a hundred and fifty miles away. Ill to death, this time, it sounded like.

'Promise her,' I said, 'that I'll come tomorrow.' I explained where I was. 'I have to be in court tomorrow morning, in Reading, but I'll come to see Rachel as soon as I get out. Promise her. Tell her I'm going to be there. Tell her I'll bring six wigs and an angel fish.'

The efficient voice said, 'I'll tell her,' and then added, 'Is it true that Ellis Quint's mother has killed herself? Mrs Ferns says someone heard it on the radio news and repeated it to her. She wants to know if it's true.'

'It's true.'

'Come as soon as you can,' the nurse said, and disconnected.

I put down the receiver. Charles said, 'The child?'

'It sounds as if she's dying.'

'You knew it was inevitable.'

'It doesn't make it any easier for the parents.' I sat down again slowly in the gold armchair. 'I would go tonight if it would save her life, but I . . .' I stopped, not knowing what to say, how to explain that I wouldn't go. Couldn't go. Not except to save her life, which no one could do however much they ached to.

Charles said briefly, 'You've only just got here.'

'Yeah.'

'And what else is there, that you haven't told me?'

I looked at him.

'I know you too well, Sid,' he said. 'You didn't come all this way just because of Ginnie. You could have told me about her on the telephone.' He paused. 'From the look of you, you came for the oldest of reasons.' He paused again, but I didn't say anything. 'For sanctuary,' he said.

I shifted in the chair. 'Am I so transparent?'

'Sanctuary from what?' he asked. 'What is so sudden . . . and urgent?'

I sighed. I said with as little heat as possible, 'Gordon Quint tried to kill me.'

Gordon Quint was Ginnie's husband. Ellis was their son.

14

It struck Charles silent, open mouthed: and it took a great deal to do that.

After a while I said, 'When they adjourned the trial I went home by train and taxi. Gordon Quint was waiting there in Pont Square for me. God knows how long he'd been there, how long he would have waited, but anyway, he was there, with an iron bar.' I swallowed. 'He aimed it at my head, but I sort of ducked, and it hit my shoulder. He tried again... Well, this mechanical hand has its uses. I closed it on his wrist and put into practice some of the judo I've spent so many hours learning, and I tumbled him onto his back... and he was screaming at me all the time that I'd killed Ginnie... I'd killed her.'

'*Sid.*'

'He was half mad... raving, really... He said I'd destroyed his whole family. I'd destroyed all their lives... he swore I would die for it... that he would get me... get me... I don't think he knew what he was saying, it just poured out of him.'

Charles said dazedly, 'So what did you do?'

'The taxi driver was still there, looking stunned, so... er... I got back into the taxi.'

'You got back...? But... what about Gordon?'

'I left him there. Lying on the pavement. Screaming revenge... starting to stand up... waving the iron bar. I... er... I don't think I'll go home tonight, if I can stay here.'

Charles said faintly, 'Of course you can stay. It's

15

taken for granted. You told me once that this was your home.'

'Yeah.'

'Then believe it.'

I did believe it, or I wouldn't have gone there. Charles and his certainties had in the past saved me from inner disintegration, and my reliance on him had oddly been strengthened, not evaporated, by the collapse of my marriage to his daughter Jenny, and our divorce.

Aynsford offered respite. I would go back soon enough to defuse Gordon Quint; I would swear an oath in court and tear a man to shreds; I would hug Linda Ferns and, if I were in time, make Rachel laugh; but for this one night I would sleep soundly in Charles's house in my own accustomed room – and let the dry well of mental stamina refill.

Charles said, 'Did Gordon . . . er . . . hurt you, with his bar?'

'A bruise or two.'

'I know your sort of bruises.'

I sighed again. 'I think . . . um . . . he's cracked a bone. In my arm.'

His gaze flew instantly to the left arm, the plastic job.

'No,' I said, 'the other one.'

Aghast, he said, 'Your *right* arm?'

'Well, yeah. But only the ulna, which goes from the little finger side of the wrist up to the elbow. Not

16

the radius as well, luckily. The radius will act as a natural splint.'

'But *Sid* . . .'

'Better than my skull. I had the choice.'

'How can you *laugh* about it?'

'A bloody bore, isn't it?' I smiled without stress. 'Don't *worry* so, Charles. It'll heal. I broke the same bone worse once before, when I was racing.'

'But you had two hands then.'

'Yes, so I did. So would you mind picking up that damned heavy brandy decanter and sloshing half a pint of anaesthetic into a glass?'

Wordlessly he got to his feet and complied. I thanked him. He nodded. End of transaction.

When he was again sitting down, he said, 'So the taxi driver was a witness.'

'The taxi driver is a "don't-get-involved" man.'

'But if he *saw* . . . He must have heard . . .'

'Blind and deaf, he insisted he was.' I drank fiery neat liquid gratefully. 'Anyway, that suits me fine.'

'But, Sid . . .'

'Look,' I said reasonably, 'what would you have me do? Complain? Prosecute? Gordon Quint is normally a level-headed worthy sixty-ish citizen. He's not your average murderer, Besides, he's your own personal long-time friend, and I, too, have eaten in his house. But he already hates me for attacking Ellis, the light of his life, and he'd not long learned that Ginnie, his adored wife, had killed herself because she couldn't bear what lies ahead. So how do you think Gordon feels?' I paused. 'I'm just glad he didn't succeed in smashing my brains in. And, if you can believe it, I'm almost as glad for *his* sake that he didn't, as for my own.'

Charles shook his head resignedly.

'Grief can be dangerous,' I said.

He couldn't dispute it. Deadly revenge was as old as time.

We sat companionably in silence. I drank brandy and felt marginally saner. Knots of tension relaxed in my stomach. I made various resolutions to give up chasing the deadlier crooks – but I'd made resolutions like that before, and hadn't kept them.

I'd stopped asking myself why I did it. There were hundreds of other ways of passing the time and earning one's keep. Other ex-jockeys became trainers or commentators or worked in racing in official capacities and only I, it seemed, felt impelled to swim round the hidden fringes, attempting to sort out doubts and worries for people who for any reason didn't want to bother the police or the racing authorities.

There was a need for me and what I could do, or I would have sat around idle, twiddling my thumbs. Instead, even in the present general climate of ostracism, I had more offers of work than I could accept.

Most jobs took me less than a week, particularly those that involved looking into someone's credit and credibility rating: bookmakers asked me to do that frequently, before taking on new account customers, and trainers paid me fees to assure them that if they bought expensive two-year-olds for new owners at the Sales, they wouldn't be left with broken promises and a mountain of debt. I'd checked on all sorts of proposed business plans and saved a lot of people from confidence tricksters, and I'd uncovered absconding debtors, and thieves of all sorts, and had proved a confounded nuisance to imaginative felons.

People had sobbed on my shoulders from joy and deliverance: others had threatened and battered to make me quit: Linda Ferns would hug me and Gordon Quint hate me; and I also had two more investigations in hand that I'd spent too little time on. So why didn't I give it up and change to a life of quiet safe financial management, which I wasn't bad at either? I felt the effects of the iron bar from neck to fingers ... and didn't know the answer.

The mobile phone on my belt buzzed and I answered it as before, finding on the line the senior lawyer I'd talked to in the corridor in the law courts.

'Sid, this is Davis Tatum. I've news for you,' he said.

'Give me your number and I'll call you back.'

'Oh? Oh, OK.' He read off his number, which I copied as before, and also as before I borrowed Charles's phone on the desk to get back to square one.

'Sid,' said Tatum, coming as usual straight to the point, 'Ellis Quint is changing his plea from not guilty to guilty by reason of diminished responsibility. It

19

seems his mother's powerful statement of no confidence in his innocence has had a laxative effect on the bowels of the counsel for the defence.'

'Jeez,' I said.

Tatum chuckled. I imagined his double chin wobbling. He said, 'The trial will now be adjourned for a week to allow expert psychiatric witnesses to be briefed. In other words, you don't have to turn up tomorrow.'

'Good.'

'But I hope you will.'

'How do you mean?'

'There's a job for you.'

'What sort of job?'

'Investigating, of course. What else? I'd like to meet you somewhere privately.'

'All right,' I said, 'but sometime tomorrow I have to go to Kent to see the child, Rachel Ferns. She's back in hospital and it doesn't sound good.'

'Hell.'

'Yeah.'

'Where are you?' he asked. 'The Press are looking for you.'

'They can wait a day.'

'I told the people from *The Pump* that after the mauling they've given you they haven't a prayer of you talking to them.'

'I appreciate that,' I said, smiling.

He chuckled. 'About tomorrow . . .'

'I'll go to Kent in the morning,' I said. 'I don't know how long I'll stay, it depends on Rachel. How about five o'clock in London? Would that do you? The end of your business day.'

'Right. Where? Not in my office. How about your place? No, perhaps not, if *The Pump*'s after you.'

'How about, say, the bar leading to the second-floor restaurant of the Le Meridien Hotel in Piccadilly?'

'I don't know it.'

'All the better.'

'If I need to change it,' he said, 'can I still get you on your mobile phone?'

'Always.'

'Good. See you tomorrow.'

I replaced Charles's receiver and sat on the gold armchair as before. Charles looked at the mobile instrument I'd lain this time on the table beside my glass and asked the obvious question.

'Why do you ring them back? Why don't you just talk?'

'Well,' I said, 'someone is listening to this gadget.'

'*Listening?*'

I explained about the insecurity of open radio transmission, that allowed anyone clever and expert to hear what they shouldn't.

Charles said, 'How do you know someone's listening to you?'

'A lot of small things people have recently learned that I haven't told them.'

'Who is it?'

'I don't actually know. Someone has also accessed my computer over the phone lines. I don't know who did that, either. It's disgustingly easy nowadays – but again, only if you're expert – to suss out people's private passwords and read their secret files.'

He said with slight impatience, 'Computers are beyond me.'

'I've had to learn,' I said, grinning briefly. 'A bit different from scudding over hurdles at Plumpton on a wet day.'

'Everything you do astounds me.'

'I wish I was still racing.'

'Yes, I know. But if you were, you'd anyway be coming to the end of it soon, wouldn't you? How old are you now? Thirty-four?'

I nodded. Thirty-five loomed.

'Not many top jump jockeys go on much after that.'

'You put things so delightfully bluntly, Charles.'

'You're of more use to more people the way you are.'

Charles tended to give me pep talks when he thought I needed them. I could never work out how he knew. He'd said something once about my looking like a brick wall: that when I shut out the world and retreated into myself, things were bad. Maybe he was right. Retreat inwards meant for me not retreating outwardly, and I supposed I'd learned the technique almost from birth.

Jenny, my loved and lost wife, had said she couldn't

live with it. She'd wanted me to give up race-riding and become a softer shelled person, and when I wouldn't – or couldn't – we had shaken acridly apart. She had recently remarried, and this time she'd tied herself not to a thin dark-haired risk-taking bundle of complexes, but to a man to fit her needs, a safe, greying, sweet-natured uncomplicated fellow with a knighthood. Jenny, the warring unhappy Mrs Halley, was now serenely Lady Wingham. A photograph of her with her handsome beaming Sir Anthony stood in a silver frame next to the telephone on Charles's desk.

'How's Jenny?' I asked politely.

'Fine,' Charles answered without expression.

'Good.'

'He's a bore, after you,' Charles observed.

'You can't say such things.'

'I can say what I bloody well like in my own house.'

In harmony and mutual regard we passed a peaceful evening, disturbed only by five more calls on my mobile phone, all demanding to know, with varying degrees of peremptoriness, where they could find Sid Halley.

I said each time, 'This is an answering service. Leave your number and we'll pass on your message.'

All of the callers, it seemed, worked for newspapers, a fact that particularly left me frowning.

'I don't know where they all got this number from,' I told Charles. 'It's not in any directory. I give it only to people I'm working for, so they can reach me day or night, and only to others whose calls I wouldn't want to miss. I tell them it's a private line for their use only. I don't hand this number out on printed cards, and I don't have it on my writing paper. Quite often I re-route calls to this phone from my phone in the flat, but I didn't today because of Gordon Quint bashing away outside and preventing me from going in. So how do half the newspapers in London know it?'

'How will you find out?' Charles asked.

'Um ... engage Sid Halley to look into it, I dare say'.

Charles laughed. I felt uneasy, all the same. Someone had been listening on that number, and now someone had broadcast it. It wasn't that my phone conversations were excessively secret – and I'd started the semi-exclusive number anyway solely so that the machine didn't buzz unnecessarily at awkward moments – but now I had a sense that someone was deliberately crowding me. Tapping into my computer – which wouldn't get anyone far, as I knew a lot of defences. Assaulting me electronically. *Stalking*.

Enough was enough. Five newspapers were too much. Sid Halley, as I'd said, would have to investigate his own case.

Charles's long-time live-in housekeeper, Mrs Cross, all dimples and delight, cooked us a simple supper and fussed over me comfortably like a hen. I guiltily found her a bit smothering sometimes, but always sent her a card for her birthday.

I went to bed early and found that, as usual, Mrs

Cross had left warm welcoming lights on in my room and had put out fresh pyjamas and fluffy towels.

A pity the day's troubles couldn't be as easily cosseted into oblivion.

I undressed and brushed my teeth and eased off the artificial hand. My left arm ended uselessly four inches below the elbow; a familiar punctuation, but still a sort of bereavement.

My right arm now twinged violently at every use.

Damn the lot, I thought.

CHAPTER TWO

The morning brought little improvement.

I sometimes used a private chauffeur-driven car hire firm based in London to ferry around people and things I wanted to keep away from prying eyes and, consequently, waking to a couple of faulty arms, I telephoned from Charles's secure number and talked to my friends at TeleDrive.

'Bob?' I said. 'I need to get from north-west of Oxford to Kent, Canterbury. There'll be a couple of short stops on the journey. And, sometime this afternoon, a return to London. Can anyone do it at such short notice?'

'Give me the address,' he said briefly. 'We're on our way.'

I breakfasted with Charles. That is to say, we sat in the dining-room where Mrs Cross, in her old-fashioned way, had set out toast, coffee and cereals and a warming dish of scrambled eggs.

Charles thought mornings hadn't begun without scrambled eggs. He ate his on toast and eyed me drinking coffee left-handedly. From long acquaintance with my preference for no fuss, he made no comment on the consequences of iron bars.

He was reading a broad-sheet newspaper which, as he showed me, was making a good-taste meal of Ginnie Quint's death. Her pleasant, smiling face inappropriately spread across two columns. I shut out of my mind any image of what she might look like sixteen floors down.

Charles said, reading aloud, ' "Friends say she appeared depressed about her son's forthcoming trial. Her husband, Gordon, was unavailable for comment." In other words, the Press couldn't find him.'

Ordeal by newsprint, I thought; the latter-day torture.

'Seriously, Sid,' Charles said in his most calm civilised voice, 'was Gordon's rage at you transient or . . . er . . . obsessive?'

'Seriously,' I echoed him, 'I don't know.' I sighed. 'I should think it's too soon to tell. Gordon himself probably doesn't know.'

'Do take care, Sid.'

'Sure.' I sorted through the flurry of impressions I'd gathered in the brief seconds of violence in Pont Square. 'I don't know where Ginnie was when she jumped,' I said, 'but I don't think Gordon was with her. I mean, when he leaped at me he was wearing country clothes. Work-day clothes: mud on his boots, corduroy trousers, old tweed jacket, open-necked blue shirt. He

27

hadn't been staying in any sixteen-storey hotel. And the metal bar he hit me with . . . it wasn't a smooth rod, it was a five-foot piece of angle iron, the sort you thread wire through or fencing. I saw the holes in it.'

Charles stared.

I said, 'I'd say he was at home in Berkshire when he was told about Ginnie. I think if I'd loitered around to search, I would have found Gordon's Land-Rover parked near Pont Square.'

Gordon Quint, though a landowner, was a hands-on custodian of his multiple acres. He drove tractors, scythed weeds to clear streams, worked alongside his men to repair his boundaries, re-fence his sheep fields and thin out his woodlands, enjoying both the physical labour and the satisfaction of a job most competently done.

I knew him also as self-admiring and as expecting – and receiving – deference from everyone, including Ginnie. It pleased him to be a generous host while leaving his guests in no doubt of his superior worth.

The man I'd seen in Pont Square, all 'squire' manner stripped away, had been a raw, hurt, *outraged* and oddly more genuine person than the Gordon I'd known before: but until I learned for sure which way the explosively tossed-up bricks of his nature would come down, I would keep away from fencing posts and any other agricultural hardware he might be travelling with.

I told Charles I'd engaged TeleDrive to come and pick me up. To his raised eyebrows I explained I would

28

put the cost against expenses. Whose expenses? General running expenses, I said.

'Is Mrs Ferns paying you?' Charles neutrally asked.

'Not any more.'

'Who is, exactly?' He liked me to make a profit. I did, but he seldom believed it.

'I don't starve,' I said, drinking my coffee. 'Have you ever tried three or four eggs whipped up in mushroom soup? Instant mushroom omelette, not at all bad.'

'Disgusting,' Charles said.

'You get a different perspective, living alone.'

'You need a new wife,' Charles said. 'What about that girl who used to share a flat with Jenny in Oxford?'

'Louise McInnes?'

'Yes. I thought you and she were having an affair.'

No one had affairs any more. Charles's words were half a century out of date. But though the terms might now be different, the meaning was eternal.

'A summer picnic,' I said. 'The frosts of winter killed it off.'

'Why?'

'What she felt for me was more curiosity than love.'

He understood that completely. Jenny had talked about me so long and intimately to her friend Louise, mostly to my detriment, that I recognised – in retrospect – that the friend had chiefly been fascinated in checking out the information personally. It had been a lighthearted passage from mating to parting. Nice while it lasted, but no roots.

When the car came for me I thanked Charles for his sanctuary.

'Any time,' he said, nodding.

We parted as usual without physically touching. Eye contact said it all.

Getting the driver to thread his way back and forth through the maze of shopping dead-ends in the town of Kingston in Surrey, I acquired six dressing-up party wigs from a carnival store and an angel fish in a plastic tub from a pet shop; and, thus armed, arrived eventually at the children's cancer ward that held Rachel Ferns.

Linda greeted my arrival with glittering tears, but her daughter still lived. Indeed, in one of those unpredictable quirks that made leukaemia such a roller-coaster of hope and despair, Rachel was marginally better. She was awake, semi-sitting up in bed and pleased at my arrival.

'Did you bring the angel fish?' she demanded by way of greeting.

I held up the plastic bucket, which swung from my plastic wrist. Linda took it and removed the watertight lid, showing her daughter the shining black-and-silver fish that swam vigorously inside.

Rachel relaxed. 'I'm going to call him Sid,' she said.

She'd been a lively, blonde, pretty child once, according to her photographs: now she seemed all huge eyes in a bald head. Lassitude and anaemia had made her frighteningly frail.

When her mother had first called me in to investigate an attack on Rachel's pony, the illness had been in remission, the dragon temporarily sleeping. Rachel had become someone special to me and I'd given her a fish tank complete with lights, aeration, water plants, Gothic castle arches, sand and brilliant tropical swimming inhabitants. Linda had wept. Rachel had spent hours getting to know her new friends' habits; the ones that skulked in corners, the one who bossed all the rest. Half of the fish were called Sid.

The fish tank stood in the Ferns' sitting-room at home and it seemed uncertain now whether Rachel would see the new Sid among his mates.

It was there, in the comfortable middle-sized room furnished with unaggressively expensive modern sofas, with glass-topped end tables and stained-glass Tiffany lamps, that I had first met my clients, Linda and Rachel Ferns.

There were no books in the room, only a few magazines; dress fashions and horses. Shiny striped curtains in crimson and cream; geometrically patterned carpet in merging fawn and grey; flower prints on pale pink walls. Overall the impression was a degree of lack of coordination which probably indicated impulsive inhabitants without strongly formed characters. The Ferns weren't 'old' money, I concluded, but there appeared to be plenty of it.

31

Linda Ferns, on the telephone, had begged me to come. Five or six ponies in the district had been attacked by vandals, and one of the ponies belonged to her daughter, Rachel. The police hadn't found out who the vandals were and now months had gone by, and her daughter was still very distressed and would I *please, please*, come and see if I could help.

'I've heard you're my only hope. I'll pay you, of course. I'll pay you *anything* if you help Rachel. She has these terrible nightmares. *Please*.'

I mentioned my fee.

'Anything,' she said.

She hadn't told me, before I arrived in the far-flung village beyond Canterbury, that Rachel was ill unto death.

When I met the huge-eyed bald-headed slender child she shook hands with me gravely.

'Are you really Sid Halley?' she asked.

I nodded.

'Mum said you would come. Daddy said you didn't work for kids.'

'I do sometimes.'

'My hair is growing,' she said; and I could see the thin fine blonde fuzz just showing over the pale scalp.

'I'm glad.'

She nodded. 'Quite often I wear a wig, but they itch. Do you mind if I don't?'

'Not in the least.'

'I have leukaemia,' she said calmly.

32

'I see.'

She studied my face, a child old beyond her age, as I'd found all sick young people to be.

'You will find out who killed Silverboy, won't you?'

'I'll try,' I said. 'How did he die?'

'No, no,' Linda interrupted. 'Don't ask her. I'll tell you. It upsets her. Just say you'll sort them out, those *pigs*. And Rachel, you take Pegotty out into the garden and push him round so that he can see the flowers.'

Pegotty, it transpired, was a contented-looking baby strapped into a buggy. Rachel without demur pushed him out into the garden and could presently be seen through the window giving him a close-up acquaintance with an azalea.

Linda Ferns watched and wept the first of many tears.

'She needs a bone marrow transplant,' she said, trying to suppress sobs. 'You'd think it would be simple, but no one so far can find a match to her, not even in the international register set up by the Anthony Nolan Trust.'

I said inadequately, 'I'm sorry.'

'Her father and I are divorced,' Linda said. 'We divorced five years ago, and he's married again.' She spoke without bitterness. 'These things happen.'

'Yes,' I said.

I was at the Ferns' house early in a June of languorous days and sweet-smelling roses, a time for the lotus, not horrors.

33

'A bunch of vandals,' Linda said with a fury that set her whole body trembling, 'they maimed a lot of ponies in Kent... in this area particularly... so that poor loving kids went out into their paddocks and found their much loved ponies *mutilated*. What sick, sick mind would *blind* a poor inoffensive pony that had never done anyone any harm? Three ponies round here were blinded and o.ers had had knives stuck up their back passages.' She blinked on her tears. 'Rachel was terribly upset. All the children for miles were crying inconsolably. And the police couldn't find who'd done any of it.'

'Was Silverboy blinded?' I asked.

'No... no... It was worse... For Rachel, it was worse. She found him, you see ... out in the paddock...' Linda openly sobbed. 'Rachel wanted to sleep in a makeshift stable... a lean-to shed, really. She wanted to sleep there at nights with Silverboy tied up there beside her, and I wouldn't let her. She's been ill for nearly three years. It's such a *dreadful* disease, and I feel so helpless...' She wiped her eyes, plucking a tissue from a half-empty box. 'She keeps saying it wasn't my fault, but I know she thinks Silverboy would be alive if I'd let her sleep out there.'

'What happened to him?' I asked neutrally.

Linda shook her head miserably, unable still to tell me. She was a pretty woman in a conventional thirty-something way: trim figure, well-washed short fair hair, all the health and beauty magazine tips come to admirable life. Only the dullness in the eyes and the intermittent vibrations in many of her muscles spoke plainly of the long strain of emotional buffeting still assailing her.

'She went out,' she said eventually, 'even though it was bitter cold, and beginning to rain ... February ... she always went to see that his water trough was filled and clean and not frozen over ... and I'd made her put on warm clothes and gloves and a scarf and a real thick woolly hat ... and she came back running, and screaming ... *screaming* ...'

I waited through Linda's unbearable memories.

She said starkly, 'Rachel found his *foot.*'

There was a moment of utter stillness, an echo of the stunned disbelief of that dreadful morning.

'It was in all the papers,' Linda said,

I moved and nodded. I'd read – months ago – about the blinded Kent ponies. I'd been busy, inattentive: hadn't absorbed names or details, hadn't realised that one of the ponies had lost a foot.

'I've found out since you telephoned,' I said, 'that round the country, not just here in Kent, there have been another half a dozen or so scattered vandalising attacks on ponies and horses in fields.'

She said unhappily, 'I did see a paragraph about a horse in Lancashire, but I threw the paper away so that Rachel wouldn't read it. Every time anything reminds her of Silverboy, she has a whole week of nightmares. She wakes up sobbing. She comes into my bed, shivering, crying. Please, please find out why ... find out *who* ... She's so ill ... and although she's in remission just now and able to live fairly normally, it almost certainly won't last. The doctors say she needs the transplant.'

I said, 'Does Rachel know any of the other children whose ponies were attacked?'

Linda shook her head. 'Most of them belonged to the Pony Club, I think, but Rachel didn't feel well enough to join the Club. She loved Silverboy – her father gave him to her – but all she could do was sit in the saddle while we led her round. He was a nice quiet pony, a very nice-looking grey with a darker smoky-coloured mane. Rachel called him Silverboy, but he had a long pedigree name really. She needed something to *love*, you see, and she wanted a pony so *much*.'

I asked, 'Did you keep any of the newspaper accounts of Silverboy and the other local ponies being attacked? If you did, can I see them?'

'Yes,' she answered doubtfully, 'but I don't see how they could help. They didn't help the police.'

'They'd be a start,' I said.

'All right, then.' She left the room and after a while returned with a small blue suitcase, the size for stowing under the seats of aircraft. 'Everything's in here,' she said, passing me the case, 'including a tape of a programme a television company made. Rachel and I are in it. You won't lose it, will you? We never show it, but I wouldn't want to lose it.' She blinked against tears. 'It was actually the only good thing that happened.

36

Ellis Quint came to see the children and he was utterly sweet with them. Rachel loved him. He was so *kind*.'

'I know him quite well,' I said. 'If anyone could comfort the children, he could.'

'A really *nice* man,' Linda said.

I took the blue suitcase with its burden of many small tragedies back with me to London and spent indignant hours reading muted accounts of a degree of vandalism that must have been mind-destroying when fresh and bloody and discovered by loving children.

The twenty-minute video tape showed Ellis Quint at his best: the gentle sympathetic healer of unbearable sorrows; the sensible, caring commentator urging the police to treat these crimes with the seriousness given to murders. How good he was, I thought, at pitching his responses exactly right. He put his arms round Rachel and talked to her without sentimentality, not mentioning, until right at the end of the programme when the children were off the screen, that for Rachel Ferns the loss of her pony was just one more intolerable blow in a life already full of burdens.

For that programme, Rachel had chosen to wear the pretty blonde wig that gave her back her pre-chemo-therapy looks. Ellis, as a final dramatic impact, had shown for a few seconds a photo of Rachel bald and vulnerable: an ending poignant to devastation.

I hadn't seen the programme when it had been broadcast: from the March date on the tape, I'd been away in America trying to find an absconding owner

37

who'd left a monstrous training account unpaid. There were, anyway, many of Ellis's programmes I hadn't seen: he presented his twenty-minute twice-weekly journalistic segments as part of an hour-long sports news medley, and was too often on the screen for any one appearance to be especially fanfared.

Meeting Ellis, as I often did at the races, I told him about Linda Ferns calling me in, and asked him if he'd learned any more on the subject of who had mutilated the Kent ponies.

'My dear old Sid,' he said, smiling, 'all of that was months ago, wasn't it?'

'The ponies were vandalised in January and February and your programme was aired in March.'

'And it's now June, right?' He shook his head, neither distressed nor surprised. 'You know what my life's like, I have *researchers* digging out stories for me. Television is insatiably hungry. Of course, if there were any more discoveries about these ponies, I would have been told, and I would have done a follow-up, but I've heard nothing.'

I said, 'Rachel Ferns, who has leukaemia, still has nightmares.'

'Poor little kid.'

'She said you were very kind.'

'Well . . .' He made a ducking, self-deprecating movement of his head, 'It isn't so very difficult. Actually that programme did marvels for my ratings.' He paused. 'Sid, do you know anything about this bookmaker kickback scandal I'm supposed to be doing an exposé on next week?'

'Nothing at all,' I regretted. 'But Ellis, going back to the mutilations, did you chase up those other scattered cases of foals and two-year-old thoroughbreds that suffered from vandalism?'

He frowned lightly, shaking his head. 'The researchers didn't think them worth more than a mention or two. It was copycat stuff. I mean, there wasn't anything as strong as that story about the children.' He grinned. 'There were no heartstrings attached to the others.'

'You're a cynic,' I said.

'Aren't we all?'

We had been close friends for years, Ellis and I. We had ridden against each other in races, he as a charismatic amateur, I as a dedicated pro, but both with the inner fire that made hurtling over large jumps on semi-wild half-ton horses at thirty miles an hour seem a wholly reasonable way of passing as many afternoons as possible.

Thinking, after three or four months of no results from the police or the Ellis Quint programme, that I would probably fail also in the search for vandals, I nevertheless did my best to earn my fee by approaching the problem crabwise, from the side, not by asking questions of the owners of the ponies, but of the newspapermen who had written the columns in the papers.

I did it methodically on the telephone, starting with

the local Kent papers, then chasing up the by-line reporters in the London dailies. Most of the replies were the same: the story had originated from a news agency that supplied all papers with condensed factual information. Follow-ups and interpretation were the business of the papers themselves.

Among the newspapers Linda Fern had given me, *The Pump* had stirred up most disgust, and after about six phone calls I ran to earth the man who'd practically burned holes in the page with the heat of his prose; Kevin Mills, *The Pump*'s chief bleeding hearts reporter.

'A jar?' he said, to my invitation. 'Don't see why not.'

He met me in a pub (nice anonymous surroundings) and he told me he'd personally been down to Kent on that story. He'd interviewed all the children and their parents and also a fierce lady who ran one of the branches of the Pony Club, and he'd pestered the police until they'd thrown him out.

'Zilch,' he said, downing a double gin and tonic. 'No one saw a thing. All those ponies were out in fields and all of them were attacked some time between sunset and dawn, which in January and February gave the vandals hours and hours to do the job and vamoose.'

'All dark, though,' I said.

He shook his head. 'They were all done over on fine nights, near the full moon in each month.'

'How many, do you remember?'

'Four altogether in January. Two of them were

40

blinded. Two were mares with torn knife wounds up their ... well, *birth passages*, as our squeamish editor had me put it.'

'And February?'

'One blinded, two more chopped up mares, one cut-off foot. A poor little girl found the foot near the water trough where her pony used to drink. Ellis Quint did a brilliant TV programme about it. Didn't you see it?'

'I was in America, but I've heard about it since.'

'There were trailers of that programme all week. Almost the whole nation watched it. It made a hell of an impact. That pony was the last one in Kent, as far as I know. The police think it was a bunch of local thugs who got the wind up when there was so much fuss. And people stopped turning ponies out into unguarded fields, see?'

I ordered him another double. He was middle-aged, half bald, doing nicely as to paunch. He wiped an untidy moustache on the back of his hand and said that in his career he'd interviewed so many parents of raped and murdered girls that the ponies had been almost a relief.

I asked him about the later copycat attacks on thoroughbreds in other places, not Kent.

'Copycat?' he repeated. 'So they say.'

'But?' I prompted.

He drank, thought it over, confided.

'All the others,' he said, 'are not in bunches, like Kent. As far as I know – and there may be still others – there were about five very young horses, foals and

41

yearlings, that had things done to them, bad enough mostly for them to have to be put down, but none of them was blinded. One had his muzzle hacked off. None of them were mares. But . . .' He hesitated, sure of his facts, I thought, but not of how I would react to them.

'Go on.'

'See, three others were two-year-olds, and all of those had a foot off.'

I felt the same revulsion that I saw in his face.

'One in March,' he said. 'One in April. One last month.'

'Not,' I said slowly, 'at the full moon?'

'Not precisely. Just on moonlit nights.'

'But why haven't you written about it?'

'I get sent to major disasters,' he said patiently. 'Air crashes, multiple deaths, dozens of accidents and murders. Some nutter driving around chopping off a horse's foot now and again – it's not my absolute priority, but maybe I'll get round to it. The news agency hasn't picked up on it, but I tend to read provincial papers. Old habit. There has been just a par or two here and there about animal vandals. It's always happening. Horses, sheep, dogs – weirdos get their mucky hands on them. Come to think of it, though, if there's another one this month I'll insist on giving it the both-barrel treatment. And now don't you go feeding this to other papers. I want my scoop.'

'Silence,' I promised, 'if . . .'

He asked suspiciously 'If what?'

'If you could give me a list of the people whose thoroughbreds have been damaged.'

He said cautiously, 'It'll cost you.'

'Done,' I said, and we agreed both on a fee and on my giving him first chance at any story I might come up with.

He fulfilled his commitment that same afternoon by sending a motorbike courier bearing a sealed brown envelope containing photocopies of several inconspicuous small paragraphs culled from provincial papers in Liverpool, Reading, Shrewsbury, Manchester, Birmingham and York. All the papers gave the names and vague addresses of the owners of vandalised thoroughbreds, so I set off by car and visited them.

Four days later, when I returned to Linda Ferns' house in Kent, I had heard enough about man's inhumanity to horses to last me for life. The injuries inflicted, from the hacked-off muzzle onwards, were truly beyond comprehension but, compared with the three two-year-olds, were all random and without pattern. It was the severed feet that were connected.

'I came across his foot by the water trough in the field,' one woman said, her eyes screwing up at the memory. 'I couldn't *believe* it. Just a *foot*. Tell you the truth, I brought up my breakfast. He was a really nice two-year-old colt.' She swallowed. 'He wasn't standing anywhere near his foot. The off-fore, it was. He'd wandered away on three legs and he was eating grass. Just *eating*, as if nothing had happened. He didn't seem to feel any pain.'

'What did you do?' I asked.

'I called the vet. He came ... He gave *me* a tranquilliser. He said I needed it more than the colt did. He looked after everything for me.'

'Was the colt insured?' I asked.

She took no offence at the question. I guessed it had been asked a dozen times already. She said there had been no insurance. They had bred the two-year-old themselves. They had been going to race him later in the year. They had been to Cheltenham races and had backed the winner of the Gold Cup, a great day, and the very next morning ...

I asked her for the vet's name and address, and I went to see him at his home.

'How was the foot taken off?' I asked.

He wrinkled his forehead. 'I don't rightly know. It was neat. The colt had bled very little. There was a small pool of blood on the grass about a yard away from the foot, and that was all. The colt himself let me walk right up to him. He looked calm and normal, except that his off-fore ended at the fetlock.'

'Was it done with an axe?'

He hesitated. 'I'd say more like a machete. Just the one cut, fast and clean. Whoever did it knew just where to aim for, unless he was simply lucky.'

'Did you tell the police?'

'Sure. A detective sergeant came out. He vomited

44

too. Then I called the knackers and put the colt down. Bloody vandals! I'd like to cut off *their* foot, see if they liked life with a stump.' He remembered suddenly about my own sliced off hand, and reddened, looking confused and embarrassed. There had been a much publicised court case about my hand. Everyone knew what had happened. I had finally stopped wincing visibly when people referred to it.

'It's all right,' I said mildly.

'I'm sorry. My big mouth . . .'

'Do you think the colt's amputation was done by a vet? By any sort of surgical expert? Was it done with a scalpel? Was the colt given a local anaesthetic?'

He said, disturbed, 'I don't know the answers. I'd just say that whoever did it was used to handling horses. That colt was loose in the field, though wearing a head-collar.'

I went to see the detective sergeant, who looked as if he might throw up again at the memory.

'I see a lot of injured people. Dead bodies, too,' he said, 'but that was different. Mindless. Fair turned my stomach.'

The police had found no culprit. It had been an isolated event, not part of a pattern. The only report they'd had was of the presence of a blue Land-Rover driving away along the lane from the colt's field; and Land-Rovers were two a penny in the countryside. Case not closed, but also not being actively investigated. The colt and his hoof had long gone to the glue factory.

45

'Are there any photographs?' I asked.

The sergeant said that the photographs were a police matter, not open to the general public.

'I do know who you are,' he said, not abrasively, 'but to us you're the general public. Sorry.'

The colt's owner, consulted, said she had been too upset to want photographs.

I drove onwards, northwards to Lancashire, into a gale of anger. Big, blustery and impressively furious, a hard competent large-scale farmer let loose his roaring sense of injustice, yelling in my face, spraying me with spittle, jabbing the air with a rigid forefinger, pushing his chin forward in a classic animal gesture of aggression.

'Best colt I ever owned,' he bellowed. 'He cost me a packet, but he was a good 'un. Breeding, conformation, the lot. And he was *fast*, I'll tell you. He was going to Newmarket the next week.' He mentioned a prestigious trainer who I knew wouldn't have accepted rubbish. 'A good 'un,' the farmer repeated. 'And then the sodding police asked if I'd killed him for the insurance. I ask you! He wasn't insured, I told them. They said I couldn't *prove* he wasn't insured. Did you know that? Did you know you can prove something *is* insured, but you can't prove it *isn't*? Did you know that?'

I said I'd heard it was so.

'I told them to bugger off. They weren't interested in finding who took my colt's foot off, only in proving

I did it myself. They made me that *angry* . . .' His words failed him. I'd met many people unjustly accused of setting fires, battering children, stealing, and taking bribes, and by then I knew the vocal vibrations of truly outraged innocence. The angry farmer, I would have staked all on it, had not taken the foot off his own colt, and I told him so. Some of his anger abated into surprise. 'So you *believe* me?'

'I sure do,' I nodded. 'The point is, who knew you'd bought a fine fast colt that you had at your farm in a field?'

'Who knew?' He suddenly looked guilty, as if he'd already had to face an unpalatable fact. 'I'd blown my mouth off a bit. Half the country knew. And I'd been boasting about him at Aintree, the day before the Grand National. I was at one of those sponsors' lunch things – Topline Foods, it was – and the colt was fine that night. I saw him in the morning. And it was the next night, after the National, that he was got at.'

He had taken his own colour photographs (out of distrust of the police) and he showed them to me readily.

'The off-fore,' he said, pointing to a close-up of the severed foot. 'He was cut just below the fetlock. Almost through the joint. You can see the white ends of the bones.'

The photographs jolted. It didn't help that I'd seen my own left wrist in much the same condition. I said, 'What was your vet's opinion?'

47

'Same as mine.'

I went to see the vet. One chop, he said. Only one. No missed shots. Straight through at the leg's most vulnerable point.

'What weapon?'

He didn't know.

I pressed onwards to Yorkshire where, barely a month earlier, at the time of the York Spring Meeting, a dark brown two-year-old colt had been deprived of his off-fore foot on a moonlit night. One chop. No insurance. Sick and angry owners. No clues.

These owners were a stiff-upper-lip couple with elderly manners and ancient immutable values who were as deeply bewildered as repelled by the level of evil that would for no clear reason destroy a thing of beauty; in this case, the fluid excellence of a fleet glossy equine princeling.

'*Why?*' they asked me insistently. '*Why* would anyone do such a pointlessly wicked thing?'

I had no answer. I prompted them only to talk, to let out their pain and deprivation. I got them to talk, and I listened.

The wife said, 'We had such a lovely week. Every year we have people to stay for the York Spring Meeting ... because, as you can see, this is quite a large house ... so we have six or eight friends staying, and we get in extra staff and have a party – such fun, you see – and this year the weather was perfect and we all had a great time.'

'Successful, don't you know,' said her husband, nodding.

'Dear Ellis Quint was one of our guests,' smiled the hostess, 'and he lifted everyone's spirits in that easy way of his so that it seemed we spent the whole week laughing. He was filming for one of his television programmes at York races, so we were all invited behind the scenes and enjoyed it all so much. And then... then... the very night after all our guests had left... well...'

'Jenkins came and told us – Jenkins is our groom – he told us while we were sitting at breakfast, that our colt... our colt...'

'We have three brood-mares,' his wife said. 'We love to see the foals and yearlings out in the fields, running free, you know... and usually we sell the yearlings, but that colt was so beautiful that we kept him, and he was going into training soon... All our guests had admired him.'

'Jenkins had made a splendid job of breaking him in.'

'Jenkins was in *tears*,' the wife said. 'Jenkins! A tough leathery old man. In *tears*.'

The husband said with difficulty, 'Jenkins found the foot by the gate, beside the water trough.'

His wife went on. 'Jenkins told us that Ellis had done a programme a few months ago about a pony's foot being cut off and the children being so devastated. So we wrote to Ellis about our colt and Ellis telephoned at once to say how *awful* for us. He couldn't have been

49

nicer. Dear Ellis. But there wasn't anything he could do, of course, except sympathise.'

'No,' I agreed, and I felt only the faintest twitch of surprise that Ellis hadn't mentioned the York colt when I'd been talking to him less than a week earlier about Rachel Ferns.

CHAPTER THREE

Back in London I met Kevin Mills, the journalist from *The Pump*, at lunchtime in the same pub as before.

'It's time for both barrels,' I said.

He swigged his double gin. 'What have you discovered?'

I outlined the rest of the pattern, beyond what he'd told me about two-year-old colts on moonlit nights. One chop from something like a machete. Always the off-fore foot. Always near a water trough. No insurance. And always just after a major local race meeting: Cheltenham, the Gold Cup Festival; the Grand National at Liverpool; the Spring Meeting at York.

'And this Saturday, two days from now,' I said levelly, 'we have the Derby.'

He put his glass down slowly, and after a full silent minute said, 'What about the kid's pony?'

I shrugged resignedly. 'It was the first that we know of.'

'And it doesn't fit the pattern. Not a two-year-old colt, was he? And no major race meeting, was there?'

'The severed foot was by the water trough. The off-fore foot. Moon in the right quarter. One chop. No insurance.'

He frowned, thinking. 'Tell you what,' he said eventually, 'it's worth a *warning*. I'm not a sports writer, as you know, but I'll get the message into the paper somewhere. "Don't leave your two-year-old colts unguarded in open fields during and after the Epsom meeting." I don't think I can do more than that.'

'It might be enough.'

'Yeah. *If* all the owners of colts read *The Pump*.'

'It will be the talk of the racecourse. I'll arrange that.'

'On Derby Day?' he looked sceptical. 'Still, it will be better than nothing.' He drank again. 'What we really need to do is catch the bugger red-handed.'

We gloomily contemplated that impossibility. Roughly fifteen thousand thoroughbred foals were born each year in the British Isles. Half would be colts. Many of those at two would already be in training for Flat racing, tucked away safely in stables; but that still left a host unattended out of doors. By June, also, yearling colts, growing fast, could be mistaken at night for two-year-olds.

Nothing was safe from a determined vandal.

Kevin Mills went away to write his column and I travelled on to Kent to report to my clients.

'Have you found out *who*?' Linda demanded.

'Not yet.'

We sat by the sitting-room window again, watching Rachel push Pegotty in his buggy round the lawn, and I told her about the three colts and their shattered owners.

'Three more,' Linda repeated numbly. 'In March, April and May? And Silverboy in February?'

'That's right.'

'And what about *now*? This month . . . *June*?'

I explained about the warning to be printed in *The Pump*.

'I'm not going to tell Rachel about the other three,' Linda said. 'She wakes up screaming as it is.'

'I enquired into other injured horses all over England,' I said, 'but they were all hurt differently from each other. I think . . . well . . . that there are several different people involved. And, I don't think the thugs that blinded and cut the ponies round here had anything to do with Silverboy.'

Linda protested. 'But they must have done! There couldn't be *two* lots of vandals.'

'I think there were.'

She watched Rachel and Pegotty, the habitual tears not far away. Rachel was tickling the baby to make him laugh.

'I'd do anything to save my daughter,' Linda said. 'The doctor said that if only she'd had several sisters, one of them might have had the right tissue type. Joe

53

– Rachel's father – is half Asian. It seems harder to find a match. So I had the baby. I had Pegotty five months ago.' She wiped her eyes. 'Joe has his new wife and he wouldn't sleep with me again, not even for Rachel. So he donated sperm and I had artificial insemination, and it worked at once. It seemed an omen ... and I had the baby ... but he doesn't match Rachel. There was only ever one chance in four that he would have the same tissue type and antigens ... I hoped and prayed ... but he *doesn't*.' She gulped, her throat closing. 'So I have Pegotty ... he's Peter, really, but we call him Pegotty ... but Joe won't bond with him ... and we still can't find a match anywhere for Rachel and there isn't much time for me to try with another baby ... and Joe *won't* anyway. His wife objects ... and he didn't want to do it the first time.'

'I'm so sorry,' I said.

'Joe's wife goes on and on about Joe having to pay child support for Pegotty ... and now she's pregnant herself.'

Life, I thought, brought unlimited and complicated cruelties.

'Joe isn't mean,' Linda said. 'He loves Rachel and he bought her the pony and he keeps us comfortable, but his wife says I could have *six* children without getting a match ...' Her voice wavered and stopped, and after a while she said, 'I don't know why I burdened you with all that. You're so easy to talk to.'

'And interested.'

She nodded, sniffing and blowing her nose. 'Go out and talk to Rachel. I told her you were coming back today. She liked you.'

Obediently I went out into the garden and gravely shook hands with Rachel, and we sat side by side on a garden bench like two old buddies.

Though still warm, the golden days of early June were greying and growing damp: good for roses perhaps, but not for the Derby.

I apologised that I hadn't yet found out who had attacked Silverboy.

'But you will in the end, won't you?'

'I hope so,' I said.

She nodded. 'I told Daddy yesterday that I was sure you would.'

'Did you?'

'Yes. He took me out in his car. He does that sometimes, when Didi goes to London to do shopping.'

'Is Didi his wife?'

Rachel's nose wrinkled in a grimace, but she made no audible judgement. She said, 'Daddy says someone chopped your hand off, just like Silverboy.'

She regarded me gravely, awaiting confirmation.

'Er,' I said, unnerved, 'not exactly like Silverboy.'

'Daddy says the man who did it was sent to prison, but he's out again now on parole.'

'Do you know what "on parole" means?' I asked curiously

'Yes. Daddy told me.'

'Your daddy knows a lot.'

'Yes, but it is *true* that someone chopped your hand off?'

'Does it matter to you?'

'Yes, it does,' she said. 'I was thinking about it in bed last night. I have awful dreams. I tried to stay awake because I didn't want to go to sleep and dream about you having your hand chopped off.'

She was trying to be grown up and calm, but I could feel screaming hysteria too near the surface; so, stifling my own permanent reluctance to talk about it, I gave her an abbreviated account of what had happened.

'I was a jockey,' I began.

'Yes, I know. Daddy said you were the champion for years.'

'Well, one day my horse fell in a race, and while I was on the ground another horse landed over a jump straight onto my wrist and . . . um . . . tore it apart. It got stitched up, but I couldn't use my hand much. I had to stop being a jockey, and I started doing what I do now, which is finding out things, like who hurt Silverboy.'

She nodded.

'Well, I found out something that an extremely nasty man didn't want me to know, and he . . . er . . . he hit my bad wrist and broke it again, and that time the doctors couldn't stitch it up, so they decided that I'd be better off with a useful plastic hand instead of the useless old one.'

'So he didn't really . . . not *really* chop it off. Not like with an axe or anything?'

'No. So don't waste dreams on it.'

She smiled with quiet relief and, as she was sitting on my left, put her right hand down delicately but without hesitation on the replacement parts. She stroked the tough plastic unfeeling skin and looked up with surprise at my eyes.

'It isn't *warm*,' she said.

'Well, it isn't cold, either.'

She laughed with uncomplicated fun. 'How does it work?'

'I tell it what to do,' I said simply. 'I send a message from my brain down my arm saying open thumb from fingers, or close thumb to fingers, to grip things, and the messages reach very sensitive terminals called electrodes, which are inside the plastic and against my skin.' I paused, but she didn't say she didn't understand. I said, 'My real arm ends about there' – I pointed – 'and the plastic arm goes up round my elbow. The electrodes are up in my forearm, there, against my skin. They feel my muscles trying to move. That's how they work.'

'Is the plastic arm tied on, or anything?'

'No. It just fits tightly and stays on by itself. It was specially made to fit me.'

Like all children she took marvels for granted, although to me, even though by then I'd had the false arm for nearly three years, the concept of nerve messages moving machinery was still extraordinary.

57

'There are three electrodes,' I said. 'One for opening the hand, one for closing, and one for turning the wrist.'

'Do electrodes work on electricity?' It puzzled her. 'I mean, you're not plugged into the wall, or anything?'

'You're a clever girl,' I told her. 'It works on a special sort of battery which slots into the outside above where I wear my watch. I charge up the batteries on a charger which *is* plugged into the wall.'

She looked at me assessingly. 'It must be pretty useful to have that hand.'

'It's brilliant,' I agreed.

'Daddy says Ellis Quint told him that you can't tell you have a plastic hand unless you touch it.'

I asked, surprised, 'Does your daddy know Ellis Quint?'

She nodded composedly. 'They go to the same place to play squash. He helped Daddy buy Silverboy. He was really really sorry when he found out it was Silverboy himself that he was making his programme about.'

'Yes, he would be.'

'I wish . . .' she began, looking down at my hand, 'I do wish Silverboy could have had a new foot . . . with electrodes and a battery.'

I said prosaically, 'He might have been able to have a false foot fitted, but he wouldn't have been able to trot or canter, or jump. He wouldn't have been happy just limping around.'

She rubbed her own fingers over the plastic ones, not convinced.

I said, 'Where did you keep Silverboy?'

'The other side of that fence at the end of the garden.' She pointed. 'You can't see it from here because of those trees. We have to go through the house and out and down the lane.'

'Will you show me?'

There was a moment of drawing back, then she said, 'I'll take you if I can hold your hand on the way.'

'Of course.' I stood up and held out my real, warm, normal arm.

'No . . .' She shook her head, standing up also. 'I mean, can I hold this hand that you can't feel?'

It seemed to matter to her that I wasn't whole; that I would understand someone ill, without hair.

I said lightly, 'You can hold which hand you like.'

She nodded, then pushed Pegotty into the house, and matter of factly told Linda she was taking me down to the field to show me where Silverboy had lived. Linda gave me a wild look but let us go, so the bald-headed child and the one-handed man walked in odd companionship down a short lane and leaned against a five-barred gate across the end.

The field was a lush paddock of little more than an acre, the grass growing strongly, uneaten. A nearby standing pipe with an ordinary tap on it stood ready to fill an ordinary galvanised water trough. The ground round the trough was churned up, the grass growing more sparsely, as always happened round troughs in fields.

'I don't want to go in,' Rachel said, turning her head away.

'We don't need to.'

'His foot was by the trough,' she said jerkily, 'I mean . . . you could see *blood* . . . and white bones.'

'Don't talk about it.' I pulled her with me and walked back along the lane, afraid I should never have asked her to show me.

She gripped my unfeeling hand in both of hers, slowing me down.

'It's all right,' she said. 'It was a long time ago. It's all right now when I'm awake.'

'Good.'

'I don't like going to sleep.'

The desperation of that statement was an open appeal, and had to be addressed.

I stopped walking before we reached the door of the house. I said, 'I don't usually tell anyone this, but I'll tell you. I still sometimes have bad dreams about my hand. I dream I can clap with two hands. I dream I'm still a jockey. I dream about my smashed wrist. Rotten dreams can't be helped. They're awful when they happen. I don't know how to stop them. But one does wake up.'

'And then you have leukaemia . . . or a plastic arm.'

'Life's a bugger,' I said.

She put her hand over her mouth and, in a fast release of tension, she giggled. 'Mum won't let me say that.'

'Say it into your pillow.'

'Do you?'

'Pretty often.'

We went on into the house and Rachel again pushed Pegotty into the garden. I stayed in the sitting-room with Linda and watched through the window.

'Was she all right?' Linda asked anxiously.

'She's a very brave child.'

Linda wept.

I said, 'Did you hear anything at all the night Silverboy was attacked?'

'Everyone asks that. I'd have said if I had.'

'No car engines?'

'The police said they must have stopped the car in the road and walked down the lane. My bedroom window doesn't face the lane, nor does Rachel's. But that lane doesn't go anywhere except to the field. As you saw, it's only a track really, it ends at the gate.'

'Could anyone see Silverboy from the road?'

'Yes, the police asked that. You could see him come to drink. You can see the water trough from the road, if you know where to look. The police say the thugs must have been out all over this part of Kent looking for unguarded ponies like Silverboy. Whatever you say about two-year-olds, Silverboy *must* have been done by thugs. Why don't you ask the police?'

'If you wholeheartedly believed the police, you wouldn't have asked me for help.'

'Joe just telephoned,' she confessed, wailing, 'and he says that calling you in to help is a waste of money.'

'Ah.'

'I don't know what to think.'

I said, 'You're paying me by the day, plus expenses. I can stop right now, if you like.'

'No. Yes. I don't *know*.' She wiped her eyes, undecided, and said, 'Rachel dreams that Silverboy is standing in the field and he's glowing bright and beautiful in the moonlight. He's *shining*, she says. And there's a dark mass of monsters oozing down the lane... oozing is what she says... and they are shapeless and devils and they're going to kill Silverboy. She says she is trying to run fast to warn him, and she can't get through the monsters, they clutch at her like cobwebs. She can't get through them and they reach Silverboy and smother his light, and all his hair falls out, and she wakes up and screams. It's always the same nightmare. I thought if you could find out who cut the poor thing's foot off, the monsters would have names and faces and would be in the papers, and Rachel would know who they were and stop thinking they're lumps that ooze without eyes and won't let her through.'

After a pause, I said, 'Give me another week.'

She turned away from me sharply and, crossing to a desk, wrote me a cheque. 'For two weeks, one gone, one ahead.'

I looked at the amount. 'That's more than we agreed on.'

'Whatever Joe says, I want you to go on trying.'

I gave her tentatively a small kiss on the cheek. She smiled, her eyes still dark and wet. 'I'll pay anything for Rachel,' she said.

I drove slowly back to London thinking of the cynical old ex-policemen who had taught me the basics of investigation. 'There are two cardinal rules in this trade,' he said. 'One. Never believe everything a client tells you, and always believe they could have told you more if you'd asked the right questions. And two. Never, never get emotionally involved with your client.'

Which was all very well, except when your client was a bright truthful nine-year-old fighting a losing battle against a rising tide of lymphoblasts.

I bought a take-out curry on the way home and ate it before spending the evening on overdue paperwork.

I much preferred the active side of the job, but clients wanted, and deserved, and paid for, detailed accounts of what I'd done on their behalf, preferably with results they liked. With the typed recital of work done, I sent also my final bill, adding a list of itemised expenses supported by receipts. I almost always played fair, even with clients I didn't like: investigators had been known to charge for seven days' work when, with a little application, they could have finished the job in three. I didn't want that sort of reputation. Speed succeeded in my new occupation as essentially as in my old.

Besides bathroom and kitchen, my pleasant (and frankly, expensive) flat consisted of three rooms; bedroom, big sunny sitting-room and a third, smaller, room that I used as an office. I had no secretary or helper; no one read the secrets I uncovered except the client and myself, and whatever the client did with the information he'd paid for was normally his or her own business. Privacy was what drove many people to consult me, and privacy was what they got.

I listened to some unexciting messages on my answering machine, typed a report on my secure word-processor, printed it and put it ready for posting. For reports and anything personal I used a computer system that wasn't connected to any phone line. No one could in consequence tap into it and, as a precaution against thieves, I used also unbreakable passwords. It was my second system that could theoretically be accessed; the one connected by modem to the big wide world of universal information. Any snooper was welcome to anything found there.

On the subject of the management of secrecy, my cynical mentor had said, 'Never ever tell your right hand what your left hand is doing. Er . . .' he added, 'whoops. Sorry, Sid.'

'It'll cost you a pint.'

'And,' he went on later, drinking, 'keep back-up copies of completed sensitive enquiries in a bank vault, and wipe the information from any computer systems in your office. If you use random passwords, and change them weekly, you should be safe enough while you're actually working on something, but once you've finished, get the back-up to the bank and wipe the office computer, like I said.'

'All right.'

'Never forget,' he told me, 'that the people you are investigating may go to violent lengths to stop you.'

He had been right about that.

'Never forget that you don't have the same protection as the police do. You have to make your own protection. You have to be careful.'

'Maybe I should look for another job.'

'No, Sid,' he said earnestly, 'you have a gift for this. You listen to what I tell you and you'll do fine.'

He had taught me for the two years I'd spent doing little but drift in the old Radnor detection agency after the end of my racing life and, for nearly three years since, I'd lived mostly by his precepts. But he was dead now, and Radnor himself also, and I had to look inwards for wisdom, which could be a variable process, not always ultra-productive.

I could try to comfort Rachel by telling her I had bad dreams also, but I could never have told her how vivid and liquefying they could be. That night, after I'd eased off the arm and showered and gone peacefully to bed, I fell asleep thinking of her, and descended after midnight into a familiar dungeon.

It was always the same.

I dreamed I was in a big dark space, and some people were coming to cut off both my hands.

Both.

They were making me wait, but they would come. There would be agony and humiliation and helplessness... and no way out.

I semi-awoke in shaking, sweating heart-thudding terror and then realised with flooding relief that it wasn't true, I was safe in my own bed: and then remembered that it had already half happened in fact, and also that I'd come within a fraction once of a villain's shooting the remaining hand off. As soon as I was awake enough to be clear about the present actual not-too-bad state of affairs I slid back reassured into sleep, and that night the whole appalling nightmare cycled again... and again.

I forced myself to wake up properly, to sit up and get out of bed and make full consciousness take over. I stood under the shower again and let cool water run through my hair and down my body. I put on a towelling bathrobe and poured a glass of milk, and sat in an armchair in the sitting-room with all the lights on.

I looked at the space where a left hand had once been, and I looked at the strong whole right hand that held a glass, and I acknowledged that often, both waking as well as sleeping, I felt, and could not repress, stabs of savage petrifying fear that one day it would indeed be both. The trick was not to let the fear show, nor to let it conquer, nor rule my life.

It was pointless to reflect that I'd brought the terrors on myself. I had chosen to be a jockey. I had chosen to go after violent crooks. I was at that moment actively seeking out someone who knew how to cut off a horse's foot with one chop.

My own equivalent of the off-fore held a glass of milk.

I had to be mentally deranged.

But then there were people like Rachel Ferns.

In one way or another I had survived many torments, and much could have been avoided but for my own obstinate nature. I knew by then that whatever came along, I would deal with it. But that child had had her hair fall out and had found her beloved pony's foot, and none of that was her fault. No nine-year-old mind could sleep sweetly under such assaults.

Oh God, Rachel, I thought, I would dream your nightmares for you, if I could.

In the morning I made a working analysis in five columns of the Ferns pony and the three two-year-olds. The analysis took the form of a simple graph, ruled in boxes. Across the top of the page I wrote: Factors, Ferns, Cheltenham, Aintree, York, and down the left-hand column, Factors, I entered 'date', 'name of owner', 'racing programme', 'motive', and finally, 'who knew of victim's availability?' I found that although I could *think* of answers to that last question, I hadn't the wish to write them in, and after a bit of indecision I phoned Kevin Mills at *The Pump* and, by persistence, reached him.

'Sid,' he said heartily, 'the warning will be in the paper tomorrow. You've done your best. Stop agitating.'

'Great,' I said, 'but could you do something else? Something that could come innocently from *The Pump*, but would raise all sorts of reverberations if I asked directly myself.'

'Such as what?'

'Such as ask Topline Foods for a list of the guests they entertained at a sponsors' lunch at Aintree the day before the National.'

'What the *hell* for?'

'Will you do it?'

He said, 'What are you up to?'

'The scoop is still yours. Exclusive.'

'I don't know why I trust you.'

'It pays off,' I said, smiling.

'It had better.' He put down his receiver with a crash, but I knew he would do what I asked.

It was Friday morning. At Epsom that day they would be running the Coronation Cup and also the Oaks, the fillies' equivalent of the Derby. It was also lightly raining: a weak warm front, it seemed, was slowly blighting southern England.

Racecourses still drew me as if I were tethered to them with bungy elastic, but before setting out I telephoned the woman whose colt's foot had been amputated during the night after the Cheltenham Gold Cup.

'I'm sorry to bother you again, but would you mind a few more questions?'

'Not if you can catch the bastards.'

'Well, was the two-year-old alone in his field?'

'Yes, he was. It was only a paddock. Railed, of course. We kept him in the paddock nearest to the house, that's what is so infuriating. We had two old hacks turned out in the field beyond him, but the vandals left them untouched.'

'And,' I said neutrally, 'how many people knew the colt was accessible? And how accessible was he?'

'Sid,' she exclaimed, 'don't think we haven't racked our brains. The trouble is, all our friends knew about him. We were excited about his prospects. And then, at the Cheltenham meeting, we had been talking to people about *trainers*. Old Gunners, who used to train for us in the past, has died, of course, and we don't like that uppity assistant of his that's taken over the stable, so we were asking around, you see.'

'Yeah. And did you decide on a trainer?'

'We did, but, of course . . .'

'Such a bloody shame,' I sympathised. 'Who did you decide on?'

She mentioned a first-class man. 'Several people said that with him we couldn't go wrong.'

'No.' I mentally sighed, and asked obliquely, 'What did you especially enjoy about the Festival meeting?'

'The Queen came,' she said promptly. 'I had thick warm boots on, and I nearly fell over them, curtseying.' She laughed. 'And oh, also, I suppose you do know you're in the Hall of Fame there?'

'It's an honour,' I said. 'They gave me an engraved glass goblet that I can see across the room right now from where I'm sitting.'

'Well, we were standing in front of that big exhibit they've put together of your life, and we were reading the captions, and dear Ellis Quint stopped beside us and put his arm round my shoulders and said that our Sid was a pretty great guy, all in all.'

Oh *shit*, I thought.

Her warm smile was audible down the line. 'We've known Ellis for years, of course. He used to ride our horses in amateur races. So he called in at our house for a drink on his way home after the Gold Cup. Such a *lovely* day.' She sighed. 'And then those *bastards* ... You will catch them, won't you, Sid?'

'If I can,' I said.

I left a whole lot of the boxes empty on my chart, and drove to Epsom Downs, spirits as grey as the skies. The bars were crowded. Umbrellas dripped. The brave colours of June dresses hid under drabber raincoats, and only the geraniums looked happy.

I walked damply to the parade ring before the two-year-old colts' six-furlong race and thoughtfully watched all the off-fore feet plink down lightheartedly. The young spindly bones of those forelegs thrust 450-kilo bodies forward at sprinting speeds near forty miles an hour. I had mostly raced on the older mature horses of steeplechasing, half a ton in weight, slightly slower, capable of four miles and thirty jumps from start to finish, but still on legs scarcely thicker than a big man's wrist.

The anatomy of a horse's foreleg consisted, from the shoulder down, of forearm, knee, cannon bone, fetlock joint (also known as the ankle), pastern bone, and hoof. The angry Lancashire farmer's coloured photograph had shown the amputation to have been effected straight through the narrowest part of the whole leg, just at the base of the fetlock joint, where the pastern emerged from it. In effect, the whole pastern and the hoof had been cut off.

Horses had very fast instincts for danger and were easily scared. Young horses seldom stood still. Yet one single chop had done the job each time. *Why* had all those poor animals stood quietly while the deed was done? None of them had squealed loud enough to alert his owner.

I went up on the stands and watched the two-year-olds set off from the spur away to the left at the top of the hill; watched them swoop down like a flock of starlings round Tattenham Corner, and sort themselves out into winner and losers along the straight with its deceptively difficult camber that could tilt a horse towards the rails if his jockey were inexperienced.

I watched, and I sighed. Five long years had passed since I'd ridden my last race. Would regret, I wondered, ever fade?

'Why so pensive, Sid, lad?' asked an elderly trainer, grasping my elbow. 'A Scotch and water for your thoughts!' He steered me round towards the nearest bar and I went with him unprotestingly, as custom came my way quite often in that casual manner. He was great with horses and famously mean with his money.

'I hear you're damned expensive,' he began inoffensively, handing me a glass. 'What will you charge me for a day's work?'

I told him.

'Too damned much. Do it for nothing, for old times' sake.'

I added, smiling, 'How many horses do you train for nothing?'

'That's different.'

'How many races would you have asked me to ride for nothing?'

'Oh, all *right* then. I'll pay your damned fee. The fact is, I think I'm being *had*, and I want you to find out.'

It seemed he had received a glowing testimonial from the present employer of a chauffeur/houseman/handyman who'd applied for a job he'd advertised. He

72

wanted to know if it was worth bringing the man up for an interview.

'She–' he said, 'his employer is a woman – I phoned her when I got the letter, to check the reference, you see. She couldn't have been more complimentary about the man if she'd tried, but . . . I don't know . . . She was *too* complimentary, if you see what I mean.'

'You mean you think she might be glad to see the back of him?'

'You don't hang about, Sid. That's exactly what I mean.'

He gave me the testimonial letter of fluorescent praise.

'No problem,' I said, reading it. 'One day's fee, plus travel expenses. I'll phone you, then send you a written report.'

'You still *look* like a jockey,' he complained. 'You're a damned sight more expensive on your feet.'

I smiled, put the letter away in a pocket, drank his Scotch and applauded the string of winners he'd had recently, cheering him up before separating him from his cash.

I drifted around pleasurably but unprofitably for the rest of the day, slept thankfully without nightmares and found on a dry and sunny Derby Day morning that my friendly *Pump* reporter had really done his stuff.

'Lock up your colts,' he directed in the paper. 'You've heard of foot-fetishists? This is one beyond belief.'

73

He outlined in succinct paragraphs the similarities in 'the affair of the four severed fetlocks' and pointed out that on that very night after the Derby – the biggest race of all – there would be moonlight enough at 3.00 a.m. for torches to be unnecessary. All two-year-old colts should, like Cinderella, be safe indoors by midnight. 'And if . . .' he finished with a flourish, '. . . you should spy anyone creeping through the fields armed with a machete, phone ex-jockey turned gumshoe Sid Halley, who provided the information gathered here and can be reached via *The Pump*'s special Hotline. Phone *The Pump*! Save the colts! Halley to the rescue!'

I couldn't imagine how he had got that last bit – including a telephone number – past any editor, but I needn't have worried about spreading the message on the racecourse. No one spoke to me about anything else all afternoon.

I phoned *The Pump* myself and reached someone eventually who told me that Kevin Mills had gone to a train crash; sorry.

'Damn,' I said. 'So how are you re-routing calls about colts to me? I didn't arrange this. How will it work?'

'Hold on.'

I held on. A different voice came back.

'As Kevin isn't available, we're re-routing all Halley Hotline calls to this number,' he said, and he read out my own Pont Square number.

'Where's your bloody Mills? I'll wring his neck.'

'Gone to the train crash. Before he left he gave us this number for reaching you. He said you would want to know at once about any colts.'

That was true enough – but hell's bloody bells, I thought, I could have set it up better if he'd warned me.

I watched the Derby with inattention. An outsider won.

Ellis teased me about the piece in *The Pump*.

'Hotline Halley,' he said, laughing and clapping me on the shoulder, tall and deeply friendly and wiping out in a flash the incredulous doubts I'd been having about him. 'It's an extraordinary coincidence, Sid, but I actually *saw* one of those colts. Alive, of course. I was staying with some chums for York, and after we'd gone home someone vandalised their colt. Such fun people. They didn't deserve anything like that.'

'No one does.'

'True.'

'The really puzzling thing is motive,' I said. 'I went to see all the owners. None of the colts was insured. Nor was Rachel Ferns' pony, of course.'

He said interestedly, 'Did you think it was an insurance scam?'

'It jumps to mind, doesn't it? Theoretically it's possible to insure a horse and collect the lucre without the owner knowing anything about it. It's been done. But if that's what this is all about, perhaps someone in an insurance company somewhere will see the piece in

The Pump and connect a couple of things. Come to think of it,' I finished slowly, 'I might send a copy to every likely insurance company's board of directors, asking, and warning them.'

'Good idea,' he said. 'Does insurance and so on really take the place of racing? It sounds a pretty dull life for you, after what we used to do.'

'Does television replace it for you?'

'Not a hope.' He laughed. 'Danger is addictive, wouldn't you say? The only dangerous job in television is reporting wars and – have you noticed – the same few war reporters get out there all the time, talking with their earnest committed faces about this or that month's little dust-up, while bullets fly and chip off bits of stone in the background to prove how brave they are.'

'You're jealous,' I smiled.

'I get sodding bored sometimes with being a chat-show celebrity, even if it's nice being liked. Don't you ache for speed?'

'Every day,' I said.

'You're about the only person who understands me. No one else can see that fame's no substitute for danger.'

'It depends what you risk.'

Hands, I thought. One could risk hands.

'Good luck, Hotline,' Ellis said.

It was the owners of two-year-old colts that had the good luck. My telephone jammed and rang non-stop all evening and all night when I got home after the Derby, but the calls were all from people enjoying their shivers and jumping at shadows. The moonlight shone on quiet fields, and no animal, whether colt or two-year-old thoroughbred or children's pony, lost a foot.

In the days that followed, interest and expectation dimmed and died. It was twelve days after the Derby, on the last night of the Royal Ascot meeting, that the screaming heeby-jeebies reawoke.

CHAPTER FOUR

On the Monday after the Derby I trailed off on the one-day dig into the overblown reference and, without talking to the lady-employer herself (which would clearly have been counter-productive) I uncovered enough to phone the tight-fisted trainer with sound advice.

'She wants to get rid of him without the risk of being accused of unfair dismissal,' I said. 'He steals small things from her house which pass through a couple of hands and turn up in the local antique shop. She can't prove they were hers. The antique shop owner is whining about his innocence. The lady has apparently said she won't try to prosecute her houseman if he gets the heck out. Her testimonial is part of the bargain. The houseman is a regular in the local betting shop, and gambles heavily on horses. Do you want to employ him?'

'Like hell.'

'The report I'll write and send to you,' I told him, 'will say only, "Work done on recruitment of staff." You can claim tax relief on it.'

He laughed dryly. 'Any time you want a reference,' he said, pleased, 'I'll write you an affidavit.'

'You never know,' I said, 'and thanks.'

I had phoned the report from the car park of a motorway service station on my way home late in the dusky evening, but it was when I reached Pont Square that the day grew doubly dark. There was a two-page fax waiting on my machine and I read it standing in the sitting-room with all thoughts of a friendly glass of Scotch evaporating into disbelief and the onset of misery.

The pages were from Kevin Mills. 'I don't know why you want this list of the great and good,' he wrote, 'but for what it's worth and because I promised, here is a list of the guests entertained by Topline Foods at lunch at Aintree on the day before the Grand National.'

The list contained the name of the angry Lancashire farmer, as was expected, but it was the top of the list that did the psychological damage.

'Guest of Honour,' it announced, 'Ellis Quint.'

All the doubts I'd banished came roaring back with double vigour. Back too came self-ridicule and every defence mechanism under the sun.

I couldn't, didn't, *couldn't* believe that Ellis could maim – and effectively kill – a child's pony and three young racehorses. Not Ellis! It was *impossible*.

There had to be *dozens* of other people who could have learned where to find all four of those vulnerable unguarded animals. It was *stupid* to give any weight to an unreliable coincidence. All the same, I pulled my box chart out of a drawer, and in very small letters, as if in that way I could physically diminish the implication, I wrote in each 'who knew of victim's availability?' space the unthinkable words, Ellis Quint.

The 'motive' boxes had also remained empty. There was no apparent rational motive. Why did people poke out the eyes of ponies? Why did they stalk strangers and write poison pen letters? Why did they torture and kill children and tape-record their screams?

I wrote 'self gratification', but it seemed too weak. Insanity? Psychosis? The irresistible primordial upsurge of a hunger for pointless, violent destruction?

It didn't fit the Ellis I knew. Not the man I'd raced against and laughed with, and had deemed a close friend for years. One couldn't know someone that well, and yet not know them at all.

Could one?

No.

Relentless thoughts kept me awake all night and in the morning I sent Linda Ferns' cheque back to her, uncashed.

'I've got no further,' I wrote. 'I'm exceedingly sorry.'

Two days later the same cheque returned.

'Dear Sid,' Linda replied, 'Keep the money. I know you'll find the thugs one day. I don't know what you said to Rachel but she's much happier and she hasn't had any bad dreams since you came last week. For that alone I would pay you double. Affectionately, Linda Ferns.'

80

I put the cheque in a pending file, caught up with paperwork and attended my usual judo training session.

The judo I practised was the subtle art of self-defence, the shifting of balance that used an attacker's own momentum to overcome him. Judo was rhythm, leverage and speed; a matter sometimes of applying pressure to nerves and always, in the way I learned, a quiet discipline. The yells and the kicks of karate, the arms slapped down on the padded mat to emphasise aggression, they were neither in my nature nor what I needed. I didn't seek physical domination. I didn't by choice start fights. With the built-in drawbacks of half an arm, a light frame and a height of about five feet seven, my overall requirement was survival.

I went through the routines absentmindedly. They were at best a mental crutch. A great many dangers couldn't be wiped out by an ability to throw an assailant over one's shoulder.

Ellis wouldn't leave my thoughts.

I was wrong. Of *course* I was wrong.

His face was universally known. He wouldn't risk being seen sneaking around fields at night armed with anything like a machete.

But he was bored with celebrity. Fame was no substitute for danger, he'd said. Everything he had was not enough.

All the same . . . *he couldn't.*

*

81

In the second week after the Derby I went to the four days of the Royal Ascot meeting, drifting around in a morning suit, admiring the gleaming coats of the horses and the women's extravagant hats. I should have enjoyed it, as I usually did. Instead, I felt as if the whole thing were a charade taking illusory place over an abyss.

Ellis, of course, was there every day: and, of course, he sought me out.

'How's it going, Hotline?'

'The Hotline is silent.'

'There you are, then,' Ellis said with friendly irony, 'you've frightened your foot merchant off.'

'For ever, I hope.'

'What if he can't help it?' Ellis said.

I turned my head: looked at his eyes. 'I'll catch him,' I said.

He smiled and looked away. 'Everyone knows you're a whiz at that sort of thing, but I'll bet you—'

'Don't,' I interrupted. 'Don't bet on it. It's bad luck.'

Someone came up to his other elbow, claiming his attention. He patted my shoulder, said with the usual affection, 'See you, Sid,' and was drawn away; and I couldn't believe, I *couldn't*, that he had told me *why*, even if not how.

'*What if he can't help it?*'

Could compulsion lead to cruel senseless acts?

No . . .

Yes, it could, and yes, it often did.

But not in Ellis. Not, *not* in Ellis.

Alibis, I thought, seeking for a rational way out. I would find out – somehow – exactly where Ellis had been on the nights the horses had been attacked. I would prove to my own satisfaction that it couldn't have been Ellis, and I would return with relief to the beginning, and admit I had no pointers at all, and would never find the thugs for Linda, and would quite happily chalk up a failure.

At five-thirty in the morning on the day after the Ascot Gold Cup, I sleepily awoke and answered my ringing telephone to hear a high agitated female voice saying, 'I want to reach Sid Halley.'

'You have,' I said, pushing myself up to sitting and squinting at the clock.

'What?'

'You are talking to Sid Halley.' I stifled a yawn. Five-bloody-thirty.

'But I phoned *The Pump* and asked for the Hotline!'

I said patiently, 'They re-route the Hotline calls direct to me. This is Sid Halley you're talking to. How can I help you?'

'Christ,' she said, sounding totally disorganised. 'We have a colt with a foot off.'

After a breath-catching second I said, 'Where are you?'

'At home. Oh, I see, Berkshire.'

'Where, exactly?'

'Combe Bassett, south of Hungerford.'

'And ... um ...' I thought of asking, 'What's the state of play?' and discarded it as less than tactful. 'What is ... happening?'

'We're all up. Everyone's yelling and crying.'

'And the vet?'

'I just phoned him. He's coming.'

'And the police?'

'They're sending someone. Then we decided we'd better call you.'

'Yes,' I replied. 'I'll come now, if you like.'

'That's why I phoned you.'

'What's your name then? Address?'

She gave them. 'Betty Bracken, Manor House, Combe Bassett' – stumbling on the words as if she couldn't remember.

'Please,' I said, 'ask the vet not to send the colt or his foot off to the knackers until I get there.'

'I'll try,' she said jerkily. 'For God's sakes, *why*? Why our colt?'

'I'll be there in an hour,' I said.

What if he can't help it ...

But it took such planning. Such stealth. So many crazy risks. Someone, sometime, would see him.

Let it not be Ellis, I thought. Let the compulsion be some other poor bastard's ravening subconscious. Ellis

84

would be able to control such a vicious appetite, even if he felt it.

Let it not be Ellis.

Whoever it was, he had to be stopped: and I would stop him, if I could.

I shaved in the car (a Mercedes), clasping the battery-driven razor in the battery-driven hand, and I covered the eighty miles to south-west Berkshire in a time down the comparatively empty M4 that had the speedometer needle quivering where it had seldom been before. The radar speed traps slept. Just as well.

It was a lovely high June morning, fine and fresh. I curled through the gates of Combe Bassett Manor, cruised to a stop in the drive and at six-thirty walked into a house where open doors led to movement, loud voices and a general gnashing of teeth.

The woman who'd phoned rushed over when she saw me, her hands flapping in the air, her whole demeanour in an out-of-control state of fluster.

'Sid Halley? Thank God. Punch some sense into this lot.'

This lot consisted of two uniformed policemen and a crowd of what later proved to be family members, neighbours, ramblers and half a dozen dogs.

'Where's the colt?' I asked. 'And where's his foot?'

'Out in the field. The vet's there. I told him what you wanted but he's an opinionated Scot. God knows if he'll wait, he's a cantankerous old devil. He—'

'Show me where,' I said abruptly, cutting into the flow.

She blinked. 'What? Oh, yes. This way.'

She set off fast, leading me through big-house, unevenly painted hinterland passages reminiscent of those of Aynsford, of those of any house built with servants in mind. We passed a gun-room, flower-room, and mud-room (ranks of green wellies) and emerged at last through a rear door into a yard inhabited by dustbins. From there, through a green wooden garden door, she led the way fast down a hedge-bordered grass path and through a metal-railing gate at the far end of it. I'd begun to think we were off to limbo when suddenly, there before us, was a lane full of vehicles and about ten people leaning on paddock fencing.

My guide was tall, thin, fluttery, at a guess about fifty, dressed in old cord trousers and a drab olive sweater. Her greying hair flopped, unbrushed, over a high forehead. She had been, and still was, beyond caring how she looked, but I had a powerful impression that she was a woman to whom looks mattered little anyway.

She was deferred to. The men leaning on the paddock rails straightened and all but touched their forelocks, 'Morning, Mrs Bracken.'

She nodded automatically and ushered me through the wide metal gate that one of the men swung open for her.

Inside the field, at a distance of perhaps thirty paces,

stood two more men, also a masculine-looking woman and a passive colt with three feet. All, except the colt, showed the facial and body language of impatience.

One of the men, tall, white-haired, wearing black-rimmed glasses, took two steps forward to meet us.

'Now, Mrs Bracken, I've done what you asked, but it's past time to put your poor boy out of his misery. And you'll be Sid Halley, I suppose,' he said, peering down as from a mountain top. 'There's little you can do.' He shook hands briefly as if it were a custom he disapproved of.

He had a strong Scottish accent and the manner of one accustomed to command. The man behind him, unremarkably built, self-effacing in manner, remained throughout a silent watcher on the fringe.

I walked over to the colt and found him wearing a head-collar, with a rope halter held familiarly by the woman. The young horse watched me with calm bright eyes, unafraid. I stroked my hand down his nose, talking to him quietly. He moved his head upwards against the pressure and down again as if nodding, saying hello. I let him whiffle his black lips across my knuckles. I stroked his neck and patted him. His skin was dry: no pain, no fear, no distress.

'Is he drugged?' I asked.

'I'd have to run a blood test,' the Scotsman said.

'Which you are doing, of course?'

'Of course.'

One could tell from the faces of the other man

87

and the woman that no blood test had so far been considered.

I moved round the colt's head and squatted down for a close look at his off-fore, running my hand down the back of his leg, feeling only a soft area of no resistance where normally there would be the tough bowstring tautness of the leg's main tendon. Pathetically, the fetlock was tidy, not bleeding. I bent up the colt's knee and looked at the severed end. It had been done neatly, sliced through, unsplintered ends of bone showing white, the skin cleanly cut as if a practised chef had used a disjointing knife.

The colt jerked his knee, freeing himself from my grasp.

I stood up.

'Well?' the Scotsman challenged.

'Where's his foot?'

'Over yon, out of sight behind the water trough.' He paused, then as I turned away from him, suddenly added, 'It wasn't found there. I put it there, out of sight. It was they ramblers that came to it first.'

'Ramblers?'

'Aye.'

Mrs Bracken, who had joined us, explained. 'One Saturday every year in June, all the local rambling clubs turn out in force to walk the footpaths in this part of the country, to keep them legally open for the public.'

'If they'd stay on the footpaths,' the Scot said forbiddingly, 'they be within their rights.'

Mrs Bracken agreed. 'They bring their children and their dogs and their picnics, and act as if they own the place.'

'But . . . what on earth time did they find your colt's foot?'

'They set off soon after dawn,' Mrs Bracken observed morosely. 'In the middle of June, that's four-thirty in the morning, more or less. They gather before five o'clock while it is still cool, and set off across my land first, and they were hammering on my door by five-fifteen. Three of the children were in full-blown hysteria, and a man with a beard and a pony-tail was screaming that he blamed the élite. What élite? One of the ramblers phoned the Press and then someone fanatical in animal rights, and a carload of activists arrived with "ban horse racing" banners.' She rolled her eyes. 'I *despair*,' she said. 'It's bad enough losing my glorious colt. These people are turning it into a *circus*.'

Hold on to the real tragedy at the heart of the farce, I thought briefly, and walked over to the water trough to look at the foot that lay behind it. There were horse-feed nuts scattered everywhere around. Without expecting much emotion, I bent and picked the foot up.

I hadn't seen the other severed feet. I'd actually thought some of the reported reactions excessive. But the reality of that poor, unexpected, curiously lonely lump of bone, gristle and torn ends of blood vessels, that wasted miracle of anatomical elegance, moved me close to the fury and grief of all the owners.

There was a shoe on the hoof; the sort of small light shoe fitted to youngsters to protect their fore feet out in the field. There were ten small nails tacking the shoe to the hoof. The presence of the shoe brought its own powerful message: civilisation had offered care to the colt's foot, barbarity had hacked it off.

I'd loved horses always: it was hard to explain the intimacy that grew between horses and those who tended or rode them. Horses lived in a parallel world, spoke a parallel language, were a mass of instincts, lacked human perceptions of kindness or guilt, and allowed a merging on an untamed, untamable mysterious level of spirit. The Great God Pan lived in racehorses. One cut off his foot at one's peril.

On a more prosaic level I put the hoof back on the ground, unclipped the mobile phone I wore on my belt and, consulting a small diary/notebook for the number, connected myself to a veterinary friend who worked as a surgeon in an equine hospital in Lambourn.

'Bill?' I said. 'This is Sid Halley.'

'Go to sleep,' he said.

'Wake up. It's six-fifty and I'm in Berkshire with the severed off-fore hoof of a two-year-old colt.'

'Jesus.' He woke up fast.

'I want you to look at it. What do you advise?'

'How long has it been off? Any chance of sewing it back on?'

'It's been off at least three hours, I'd say. Probably more. There's no sign of the achilles tendon. It's contracted up inside the leg. The amputation is through the fetlock joint itself.'

'One blow, like the others?'

I hesitated. 'I didn't see the others.'

'But something's worrying you?'

'I want you to look at it,' I said.

Bill Ruskin and I had worked on other, earlier puzzles, and got along together in a trusting undemanding friendship that remained unaltered by periods of non-contact.

'What shape is the colt in generally?' he asked.

'Quiet. No visible pain.'

'Is the owner rich?'

'It looks like it.'

'See if he'll have the colt – and his foot, of course – shipped over here.'

'She,' I said. 'I'll ask her.'

Mrs Bracken gaped at me mesmerised when I relayed the suggestion, and said 'Yes' faintly.

Bill said, 'Find a sterile surgical dressing for the leg. Wrap the foot in another dressing and a polythene bag and pack it in a bucket of ice cubes. Is it clean?'

'Some early morning ramblers found it.'

He groaned. 'I'll send a horse ambulance,' he said. 'Where to?'

I explained where I was, and added, 'There's a Scots

vet here that's urging to put the colt down at once. Use honey-tongued diplomacy.'

'Put him on.'

I returned to where the colt still stood and, explaining who he would be talking to, handed my phone to the vet. The Scot scowled. Mrs Bracken said 'Anything, anything,' over and over again. Bill talked.

'Very well,' the Scot said frostily, finally, 'but you do understand, don't you, Mrs Bracken, that the colt won't be able to race, even if they do succeed in reattaching his foot, which is very, very doubtful.'

She said simply, 'I don't want to lose him. It's worth a try.'

The Scot, to give him his due, set about enclosing the raw leg efficiently in a dressing from his surgical bag and in wrapping the foot in a businesslike bundle. The row of men leaning on the fence watched with interest. The masculine-looking woman holding the head-collar wiped a few tears from her weatherbeaten cheeks while crooning to her charge, and eventually Mrs Bracken and I returned to the house, which still rang with noise. The ramblers, making the most of the drama, seemed to be rambling all over the ground floor and were to be seen assessing their chances of penetrating upstairs. Mrs Bracken clutched her head in distraction and said, 'Please will everyone leave,' but without enough volume to be heard.

I begged one of the policemen, 'Shoo the lot out, can't you?' and finally most of the crowd left, the ebb revealing a large basically formal pale green and gold drawing-room inhabited by five or six humans, three dogs and a clutter of plastic cups engraving wet rings on ancient polished surfaces. Mrs Bracken, like a somnambulist, drifted around picking up cups from one place only to put them down in another. Ever tidy-minded, I couldn't stop myself twitching up a waste-paper basket and following her, taking the cups from her fingers and collecting them all together.

She looked at me vaguely. She said, 'I paid a quarter of a million for that colt.'

'Is he insured?'

'No. I don't insure my jewellery either.'

'Or your health?'

'No, of course not.'

She looked unseeingly round the room. Five people now sat on easy chairs, offering no help or succour.

'Would someone make a cup of tea?' she asked.

No one moved.

She said to me, as if it explained everything, 'Esther doesn't start work until eight.'

'Mm,' I said. 'Well . . . er . . . who is everybody?'

'Goodness, yes. Rude of me. That's my husband.' Her gaze fell affectionately on an old bald man who looked as if he had no comprehension of anything. 'He's deaf, the dear man.'

'I see.'

'And that's my aunt, who mostly lives here.'

The aunt was also old and proved unhelpful and selfish.

'Our tenants.' Mrs Bracken indicated a stolid couple. 'They live in part of the house. And my nephew.'

Even her normal good manners couldn't keep the irritation from either her voice or her face at this last identification. The nephew was a teenager with a loose mouth and an attitude problem.

None of this hopeless bunch looked like an accomplice in a spite attack on a harmless animal, not even the unsatisfactory boy, who was staring at me intensely as if demanding to be noticed: almost, I thought fleetingly, as if he wanted to tell me something by telepathy. It was more than an interested inspection, but also held neither disapproval nor fear, as far as I could see.

I said to Mrs Bracken, 'If you tell me where the kitchen is, I'll make you some tea.'

'But you've only one hand.'

I reassured her, 'I can't climb Everest but I can sure make tea.'

A streak of humour began to banish the morning's shocks from her eyes. 'I'll come with you,' she said.

The kitchen, like the whole house, had been built on a grand scale for a cast of dozens. Without difficulties we made tea in a pot and sat at the well-scrubbed old wooden central table to drink it from mugs.

'You're not what I expected,' she said. 'You're *cosy*.'

I liked her: couldn't help it.

She went on, 'You're not like my brother said. I'm afraid I didn't explain that it is my brother who is out in the field with the vet. It was he who said I should phone you. He didn't say you were cosy, he said you were flint. I should have introduced you to him, but you can see how things are ... Anyway, I rely on him dreadfully. He lives in the next village. He came at once when I woke him.'

'Is he,' I asked neutrally, 'your nephew's father?'

'Goodness, no. My nephew ... Jonathan ...' She stopped, shaking her head. 'You don't want to hear about Jonathan.'

'Try me.'

'He's our sister's son. Fifteen. He got into trouble, expelled from school ... on probation ... his step-father can't stand him. My sister was at her wits' end so I said he could come here for a bit. It's not working out, though. I can't get through to him.' She looked suddenly aghast. 'You don't think he had anything to do with the colt?'

'No, no. What trouble did he get into? Drugs?'

She sighed, shaking her head. 'He was with two other boys. They stole a car and crashed it. Jonathan was in the back seat. The boy driving was also fifteen and broke his neck. Paralysed. Joy-riding, they called it. Some joy! Stealing, that's what it was. And Jonathan isn't repentant. Really, he can be a *pig*. But not the colt ... not that?'

'No,' I assured her, 'positively not.' I drank hot tea

95

and asked, 'Is it well known hereabouts that you have this great colt in that field?'

She nodded. 'Eva, who looks after him, she talks of nothing else. All the village knows. That's why there are so many people here. Half the men from the village, as well as the ramblers. Even so early in the morning.'

'And your friends?' I prompted.

She nodded gloomily. 'Everyone. I bought him at the Premium Yearling Sales last October. His breeding is a dream. He was a late foal – end of April – he's ... he *was* going into training next week. Oh *dear*.'

'I'm so sorry,' I said. I screwed myself unhappily to ask the unavoidable question, 'Who, among your friends, came here in person to admire the colt?'

She was far from stupid, and also vehement. 'No one who came here could *possibly* have done this! People like Lord and Lady Dexter? Of course not! Gordon and Ginnie Quint, and darling Ellis? Don't be silly. Though I suppose,' she went on doubtfully, 'they could have mentioned him to other people. He wasn't a *secret*. Anyone since the Sales would know he was here, like I told you.'

'Of course,' I said.

Ellis.

We finished the tea and went back to the drawing-room. Jonathan, the nephew, stared at me again unwaveringly, and after a moment, to test my own impression, I jerked my head in the direction of the door, walking that way; and, with hardly a hesitation, he stood up and followed.

I went out of the drawing-room, across the hall and through the still wide-open front door onto the drive.

'Sid Halley,' he said behind me.

I turned. He stopped four paces away, still not wholly committed. His accent and general appearance spoke of expensive schools, money and privilege. His mouth and his manner said slob.

'What is it that you know?' I asked.

'Hey! Look here! What do you mean?'

I said without pressure, 'You want to tell me something, don't you?'

'I don't know. Why do you think so?'

I'd seen that intense bursting-at-the-seams expression too often by then to mistake it. He knew something that he ought to tell: it was only his own contrary rebelliousness that had kept him silent so far.

I made no appeal to a better nature that I wasn't sure he had.

I said, guessing, 'Were you awake before four o'clock?'

He glared, but didn't answer.

I tried again. 'You hate to be helpful, is that it? No one is going to catch you behaving well – that sort of thing? Tell me what you know. I'll give you as bad a press as you want. Your obstructive reputation will remain intact.'

'Sod you,' he said.

I waited.

'She'd kill me,' he said. 'Worse, she'd pack me off home.'

'Mrs Bracken?'

He nodded. 'My Aunt Betty.'

'What have you done?'

He used a few old Anglo-Saxon words: bluster to impress me with his virility, I supposed. Pathetic, really. Sad.

'She has these effing stupid rules,' he said. 'Be back in the house at night by eleven-thirty.'

'And last night,' I suggested, 'you weren't?'

'I got probation,' he said. 'Did she tell you?'

'Yeah.'

He took two more steps towards me, into normal talking distance.

'If she knew I went out again,' he said, 'I could get youth custody.'

'If she shopped you, you mean?'

He nodded. 'But ... sod it ... to cut a foot off a horse ...'

Perhaps the better nature was somewhere there after all. Stealing cars was OK, maiming racehorses wasn't. He wouldn't have blinded those ponies: he wasn't that sort of lout.

'If I fix it with your aunt, will you tell me?' I asked.

'Make her promise not to tell Archie. He's worse.'

'Er,' I said, 'who is Archie?'

'My uncle. Aunt Betty's brother. He's Establishment, man. He's the flogging classes.'

I made no promises. I said, 'Just spill the beans.'

'In three weeks I'll be sixteen.' He looked at me intently for reaction, but all he'd caused in me was puzzlement. I thought the cut-off age for crime to be considered 'juvenile' was two years older. He wouldn't be sent to an adult jail.

Jonathan saw my lack of understanding. He said impatiently, 'You can't be under age for sex if you're a man, only if you're a girl.'

'Are you sure?'

'*She* says so.'

'Your Aunt Betty?' I felt lost.

'No, stupid. The woman in the village.'

'Oh . . . ah.'

'Her old man's a long-distance lorry driver. He's away for nights on end. He'd kill me. Youth custody would be apple-pie.'

'Difficult,' I said.

'She *wants* it, see? I'd never done it before. I bought her a gin in the pub.' Which, at fifteen, was definitely illegal to start with.

'So . . . um . . .' I said, 'last night you were coming back from the village . . . When, exactly?'

'It was dark. Just before dawn. There had been more moonlight earlier, but I'd left it late. I was *running*. She – Aunt Betty – she wakes with the cocks. She lets

99

the dogs out before six.' His agitation, I thought, was producing what sounded like truth.

I thought, and asked, 'Did you see any ramblers?'

'No. I was earlier than them.'

I held my breath. I had to ask the next question, and dreaded the answer.

'So, who was it that you saw?'

'It wasn't a "who", it was a "what".' He paused and reassessed his position. 'I didn't go to the village.' He said, 'I'll deny it.'

I nodded. 'You were restless. Unable to sleep. You went for a walk.'

He said, 'Yeah, that's it,' with relief.

'And you saw?'

'A Land-Rover.'

Not a who. A what. I said, partly relieved, partly disappointed, 'That's not so extraordinary, in the country.'

'No, but it wasn't Aunt Betty's Land-Rover. It was much newer, and blue, not green. It was standing in the lane not far from the gate into the field. There was no one in it. I didn't think much of it. There's a path up to the house from the lane. I always go out and in that way. It's miles from Aunt Betty's bedroom.'

'Through the yard with all the dustbins?' I asked.

He was comically astounded. I didn't explain that his aunt had taken me out that way. I said, 'Couldn't it have been a rambler's Land-Rover?'

100

He said sullenly, 'I don't know why I bothered to tell you.'

I asked, 'What else did you notice about the Land-Rover, except for its colour?'

'Nothing. I told you, I was more interested in getting back into the house without anyone spotting me.'

I thought a bit and said, 'How close did you get to it?'

'I touched it. I didn't see it until I was almost on top of it. Like I told you, I was running along the lane. I was mostly looking at the ground, and it was still almost dark.'

'Was it facing you, or did you run into the back of it?'

'Facing. There was still enough moonlight to reflect off the windscreen. That's what I saw first, the reflection.'

'What part of it did you touch?'

'The bonnet.' Then he added as if surprised by the extent of his memory, 'It was quite hot.'

'Did you see a number plate?'

'Not a chance. I wasn't hanging about for things like that.'

'What else did you see?'

'Nothing.'

'How did you know there was no one in the cab? There might have been a couple lying in there snogging.'

'Well, there wasn't. I looked through the window.'

'Open or shut windows?'

'Open.' He surprised himself again. 'I looked in fast, on the way past. No people, just a load of machinery behind the front seats.'

'What sort of machinery?'

'How the eff do I know? It had handles sticking up. Like a lawn mower. I didn't look. I was in a hurry. I didn't want to be seen.'

'No,' I agreed. 'How about an ignition key?'

'Hey?' It was a protest of hurt feelings. 'I didn't drive it away.'

'Why not?'

'I don't take every car I see. Not alone, ever.'

'There's no fun in it if you're alone?'

'Not so much.'

'So there *was* a key in the ignition?'

'I suppose so. Yah.'

'Was there one key, or a bunch?'

'Don't know.'

'Was there a key-ring?'

'You don't ask much!'

'Think, then.'

He said unwillingly, 'See, I *notice* ignition keys.'

'Yes.'

'It was a bunch of keys, then. They had a silver horseshoe dangling from them on a little chain. A little horseshoe. Just an ordinary key-ring.'

We stared at each other briefly.

He said, 'I didn't think anything of it.'

'No,' I agreed. 'You wouldn't. Well, go back a bit. When you put your hand on the bonnet, were you looking at the windscreen?'

'I must have been.'

'What was on it?'

'Nothing. What do you mean?'

'Did it have a tax disc?'

'It must have done, mustn't it?' he said.

'Well, did it have anything else? Like, say, a sticker saying "Save the Tigers"?'

'No, it didn't.'

'Shut your eyes and think,' I urged him. 'You're running. You don't want to be seen. You nearly collide with a Land-Rover. Your face is quite near the windscreen—'

'There was a red dragon,' he interrupted. 'A red circle with a dragon thing in it. Not very big. One of those sort of transparent transfers that stick to glass.'

'Great,' I said. 'Anything else?'

For the first time he gave it concentrated thought, but came up with nothing more.

'I'm nothing to do with the police,' I said, 'and I won't spoil your probation and I won't give you away to your aunt, but I'd like to write down what you've told me, and if you agree that I've got it right, will you sign it?'

'Hey. I don't know. I don't know why I told you.'

'It might matter a lot. It might not matter at all. But

I'd like to find this bugger . . .' God help me, I thought. I have to.

'So would I.' He meant it. Perhaps there was hope for him yet.

He turned on his heel and went rapidly alone into the house, not wanting to be seen in even semi-reputable company, I assumed. I followed more slowly. Jonathan had not returned to the drawing-room, where the tenants still sat stolidly, the difficult old aunt complained about being woken early, the deaf husband said, 'Eh?' mechanically at frequent intervals and Betty Bracken sat looking into space. Only the three dogs, now lying down and testing their heads on their front paws, seemed fully sane.

I said to Mrs Bracken, 'Do you by any chance have a typewriter?'

She said incuriously, 'There's one in the office.'

'Er . . .'

'I'll show you.' She rose and led me to a small, tidy back room containing the bones of communication but an impression of under-use.

'I don't know how anything works,' Betty Bracken said frankly. 'We have a part-time secretary, once a week. Help yourself.'

She left, nodding, and I thanked her, and I found an electric typewriter under a fitted dust-cover, plugged ready into the current.

I wrote:

Finding it difficult to sleep I went for a short walk in the grounds of Combe Bassett Manor at about three-thirty in the morning. [I inserted the date.] In the lane near to the gate of the home paddock I passed a Land-Rover that was parked there. The vehicle was blue. I did not look at the number plate. The engine was still hot when I touched the bonnet in passing. There was a key in the ignition. It was one of a bunch of keys on a key-ring which had a silver horseshoe on a chain. There was no one in the vehicle. There was some sort of equipment behind the front seat, but I did not take a close look. On the inside of the windscreen I observed a small transfer of a red dragon in a red circle. I went past the vehicle and returned to the house.

Under another fitted cover I located a copier, so I left the little office with three sheets of paper and went in search of Jonathan, running him to earth eating a haphazard breakfast in the kitchen. He paused over his cereal, spoon in air, while he read what I'd written. Wordlessly, I produced a ballpoint pen and held it out to him.

He hesitated, shrugged and signed the first of the papers with loops and a flourish.

'Why *three*?' he asked suspiciously, pushing the copies away.

'One for you,' I said calmly. 'One for my records.

One for the on-going file of bits and pieces which may eventually catch our villain.'

'Oh.' He considered. 'All right then.' He signed the other two sheets and I gave him one to keep. He seemed quite pleased with his civic-mindedness. He was re-reading his edited deposition over his flakes as I left.

Back in the drawing-room, looking for her, I asked where Mrs Bracken had gone. The aunt, the tenants and the deaf husband made no reply.

Negotiating the hinterland passage and the dustbin yard again, I arrived back at the field, to see Mrs Bracken herself, the fence-leaners, the Scots vet and her brother watching the horse ambulance drive into the field and draw up conveniently close to the colt.

The horse ambulance consisted of a narrow low-slung trailer pulled by a Range Rover. There was a driver and a groom used to handling sick and injured horses and, with crooning noises from the solicitous Eva, the poor young colt made a painful-looking, head-bobbing stagger up a gentle ramp into the waiting stall.

'Oh *dear*, oh *dear*,' Mrs Bracken whispered beside me. 'My dear, dear, young fellow . . . how *could* they?'

I shook my head. Rachel Ferns' pony and four prized colts . . . How could *anyone*.

The colt was shut into the trailer, the bucket containing the foot was loaded, and the pathetic twelve-mile journey to Lambourn began.

The Scots vet patted Betty Bracken sympathetically on the arm, gave her his best wishes for the colt, claimed his car from the line of vehicles in the lane and drove away.

I unclipped my mobile phone and got through to *The Pump*, who forwarded my call to an irate newspaperman at his home in Surrey.

Kevin Mills yelled, 'Where the hell are you? They say all anyone gets on the Hotline now is your answering machine, saying you'll call back. About fifty people have phoned. They're all rambling.'

'Ramblers,' I said.

'What?'

I explained.

'It's supposed to be my day off,' he grumbled. 'Can you meet me in the pub? What time? Five o'clock?'

'Make it seven,' I suggested.

'It's no longer a *Pump* exclusive, I suppose you realise?' he demanded. 'But save yourself for me alone, will you, buddy? Give me the inside edge?'

'It's yours.'

I closed my phone and warned Betty Bracken to expect the media on her doorstep.

'Oh no!'

'Your colt is one too many.'

'Archie!' She turned to her brother for help with a beseeching gesture of the hand and, as if for the thousandth time in their lives, he responded with comfort and competent solutions.

'My dear Betty,' he said, 'if you can't bear to face the Press, simply don't be here.'

'But . . .' she wavered.

'I shouldn't waste time,' I said.

The brother gave me an appraising glance. He himself was of medium height, lean of body, grey in colour, a man to get lost in a crowd. His eyes alone were notable: brown, bright and *aware*. I had an uncomfortable feeling that, far beyond having his sister phone me, he knew a good deal about me.

'We haven't actually met,' he said to me civilly. 'I'm Betty's brother. I'm Archie Kirk.'

I said, 'How do you do,' and I shook his hand.

CHAPTER FIVE

Betty Bracken, Archie Kirk and I returned to the house, again circumnavigating the dustbins. Archie Kirk's car was parked outside the Manor's front door, not far from my own.

The lady of the Manor refusing to leave without her husband, the uncomprehending old man, still saying 'Eh?', was helped with great solicitude across the hall, through the front door and into an ancient Daimler, an Establishment-type conservative-minded political statement if ever I saw one.

My own Mercedes, milk-coffee-coloured, stood beyond: and what, I thought astringently, was it saying about *me*? Rich enough, sober enough, preferring reliability to flash? All spot on, particularly the last. And speed, of course.

Betty spooned her beloved into the back seat of the Daimler and folded herself in beside him, patting him gently. Touch, I supposed, had replaced speech as their means of communication. Archie Kirk took his place behind the wheel as natural commander-in-chief, and drove away, leaving for me the single short parting remark, 'Let me know.'

I nodded automatically. Let him know *what*? Whatever I learned, I presumed.

I returned to the drawing-room. The stolid tenants, on their feet, were deciding to return to their own wing of the house. The dogs snoozed. The cross aunt crossly demanded Esther's presence. Esther, on duty at eight and not a moment before, come ramblers, police or whatever, appeared forbiddingly in the doorway, a small, frizzy-haired worker, clear about her 'rights'.

I left the two quarrelsome women pitching into each other and went in search of Jonathan. What a household! The media were welcome to it. I looked but couldn't find Jonathan, so I just had to trust that his boorishness would keep him well away from inquisitive reporters with microphones. The Land-Rover he'd seen might have brought the machete to the colt, and I wanted, if I could, to find it before its driver learned there was a need for rapid concealment.

The first thing in my mind was the colt himself. I started the car and set off north to Lambourn, driving thoughtfully, wondering what was best to do concerning the police. I had had varying experiences with the Force, some good, some rotten. They did not, in general, approve of freelance investigators like myself, and could be downright obstructive if I appeared to be working on something they felt belonged to them alone. Sometimes, though, I'd found them willing to take over

110

if I'd come across criminal activity that couldn't go unprosecuted. I stepped gingerly round their sensitive areas, and also those of racing's own security services run by the Jockey Club and the British Horse-racing Board. I was careful always not to claim credit for clearing up three-pipe problems. Not even one-pipe problems, hardly worthy of Sherlock Holmes.

Where the Jockey Club itself was concerned, I fluctuated in their view between flavour of the month and anathema, according as to who currently reigned as Senior Steward. With the police, collaboration depended very much on which individual policeman I reached and his private-life stress level at the moment of contact.

The rules governing evidence, moreover, were growing ever stickier. Juries no longer without question believed the police. For an object to be admitted for consideration in a trial it had to be ticketed, docketed and continuously accounted for. One couldn't, for instance, flourish a machete and say, 'I found it in X's Land-Rover, therefore it was X who cut off a colt's foot.' To get even within miles of conviction one needed a specific search warrant before one could even *look* in the Land-Rover for a machete, and search warrants weren't granted to Sid Halleys, and sometimes not to the police.

The police force as a whole was divided into autonomous districts, like the Thames Valley Police, who solved crimes in their own area but might not take

111

much notice outside. A maimed colt in Lancashire might not have been heard of in Yorkshire. Serial rapists had gone for years uncaught because of the slow flow of information. A serial horse maimer might have no central file.

Dawdling along up the last hill before Lambourn I became aware of a knocking in the car and pulled over to the side with gloomy thoughts of broken shock absorbers and misplaced trust in reliability, but after the car stopped the knocking continued. With awakening awareness, I climbed out, went round to the back and with difficulty opened the boot. There was something wrong with the lock.

Jonathan lay curled in the space for luggage. He had one shoe off, with which he was assaulting my milk-coffee bodywork. When I lifted the lid he stopped banging and looked at me challengingly.

'What the hell are you doing there?' I demanded.

Silly question. He looked at his shoe. I rephrased it. 'Get out.'

He manoeuvred himself out onto the road and calmly replaced his shoe with no attempt at apology. I slammed the boot lid shut at the second try and returned to the driver's seat. He walked to the passenger side, found the door there locked and tapped on the window to draw my attention to it. I started the engine, lowered the electrically controlled window a little, and shouted to him, 'It's only three miles to Lambourn.'

'No. Hey! You can't leave me here!'

Want to bet, I thought, and set off along the deserted downland road. I saw him, in the rear-view mirror, running after me determinedly. I drove slowly, but faster than he could run. He went on running, nevertheless.

After nearly a mile a curve in the road took me out of his sight. I braked and stopped. He came round the bend, saw my car and put on a spurt, racing this time up to the driver's side. I'd locked the door but lowered the window three or four inches.

'What's all that for?' he demanded.

'What's all what for?'

'Making me run.'

'You've broken the lock on my boot.'

'What?' He looked baffled. 'I only gave it a clout. I didn't have a key.' No key; a clout. Obvious, his manner said.

'Who's going to pay to get it mended?' I asked.

He said impatiently, as if he couldn't understand such small-mindedness, 'What's that got to do with it?'

'With what?'

'With the colt.'

Resignedly I leaned across and pulled up the locking knob on the front passenger door. He went round there and climbed in beside me. I noted with interest that he was hardly out of breath.

Jonathan's haircut, I thought as he settled into his seat and neglected to buckle the seat-belt, shouted an indication of his adolescent insecurity, of his desire to shock or at least to be *noticed*. He had, I thought, bleached inexpert haphazard streaks into his hair with a comb dipped in something like hydrogen peroxide. Straight and thick, the mop was parted in the centre with a wing each side curving down to his cheek, making a curtain beside his eye. From one ear backwards, and round to the other ear, the hair had been sliced off in a straight line. Below the line, his scalp was shaven. To my eyes it looked ugly, but then I wasn't fifteen.

Making a statement through hairstyle was universal, after all. Men with bald crowns above pigtails, men with plaited beards, women with severely scraped back pinnings, all were saying 'This is *me*, and I'm *different*.' In the days of Charles I, when long male hair was normal, rebellious sons had cut off their curls to have roundheads. Archie Kirk's grey hair had been short, neat and controlled. My own dark hair would have curled girlishly if allowed to grow. A haircut was still the most unmistakable give-away of the person inside.

Conversely, a wig could change all that.

I asked Jonathan, 'Have you remembered something else?'

'No, not really.'

'Then why did you stow away?'

'Come on, man, give me a break. What am I supposed to do all day in that graveyard of a house? The

114

aunt's whinging drives me insane and even Karl Marx would have throttled Esther.'

He did, I suppose, have a point.

I thoughtfully coasted down the last hill towards Lambourn.

'Tell me about your uncle, Archie Kirk,' I said.

'What about him?'

'You tell me. For starters, what does he do?'

'He works for the government.'

'What as?'

'Some sort of civil servant. Dead boring.'

Boring, I reflected, was the last adjective I would have applied to what I'd seen in Archie Kirk's eyes.

'Where does he live?' I asked.

'Back in Shelley Green, a couple of miles from Aunt Betty. She can't climb a ladder unless he's holding it.'

Reaching Lambourn itself I took the turn that led to the equine hospital. Slowly though I had made the journey, the horse-ambulance had been slower. They were still unloading the colt.

From Jonathan's agog expression, I guessed it was in fact the first view he'd had of a shorn-off leg, even if all he could now see was a surgical dressing.

I said to him, 'If you want to wait half an hour for me, fine. Otherwise, you're on your own. But if you try stealing a car, I'll personally see you lose your probation.'

'Hey. Give us a break.'

'You've had your share of good breaks. Half an hour. OK?'

He glowered at me without words. I went across to where Bill Ruskin, in a white coat, was watching his patient's arrival. He said, 'Hello, Sid,' absentmindedly, then collected the bucket containing the foot and, with me following, led the way into a small laboratory full of weighing and measuring equipment and microscopes.

Unwrapping the foot, he stood it on the bench and looked at it assessingly.

'A good clean job,' he said.

'There's nothing good about it.'

'Probably the colt hardly felt it.'

'How was it done?' I asked.

'Hm.' He considered. 'There's no other point on the leg that you could amputate a foot without using a saw to cut through the bone. I doubt if a single swipe with a heavy knife would achieve this precision. And achieve it several times, on different animals, right?'

I nodded.

'Yes, well, I think we might be looking at game shears.'

'*Game shears?*' I exclaimed. 'Do you mean those sort of heavy scissors that will cut up duck and pheasant?'

'Something along those lines, yes.'

'But those shears aren't anywhere near big enough for this.'

He pursed his mouth. 'How about a gralloching

knife, then? The sort used for disembowelling deer out on the mountains?'

'Jeez.'

'There are signs of *compression*, though. On balance, I'd hazard heavy game shears. How did he get the colt to stand still?'

'There were horse-nuts on the ground.'

He nodded morosely. 'Slime ball.'

'There aren't any words for it.'

He peered closely at the raw red and white end of the pastern. 'Even if I can reattach the foot, the colt will never race.'

'His owner knows that. She wants to save his life.'

'Better to collect the insurance.'

'No insurance. A quarter of a million down the drain. But it's not the money she's grieving over. What she's feeling is guilt.'

He understood. He saw it often.

Eventually he said, 'I'll give it a try. I don't hold out much hope.'

'You'll photograph this as it is?'

He looked at the foot. 'Oh, sure. Photos, X-rays, blood tests on the colt, micro-stitching, every luxury. I'll get on with anaesthetising the colt as soon as possible. The foot's been off too long . . .' He shook his head. 'I'll try.'

'Phone my mobile.' I gave him the number. 'Any time.'

'See you, Sid. And catch the bugger.'

He bustled away, taking the foot with him, and I returned to my car to find Jonathan not only still there but jogging around with excitement.

'What's up?' I asked.

'That Range Rover that pulled the trailer that brought the colt . . .'

'What about it?'

'It's got a red dragon on the windscreen!'

'What? But you said a *blue*—'

'Yeah, yeah, it wasn't the vet's Range Rover I saw in the lane, but it's got a red dragon transfer on it. Not exactly the same, I don't think, but definitely a red dragon.'

I looked round, but the horse-ambulance was no longer in sight.

'They drove it off,' Jonathan said, 'but I saw the transfer close to, and it has *letters* in it.' His voice held triumph, which I allowed was justified.

'Go on, then,' I said. 'What letters?'

'Aren't you going to say "well done"?'

'Well done. What letters?'

'E.S.M. They were cut out of the red circle. Gaps, not printed letters.' He wasn't sure I understood.

'I do see,' I assured him.

I returned to the hospital to find Bill and asked him when he'd bought his Range Rover.

'Our local garage got it for us from a firm in Oxford.'

'What does E.S.M. stand for?'

'God knows.'

'I can't ask God. What's the name of the Range-Rover firm in Oxford?'

He laughed and thought briefly. 'English Sporting Motors. E.S.M. Good Lord.'

'Can you give me the name of someone there? Who did you actually deal with?'

With impatience he said, 'Look, Sid, I'm trying to scrub up to see what I can do about sticking the colt's foot back on.'

'And I'm trying to catch the bugger that took it off. And it's possible he travelled in a Land-Rover sold by English Sporting Motors.'

He said 'Christ' wide-eyed and headed for what proved to be the hospital's record office, populated by filing cabinets. Without much waste of time he flourished a copy of a receipted account, but shook his head.

'Ted James in the village might help you. I paid *him*. He dealt direct with Oxford. You'd have to ask Ted James.'

I thanked him, collected Jonathan, drove into the small town of Lambourn and located Ted James, who would do a lot for a good customer like Bill Ruskin, it seemed.

'No problem,' he assured me. 'Ask for Roger Brook in Oxford. Do you want me to phone him?'

'Yes, please.'

'Right-oh.' He spoke briefly on the phone and reported back. 'He's busy. Saturday's always a busy sales day. He'll help you if it doesn't take long.'

The morning seemed to have been going on for ever, but it was still before eleven o'clock when I talked to Roger Brook, tubby, smooth and self-important in the carpeted sales office of English Sporting Motors.

Roger Brook pursed his lips and shook his head; not the firm's policy to give out information about its customers.

I said ruefully, 'I don't want to bother the police . . .'

'Well . . .'

'And, of course, there would be a fee for your trouble.'

A fee was respectable where a bribe wasn't. In the course of life I disbursed a lot of fees.

It helpfully appeared that the red-dragon transparent transfers were slightly differently designed each year: *improved* as time went on, did I see?

I fetched Jonathan in from outside for Roger Brook to show him the past and present dragon logos, and Jonathan with certainty picked the one that had been, Brook said, that of the year before last.

'Great,' I said with satisfaction. 'How many blue Land-Rovers did you sell in that year? I mean, what are the names of the actual buyers, not the middlemen like Ted James?'

An open-mouthed silence proved amenable to a larger fee. 'Our Miss Denver' helped with a computer print-out. Our Miss Denver got a kiss from me. Roger Brook with dignity took his reward in readies, and Jonathan and I returned to the Mercedes with the names and addresses of two hundred and eleven purchasers of blue Land-Rovers a little back in time.

Jonathan wanted to read the list when I'd finished. I handed it over, reckoning he'd deserved it. He looked disappointed when he reached the end, and I didn't point out to him the name that had made my gut contract.

One of the Land-Rovers had been delivered to Twyford Lower Farms Ltd.

I had been to Twyford Lower Farms to lunch. It was owned by Gordon Quint.

Noon, Saturday. I sat in my parked car outside English Sporting Motors, while Jonathan fidgeted beside me, demanding 'What next?'

I said, 'Go and eat a hamburger for your lunch and be back here in twenty minutes.'

He had no money. I gave him some. 'Twenty minutes.'

He promised nothing, but returned with three minutes to spare. I spent his absence thinking highly unwelcome thoughts and deciding what to do, and when he slid in beside me smelling of raw onions and chips I set off southwards again, on the roads back to Combe Bassett.

'Where are we going?'

'To see your Aunt Betty.'

'But hey! She's not at home. She's at Archie's.'

'Then we'll go to Archie's. You can show me the way.'

He didn't like it, but he made no attempt to jump ship when we were stopped by traffic lights three times on the way out of Oxford. We arrived together in due course outside a house an eighth the size of Combe Bassett Manor; a house, moreover, that was frankly modern and not at all what I'd expected.

I said doubtfully, 'Are you sure this is the place?'

'The lair of the wolf. No mistake. He won't want to see me.'

I got out of the car and pressed the thoroughly modern doorbell beside a glassed-in front porch. The woman who came to answer the summons was small and wrinkled like a drying apple, and wore a sleeveless sundress in blue and mauve.

'Er . . .' I said to her enquiring face, 'Archie Kirk?'

Her gaze lengthened beyond me to include Jonathan in my car, a sight that pinched her mouth and jumped her to an instant wrong conclusion. She whirled away and returned with Archie, who said repressively, 'What is *he* doing here?'

'Can you spare me half an hour?' I asked.

'What's Jonathan done?'

'He's been extraordinarily helpful. I'd like to ask your advice.'

'*Helpful!*'

'Yes. Could you hold your disapproval in abeyance for half an hour while I explain?'

He gave me an intense inspection, the brown eyes

sharp and knowing, as before. Decision arrived there plainly.

'Come in,' he said, holding his front door wide.

'Jonathan's afraid of you,' I told him. 'He wouldn't admit it but he is. Could I ask you not to give him the normal tongue-lashing? Will you invite him in and leave him alone?'

'You don't know what you're asking.'

'I do,' I said.

'No one speaks to me like this.' He was, however, only mildly affronted.

I smiled at his eyes. 'That's because they know you. But I met you only this morning.'

'And,' he said, 'I've heard about your lightning judgements.'

I felt, as on other occasions with people of his sort, a deep thrust of mental satisfaction. Also, more immediately, I knew I had come to the right place.

Archie Kirk stepped out from his door, took the three paces to my car, and said through the window, 'Jonathan, please come into the house.'

Jonathan looked past him to me. I jerked my head, as before, to suggest that he complied, and he left the safe shelter and walked to the house, even if reluctantly and frozen-faced.

Archie Kirk led the way across a modest hallway into a middle-sized sitting-room where Betty Bracken, her husband, and the small woman who'd answered my ring were sitting in armchairs drinking cups of coffee.

The room's overall impression was of old oak and books, a room for dark winter evenings and lamps and log fires, not fitted to the dazzle of June. None of the three faces turned towards us could have looked welcoming to the difficult boy.

The small woman, introducing herself as Archie's wife, stood up slowly and offered me coffee, 'And ... er ... Jonathan ... Coca-Cola?'

Jonathan, as if reprieved, followed her out to the next door kitchen, and I told Betty Bracken that her colt was at that moment being operated on, and that there should be news of him soon. She was pathetically pleased: too pleased, I was afraid.

I said casually to Archie, 'Can I talk to you in private?' and without question he said, 'This way,' and transferred us to a small adjacent room, again all dark oak and books, that he called his study.

'What is it?' he asked.

'I need a policeman,' I said.

He gave me a long level glance and waved me to one of the two hard oak chairs, himself sitting in the other, beside a paper-strewn desk.

I told him about Jonathan's night walk (harmless version) and about our tracing the Land-Rover to the suppliers at Oxford. I said that I knew where the Land-Rover might now be, but that I couldn't get a search warrant to examine it. For a successful prosecution, I mentioned, there had to be integrity of evidence; no chance of tampering or substitution. So I needed a policeman, but one that would listen and cooperate, not one that would either brush me off altogether or one that would do the police work sloppily.

'I thought you might know someone,' I finished. 'I don't know who else to ask, as at the moment this whole thing depends on crawling up to the machine-gun nest on one's belly, so to speak.'

He sat back in his chair staring at me vacantly while the data got processed.

At length he said, 'Betty called in the local police this morning early, but . . . ' he hesitated, 'they hadn't the clout you need.' He thought some more, then picked up an address book. He leafed through it for a number and made a phone call.

'Norman, this is Archie Kirk.'

Whoever Norman was, it seemed he was unwilling.

'It's extremely important,' Archie said.

Norman apparently capitulated, but with protest, giving directions.

'You had better be right,' Archie said to me, disconnecting. 'I've just called in about a dozen favours he owed me.'

'Who is he?'

'Detective Inspector Norman Picton, Thames Valley Police.'

'Brilliant,' I said.

'He's off duty. He's on the gravel pit lake. He's a clever and ambitious young man. And I,' he added with a glimmer, 'am a magistrate, and I may sign a search warrant myself, if he can clear it with his superintendent.'

He rendered me speechless, which quietly amused him.

'You didn't know?' he asked.

I shook my head and found my voice, 'Jonathan said you were a civil servant.'

'That too,' he agreed. 'How did you get that boorish young man to talk?'

'Er . . .' I said. 'What is Inspector Picton doing on the gravel pit lake?'

'Water ski-ing,' Archie said.

There were speedboats, children, wet-suits, picnics. There was a club house in a sea of scrubby grass and people sliding over the shining water pulled by strings.

Archie parked his Daimler at the end of a row of cars, and I, with Jonathan beside me, parked my Mercedes alongside. We had agreed to bring both cars so that I could go on eventually to London, with Archie ferrying Jonathan back to pick up the Brackens and take them all home to Combe Bassett. Jonathan hadn't warmed to the plan, but had ungraciously accompanied me as being a lesser horror than spending the afternoon mooching aimlessly round Archie's aunt-infested house.

Having got as far as the lake, he began looking at the harmless physical activity all around him, not with a sneer but with something approaching interest. On the shortish journey from Archie's house he had asked three moody questions, two of which I answered.

First: 'This is the best day for a long time. How come you get so much done so quickly?'

No answer possible.

And second: 'Did you ever steal anything?'

'Chocolate bars,' I said.

And third: 'Do you mind having only one hand?'

I said coldly, 'Yes.'

He glanced with surprise at my face and I saw that he'd expected me to say no. I supposed he wasn't old enough to know it was a question one shouldn't ask; but then, perhaps he would have asked it anyway.

When we climbed out of the car at the water-ski club I said, 'Can you swim?'

'Do me a favour.'

'Then go jump in the lake.'

'Sod you,' he said, and actually laughed.

Archie had meanwhile discovered that one of the scudding figures on the water was the man we'd come to see. We waited a fair while until a large presence in a blue wet-suit with scarlet stripes down arms and legs let go of the rope pulling him and skied free and gracefully to a sloping landing place on the edge of the water. He stepped off his skis grinning, knowing he'd shown off his considerable skill, and wetly shook Archie's hand.

'Sorry to keep you waiting,' he said, 'but I reckoned once you got here I'd have had it for the day.'

His voice, with its touch of Berkshire accent, held self-confidence and easy authority.

Archie said formally, 'Norman, this is Sid Halley.'

I shook the offered hand, which was cold besides wet. I received the sort of slow searching inspection I'd had from Archie himself: and I had no idea what the policeman thought.

'Well,' he said finally, stirring, 'I'll get dressed.'

We watched him walk away, squelching, gingerly barefooted, carrying his skis. He was back within five minutes, clad now in jeans, sneakers, open-necked shirt and sweater, his dark hair still wet and spiky, uncombed.

'Right,' he said to me. 'Give.'

'Er . . .' I hesitated. 'Would it be possible for Mr Kirk's nephew, Jonathan, to go for a ride in a speedboat?'

Both he and Archie looked over to where Jonathan, not far away, lolled unprepossessingly against my car. Jonathan did himself no favours, I thought; self-destruction rampant in every bolshie tilt of the anti-authority haircut.

'He doesn't deserve any ride in a speedboat,' Archie objected.

'I don't want him to overhear what I'm saying.'

'That's different,' Norman Picton decided. 'I'll fix it.'

Jonathan ungraciously allowed himself to be driven

128

round the lake by Norman Picton's wife in Norman Picton's boat, accompanied by Norman Picton's son. We watched the boat race past with a roar, Jonathan's streaky mop blown back in the wind.

'He's on the fence,' I said mildly to Archie. 'There's a lot of good in him.'

'You're the only one who thinks so.'

'He's looking for a way back without losing face.'

Both men gave me the slow assessment and shook their heads.

I said, bringing Jonathan's signed statement from my pocket, 'Try this on for size.'

They both read it, Picton first, Archie after.

Archie said in disbelief, 'He never talks. He wouldn't have said all this.'

'I asked him questions,' I explained. 'Those are his answers. He came with me to the Land-Rover central dealers in Oxford who put that red dragon transfer on the windscreen of every vehicle they sell. And we wouldn't know of the Land-Rover's presence in the lane, or its probable owner and whereabouts now, except for Jonathan. So I really do think he's earned his ride on the lake.'

'What exactly do you want the search warrant *for*?' Picton asked. 'One can't get search warrants unless one can come up with a good reason – or at least a convincing possibility or probability of finding something material to a case.'

'Well,' I said, 'Jonathan put his hand on the bonnet

of the vehicle standing right beside the gate to the field where Betty Bracken's colt lost his foot. If you search a certain Land-Rover and find Jonathan's hand-print on the bonnet, would that be proof enough that you'd found the right wheels?'

Picton said, 'Yes.'

'So,' I went on without emphasis, 'if we leave Jonathan here by the lake while your people fingerprint the Land-Rover, there could be no question of his having touched it this afternoon, and not last night.'

'I've heard about you,' Picton said.

'I think,' I said, 'that it would be a good idea to fingerprint that bonnet before it rains, don't you? Or before anyone puts it through a car-wash?'

'Where is it?' Picton asked tersely.

I produced the English Sporting Motors' print-out, and pointed. 'There,' I said. 'That one.'

Picton read it silently, Archie aloud.

'But I know the place. You're quite *wrong*. I've been a guest there. They're friends of Betty's.'

'And of mine,' I said.

He listened to the bleakness I could hear in my own voice.

'Who are we talking about?' Picton asked.

'Gordon Quint,' Archie said. 'It's rubbish.'

'Who is Gordon Quint?' Picton asked again.

'The father of Ellis Quint,' Archie said. 'And you must have heard of *him*.'

Picton nodded. He had indeed.

'I suppose it's possible,' I suggested tentatively, 'that someone *borrowed* the Land-Rover for the night.'

'But you don't believe it,' Picton remarked.

'I wish I did.'

'But where's the connection?' Picton asked. 'There has to be *more*. The fact that Twyford Lower Farms Ltd owned a blue Land-Rover of the relevant year isn't enough on its own. We cannot search that vehicle for hand-prints unless we have good reason to believe that it was that one and no other that we are looking for.'

Archie said thoughtfully, 'Search warrants have been issued on flimsier grounds before now.'

He and Picton walked away from me, the professionals putting their distance between themselves and Sid Public. I thought that if they refused to follow the trail it would be a relief, on the whole. It would let me off the squirming hook. But there could be another month and another colt . . . and an obsession feeding and fattening on success.

They came back, asking why I should link the Quint name to the deed. I described my box chart. Not conclusive, Archie said judiciously, and I agreed, no.

Picton repeated what I'd just said, 'Rachel's pony was bought by her father, Joe, on the advice of Ellis Quint?'

I said, 'Ellis did a broadcast about Rachel's pony losing his foot.'

'I saw it,' Picton said.

They didn't want to believe it any more than I did. There was a fairly long indeterminate silence.

Jonathan came back looking uncomplicatedly happy from his fast laps round the lake, and Norman Picton abruptly went into the club house, returning with a can of Coke which he put into Jonathan's hands. Jonathan held it in his left hand to open it and his right hand to drink. Norman took the empty can from him casually but carefully by the rim, and asked if he would like to try the skiing itself, not just a ride in the boat.

Jonathan, on the point of enthusiastically saying, '*Yes,*' remembered his cultivated disagreeableness and said, 'I don't mind. If you insist, I suppose I'll have to.'

'That's right,' Picton said cheerfully. 'My wife will drive. My son will watch the rope. We'll find you some swimming trunks and a wet-suit.'

He led Jonathan away. Archie watched inscrutably.

'Give him a chance,' I murmured. 'Give him a challenge.'

'Pack him off to the colonies to make a man of him?'

'Scoff,' I smiled. 'But long ago it often worked. He's bright and he's bored and he's not yet a totally confirmed delinquent.'

'You'd make a soft and rotten magistrate.'

'I expect you're right.'

Picton returned, saying, 'The boy will stay here until I get back, so we'd better get started. We'll take two cars, mine and Mr Halley's. In that way he can go on to London when he wants. We'll leave your car here, Archie. Is that all right?'

Archie said he didn't trust Jonathan not to steal it.

'He doesn't think stealing's much fun without his pals,' I said.

Archie stared. 'That boy never says *anything*.'

'Find him a dangerous job.'

Picton, listening, said, 'Like what?'

'Like,' I said, unprepared, 'like ... well ... on an oil rig. Two years of that. Tell him to keep a diary. Tell him to write.'

'Good God,' Archie said, shaking his head, 'he'd have the place in flames.'

He locked his car and put the keys in his pocket, climbing into the front passenger seat beside me as we followed Norman Picton into Newbury, to his official place of work.

I sat in my car outside the police station while Archie and Picton, inside, arranged the back-ups: the photographer, the fingerprinter, the detective constable to be Inspector Picton's note-taking assistant.

I sat with the afternoon sun falling through the windscreen and wished I were anywhere else, engaged on any other mission.

All the villains I'd caught before hadn't been people I knew. Or people – one had to face it – people I'd thought I'd known. I'd felt mostly satisfaction, sometimes relief, occasionally even regret, but never anything approaching this intensity of entrapped despair.

Ellis was loved. I was going to be hated.

Hatred was inevitable.

Could I bear it?

There was no choice, really.

Archie and Picton came out of the police station followed by their purposeful troop.

Archie, sliding in beside me, said the search warrant was signed, the Superintendent had given the expedition his blessing, and off we could go to the Twyford Lower Farms.

I sat without moving, without starting the car.

'What's the matter?' Archie demanded, looking at my face.

I said with pain, 'Ellis is my friend.'

CHAPTER SIX

Ginnie Quint was gardening in a large straw hat, businesslike gloves and grey overall dungarees, waging a losing war on weeds in flower beds in front of the comfortable main house of Twyford Lower Farms.

'Hello, dear Sid!' She greeted me warmly, standing up, holding the dirty gloves wide and putting her soft cheek forward for a kiss of greeting. 'What a nice surprise. But Ellis isn't here, you know. He went to the races, then he was going up to the Regent's Park flat. That's where you'll find him, dear.'

She looked in perplexity over my shoulder to where the Norman Picton contingent were erupting from their transport.

Ginnie said uncertainly, 'Who are your friends, dear?' Her face cleared momentarily in relief, and she exclaimed, 'Why, it's Archie Kirk! My dear man. How nice to see you.'

Norman Picton, carrying none of Archie's or my social-history baggage, came rather brutally to the point.

'I'm Detective Inspector Picton, madam, of the Thames Valley Police. I've reason to believe you own a blue Land-Rover, and I have a warrant to inspect it.'

Ginnie said in bewilderment, 'It's no secret we have a Land-Rover. Of course we have. You'd better talk to my husband. Sid ... Archie ... what's all this about?'

'It's possible,' I said unhappily, 'that someone borrowed your Land-Rover last night and ... er ... committed a crime.'

'Could I see the Land-Rover, please, madam?' Picton insisted.

'It will be in the farmyard,' Ginnie said. 'I'll get my husband to show you.'

The scene inexorably unwound. Gordon, steaming out of the house to take charge, could do nothing but protest in the fact of a properly executed search warrant. The various policemen went about their business, photographing, fingerprinting and collecting specimens of dusty earth from the tyre treads. Every stage was carefully documented by the assisting constable.

The warrant apparently covered the machinery and anything else behind the front seat. The two sticking up handles that had looked to Jonathan like those of a lawn mower were, in fact, the handles of a lawn mower – a light electric model. There were also a dozen or so angled iron posts for fencing, also a coil of fencing wire and the tools needed for fastening the wire through the posts. There was an opened bag of horse-feed nuts. There was a rolled leather apron, like those

136

used by farriers. There were two spades, a heavy four-pronged fork and a large knife like a machete wrapped in sacking.

The knife was clean, sharp and oiled.

Gordon, questioned, growled impatiently that a good workman looked after his tools. He picked up a rag and a can of oil, to prove his point. What was the knife for? Clearing ditches, thinning woodland, a hundred small jobs around the fields.

There was a second, longer bundle of sacking lying beneath the fencing posts. I pointed to it non-committally, and Norman Picton drew it out and unwrapped it.

Inside there were two once-varnished wooden handles a good metre in length, with, at the business end, a heavy arrangement of metal.

'Lopping shears,' Gordon pronounced. 'For lopping off small branches of trees in the woods. Have to keep young trees pruned, you know, or you get a useless tangle where nothing will grow.'

He took the shears from Picton's hands to show him how they worked. The act of parting the handles widely away from each other opened heavy metal jaws at the far end; sharp, clean and oiled jaws with an opening wide enough to grip a branch three inches thick. Gordon, with a strong quick motion, pulled the handles towards each other, and the metal jaws closed with a snap.

'Very useful,' Gordon nodded, and rewrapped the shears in their sacking.

Archie, Picton and I said nothing.

I felt faintly sick.

Archie walked away speechless and Gordon, not understanding, laid the sacking parcel back in the Land-Rover and walked after him, saying, puzzled, 'Archie! What is it?'

Picton said to me, 'Well?'

'Well,' I said, swallowing, 'what if you took those shears apart? They look clean, but in the jaws ... in that hinge ... just one drop of blood ... or one hair ... that would do, wouldn't it?'

'So these shears fit the bill?'

I nodded faintly. 'Mr Kirk saw the colt's leg, like I did. And he saw the foot.' I swallowed again. '*Lopping* shears. Oh Christ.'

'It was only a *horse*,' he protested.

'Some people love their horses like they do their children,' I said. 'Suppose someone lopped off your son's foot?'

He stared. I said wryly, 'Betty Bracken is the fifth bereaved owner I've met in the last three weeks. Their grief gets to you.'

'My son,' he said slowly, 'had a dog that got run over. He worried us sick ... wouldn't eat properly ...' He stopped, then said, 'You and Archie Kirk are too close to this.'

'And the Great British public,' I reminded him, 'poured their hearts out to those cavalry horses maimed by terrorists in Hyde Park.'

138

He was old enough to remember the carnage that had given rise to the daily bulletins and to medals and hero-status bestowed on Sefton, the wonderful survivor of heartless bombs set off specifically to kill harmless horses used by the army solely as a spectacle in plumed parades.

This time the Great British public would vilify the deed, but wouldn't, and couldn't, believe a national idol guilty. Terrorists, yes. Vandals, yes. Idol . . . *no*.

Picton and I walked in the wake of Archie and Gordon, returning to Ginnie in front of the house.

'I don't understand,' Ginnie was saying plaintively. 'When you say the Land-Rover may have been taken and used in a crime . . . what crime do you mean?'

Gordon jumped in without waiting for Picton to explain.

'It's always for robbery,' he said confidently. 'Where did the thieves take it?'

Instead of answering, Norman Picton asked if it was Gordon Quint's habit to leave the ignition key in the Land-Rover.

'Of course not,' Gordon said, affronted. 'Though a little thing like no ignition key never stops a practised thief.'

'If you did by any chance leave the key available – which I'm sure you didn't, sir, please don't get angry – but if anyone could have found and used your key, would it have been on a key-ring with a silver chain and a silver horseshoe?'

'Oh no,' Ginnie interrupted utterly guilelessly. 'That's Ellis's key-ring. And it's not a silver horseshoe, it's white gold. I had it made especially for him last Christmas.'

I drove Archie Kirk back to Newbury. The unmarked car ahead of us carried the four policemen and a variety of bagged, docketed, documented objects for which receipts had been given to Gordon Quint.

Lopping shears in sacking. Machete, the same. Oil rag and oil-can. Sample of horse-feed nuts. Instant photos of red-dragon logo. Careful containers of many lifted fingerprints, including one sharply defined right full hand-print from the Land-Rover's bonnet that, on first inspection, matched exactly the right hand-print from the Coke can held by Jonathan at the lake.

'There's no doubt that it was the Quint Land-Rover in my sister's lane,' Archie said. 'There's no doubt Ellis's keys were in the ignition. But there's no proof that Ellis himself was anywhere near.'

'No,' I agreed. 'No one saw him.'

'Did Norman ask you to write a report?'

'Yes.'

'He'll give your report and Jonathan's statement to the Crown Prosecution Service, along with his own findings. After that, it's up to them.'

'Mm.'

After a silence, as if searching for words of comfort, Archie said, 'You've done wonders.'

'I hate it.'

'But it doesn't stop you.'

What if he can't help it...? What if I couldn't help it, either?

At the police station, saying goodbye, Archie said, 'Sid... you don't mind if I call you Sid? And I'm Archie, of course, as you know ... I do have some idea of what you're facing. I just wanted you to know.'

'I ... er ... thanks,' I said. 'If you wait a minute, I'll phone the equine hospital and find out how the colt is doing.'

His face lightened but the news was moderate.

'I've re-attached the tendon,' Bill reported. 'I grafted a couple of blood vessels so there's now an adequate blood supply to the foot. Nerves are always difficult. I've done my absolute best and, bar infection, the foot could technically stay in place. The whole leg is now in a cast. The colt is semi-conscious. We have him in slings. But you know how unpredictable this all is. Horses don't recover as easily as humans. There'll be no question of racing, of course, but breeding ... I understand he's got the bloodlines of champions. Absolutely no promises, mind.'

'You're brilliant,' I said.

'It's nice,' he chuckled, 'to be appreciated.'

141

I said, 'A policeman will come and collect some of the colt's hair and blood.'

'Good. Catch the bugger,' he said.

I drove willy nilly without haste in heavy traffic to London. By the time I reached the pub I was half an hour late for my appointment with Kevin Mills of *The Pump*, and he wasn't there. No balding head, no paunch, no drooping beer-frothed moustache, no cynical world-weariness.

Without regret I mooched tiredly to the bar, bought some whisky and poured into it enough London tap water to give the distiller fits.

All I wanted was to finish my mild tranquilliser, go home, find something to eat, and sleep. Sleep, I thought, yawning, had overall priority.

A woman's voice at my side upset those plans.

'Are you Sid Halley?' it said.

I turned reluctantly. She had shining black shoulder-length hair, bright light-blue eyes and dark red lipstick, sharply edged. Naturally unblemished skin had been given a matt porcelain powdering. Black eyebrows and eyelashes gave her face strong definition, an impression her manner reinforced. She wore black clothes in June. I found it impossible to guess her age, within ten years, from her face, but her manicured red-nailed hands said no more than thirty.

'I'm from *The Pump*,' she said. 'My colleague, Kevin Mills, has been called away to a rape.'

I said, 'Oh,' vaguely.

'I'm India Cathcart,' she said.

I said 'Oh' again, just as vaguely, but I knew her by her name, by her reputation and by her writing. She was a major columnist, a ruthless interviewer, a deconstructing nemesis, a pitiless exposer of pathetic human secrets. They said she kept a penknife handy for sharpening her ballpoints. She was also funny, and I, like every *Pump* addict, avidly read her stuff and laughed even as I winced.

I did not, however, aim to be either her current or future quarry.

'I came to pick up our exclusive,' she said.

'Ah. 'Fraid there isn't one.'

'But you *said*.'

'I hoped,' I agreed.

'And you haven't answered your phone all day.'

I unclipped my mobile phone and looked at it as if puzzled, which I wasn't. I said, making a discovery, 'It's switched off.'

She said, disillusioned, 'I was warned you weren't dumb.'

There seemed to be no answer to that, so I didn't attempt one.

'We tried to reach you. Where have you been?'

'Just with friends,' I said.

'I went to Combe Bassett. What did I find? No colt,

with or without feet. No Sid Halley. No sobbing colt-owner. I find some batty old fusspot who says everyone went to Archie's house.'

I gazed at her with a benign expression. I could do a benign expression rather well.

'So,' continued India Cathcart with visible disgust, 'I go to the house of a Mr Archibald Kirk in the village of Shelley Green, and what do I find *there*?'

'What?'

'I find about five other newspapermen, sundry photographers, a Mrs Archibald Kirk and a deaf old gent saying "Eh?" '

'So then what?'

'Mrs Kirk is lying, all wide-eyed and helpful. She's saying she doesn't know where anyone is. After three hours of that, I went back to Combe Bassett to look for ramblers.'

'Did you find any?'

'They had rambled twenty miles and had climbed a stile into a field with a resident bull. A bunch of ramblers crashed out in panic through a hedge backwards and the rest are discussing suing the farmer for letting a dangerous animal loose near a public footpath. A man with a pony-tail says he's also suing Mrs Bracken for not keeping her colt in a stable, thus preventing an amputation that gave his daughter hysterics.'

'Life's one long farce,' I said.

A mistake. She pounced on it. 'Is that your comment on the maltreatment of animals?'

'No.'

'Your opinion of ramblers?'

'Footpaths are important,' I said.

She looked past me to the bartender. 'Sparkling mineral water, ice and lemon, please.'

She paid for her own drink as a matter of course. I wondered how much of her challenging air was unconscious and habitual, or whether she volume-adjusted it according to who she was talking to. I often learned useful things about people's characters by watching them talk to others than myself, and comparing the response.

'You're not playing fair,' she said, judging me over the wedge of lemon bestriding the rim of her glass. 'It was *The Pump*'s Hotline that sent you to Combe Bassett. Kevin says you pay your debts. So pay.'

'The Hotline was his own idea. Not a bad one, except for about a hundred false alarms. But there's nothing I can tell you this evening.'

'Not can't. Won't.'

'It's often the same thing.'

'Spare me the philosophy!'

'I enjoy reading your page every week,' I said.

'But you don't want to figure in it?'

'That's up to you.'

She raised her chin. 'Strong men *beg* me not to print what I know.'

I didn't want to antagonise her completely and I could forgo the passing pleasure of banter, so I gave her the benign expression and made no comment.

She said abruptly, 'Are you married?'

'Divorced.'

'Children?'

I shook my head. 'How about you?'

She was more used to asking questions than answering. There was perceptible hesitation before she said, 'The same.'

I drank my Scotch. I said, 'Tell Kevin I'm very sorry I can't give him his inside edge. Tell him I'll talk to him on Monday.'

'Not good enough.'

'No, well . . . I can't do more.'

'Is someone *paying* you?' she demanded. 'Another paper?'

I shook my head. 'Maybe Monday,' I said. I put my empty glass on the bar. 'Goodbye.'

'Wait!' She gave me a straight stare, not overtly or aggressively feminist, but one that saw no need to make points in a battle that had been won by the generation before her. I thought that perhaps India Cathcart wouldn't have made it a condition of continued marriage that I should give up the best skill I possessed. I'd married a loving and gentle girl and turned her bitter: the worst, the most miserable failure of my life.

India Cathcart said, 'Are you hungry? I've had nothing to eat all day. My expense account would run to two dinners.'

There were many worse fates. I did a quick survey of the possibility of being deconstructed all over page fifteen, and decided as usual that playing safe had its limits. Take risks with caution: a great motto.

'Your restaurant or mine?' I said, smiling, and was warned by the merest flash of triumph in her eyes that she thought the tarpon hooked and as good as landed.

We ate in a noisy brightly lit large and crowded black-mirrored restaurant that was clearly the in-place for the in-crowd. India's choice. India's habitat. A few sycophantic hands shot out to make contact with her as we followed a lisping young greeter to a central, noteworthy table. India Cathcart acknowledged the plaudits and trailed me behind her like a comet's tail (Halley's?) while introducing me to no one.

The menu set out to amaze, but from long habit I ordered fairly simple things that could reasonably be dealt with one-handed: watercress mousse, then duck curry with sliced baked plantains. India chose baby aubergines with oil and pesto, followed by a large mound of crisped frogs' legs that she ate uninhibitedly with her fingers.

The best thing about the restaurant was that the decibel level made private conversation impossible: everything anyone said could be overheard by those at the next table.

'So,' India raised her voice, teeth gleaming over a herb-dusted *cuisse*, 'was Betty Bracken in tears?'

'I didn't see any tears.'

'How much was the colt worth?'

I ate some plantain and decided they'd overdone the caramel. 'No one knows,' I said.

'Kevin told me it cost a quarter of a million. You're simply being evasive.'

'What it cost and what it was worth are different. It might have won the Derby. It might have been worth millions. No one knows.'

'Do you always play word games?'

'Quite often,' I nodded. 'Like you do.'

'Where did you go to school?'

'Ask Kevin,' I said, smiling.

'Kevin's told me things about you that you wouldn't want me to know.'

'Like what?'

'Like it's easy to be taken in by your peaceful front. Like you having tungsten where other people have nerves. Like you being touchy about losing a hand. That's for starters.'

I would throttle Kevin, I thought. I said, 'How are the frogs' legs?'

'Muscular.'

'Never mind,' I said. 'You have sharp teeth.'

Her mind quite visibly changed gears from patronising to uncertain, and I began to like her.

Risky to like her, of course.

After the curry and the frogs we drank plain black coffee and spent a pause or two in eye-contact appraisal. I expected she saw me in terms of adjectives and paragraphs. I saw her with appeased curiosity. I now knew what the serial reputation-slasher looked like at dinner.

In the way one does, I wondered what she looked like in bed; and in the way that one doesn't cuddle up to a potential cobra, I made no flicker of an attempt to find out.

She seemed to take this passivity for granted. She paid for our meal with a *Pump* business credit card, as promised, and crisply expected I would kick in my share on Monday as an exclusive for Kevin.

I promised what I knew I wouldn't be able to deliver, and offered her a lift home.

'But you don't know where I live!'

'Wherever,' I said.

'Thanks. But there's a bus.'

I didn't press it. We parted on the pavement outside the restaurant. No kiss. No handshake. A nod from her. Then she turned and walked away, not looking back: and I had no faith at all in her mercy.

On Sunday morning I reopened the small blue suitcase Linda had lent me, and read again through all the clippings that had to do with the maimed Kent ponies.

I played again the video tape of the twenty-minute programme Ellis had made of the child owners, and watched it from a different, and sickened, perspective.

There on the screen he looked just as friendly, just as charismatic, just as expert. His arms went round

Rachel in sympathy. His good-looking face filled with compassion and outrage. Blinding ponies, cutting off a pony's foot, he said, those were crimes akin to murder.

Ellis, I thought in wretchedness, how *could* you?

What if he can't help it?

I played the tape a second time, taking in more details and attentively listening to what he had actually said.

His instinct for staging was infallible. In the shot where he'd commiserated with the children all together, he had had them sitting around on hay bales in a tack room, the children dressed in riding breeches, two or three wearing black velvet riding hats. He himself had sat on the floor among them, casual in a dark open-necked jogging suit, a peaked cap pushed back on his head, sunglasses in pocket. Several of the children had been in tears. He'd given them his handkerchief and helped them cope with grief.

There were phrases he had used when talking straight to camera that had brought the children's horrors sharply to disturbingly visual life: 'pierced empty sockets, their eyesight running down their cheeks', and 'a pure-bred silver pony proud and shining in the moonlight'.

His caring tone of voice alone had made the word-pictures bearable.

'A silver pony shining in the moonlight.' The basis of Rachel's nightmare.

'In the moonlight.' He had *seen* the pony in the moonlight.

I played the tape a third time, listening with my eyes shut, undistracted by the familiar face, or by Rachel in his comforting hug.

He said, 'A silver pony trotting trustfully across the field lured by a handful of horse-nuts.'

He shouldn't have known that.

He could have known it if any of the Ferns had suggested it.

But the Ferns themselves wouldn't have said it. They hadn't fed Silverboy on nuts. The agent of destruction that had come by night had brought the nuts.

Ellis would say, of course, that he had made it up, and the fact that it might be true was simply a coincidence. I rewound the tape and stared for a while into space. Ellis would have an answer to everything. Ellis would be believed.

In the afternoon I wrote a long, detailed report for Norman Picton: not a joyous occupation.

Early Monday morning, as he had particularly requested it, I drove to the police station in Newbury and personally delivered the package into the Detective Inspector's own hands.

'Did you talk about this to anybody?' he asked.

'No.'

'Especially not to Quint?'

'Especially not. But . . .' I hesitated, 'they're a close family. It's more than likely that on Saturday evening or yesterday, Ginnie and Gordon told Ellis that you and I and Archie were sniffing round the Land-Rover and that you took away the shears. I think you must consider that Ellis knows the hunt is on.'

He nodded disgustedly. 'And as Ellis Quint officially lives in the Metropolitan area, we in the Thames Valley district cannot pursue our enquiries . . .'

'You mean, you can't haul him down to the local Regent's Park nick and ask him awkward questions, like what was he doing at 3.00 a.m. on Saturday?'

'That's right. We can't ask him ourselves.'

'I thought these divisions were being done away with.'

'Everything takes time.'

I left him to sort out his problems and set off to drive to Kent. On the way, wanting to give Rachel Ferns a cheering-up present, I detoured into the maze of Kingston and, having parked, walked around the precincts looking for inspiration in the shops.

A windowful of tumbling puppies made me pause; perhaps Rachel needed an animal to love, to replace the pony. And perhaps Linda would *not* be pleased at having to house-train a growing nuisance that moulted and chewed the furniture. I went into the pet shop, however, and that's how I came to arrive at Linda Fern's house with my car full of fish tank, water weeds, miniature ruined castle walls, electric pump, lights, fish food, instructions, and three large lidded buckets of tropical fish.

152

Rachel was waiting by the gate for my arrival.

'You're half an hour late,' she accused. 'You said you'd be here by twelve.'

'Have you heard of the M25?'

'*Everyone* makes that motorway an excuse.'

'Well, sorry.'

Her bald head was still a shock. Apart from that she looked well, her cheeks full and rounded by steroids. She wore a loose sundress and clumpy trainers on stick-like legs. It was crazy to love someone else's child so comprehensively, yet for the first time ever, I felt the idea of fatherhood take a grip.

Jenny had refused to have children on the grounds that any racing day could leave her a widow, and at the time I hadn't cared one way or another. If ever I married again, I thought, following Rachel into the house, I would long for a daughter.

Linda gave me a bright bright smile, a pecking kiss and the offer of a gin and tonic while she threw together some pasta for our lunch. The table was laid. She set out steaming dishes.

'Rachel was out waiting for you two hours ago!' she said. 'I don't know what you've done to the child.'

'How are things?'

'Happy.' She turned away abruptly, tears as ever near the surface. 'Have some more gin. You said you'd got news for me.'

'Later. After lunch. And I've brought Rachel a present.'

153

The fish tank after lunch was the ultimate success. Rachel was enthralled, Linda interested and helpful. 'Thank goodness you didn't give her a dog,' she said. 'I can't stand animals under my feet. I wouldn't let Joe give her a dog. That's why she wanted a pony.'

The vivid fish swam healthily through the Gothic ruins, the water weeds rose and swelled, the lights and bubbles did their stuff. Rachel sprinkled fish food and watched her new friends eat. The pet shop owner had persuaded me to take a bigger tank than I'd thought best, and he had undoubtedly been right. Rachel's pale face glowed. Pegotty, in a baby-bouncer, sat wide eyed and open mouthed beside the glass. Linda came with me into the garden.

'Any news about a transplant?' I asked.

'It would have been the first thing I'd told you.'

We sat on the bench. The roses bloomed. It was a beautiful day, heartbreaking.

Linda said wretchedly, 'In acute lymphoblastic leukaemia, which is what Rachel's got, chemotherapy causes remission almost always. More than ninety per cent of the time. In seven out of ten children, the remission lasts for ever, and after five years they can be thought of as cured for life. And girls have a better chance than boys, isn't that odd? But in thirty per cent of children, the disease comes back.'

She stopped.

'And it has come back in Rachel?'

'Oh, *Sid*!'

'Tell me.'

She tried, the tears trickling while she spoke. 'The disease came back in Rachel after less than two years, and that's not good. Her hair was beginning to grow, but it came out again with the drugs. They re-established her again in remission, and they're so good, it isn't so easy the second time. But I know from their faces – and they don't suggest transplants unless they have to, because only about half of bone marrow transplants are successful. I always talk as if a transplant will definitely save her, but it only *might*. If they found a tissue match they'd kill all her own bone marrow with radiation, which makes the children terribly nauseous and wretched, and then when the marrow's all dead they transfuse new liquid marrow into the veins and hope it will migrate into the bones and start making leukaemia-free blood there, and quite often it *works* . . . and sometimes a child can be born with one blood group and be transfused with another. It's extraordinary. Rachel now has type A blood, but she might end up with type O, or something else. They can do so *much* nowadays. One day they may cure *everybody*. But oh . . . oh . . .'

I put my arm round her shoulders while she sobbed. So many disasters were for ever. So many Edens lost.

I waited until the weeping fit had passed, and then I told her I'd discovered who had maimed and destroyed Silverboy.

'You're not going to like it,' I said, 'and it might be

best if you can prevent Rachel from finding out. Does she ever read the newspapers?'

'Only Peanuts.'

'And the television news?'

'She doesn't like news of starving children.' Linda looked at me fearfully. 'I've *wanted* her to know who killed Silverboy. That's what I'm paying you for.'

I took out of my pocket and put into her hands an envelope containing her much-travelled cheque torn now into four pieces.

'I don't like what I found, and I don't want your money. Linda . . . I'm so very sorry . . . but it was Ellis Quint himself who cut off Silverboy's foot.'

She sprang in revulsion to her feet, her immediate anger filling her, the shock hard and physical, the enormity of what I'd said making her literally shake.

I should have broken it more slowly, I thought, but the words had had to be said.

'How can you say such a thing?' she demanded. 'How *can* you? You've got it all wrong. He couldn't possibly! You're *crazy* to say such a thing.'

I stood up also. 'Linda . . .'

'Don't say anything. I won't listen. I *won't*. He is so *nice*. You're *truly* crazy. And of course I'm not going to tell Rachel what you've accused him of, because it would upset her, and you're *wrong*. And I know you've been kind to her . . . and to me . . . but I wouldn't have asked you here if I'd thought you could do so much awful harm. So please . . . *go*. Go, just *go*.'

I shrugged a fraction. Her reaction was extreme, but her emotions were always at full stretch. I understood her, but that didn't much help.

I said persuasively, 'Linda, *listen*.'

'No!'

I said, 'Ellis has been my own friend for years. This is terrible for me, too.'

She put her hands over her ears and turned her back, screaming, 'Go away. Go away.'

I said uncomfortably, 'Phone me, then,' and got no reply.

I touched her shoulder. She jerked away from me and ran a good way down the lawn, and after a minute I turned and went back into the house.

'Is Mummy crying?' Rachel asked, looking out of the window. 'I heard her shout.'

'She's upset.' I smiled, though not feeling happy. 'She'll be all right. How are the fish?'

'Cool.' She went down on her knees, peering into the wet little world.

'I have to go now,' I said.

'Goodbye.' She seemed sure I would come back. It was a temporary farewell, between friends. She looked at the fishes, not turning her head.

'Bye,' I said, and drove ruefully to London knowing that Linda's rejection was only the first: the beginning of the disbelief.

In Pont Square the telephone was ringing when I opened my front door, and continued to ring while

157

I poured water and ice from a jug in the refrigerator, and continued to ring while I drank thirstily after the hot afternoon, and continued to ring while I changed the battery in my left arm.

In the end, I picked up the receiver.

'Where the bloody hell have you *been*?'

The Berkshire voice filled my ear, delivering not contumely, but information. Norman Picton, Detective Inspector, Thames Valley Police.

'You've heard the news, of course.'

'What news?' I asked.

'Do you live with your head in the sand? Don't you own a radio?'

'What's happened?'

'Ellis Quint is in custody,' he said.

'He's *what*?'

'Yes, well, hold on, he's sort of in custody. He's in hospital, under guard.'

'Norman,' I said, disoriented. 'Start at the beginning.'

'Right.' He sounded over-patient, as if talking to a child. 'This morning two plain clothes officers of the Metropolitan Police went to Ellis Quint's flat overlooking Regent's Park intending to interview him harmlessly about his whereabouts early Saturday morning. He came out of the building before they reached the main entrance, so, knowing him by sight, they approached him, identifying themselves and showing him their badges. At which point,' Picton cleared his throat but didn't seem able to clear his account of pedestrian police phraseology, '... at which point Mr Ellis Quint pushed one of the officers away so forcefully that the officer overbalanced into the roadway and was struck by a passing car. Mr Quint himself then ran into the path of traffic as he attempted to cross the road to put distance between himself and the police officers. Mr Quint caused a bus to swerve. The bus struck Mr Quint a glancing blow, throwing him to the ground. Mr Quint was dazed and bruised. He was taken to hospital where he is now in a secure room while investigations proceed.'

I said, 'Are you reading that from a written account?'

'That's so.'

'How about an interpretation in your own earthy words?'

'I'm at work. I'm not alone.'

'OK,' I said. 'Did Ellis panic or did he think he was being mugged?'

Picton half laughed. 'I'd say the first. His lawyers will say the second. But, d'you know what? When they emptied his pockets at the hospital, they found a thick packet of cash – and his passport.'

'No!'

'It isn't illegal.'

'What does he say?'

'He hasn't said anything yet.'

'How's the officer he pushed?'

'Broken leg. He was lucky.'

'And ... when Ellis's daze wears off?'

'It'll be up to the Met. They can routinely hold him for seventy-two hours while they frame a charge. I'd say that's a toss-up. With the clout he can muster, he'll be out in hours.'

'What did you do with my report?'

'It went to the proper authorities.'

Authorities was such a vague word. Whoever described their occupation as 'an authority'?

'Thanks for phoning,' I said.

'Keep in touch.' An order, it sounded like.

I put down the receiver and found a handwritten scrawl from Kevin Mills on *Pump* note-headed paper in my fax.

He'd come straight to the point.

Sid, you're a shit.

CHAPTER SEVEN

The week got worse, slightly alleviated only by a letter from Linda on Thursday morning. Variably slanting handwriting. Jerky. A personality torn this way and that.

Dear Sid,

I'm sorry I talked to you the way I did. I still cannot believe that Ellis Quint would cut off Silverboy's foot, but I remember thinking when he came here to do the TV programme that he already knew a lot about what had happened. I mean things that hadn't been in the papers, like Silverboy liking horse-nuts, which we never gave him, so how did he know, we didn't know ourselves, and I did wonder who had told him, but of course Joe asked Ellis who to buy a pony from, so of course I thought Ellis knew things about him from way back, like Silverboy being fed on horse-nuts before he came to us.

Anyway, I can see how you got it wrong about

161

Ellis, and it was very nice of you to bring the fish tank for Rachel, I can't tear her away from it. She keeps asking when you will come back and I don't like to tell her you won't, not as things are, so if you'll visit us again I will not say any more about you being wrong about Ellis. I ask you for Rachel.

We are glad Ellis wasn't hurt today by that horrid bus.

Yours sincerely,
Linda Ferns.

I wrote back thanking her for her letter, accepting her invitation and saying I would phone her soon.

On Tuesday Ellis was charged with 'actual bodily harm' for having inadvertently and without intention pushed 'an assailant' into the path of potential danger (under the wheels of a speeding motor) and was set free 'pending enquiries'.

Norman Picton disillusionedly reported, 'The only approximately good thing is that they confiscated his passport. His lawyers are pointing their fingers up any police nose they can confront, screeching that it's a scandal.'

'Where's Ellis now?'

'Look to your back. Your report is with the Crown Prosecution Service, along with mine.'

'Do you mean you don't know where he is?'

'He's probably in Britain or anywhere he can get to where he doesn't need a passport. He told the magistrates in court that he'd decided to do a sports programme in Australia, and he had to have his passport with him because he needed it to get a visa for Australia.'

'Never underestimate his wits,' I said.

'And he'd better look out for yours.'

'He and I know each other too well.'

On Wednesday afternoon Ellis turned up at his regular television studio as if life were entirely normal and, on completion of an audience-attended recording of a sports quiz, was quietly arrested by three uniformed police officers. Ellis spent the night in custody, and on Thursday morning was charged with severing the foot of a colt: to be exact, the off-fore foot of an expensive two-year-old thoroughbred owned by Mrs Elizabeth Bracken of Combe Bassett Manor, Berkshire. To the vociferous fury of most of the nation, the magistrates remanded him in custody for another seven days, a preliminary precaution usually applied to those accused of murder.

Norman Picton phoned me privately on my home number.

'I'm not telling you this,' he said. 'Understand?'

'I've got cloth ears.'

'It would mean my job.'

'I hear you,' I said. 'I won't talk.'

'No,' he said, 'that, I believe.'

'Norman?'

'Word gets around. I looked up the transcript of the trial of that man that smashed off your hand. You didn't tell *him* what he wanted to know, did you?'

'No . . . well . . . everyone's a fool sometimes.'

'Some fool. Anyway, pin back the cloth ears. The reason why Ellis Quint is remanded for seven days is because after his arrest he tried to hang himself in his cell with his tie.'

'He *didn't!*'

'No one took his belt or tie away, because of who he was. No one in the station *believed* in the charge. There's all hell going on now. The top brass are passing the parcel like a children's party. No one's telling anyone outside anything on pain of death, so Sid . . .'

'I promise,' I said.

'They'll remand him next week for another seven days, partly to stop him committing suicide and partly because . . .' He faltered on the brink of utter trust, his whole career at risk.

'I *promise*,' I said again quickly. 'And if I know what it is you want to keep quiet, then I'll know what not to guess at publicly, won't I?'

'God,' he said, half the anxiety evaporating, 'then . . . there's horse blood in the hinges of the shears, and horse blood and hairs on the oily rag, and horse blood and hairs in the sacking. They've taken samples from

164

the colt in the hospital at Lambourn, and everything's gone away for DNA testing. The results will be back next week.'

'Does Ellis know?'

'I imagine that's why he tried the quick way out. It was an Hermès tie, incidentally, with a design of horseshoes. The simple knot he tied slid undone because the tie was pure smooth silk.'

'For God's sake . . .'

'I keep forgetting he's your friend. Anyway, his lawyers have got to him. They're six deep. He's now playing the lighthearted celebrity, and he's sorrowful about *you*, Sid, for having got him all wrong. His lawyers are demanding proof that Ellis himself was ever at Combe Bassett by night, and we are asking for proof that he wasn't. His lawyers know we would have to drop the case if they can come up with a trustable alibi for any of the other amputations, but so far they haven't managed it. It's early days, though. They'll dig and dig, you can bet on it.'

'Yeah.'

'None of the Land-Rover evidence will get into the papers because the *sub judice* rule kicked in the minute they remanded him. Mostly, that helps us but you, as Sid Halley, won't be able to justify yourself in print until after the trial.'

'Even if I can then.'

'Juries are unpredictable.'

'And the law is, frequently, an ass.'

'People in the Force are already saying you're off your rocker. They say Ellis is too well known. They say that wherever he went he would be recognised, therefore if no one recognised him, that in itself is proof he wasn't there.'

'Mm,' I said. 'I've been thinking about that. Do you have time off at the weekend?'

'Not this weekend, no. Monday do you?'

'I'll see if I can fix something up with Archie . . . and Jonathan.'

'And there's another thing,' Norman said, 'the Land-Rover's presence at Combe Bassett is solid in itself, but Jonathan, if he gets as far as the witness box, will be a *meal* for Ellis's lawyers. On probation for stealing cars! What sort of witness is that?'

'I understood the jury isn't allowed to know anything about a witness. I was at a trial once in the Central Law Courts – the Old Bailey – when a beautifully dressed and blow-dried twenty-six-year-old glamour boy gave evidence – all lies – and the jury weren't allowed to know that he was already serving a sentence for confidence tricks and had come to court straight from jail, via the barber and the wardrobe room. The jury thought him a *lovely* young man. So much for juries.'

'Don't you believe in the jury system?'

'I would believe in it if they were told more. How can a jury come to a prison-or-freedom decision if half the facts are withheld? There should be *no* inadmissable evidence.'

'You're naive.'

'I'm Sid Public, remember? The law bends over backwards to give the accused the benefit of the slightest doubt. The *victim* of murder is never there to give evidence. The colt in Lambourn can't talk. It's safer to kill animals. I'm sorry, but I can't stand what Ellis has become.'

He said flatly, 'Emotion works against you in the witness box.'

'Don't worry. In court, I'm a block of ice.'

'So I've heard.'

'You've heard too damned much.'

He laughed. 'There's an old-boy internet,' he said. 'All you need is the password and a whole new world opens up.'

'What's the password?'

'I can't tell you.'

'Don't bugger me about. What's the password?'

'Archie,' he said.

I was silent for all of ten seconds, remembering Archie's eyes the first time I met him, remembering the *awareness*, the message of knowledge. Archie knew more about me than I knew about him.

I asked, 'What exactly does Archie do in the Civil Service?'

'I reckon,' Norman said, amused, 'that he's very like

167

you, Sid. What he don't want you to know, he don't tell you.'

'Where can I reach you on Monday?'

'Police station. Say you're John Paul Jones.'

Kevin Mills dominated the front page of *The Pump* on Friday – a respite from the sexual indiscretions of cabinet ministers but a demolition job on myself. '*The Pump*', he reminded readers, 'had set up a Hotline to Sid Halley to report attacks on colts. Owners had been advised to lock their stable doors, and to great effect had done so after the Derby. *The Pump* disclaims all responsibility for Sid Halley now ludicrously fingering Ellis Quint as the demon responsible for torturing defenceless horses. Ellis Quint, whose devotion to thoroughbreds stretches back to his own starry career as the country's top amateur race-rider, the popular hero who braved all perils in the ancient tradition of gentlemen sportsmen . . .'

More of the same.

'See also "Analysis" on page 10, and India Cathcart, page 15.'

I supposed one had to know the worst. I read the leader column – 'Should an ex-jockey be allowed free rein as pseudo sleuth? (Answer: no, of course not.)' – and then, dredging deep for steel, I finally turned to India Cathcart's piece.

Sid Halley, smugly accustomed to acclaim as a
champion, in short time lost his career, his wife
and his left hand, and then weakly watched his
friend soar to super-celebrity and national star
status, all the things that he considered should be
his. Who does this pathetic little man think he's
kidding? He's no Ellis Quint. He's a has-been with
an ego problem, out to ruin what he envies.

That was for starters. The next section pitilessly but not
accurately dissected the impulse that led one to com-
pete at speed (ignoring the fact that presumably Ellis
himself had felt the same power-hungry inferiority
complex).

My ruthless will to win, India Cathcart had written,
had destroyed everything good in my own life. The
same will to win now aimed to destroy my friend Ellis
Quint. This was ambition gone mad.

The Pump would not let it happen. Sid Halley was
a beetle ripe for squashing. *The Pump* would extermi-
nate. The Halley myth was curtains.

Damn and blast her, I thought and, for the first time
in eighteen years, got drunk.

On Saturday morning, groaning around the flat with a
headache, I found a message in my fax machine.

Handwritten scrawl, *Pump*-headed paper same as
before . . . Kevin Mills.

169

Sid, sorry, but you asked for it.

You're still a shit.

Most of Sunday I listened to voices on my answering machine delivering the same opinion.

Two calls relieved the gloom.

One from Charles Roland, my ex-father-in-law. 'Sid, if you're in trouble, there's always Aynsford,' and a second from Archie Kirk, 'I'm at home. Norman Picton says you want me.'

Two similar men, I thought gratefully. Two men with cool dispassionate minds who would listen before condemning.

I phoned back to Charles, who seemed relieved I sounded sane.

'I'm all right,' I said.

'Ellis is a knight in shining armour, though.'

'Yeah.'

'Are you *sure*, Sid?'

'Positive.'

'But Ginnie . . . and Gordon . . . they're *friends*.'

'Well,' I said, 'if *I* cut the foot off a horse, what would you do?'

'But you *wouldn't*.'

'No.'

I sighed. That was the trouble. No one could believe it of Ellis.

'Sid, come, any time,' Charles said.

'You're my rock,' I said, trying to make it sound light. 'I'll come if I need to.'

'Good.'

I phoned Archie and asked if Jonathan were still staying with Betty Bracken.

Archie said, 'I've been talking to Norman. Jonathan is now addicted to water ski-ing and spends every day at the lake. Betty is paying hundreds and says it's worth it to get him out of the house. He'll be at the lake tomorrow. Shall we all meet there?'

We agreed on a time, and met.

When we arrived, Jonathan was out on the water.

'That's him,' Norman said, pointing.

The flying figure in a scarlet wet-suit went up a ramp, flew, turned a somersault in the air and landed smoothly in the water on two skis.

'*That*,' Archie said in disbelief, 'is *Jonathan*?'

'He's a natural,' Norman said. 'I've been out here for a bit most days. Not only does he know his spatial balance and attitude by instinct, but he's fearless.'

Archie and I silently watched Jonathan approach the shore, drop the rope and ski confidently up the sloping landing place with almost as much panache as Norman himself.

Jonathan grinned. Jonathan's streaky hair blew wetly back from his forehead. Jonathan, changed, looked blazingly *happy*.

A good deal of the joy dimmed with apprehension as he looked at Archie's stunned and expressionless

171

face. I took a soft sports bag out of my car and held it out to him, asking him to take it with him to the dressing-rooms.

'Hi,' he said. 'OK.' He took the grip and walked off barefooted, carrying his skis.

'Incredible,' Archie said, 'but he can't ski through life.'

'It's a start,' Norman said.

After we'd stood around for a few minutes discussing Ellis we were approached by a figure in a dark blue tracksuit, wearing also black running shoes, a navy baseball cap and sunglasses and carrying a sheet of paper. He came to within fifteen feet of us and stopped.

'Yes?' Norman asked, puzzled, as to a stranger. 'Do you want something?'

I said, 'Take off the cap and the glasses.'

He took them off. Jonathan's streaky hair shook forward into its normal startling shape and his eyes stared at my face. I gave him a slight jerk of the head, and he came the last few paces and handed the paper to Norman.

Archie for once looked wholly disconcerted. Norman read aloud what I'd written on the paper.

' "Jonathan, this is an experiment. Please put on the clothes you'll find in this bag. Put on the baseball cap, peak forward, hiding your face. Wear the sunglasses. Bring this paper. Walk towards me, stop a few feet away, and don't speak. OK. Thanks, Sid." '

Norman lowered the paper, looked at Jonathan and said blankly, 'Bloody hell.'

'Is that the lot?' Jonathan asked me.

'Brilliant,' I said.

'Shall I get dressed now?'

I nodded, and he walked nonchalantly away.

'He looked totally different,' Archie commented, still amazed. 'I didn't know him at all.'

I said to Norman, 'Did you look at the tape of Ellis's programme, that one I put in with my report?'

'The tape covered with stickers saying it was the property of Mrs Linda Ferns? Yes, I did.'

'When Ellis was sitting on the floor with those children,' I said, 'he was wearing a dark tracksuit, open at the neck. He had a peaked cap pushed back on his head. He looked young. Boyish. The children responded to him ... touched him ... *loved* him. He had a pair of sunglasses tucked into a breast pocket.'

After a silence Norman said, 'But he *wouldn't*. He wouldn't wear those clothes on television if he'd worn them to mutilate the Ferns pony.'

'Oh yes he would. It would deeply amuse him. There's nothing gives him more buzz than taking risks.'

'A baseball cap,' Archie said thoughtfully, 'entirely changes the shape of someone's head.'

I nodded. 'A baseball cap and sports clothes can reduce any man of status to anonymity.'

'We'll never prove it,' Norman said.

Jonathan slouched back in his own clothes and with

his habitual half-sneering expression firmly in place.
Archie's exasperation with him sharply returned.

'This is not the road to Damascus,' I murmured.

'Damn you, Sid.' Archie glared, and then laughed.

'What are you talking about?' Norman asked.

'St Paul's conversion on the road to Damascus happened like a thunderclap,' Archie explained. 'Sid's
telling me not to look for instant miracles by the gravel
pit lake.'

Jonathan, now listening, handed me the grip. 'Cool
idea,' he said. 'No one knew me.'

'They would, close to.'

'It was still a risk,' Norman objected.

'I told you,' I said, 'the risk is the point.'

'It doesn't make sense.'

'Cutting off a horse's foot doesn't make sense. Half
of human actions don't make sense. Sense is in the
eye of the beholder.'

I drove back to London.

My answer-phone had answered so many calls that
it had run out of recording tape.

Among the general abuse, three separate calls were
eloquent about the trouble I'd stirred up. All three of
the owners of the other colt victims echoed Linda
Ferns' immovable conviction.

The lady from Cheltenham: 'I can't believe you can
be so misguided. Ellis is absolutely innocent. I wouldn't

have thought of you as being jealous of him, but all the papers say so. I'm sorry, Sid, but you're not welcome here any more.'

The angry Lancashire farmer: 'You're a moron, do you know that? Ellis Quint! You're stupid. You were all right as a jockey. You should give up this pretence of being Sherlock Holmes. You're pitiful, lad.'

The lady from York. 'How *can* you? Dear Ellis! He's worth ten of you, I have to say.'

I switched off the critical voices, but they went on reverberating in my brain.

The Press had more or less uniformly followed *The Pump*'s lead. Pictures of Ellis at his most handsome smiled confidently from news stands everywhere. Trial by media found Ellis Quint the wronged and innocent hero, Sid Halley the twisted jealous cur snapping at his heels.

I'd known it would be bad: so why the urge to bang my head against the wall? Because I was human, and didn't have tungsten nerves, whatever anyone thought. I sat with my eyes shut, ostrich fashion.

Tuesday was much the same. I still didn't bang my head. Close run thing.

On the Wednesday Ellis appeared again before magistrates, who that time set him free on bail.

Norman phoned.

'Cloth ears?' he said. 'Same as before?'

'Deaf,' I assured him.

'It was fixed beforehand. Two minutes in court. Dif-

175

ferent time than posted. The Press arrived just after it was over. Ellis greeted them, free, smiling broadly.'

'Shit.'

Norman said, 'His lawyers have done their stuff. It's rubbish to think that the well-balanced personality intended to kill himself – his tie got caught somehow but he managed to free it. The policeman he pushed failed to identify himself adequately and is now walking about comfortably in a cast. The colt Ellis is accused of attacking is alive and recovering well. As bail is granted in cases of manslaughter, it is unnecessary to detain Ellis Quint any longer on far lesser charges. So . . . he's walked.'

'Is he still to be tried?'

'So far. His lawyers have asked for an early trial date so that he can put this unpleasantness behind him. He will plead not guilty, of course. His lawyers are already patting each other on the back. And . . . I think there's a heavyweight manoeuvring someone in this case.'

'A heavyweight? Who?'

'Don't know. It's just a feeling.'

'Could it be Ellis's father?'

'No, no. Quite different. It's just . . . since our reports, yours and mine, reached the Crown Prosecution Service, there's been a new factor. Political, perhaps. It's difficult to describe. It's not exactly a cover-up. There's already been too much publicity, it's more a sort of re-direction. Even officially, and not just to the Press, someone with muscles is trying to get you thoroughly, and I'm afraid I must say, *malignantly* discredited.'

'Thanks a bunch.'

'Sid, seriously, look out for yourself.'

I felt as prepared as one could be for some sort of catastrophic pulverisation to come my way, but in the event the process was subtler and long drawn out.

As if nothing had happened, Ellis resumed his television programme and began making jokes about Sid Halley – 'Sid Halley? That friend of mine! Have you heard that he comes from Halifax? Halley facts – he makes them up.'

And 'I like halibut – I eat it.' And the old ones that I was used to, 'Halitosis' and 'Hallelujah'.

Hilarious.

When I went to the races, which I didn't do as often as earlier, people either turned their backs or *laughed*, and I wasn't sure which I disliked more.

I took to going only to jumping meetings, knowing Ellis's style took him to the most fashionable meetings on the Flat. I acknowledged unhappily to myself that in my avoidance of him there was an element of cringe. I despised myself for it. All the same, I shrank from a confrontation with him and truly didn't know whether it was because of an ever-deepening aversion to what he had done, or because of the fear – the certainty – that he would publicly mock me.

He behaved as if there were never going to be a trial; as if awkward details like Land-Rovers, lopping shears, and confirmed matching DNA tests tying the shears to the Bracken colt were never going to surface, once the *sub judice* silence ended.

Norman, Archie and also Charles Roland worried that, for all the procedural care we had taken, Ellis's lawyers would somehow get the Land-Rover disallowed. Ellis's lawyers, Norman said, backed by the heavy unseen presence that was motivating them and possibly even paying the mounting fees, now included a defence counsel whose loss rate for the previous seven years was nil.

Surprisingly, despite the continuing barrage of ignominy, I went on being offered work. True, the approach was often tentative and apologetic – 'Whether you're right or pigheaded about Ellis Quint...' and 'Even if you've got Ellis Quint all wrong...' The nitty-gritty seemed to be that they needed me and there was no one else.

Well, hooray for that. I cleaned up minor mysteries, checked credit ratings, ditto characters, found stolen horses, caught sundry thieves, all the usual stuff.

July came in with a deluge that flooded rivers and ruined the shoes of racegoers, and no colt was attacked at the time of the full moon, perhaps because the nights were wet and windy and black dark with clouds.

The Press finally lost interest in the daily trashing of Sid Halley and Ellis Quint's show wrapped up for the summer break. I went down to Kent a couple of times, taking new fish for Rachel, sitting on the floor with her, playing draughts. Neither Linda nor I mentioned Ellis. She hugged me goodbye each time and asked when I would be coming back. Rachel, she said, had had no more nightmares. They were a thing of the past.

August came quietly and left in the same manner. No colts were attacked. The Hotline went cold. India Cathcart busied herself with a cabinet member's mistress but still had a routinely vindictive jab at me each Friday. I went to America for two short weeks and rode horses up the Teton mountains in Wyoming, letting the wide skies and the forests work their peace.

In September, one dew-laden early autumn English Saturday morning after a calm moonlit night, a colt was discovered with a foot off.

Nauseated, I heard the announcement on the radio in the kitchen while I made coffee.

Listeners would remember, the cool newsreader said, that in June Ellis Quint had been notoriously accused by ex-jockey Sid Halley of a similar attack. Quint was laughing off this latest incident, affirming his total ignorance on the matter.

There were no Hotline calls from *The Pump*, but Norman Picton scorched the wires.

'Have you heard?' he demanded.

'Yes. But no details.'

'It was a yearling colt this time. Apparently, there aren't many two-year-olds in the fields just now, but there are hundreds of yearlings.'

'Yes,' I agreed. 'The yearling sales are starting.'

'The yearling in question belonged to some people near Northampton. They're frantic. Their vet put the colt out of his misery. But get this. Ellis Quint's lawyers have already claimed he has an alibi.'

I stood in silence in my sitting-room, looking out to the unthreatening garden.

'Sid?'

'Mm.'

'You'll have to break that alibi. Otherwise, it will break *you*.'

'Mm.'

'Say something else, dammit.'

'The police can do it. Your lot.'

'Face it. They're not going to try very hard. They're going to believe in his alibi, if it's anything like solid.'

'Do you think, do you *really* think,' I asked numbly, 'that an ultra-respected barrister would connive with his client to mutilate ... to kill ... a colt – or pay someone else to do it – to cast doubt on the prosecution's case in the matter of a *different* colt?'

'Put like that, no.'

'Nor do I.'

'So Ellis Quint has set it up himself, and what he has set up, you can knock down.'

'He's had weeks – more than two months – to plan it.'

'Sid,' he said, 'it's not like you to sound defeated.'

If he, I thought, had been on the receiving end of a long pitiless barrage of systematic denigration, he might feel as I did, which, if not comprehensively defeated, was at least battle weary before I began.

'The police at Northampton,' I said, 'are not going to welcome me with open arms.'

'That's never stopped you before.'

I sighed. 'Can you find out from the Northampton police what his alibi actually is?'

'Piece of cake. I'll phone you back.'

I put down the receiver and went over to the window. The little square looked peaceful and safe, the railed garden green and grassy, a tree-dappled haven where generations of privileged children had run and played while their nursemaids gossiped. I'd spent my own childhood in Liverpool's back streets, my father dead and my mother fighting cancer. I in no way regretted the contrast in origins. I had learned self-sufficiency and survival there. Perhaps because of the back streets I now valued the little garden more. I wondered how the children who'd grown up in that garden would deal with Ellis Quint. Perhaps I could learn from them. Ellis had been that sort of child.

Norman phoned back later in the morning.

'Your friend,' he said, 'reportedly spent the night at a private dance in Shropshire, roughly a hundred miles

181

to the north-west of the colt. Endless friends will testify to his presence, including his hostess, a duchess. It was a dance given to celebrate the twenty-first birthday of the heir.'

'Damn.'

'He could hardly have chosen a more conspicuous or more watertight alibi.'

'And some poor bitch will swear she lay down for him at dawn.'

'Why dawn?'

'It's when it happens.'

'How do you know?'

'Never you mind,' I said.

'You're a bad boy, Sid.'

Long ago, I thought. Before Jenny. Summer dances, dew, wet grass, giggles and passion. Long ago and innocent.

Life's a bugger, I thought.

'Sid,' Norman's voice said, 'do you realise the trial is due to start two weeks on Monday?'

'I do realise.'

'Then get a move on, with this alibi.'

'Yes, sir, Detective Inspector.'

He laughed. 'Put the bugger back behind bars.'

On the Tuesday I went to see the Shropshire duchess, for whom I had ridden winners in that former life. She even had a painting of me on her favourite horse, but I was no longer her favourite jockey.

'Yes, of *course* Ellis was here all night,' she confirmed. Short, thin, and at first unwelcoming, she led me through the armour-dotted entrance hall of her draughty old house to the sitting-room where she had been watching the jump racing on television when I arrived.

Her front door had been opened to me by an arthritic old manservant who had hobbled away to see if Her Grace was in. Her Grace had come into the hall clearly anxious to get rid of me as soon as possible, and had then relented, her old kindness towards me resurfacing like a lost but familiar habit.

A three-mile steeplechase was just finishing, the jockeys kicking side by side to the finish line, the horses tired and straining, the race going in the end to the one carrying less weight.

The duchess turned down the volume, the better to talk.

'I cannot *believe*, Sid,' she said, 'that you've accused dear Ellis of something so *disgusting*. I know you and Ellis have been friends for years. Everyone knows that. I do think he's been a bit unkind about you on television, but you did *ask* for it, you know.'

'But he *was* here . . .?' I asked.

'Of course. All night. It was five or later when everyone started to leave. The band was playing still . . . we'd all had breakfast . . .'

'When did the dance start?' I asked.

'*Start?* The invitations were for ten. But you know how people are. It was eleven or midnight before most people came. We had the fireworks at three-thirty because rain was forecast for later, but it was fine all night, thank goodness.'

'Did Ellis say goodnight when he left?'

'My dear Sid, there were over three hundred people here last Friday night. A *succès fou*, if I say it myself.'

'So you don't actually remember when Ellis left?'

'The last I saw of him he was dancing an eightsome with that gawky Raven girl. Do drop it, Sid. I'm seeing you now for old times' sake, but you're not doing yourself any good, are you?'

'Probably not.'

She patted my hand. 'I'll always *know* you, at the races and so on.'

'Thank you,' I said.

'Yes. Be a dear and find your own way out. Poor old Stone has such bad arthritis these days.'

She turned up the volume in preparation for the next race, and I left.

The gawky Raven girl who had danced an eightsome reel with Ellis turned out to be the third daughter of an earl. She herself had gone off to Greece to join someone's yacht, but her sister (the second daughter) insisted that Ellis had danced with dozens of people

184

after that, and wasn't I, Sid Halley, being a teeny weeny *twit*?

I went to see Miss Richardson and Mrs Bethany, joint owners of the Windward Stud Farm, home of the latest colt victim: and to my dismay found Ginnie Quint there as well.

All three women were in the stud farm's office, a building separate from the rambling one-storey dwelling house. A groom long-reining a yearling had directed me incuriously and I drew up outside the pinkish brick new-looking structure without relish for my mission, but not expecting a tornado.

I knocked and entered, as one does with such offices, and found myself in the normal clutter of desks, computers, copiers, wall charts and endless piles of paper.

I'd done a certain amount of homework before I went there, so it was easy to identify Miss Richardson as the tall bulky dominant figure in tweed jacket, worn cord trousers and wiry grey short cropped curls. Fifty, I thought; despises men. Mrs Bethany, a smaller, less powerful version of Miss Richardson, was reputedly the one who stayed up at night when the mares were foaling, the one on whose empathy with horses the whole enterprise floated.

The women didn't own the farm's two stallions (they belonged to syndicates) nor any of the mares: Windward Stud was a cross between a livery stable and a

185

maternity ward. They couldn't afford the bad publicity of the victimised yearling.

Ginnie Quint, sitting behind one of the desks, leapt furiously to her feet the instant I appeared in the doorway and poured over me an accumulated concentration of verbal volcanic lava, scalding, shrivelling, sticking my feet to the ground and my tongue in dryness to the roof of my mouth.

'He *trusted* you. He would have *died* for you.'

I sensed Miss Richardson and Mrs Bethany listening in astonishment, not knowing who I was nor what I'd done to deserve such an onslaught; but I had eyes only for Ginnie, whose long fondness for me had fermented to hate.

'You're going to go into court and try to send your best friend to prison ... to destroy him ... pull him down ... ruin him. You're going to *betray* him. You're not fit to live.'

Emotion twisted her gentle features into ugliness. Her words came out spitting.

It was her own son who had done this. Her golden idolised son. He had made of me finally the traitor that would deliver the kiss.

I said absolutely nothing.

I felt, more intensely than ever, the by now accustomed and bitter awareness of the futility of rebellion. Gagged by *sub judice*, I'd been unable all along to put

186

up any defence, especially because the Press had tended to pounce on my indignant protests and label them as 'whining' and 'diddums', and 'please teacher, he hit me . . .' and 'it's not fair, I hit him first'.

A quick check with a lawyer had confirmed that though trying to sue one paper for libel might have been possible, suing the whole lot was not practical. Ellis's jokes were not actionable and, unfortunately, the fact that I was still profitably employed in my chosen occupation meant that I couldn't prove the criticism had damaged me financially.

'Grit your teeth and take it,' he'd advised cheerfully, and I'd paid him for an opinion I gave myself free every day.

As there was no hope of Ginnie's listening to anything I might say, I unhappily but pragmatically turned to retreat, intending to return another day to talk to Miss Richardson and Mrs Bethany, and found my way barred by two new burly arrivals, known already to the stud owners as policemen.

'Sergeant Smith reporting, madam,' one said to Miss Richardson.

She nodded. 'Yes, sergeant?'

'We've found an object hidden in one of the hedges round the field where your horse was done in.'

No one objected to my presence, so I remained in the office, quiet and riveted.

Sergeant Smith carried a long narrow bundle which

187

he laid on one of the desks. 'Could you tell us, madam, if this belongs to *you*?'

His manner was almost hostile: accusatory. He seemed to expect the answer to be yes.

'What is it?' Miss Richardson asked, very far from guilty perturbation.

'This, madam,' the sergeant said with a note of triumph, and lifted back folds of filthy cloth to reveal their contents, which were two long wooden handles topped by heavy metal clippers.

A pair of lopping shears.

Miss Richardson and Mrs Bethany stared at them unmoved. It was Ginnie Quint who turned slowly white and fainted.

CHAPTER EIGHT

So here we were in October, with the leaves weeping yellowly from the trees.

Here I was, perched on the end of Rachel Ferns' bed, wearing a huge fluffy orange clown wig and a red bulbous nose, making sick children laugh while feeling far from merry inside.

'Have you hurt your arm?' Rachel asked conversationally.

'Banged it,' I said.

She nodded. Linda looked surprised. Rachel said, 'When things hurt it shows in people's eyes.'

She knew too much about pain for a nine-year-old. I said, 'I'd better go before I tire you.'

She smiled, not demurring. She, like the children wearing the other wigs I'd brought, all had very short bursts of stamina. Visiting was down to ten minutes maximum.

I took off the clown wig and kissed Rachel's forehead. 'Bye,' I said.

'You'll come back?'

'Of course.'

She sighed contentedly, knowing I would. Linda walked with me from the ward to the hospital door.

'It's ... *awful*,' she said, forlorn, on the exit steps. Cold air. The chill to come.

I put my arms round her. Both arms. Hugged her.

'Rachel asks for you all the time,' she said. 'Joe cuddles her, and cries. She cuddles *him*, trying to comfort him. She's her daddy's little girl. She loves him. But you ... you're her *friend*. You make her laugh, not cry. It's you she asks for all the time – not Joe.'

'I'll always come if I can.'

She sobbed quietly on my shoulder and gulped, 'Poor Mrs Quint.'

'Mm,' I said.

'I haven't told Rachel about Ellis ...'

'No. Don't,' I said.

'I've been beastly to you.'

'No, far from it.'

'The papers have said such *dreadful* things about you.' Linda shook in my arms. 'I knew you weren't like that ... I told Joe I have to believe you about Ellis Quint and he thinks I'm stupid.'

'Look after Rachel, nothing else matters.'

She went back into the hospital and I rode dispiritedly back to London in the TeleDrive car.

Even though I'd returned with more than an hour to spare I decided against Pont Square and took the sharp memory of Gordon Quint's attack straight to the bar in the Piccadilly hotel where I'd agreed to meet the lawyer Davis Tatum.

With a smile worth millions, the French lady in charge of the restaurant arranged for me to have coffee and a sandwich in the tiny bar while I waited for my friend. The bar, in fact, looked as if it had been wholly designed as a meeting place for those about to lunch. There were no more than six tables, a bartender who brought drinks to one's elbow, and a calm atmosphere. The restaurant itself was full of daylight, with huge windows and green plants, and was sufficiently hidden from the busy artery of Mayfair downstairs as to give peace and privacy and no noisy passing trade.

I sat at a bar table in the corner with my back to the entrance, though in fact few were arriving: more were leaving after long hours of talk and lunch. I took some ibuprofen, and waited without impatience. I spent hours in my job, sometimes, waiting for predators to pop out of their holes.

Davis Tatum arrived late and out of breath from having apparently walked up the stairs instead of waiting for the lift. He wheezed briefly behind my back, then came round into view and lowered his six foot three inch bulk into the chair opposite.

He leaned forward and held out his hand for a shake. I gave him a limp approximation, which raised his eyebrows but no comment.

He was a case of an extremely agile mind in a totally unsuitable body. There were large cheeks, double chins,

191

fat-lidded eyes and a small mouth. Dark smooth hair had neither receded nor greyed. He had flat ears, a neck like a weight-lifter and a charcoal pin-striped suit straining over a copious belly. He might have difficulty, I thought, in catching sight of certain parts of his own body. Except in the brain-box, nature had dealt him a sad hand.

'First of all,' he said, 'I have some bad news, and I possibly shouldn't be here talking to you at all, according to how you read *Archbold*.'

'*Archbold* being the dos and don'ts manual for trial lawyers?'

'More or less.'

'What's the bad news, then?' I asked. There hadn't been much that was good.

'Ellis Quint has retracted his "guilty" plea, and has gone back to "not guilty".'

'*Retracted?*' I exclaimed. 'How can one retract a confession?'

'Very easily.' He sighed. 'Quint says he was upset yesterday about his mother's death, and what he said about feeling guilty was misinterpreted. In other words, his lawyers have got over the shock and have had a re-think. They apparently know you have so far not been able to break Ellis Quint's alibi for the night that last colt was attacked in Northamptonshire, and they think they can therefore get the Bracken colt charge dismissed, despite the Land-Rover and circumstantial evidence, so they are aiming for a complete acquittal, not

192

psychiatric treatment, and, I regret to tell you, they are likely to succeed.'

He didn't have to tell me that my own reputation would never recover if Ellis emerged with his intact.

'And *Archbold*?'

'If I were the crown prosecuting counsel in this case I could be struck off for talking to you, a witness. As you know, I am the senior barrister in the chambers where a colleague prosecuting Ellis Quint works. I have seen his brief and discussed the case with him. I can absolutely properly talk to you, though perhaps some people might not think it prudent.'

I smiled. 'Bye bye, then.'

'I may not discuss with you a case in which I may be examining you as a witness. But of course I will not be examining you. Also, we can talk about anything else. Like, for instance, a recent game of golf.'

'I don't play golf.'

'Don't be obtuse, my dear fellow. Your perceptions are acute.'

'Are we talking about angles?'

His eyes glimmered behind the folds of fat. 'I saw the report package that you sent to the CPS.'

'The Crown Prosecution Service?'

'The same. I happened to be talking to a friend. I said your report had surprised me, both by its thoroughness and by your deductions and conclusions. He said I shouldn't be surprised. He said you'd had the whole top echelon of the Jockey Club hanging on your every word. He said that, about a year ago, you'd cleared up two major racing messes at the same time. They've never forgotten it.'

'A year last May,' I said. 'Is that what he meant?'

'I expect so. He said you had an assistant then that isn't seen around any more. The job I'd like you to do might need an assistant for the leg-work. Don't you have your assistant nowadays?'

'Chico Barnes?'

He nodded. 'A name like that.'

'He got married,' I said briefly. 'His wife doesn't like what I do, so he's given it up. He teaches judo. I still see him – he gives me a judo lesson most weeks, but I can't ask him for any other sort of help.'

'Pity.'

'Yes. He was good. Great company and bright.'

'And he got *deterred*. That's why he gave it up.'

I went, internally, very still. I said, 'What do you mean?'

'I heard,' he said, his gaze steady on my face, 'that he got beaten with some sort of thin chain to deter him from helping you. To deter him from all detection. And it worked.'

'He got married,' I said.

David Tatum leaned back in his chair, which creaked under his weight.

'I heard,' he said, 'that the same treatment was doled out to you, and in the course of things the Jockey Club mandarins made you take your shirt off. They said they had never seen anything like it. The whole of your upper body, arms included, was black with bruising, and there were vicious red weals all over you. And with your shirt hiding all that you'd calmly explained to them how and why you'd been attacked and how one of their number, who had arranged it, was a villain. You got one of the big shots chucked out.'

'Who told you all that?'

'One hears things.'

I thought in unprintable curses. The six men who'd seen me that day with my shirt off had stated their intention of never talking about it. They'd wanted to keep to themselves the villainy I'd found within their own walls; and nothing had been more welcome to me than that silence. It had been bad enough at the time. I didn't want continually to be reminded.

'Where does one hear such things?' I asked.

'Be your age, Sid. In the clubs . . . Buck's, the Turf, the RAC, the Garrick . . . these things get mentioned.'

'How often . . . do they get mentioned? How often have you heard that story?'

He paused as if checking with an inner authority, and then said, 'Once.'

'Who told you?'

'I gave my word.'

'One of the Jockey Club?'

'I gave my word. If you'd given your word, would *you* tell *me*?'

'No.'

He nodded. 'I asked around, about you. And that's what I was told. Told in confidence. If it matters to you, I've heard it from no one else.'

'It matters.'

'It reflects to your credit,' he protested. 'It obviously didn't stop you.'

'It could give other villains ideas.'

'And do villains regularly attack you?'

'Well, no,' I said. 'Physically no one's laid a finger on me since that time.' Not until yesterday, I thought. 'If you're talking about non-physical assaults . . . Have you read the papers?'

'Scurrilous.' Davis Tatum twisted in his seat until he could call the barman. 'Tanqueray and tonic, please – and for you, Sid?'

'Scotch. A lot of water.'

The barman brought the glasses, setting them out on little round white mats.

'Health,' Davis Tatum toasted, raising his gin.

'Survival,' I responded, and drank to both.

He put down his glass and came finally to the point.

'I need someone,' he said, 'who is clever, unafraid and able to think fast in a crisis.'

'No one's like that.'

'What about you?'

I smiled. 'I'm stupid, scared silly a good deal of the time, and I have nightmares. What you think you see, is not what you get.'

'I get the man who wrote the Quint report.'

I looked benignly at my glass and not at his civilised face.

'If you're going to do something to a small child that you know he won't like,' I said, 'such as sticking a needle into him, you *first* tell him what a brave little boy he is – in the hope that he'll then let you make a pincushion of him without complaint.'

There was a palpable silence, then he chuckled, the low rich timbre filling the air. There was embarrassment in there somewhere; a ploy exposed.

I said prosaically, 'What's the job?'

He waited while four businessmen arrived, arranged their drinks and sank into monetary conversation at the table furthest from where we sat.

'Do you know who I mean by Owen Yorkshire?' Tatum asked, looking idly at the newcomers, not at me.

'Owen Yorkshire,' I rolled the name around in memory and came up with only doubts. 'Does he own a horse or two?'

'He does. He also owns Topline Foods.'

'Topline . . . as in sponsored race at Aintree? As in Ellis Quint, guest of honour at the Topline Foods lunch the day before the Grand National?'

'That's the fellow.'

'And the enquiry?'

'Find out if he's manipulating the Quint case to his own private advantage.'

I said thoughtfully, 'I did hear that there's a heavy-weight abroad.'

197

'Find out who it is, and why.'

'What about poor old Archbold? He'd turn in his grave.'

'So you'll do it!'

'I'll try. But why me? Why not the police? Why not the old boy internet?'

He looked at me straightly. 'Because you include silence in what you sell.'

'And I'm expensive,' I said.

'Retainer and refreshers,' he promised.

'Who's paying?'

'The fees will come through me.'

'And it's agreed,' I said, 'that the results, if any, are yours. Prosecution or otherwise will normally be your choice.'

He nodded.

'In case you're wondering,' I said, 'when it comes to Ellis Quint, I gave the client's money back, in order to be able to stop him myself. The client didn't at first believe in what he'd done. I made my own choice. I have to tell you that you'd run that risk.'

He leaned forward and extended his pudgy hand.

'We'll shake on it,' he said, and grasped my palm with a firmness that sent a shockwave fizzing clear up to my jaw.

'What's the matter?' he said, sensing it.

'Nothing.'

He wasn't getting much of a deal, I thought. I had a reputation already in tatters, a crackled ulna playing up, and the prospect of being chewed to further shreds by Ellis's defence counsel. He'd have done as well to engage my pal Jonathan of the streaky hair.

'Mr Tatum,' I began.

'Davis. My name's Davis.'

'Will you give me your *assurance* that you won't speak of that Jockey Club business around the clubs?'

'Assurance?'

'Yes.'

'But I told you . . . it's to your credit.'

'It's a private thing. I don't like *fuss*.'

He looked at me thoughtfully. He said, 'You have my assurance.' And I wanted to believe in it, but I wasn't sure that I did. He was too intensely a club man, a filler of large armchairs in dark panelled rooms full of old exploded reputations and fruitily repeated secrets. 'Won't say a word, old boy.'

'Sid.'

'Mm?'

'Whatever the papers say, where it really counts, you are respected.'

'Where's that?'

'The clubs are good for gossip, but these days that's not where the power lies.'

'Power wanders round like the magnetic North Pole.'

'Who said that?'

'I just did,' I said.

'No, I mean, did you make it up?'

'I've no idea.'

'Power, these days, is fragmented,' he said.

I added, 'And where the power is at any one time is not necessarily where one would want to be.'

He beamed proprietorially as if he'd invented me himself.

There was a quick rustle of clothes beside my ear and a drift of flowery scent, and a young woman tweaked a chair round to join our table and sat in it, looking triumphant.

'Well, well, well,' she said. 'Mr Davis Tatum and Sid Halley! What a surprise!'

I said, to Davis Tatum's mystified face, 'This is Miss India Cathcart, who writes for *The Pump*. If you say nothing you'll find yourself quoted repeating things you never thought, and if you say anything at all, you'll wish you hadn't.'

'Sid,' she said mock-sorrowfully, 'can't you take a bit of kicking around?'

Tatum opened his mouth indignantly and, as I was afraid he might try to defend me, I shook my head. He stared at me, then with a complete change of manner said in smooth lawyerly detachment, 'Miss Cathcart, why are you here?'

'Why? To see you, of course.'

'But why?'

She looked from him to me and back again, her appearance just as I remembered it: flawless porcelain skin, light-blue eyes, cleanly outlined mouth, black

200

shining hair. She wore brown and red, with amber beads.

She said, 'Isn't it improper for a colleague of the Crown Prosecutor to be seen talking to one of the witnesses?'

'No, it isn't,' Tatum said, and asked me, 'Did you tell her we were meeting here?'

'Of course not.'

'Then how . . . why, Miss Cathcart, are you here?'

'I told you. It's a story.'

'Does *The Pump* know you're here?' I asked.

A shade crossly she said, 'I'm not a child. I'm allowed out on my own, you know. And anyway, the paper sent me.'

'*The Pump* told you we'd be here?' Tatum asked.

'My editor said to come and see you. And he was right!'

Tatum said, 'Sid?'

'Mm,' I said. 'Interesting.'

India said to me, 'Kevin says you went to school in Liverpool.'

Tatum, puzzled, asked, 'What did you say?'

She explained, 'Sid wouldn't tell me where he went to school, so I found out.' She looked at me accusingly. 'You don't sound like Liverpool.'

'Don't I?'

'You sound more like Eton. How come?'

'I'm a mimic,' I said.

If she really wanted to, she could find out also that

between the ages of sixteen and twenty-one I'd been more or less adopted by a Newmarket trainer (who *had* been to Eton) who made me into a good jockey and by his example changed my speech and taught me how to live and how to behave and how to manage the money I earned. He'd been already old then, and he died. I often thought of him. He opened doors for me still.

'Kevin told me you were a slum child,' India said.

'Slum is an attitude, not a place.'

'Prickly, are we?'

Damn, I thought. I will *not* let her goad me. I smiled, which she didn't like.

Tatum, listening with disapproval, said, 'Who is Kevin?'

'He works for *The Pump*,' I told him.

India said, 'Kevin Mills is *The Pump*'s chief reporter. He did favours for Halley and got kicked in the teeth.'

'Painful,' Tatum commented dryly.

'This conversation's getting nowhere,' I said. 'India, Mr Tatum is not the prosecutor in any case where I am a witness, and we may talk about anything we care to, including, as just now before you came, golf.'

'You can't play golf with one hand.'

It was Tatum who winced, not I. I said, 'You can watch golf on television without arms, legs or ears. Where did your editor get the idea that you might find us here?'

'He didn't say. It doesn't matter.'

202

'It is of the essence,' Tatum said.

'It's interesting,' I said, 'because to begin with it was *The Pump* that worked up the greatest head of steam about the ponies mutilated in Kent. That was why I got in touch with Kevin Mills. Between us we set up a Hotline, as a "Save the *Tussilago farfara*" sort of thing.'

India demanded, 'What did you say?'

'*Tussilago farfara*,' Tatum repeated, amused. 'It's the botanical name of the wildflower, coltsfoot.'

'How did you know that?' she asked me fiercely.

'I looked it up.'

'Oh.'

'Anyway, the minute I linked Ellis Quint, even tentatively, to the colts, and to Rachel Ferns' pony, *The Pump* abruptly changed direction and started tearing me apart with crusading claws. I can surely ask, India, why do you write about me so ferociously? Is it just your way? Is it that you do so many hatchet jobs that you can't do anything else? I didn't expect kindness, but you are ... every week ... extreme.'

She looked uncomfortable. She did what she had one week called me 'diddums' for doing: she defended herself.

'My editor gives me guidelines.' She almost tossed her head.

'You mean he tells you what to write?'

'Yes. No.'

'Which?'

She looked from me to Tatum and back.

203

She said, 'He subs my piece to align it with overall policy.'

I said nothing. Tatum said nothing. India, a shade desperately, said, 'Only saints get themselves burned at the stake.'

Tatum said with gravitas, 'If I read any lies or innuendoes about my having improperly talked to Sid Halley about the forthcoming Quint trial, I will sue you personally for defamation, Miss Cathcart, and I will ask for punitive damages. So choose your stake. Flames seem inevitable.'

I felt almost sorry for her. She stood up blankly, her eyes wide.

'Say we weren't here,' I said.

I couldn't read her frozen expression. She walked away from us and headed for the stairs.

'A confused young woman,' Tatum said. 'But how did she – or her paper – know we would be here?'

I asked, 'Do you feed your appointments into a computer?'

He frowned. 'I don't do it personally. My secretary does it. We have a system which can tell where all the partners are, if there's a crisis. It tells where each of us can be found. I did tell my secretary I was coming here, but not who I was going to meet. That still doesn't explain . . .'

I sighed. 'Yesterday evening you phoned my mobile number.'

'Yes, and you phoned me back.'

'Someone's been listening on my mobile phone's frequency. Someone heard you call me.'

'Hell! But you called me back. They heard almost nothing.'

'You gave your name . . . How secure is your office computer?'

'We change passwords every three months.'

'And you use passwords that everyone can remember easily?'

'Well . . .'

'There are people who crack passwords just for the fun of it. And others hack into secrets. You wouldn't believe how *careless* some firms are with their most private information. Someone has recently accessed my own on-line computer – during the past month. I have a detector program that tells me. Much good it will do any hacker as I never keep anything personal there. But a combination of my mobile phone and your office computer must have come up with the *possibility* that your appointment was with me. Someone in *The Pump* did it. So they sent India along to find out . . . and here we are. And because they succeeded, we now know they tried.'

'It's incredible.'

'Who runs *The Pump*? Who sets the policy?'

Tatum said thoughtfully, 'The editor is George Godbar. The proprietor's Lord Tilepit.'

'Any connection with Ellis Quint?'

He considered the question and shook his head. 'Not that I know of.'

'Does Lord Tilepit have an interest in the television company that puts on Ellis Quint's programme? I think I'd better find out.'

Davis Tatum smiled.

Reflecting that, as about thirty hours had passed since Gordon Quint had jumped me in Pont Square, he was unlikely still to be hanging about there with murderous feelings and his fencing post (not least because with Ginnie dead he would have her inquest to distract him) and also feeling that one could take self-preservation to shaming lengths, I left the Piccadilly restaurant in a taxi and got the driver to make two reconnoitring passes round the railed central garden.

All seemed quiet. I paid the driver, walked without incident up the steps to the front door, used my key, went up to the next floor and let myself into the haven of home.

No ambush. No creaks. Silence.

I retrieved a few envelopes from the wire basket clipped inside the letter box and found a page in my fax. It seemed a long time since I'd left, but it had been only the previous morning.

My cracked arm hurt. Well, it would. I'd ridden races – and winners – now and then with cracks: disguising them, of course, because the betting public deserved healthy riders to carry their money. The odd thing was that in the heat of a race one didn't feel an injury. It was in the cooler ebbing of excitement that the discomfort returned.

The best way, always, to minimise woes was to concentrate on something else. I looked up a number and phoned the handy acquaintance who had set up my computers for me.

'Doug,' I said, when his wife had fetched him in from an oil change, 'tell me about listening in to mobile phones.'

'I'm covered in grease,' he complained. 'Won't this do another time?'

'Someone is listening to my mobile.'

'Oh.' He sniffed. 'So you want to know how to stop it?'

'You're dead right.'

He sniffed again. 'I've got a cold,' he said, 'my wife's mother is coming to dinner and my sump is filthy.'

I laughed: couldn't help it. 'Please, Doug.'

He relented. 'I suppose you've got an analog mobile. They have radio signals that can be listened to. It's difficult, though. Your average bloke in the pub couldn't do it.'

'Could you?'

'I'm not your average bloke in the pub. I'm a walking mid-life crisis halfway through an oil change. I could do it if I had the right gear.'

'How do I deal with it?'

'Blindingly simple.' He sneezed and sniffed heavily. 'I need a tissue.' There was a sudden silence on the line, then the distant sound of a nose being vigorously blown, then the hoarse voice of wisdom in my ear.

'OK,' he said. 'You ditch the analog, and get a digital.'

'I do?'

'Sid, being a jockey does not equip the modern man to live in tomorrow's world.'

'I do see that.'

'Everyone,' he sniffed, 'if they had any sense, would go digital.'

'Teach me.'

'The digital system,' he said, 'is based on two numbers, nought and one. Nought and one have been with us from the dawn of computers, and no one has ever invented anything better.'

'They haven't?'

He detected my mild note of irony. 'Has anyone,' he asked, 're-invented the wheel?'

'Er, no.'

'Quite. One cannot improve on an immaculate conception.'

'That's blasphemous.' I enjoyed him always.

'Certainly not,' he said, 'Some things are perfect to begin with. $E = mc^2$, and all that.'

'I grant that. How about my mobile?'

'The signal sent to a digital telephone,' he said, 'is

not one signal, as in analog, but is eight simultaneous signals, each transmitting one eighth of what you hear.'

'Is that so?' I asked dryly.

'You may bloody snigger,' he said, 'but I'm giving you the goods. A digital phone receives eight simultaneous signals, and it is *impossible* for anyone to decode them, except the receiving mobile. Now, because the signal arrives in eight pieces, the reception isn't always perfect. You don't get the crackle or the fading in and out that you get on analog phones, but you do sometimes get bits of words missing. Still, *no one* can listen in. Even the police can never tap a digital mobile number.'

'So,' I said, fascinated, 'where do I get one?'

'Try Harrods,' he said.

'*Harrods?*'

'Harrods is just round the corner from where you live, isn't it?'

'More or less.'

'Try there, then. Or anywhere else that sells phones. You can use the same number that you have now. You just need to tell your service provider. And, of course, you'll need an SIM card. You have one, of course?'

I said meekly, 'No.'

'Sid!' he protested. He sneezed again. 'Sorry. An SIM card is a Subscribers Identity Module. You can't live without one.'

'I can't?'

'Sid, I despair of you. Wake up to technology.'

'I'm better at knowing what a horse thinks.'

Patiently he enlightened me, 'An SIM card is like a credit card. It actually *is* a credit card. Included on it are your name and mobile phone number and other details, and you can slot it into any mobile that will take it. For instance, if you are someone's guest in Athens and he has a mobile that accepts an SIM card, you can slot *your* card into *his* phone and the charge will appear on your account, not his.'

'Are you serious?' I asked.

'With my problems, would I joke?'

'Where do I get an SIM card?'

'Ask Harrods.' He sneezed. 'Ask anyone who travels for a living. Your service provider will provide.' He sniffed. 'So long, Sid.'

Amused and grateful, I opened my post and read the fax. The fax being most accessible got looked at first.

Handwritten, it scrawled simply, 'Phone me,' and gave a long number.

The writing was Kevin Mills', but the fax machine he'd sent it from was anonymously not *The Pump*'s.

I phoned the number given, which would have connected me to a mobile, and got only the infuriating instruction, 'Please try later.'

There were a dozen messages I didn't much want on my answering machine and a piece of information I *definitely* didn't want in a large brown envelope from Shropshire.

The envelope contained a copy of a glossy county magazine, one I'd sent for as I'd been told it included lengthy coverage of the heir-to-the-dukedom's coming-of-age dance. There were, indeed, four pages of pictures, mostly in colour, accompanied by prose gush about the proceedings and a complete guest list.

A spectacular burst of fireworks filled half a page, and there in a group of heaven-gazing spectators, there in white dinner jacket and all his photogenic glory, there unmistakably stood Ellis Quint.

My heart sank. The fireworks had started at three-thirty. At three-thirty, when the moon was high, Ellis had been a hundred miles north-west of the Windward Stud's yearling.

There were many pictures of the dancing, and a page of black and white shots of the guests, names attached. Ellis had been dancing. Ellis smiled twice from the guests' page, carefree, having a good time.

Damn it to hell, I thought. He had to have taken the colt's foot off early. Say by one o'clock. He could then have arrived for the fireworks by three-thirty. I'd found no one who'd seen him *arrive*, but several who swore to his presence after five-fifteen. At five-fifteen he had helped the heir to climb onto a table to make a drunken speech. The heir had poured a bottle of champagne over Ellis's head. Everyone remembered *that*. Ellis could not have driven back to Northampton before dawn.

For two whole days the previous week I'd traipsed

211

round Shropshire, and next door Cheshire, handed on from grand house to grander, asking much the same questions (according to sex) – did you dance with Ellis Quint or did you drink/eat with him. The answers at first had been freely given, but, as time went on, news of my mission spread before me until I was progressively met by hostile faces and frankly closed doors. Shropshire was solid Ellis country. They'd have stood on their heads to prove him unjustly accused. They were not going to say that they didn't know when he'd arrived.

In the end I returned to the duchess's front gates, and from there drove as fast as prudence allowed, to the Windward Stud Farm, timing the journey at two hours and five minutes. On empty roads at night, Northampton to the duchess might have taken ten minutes less. I'd proved nothing except that Ellis had had time.

Enough time was not enough.

As always before gathering at such dances, the guests had given and attended dinner parties both locally and further away. No one that I'd asked had entertained Ellis to dinner.

No dinner was not enough.

I went through the guest list crossing off the people I'd seen. There were still far more than half unconsulted, most of whom I'd never heard of.

Where was Chico? I needed him often. I hadn't the time, or to be frank, the appetite to locate and question all the guests, even if they would answer. There must have been people – local people – helping with the parking of cars that night. Chico would have chatted people up in the local pubs and found out if any of the car-parkers remembered Ellis's arrival. Chico was good at pubs, and I wasn't in his class.

The police might have done it, but they wouldn't. The death of a colt still didn't count like murder.

The police.

I phoned Norman Picton's police station number and gave my name as John Paul Jones.

He came on the line in a good humour and listened to me without protest.

'Let me get this straight,' he said. 'You want me to ask favours of the Northamptonshire police? What do I offer in return?'

'Blood in the hinges of lopping shears.'

'They'll have made their own tests.'

'Yes, and that Northamptonshire colt is dead and gone to the glue factory. An error, wouldn't you say? Might they not do you a favour in exchange for commiseration?'

'You'll have my head off. What is it you actually *want*?'

'Er ...' I began, 'I was there when the police found the lopping shears in the hedge.'

'Yes, you told me.'

'Well, I've been thinking. Those shears weren't wrapped in sacking, like the ones we took from the Quints.'

'No, and the shears weren't the same, either. The

213

ones at Northampton are a slightly newer model. They're on sale everywhere in garden centres. The problem is that Ellis Quint hasn't been reported as buying any, not in the Northamptonshire police district, nor ours.'

'Is there any chance,' I asked, 'of my looking again at the material used for wrapping the shears?'

'If there are horse hairs in it, there's nothing left to match them to, same as the blood.'

'All the same, the cloth might tell us where the shears came from. *Which* garden centre, do you see?'

'I'll see if they've done that already.'

'Thanks, Norman.'

'Thank Archie. He drives me to help you.'

'Does he?'

He heard my surprise. 'Archie has *influence*,' he said, 'and I do what the magistrate tells me.'

When he'd gone off the line I tried Kevin Mills again and reached the same electronic voice: 'Please try later.'

After that I sat in an armchair while the daylight faded and the lights came on in the peaceful square. We were past the equinox, back in winter thoughts, the year dying ahead. Autumn for me had for almost half my life meant the longed-for resurgence of major jump racing, the time of big winners and speed and urgency in the blood. Winter now brought only nostalgia and heating bills. At thirty-four I was growing old.

I sat thinking of Ellis and the wasteland he had made of my year. I thought of Rachel Ferns and Silverboy, and lymphoblasts. I thought of the Press, and especially *The Pump* and India Cathcart and the orchestrated months of vilification. I thought of Ellis's relentless jokes.

I thought for a long time about Archie Kirk, who had drawn me to Combe Bassett and given me Norman Picton. I wondered if it had been from Archie that Norman had developed a belief in a heavy presence behind the scenes. I wondered if it could possibly be Archie who had prompted Davis Tatum to engage me to find that heavyweight. I wondered if it could possibly have been Archie who told Davis Tatum about my run-in with the bad hat at the Jockey Club, and if so, how did *he* know?

I trusted Archie. He could pull my strings, I thought, as long as I was willing to go where he pointed, and as long as I was sure no one was pulling *his*.

I thought about Gordon Quint's uncontrollable rage, and the practical difficulties his fencing post had inflicted. I thought of Ginnie Quint and despair and sixteen floors down.

I thought of the colts and their chopped-off feet.

When I went to bed I dreamed the same old nightmare.

Agony. Humiliation. Both hands.

I awoke sweating.

Damn it all to hell.

CHAPTER NINE

In the morning, when I'd failed yet again to get an answer from Kevin Mills, I shunted by tube across central London and emerged not far from Companies House at 55 City Road, E.C.

Companies House, often my friend, contained the records of all public and private limited companies active in the United Kingdom, including the audited annual balance sheets, investment capital, fixed assets and the names of major shareholders and the directors of the boards.

Topline Foods, I soon learned, was an old company recently taken over by a few new big investors and a bustling new management. The chief shareholder and managing director was listed as Owen Cliff Yorkshire. There were fifteen non-executive directors, of whom one was Lord Tilepit.

The premises at which business was carried out were located at Frodsham in Cheshire. The registered office was at the same address.

The product of the company was foodstuffs for animals.

After Topline, I looked up Village Pump Newspapers (they'd dropped the 'Village' in about 1900, but retained the idea of a central meeting place for gossip) and found interesting items, and after Village Pump Newspapers I looked up the TV company that aired Ellis's sports programme, but found no sign of Tilepit or Owen Yorkshire in its operations.

I travelled home (safely) and phoned Archie, who was, his wife reported, at work.

'Can I reach him at work?' I asked.

'Oh no, Sid. He wouldn't like it. I'll give him a message when he gets back.'

Please try later.

I tried Kevin Mills later and this time nearly got my eardrums perforated. 'At last!'

'I've tried you a dozen times,' I said.

'I've been in an old people's home.'

'Well, bully for you.'

'A nurse hastened three harpies into the hereafter.'

'Poor old sods.'

'If you're in Pont Square,' he said, 'can I call round and see you? I'm in my car not far away.'

'I thought I was *The Pump*'s number one all-time shit.'

'Yeah. Can I come?'

'I suppose so.'

217

'Great.' He clicked off before I could change my mind and he was at my door in less than ten minutes.

'This is *nice*,' he said appreciatively, looking round my sitting-room. 'Not what I expected.'

There was a Sheraton writing-desk and buttoned brocade chairs and a couple of modern exotic wood inlaid tables by Mark Boddington. The overall colours were greyish blue, soft and restful. The only brash intruder was an ancient fruit machine that worked on tokens.

Kevin Mills made straight towards it, as most visitors did. I always left a few tokens haphazardly on the floor, with a bowl of them nearby on a table. Kevin picked a token from the carpet, fed it into the slot, and pulled the handle. The wheels clattered and clunked. He got two cherries and a lemon. He picked up another token and tried again.

'What wins the jackpot?' he asked, achieving an orange, a lemon and a banana.

'Three horses with jockeys jumping fences.'

He looked at me sharply.

'It used to be the bells,' I said. 'That was boring, so I changed it.'

'And do the three horses ever come up?'

I nodded. 'You get a fountain of tokens all over the floor.'

The machine was addictive. It was my equivalent of the psychiatrist's couch. Kevin played throughout our conversation but the nearest he came was two horses and a pear.

'The trial has started, Sid,' he said, 'so give us the scoop.'

'The trial's only technically started. I can't tell you a thing. When the adjournment's over, you can go to court and listen.'

'That's not exclusive,' he complained.

'You know damned well I can't tell you.'

'I gave you the story to begin with.'

'I sought you out,' I said. 'Why did *The Pump* stop helping the colt owners and shaft me instead?'

He concentrated hard on the machine. Two bananas and a blackberry.

'Why?' I asked.

'Policy.'

'Whose policy?'

'The public wants demolition, they gobble up spite.'

'Yes, but—'

'Look, Sid, we get the word from on high. And don't ask *who* on high. I don't know. I don't like it. None of us likes it. But we have the choice, go along with overall policy or go somewhere else where we feel more in tune. And do you know where that gets you? I work for *The Pump* because it's a good paper with, on the whole, fair comment. OK, so reputations topple. Like I said, that's what Mrs Public wants. Now and then we get a *request*, such as "lean hard on Sid Halley". I did it without qualms, as you'd clammed up on me.'

He looked all the time at the machine, playing fast.

'And India Cathcart?' I asked.

He pulled the lever and waited until two lemons and a jumping horse came to rest in a row.

'India . . .' he said slowly. 'For some reason she didn't want to trash you. She said she'd enjoyed her dinner with you and you were quiet and kind. Kind! I ask you! Her editor had to squeeze the poison out of her drop by drop for that first long piece. In the end he wrote most of her page himself. She was furious the next day when she read it, but it was out on the streets by then and she couldn't do anything about it.'

I was more pleased than I would have expected, but I wasn't going to let Kevin see it. I said, 'What about the continued stab wounds almost every week?'

'I guess she goes along with the policy. Like I said, she has to eat.'

'Is it George Godbar's policy?'

'The big white chief himself? Yes, you could say the editor of the paper has the final say.'

'And Lord Tilepit?'

He gave me an amused glance. Two pears and a lemon. 'He's not a hands-on proprietor of the old school. Not a Beaverbrook or a Harmsworth. We hardly know he's alive.'

'Does he give the overall policy to George Godbar?'

'Probably.' A horse, a lemon and some cherries. 'Why do I get the idea that *you* are interviewing *me*, instead of the other way round?'

'I cannot imagine. What do you know about Owen Cliff Yorkshire?'

'Bugger all. Who is he?'

'Quite likely a friend of Lord Tilepit.'

'Sid,' he protested. 'I do my job. Rapes, murders, little old ladies smothered in their sleep. I do *not* chew off the fingernails of my pay cheque.'

He banged the fruit machine frustratedly. 'The bloody thing hates me.'

'It has no soul,' I said. I fed in a stray token myself with my plastic fingers and pulled the handle. Three horses. Fountains of love. Life's little irony.

Kevin Mills took his paunch, his moustache and his disgusted disgruntlement off to his word-processor, and I again phoned Norman as John Paul Jones.

'My colleagues now think John Paul Jones is a snitch,' he said.

'Fine.'

'What is it this time?'

'Do you still have any of those horse-nuts I collected from Betty Bracken's field, and those others we took from the Land-Rover?'

'Yes, we do. And as you know, they're identical in composition.'

'Then could you find out if they were manufactured by Topline Foods Ltd, of Frodsham in Cheshire?'

After a short silence he said cautiously, 'It could be done, but is it necessary?'

221

'If you could let me have some of the nuts I could do it myself.'

'I can't let you have any. They are bagged and counted.'

'Shit.' And I could so easily have kept some in my own pocket. Careless. Couldn't be helped.

'Why does it matter where they came from?' Norman asked.

'Um ... You know you told me you thought there might be a heavyweight somewhere behind the scenes? Well, I've been asked to find out.'

'Jeez,' he said. 'Who asked you?'

'Can't tell you. Client confidentiality and all that.'

'Is it Archie Kirk?'

'Not so far as I know.'

'Huh!' He sounded unconvinced. 'I'll go this far. If you get me some authenticated Topline nuts I'll see if I can run a check on them to find out if they match the ones we have. That's the best I can do, and that's stretching it, and you wouldn't have a prayer if you hadn't been the designer of our whole prosecution – and you can *not* quote me on that.'

'I'm truly grateful. I'll get some Topline nuts, but they probably won't match the ones you have.'

'Why not?'

'The grains – the balance of ingredients – will have changed since those were manufactured. Every batch must have its own profile, so to speak.'

He well knew what I meant, as an analysis of ingredi-

222

ents could reveal their origins as reliably as grooves on a bullet.

'What interests you in Topline Foods?' Norman asked.

'My client.'

'Bugger your client. Tell me.' I didn't answer and he sighed heavily. 'All right. You can't tell me now. I hate amateur detectives. I've got you a strip off that dirty Northampton material. At least, it's promised for later today. What are you going to do about it, and have you cracked Ellis Quint's alibi yet?'

'You're *brilliant*,' I said. 'Where can I meet you? And no, I haven't cracked the alibi.'

'Try harder.'

'I'm only an amateur.'

'Yeah, yeah. Come to the lake at five o'clock. I'm picking up the boat to take it home for winter storage. OK?'

'I'll be there.'

'See you.'

I phoned the hospital in Canterbury. Rachel, the ward sister told me, was 'resting comfortably'.

'What does that mean?'

'She's no worse than yesterday, Mr Halley. When can you return?'

'Sometime soon.'

'Good.'

I spent the afternoon exchanging my old vulnerable analog mobile cellular telephone for a digital receiving

223

eight splintered transmissions that would baffle even the Thames Valley stalwarts, let alone *The Pump*.

From my flat I then phoned Miss Richardson of Northamptonshire, who said vehemently that *no*, I certainly might *not* call on her again. Ginnie and Gordon Quint were her dear friends and it was *unthinkable* that Ellis could harm horses, and I was foul and *wicked* even to think it. Ginnie had told her about it. Ginnie had been very distressed. It was all my fault that she had killed herself.

I persevered with two questions, however, and did get answers of sorts.

'Did your vet say how long he thought the foot had been off when the colt was found at seven o'clock?'

'No, he didn't.'

'Could you give me his name and phone number?'

'No.'

As I had over the years accumulated a whole shelfful of area telephone directories, it was not so difficult, via the Northamptonshire Yellow Pages, to find and talk to Miss Richardson's vet. He would, he said, have been helpful if he could. All he could with confidence say was that neither the colt's leg nor the severed foot had shown signs of recent bleeding. Miss Richardson herself had insisted he put the colt out of his misery immediately, and, as it was also his own judgement, he had done so.

He had been unable to suggest to the police any particular time for the attack; earlier rather than later was as far as he could go. The wound had been clean: one chop. The vet said he was surprised a yearling would have stood still long enough for shears to be applied. Yes, he confirmed, the colt had been lightly shod, and yes, there had been horse-nuts scattered around, but Miss Richardson often gave her horses nuts as a supplement to grass.

He'd been helpful, but no help.

After that I had to decide how to get to the lake, as the normal taken-for-granted act of driving now had complications. I had a knob fixed on the steering wheel of my Mercedes which gave me a good grip for one-(right)handed operation. With my left unfeeling hand I shifted the automatic gear lever.

I experimentally flexed and clenched my right hand. Sharp protests. Boring. With irritation I resorted to ibuprofen and drove to the lake wishing Chico were around to do it.

Norman had winched his boat onto its trailer by the edge of the water. Big, competent and observant, he watched my slow emergence to upright and frowned.

'What hurts?' he asked.

'Self-esteem.'

He laughed. 'Give me a hand with the boat, will you? Pull when I lift.'

I looked at the job and said briefly that I couldn't.

'You only need one hand for pulling.'

I told him unemotionally that Gordon Quint had aimed for my head and done lesser but inconvenient damage. 'I'm telling you in case he tries again and succeeds. He was slightly out of his mind over Ginnie.'

Norman predictably said I should make an official complaint.

'No,' I said. 'This is unofficial, and ends right here.'

He went off to fetch a friend to help him with the boat, and then busied himself with enclosing his powerful outboard engine into a fitted zipped cover.

I said, 'What first gave you the feeling that there was some heavyweight meandering behind the scenes?'

'First?' He went on working while he thought. 'It's months ago. I talked it over with Archie. I expect it was because one minute I was putting together an ordinary case – even if Ellis Quint's fame made it newsworthy – and the next I was being leaned on by the Superintendent to find some reason to drop it, and when I showed him the strength of the evidence, he said the Chief Constable was unhappy, and the reason for the Chief Constable's unhappiness was always the same, which was political pressure from outside.'

'What sort of political?'

Norman shrugged. 'Not party politics especially. A pressure group. Lobbying. A bargain struck somewhere, along the lines of "Get the Quint prosecution aborted and such-and-such a good thing will come your way!" '

'But not a direct cash advantage?'

'Sid!'

'Well, sorry.'

'I should frigging well hope so.' He wrapped thick twine round the shrouded engine. 'I'm not asking cash for a strip of rag from Northamptonshire.'

'I grovel,' I said.

He grinned. 'That'll be the day.' He climbed into his boat and secured various bits of equipment against movement en route.

'No one has entirely given in to the pressure,' he pointed out. 'The case against Ellis Quint has not been dropped. True, it's now in a ropey state. You yourself have been relentlessly discredited to the point where you're almost a liability to the prosecution, and even though that's brutally unfair, it's a fact.'

'Mm.'

In effect, I thought, I'd been commissioned by Davis Tatum to find out who had campaigned to defeat me. It wasn't the first time I'd faced campaigns to enforce my inactivity, but it was the first time I'd been offered a fee to save myself. To save myself, in this instance, meant to defeat Ellis Quint: so I was being paid for *that*, in the first place. And for what *else*?

Norman backed his car up to the boat trailer and hitched them together. Then he leaned through the open front passenger window of the car, unlocked the glove compartment there, and drew out and handed me a plastic bag.

'One strip of dirty rag,' he said cheerfully. 'Cost to you, six grovels before breakfast for a week.'

I took the bag gratefully. Inside, the filthy strip, about

227

three inches wide, had been loosely folded until it was several layers thick.

'It's about a metre long,' Norman said. 'It was all they would let me have. I had to sign for it.'

'Good.'

'What are you going to do with it?'

'Clean it, for a start.'

Norman said doubtfully, 'It's got some sort of pattern in it but there wasn't any printing on the whole wrapping. Nothing to say where it came from. No garden centre name, or anything.'

'I don't have high hopes,' I said, 'but, frankly, just now every straw's worth clutching.'

Norman stood with his legs apart and his hands on his hips. He looked like a pillar of every possible police strength but what he was actually feeling turned out to be indecision.

'How far can I trust you?' he asked.

'For silence?'

He nodded.

'I thought we'd discussed this already.'

'Yes, but that was months ago.'

'Nothing's changed,' I said.

He made a decision, stuck his head into his car again and this time brought out a business-sized brown envelope which he held out to me.

'It's a copy of the analysis done on the horse-nuts,' he said. 'So read it and shred it.'

'OK. And thanks.'

I held the envelope and plastic bag together and knew I couldn't take such trust lightly. He must be very sure of me, I thought; and felt not complimented but apprehensive.

'I've been thinking,' I said, 'do you remember, way back in June, when we took those things out of Gordon Quint's Land-Rover?'

'Of course I remember.'

'There was a farrier's apron in the Land-Rover. Rolled up. We didn't take that, did we?'

He frowned. 'I don't remember it, but no, it's not among the things we took. What's significant about it?'

I said, 'I've always thought it odd that the colts should stand still long enough for the shears to close round the ankle, even with head-collars and those nuts. But horses have an acute sense of smell ... and all those colts had shoes on – I checked with their vets – and they would have known the smell of a blacksmith's apron. I think Ellis might have worn that apron to reassure the colts. They may have thought he was the man who shod them. They would have *trusted* him. He could have lifted a fetlock and gripped it with the shears.'

He stared.

'What do you think?' I asked.

'It's you who knows horses.'

'It's how I might get a two-year-old to let me near his legs.'

229

'As far as I'm concerned,' he said, 'that's how it was done.'

He held out his hand automatically to say goodbye, then remembered Gordon Quint's handiwork, shrugged, grinned, and said instead, 'If there's anything interesting about that strip of rag, you'll let me know?'

'Of course.'

'See you.'

He drove off with a wave, trailing his boat, and I returned to my car, stowed away the bag and the envelope and made a short journey to Shelley Green, the home of Archie Kirk.

He had returned from work. He took me into his sitting-room while his smiling wife cooked in the kitchen.

'How's things?' Archie asked. 'Whisky?'

I nodded. 'A lot of water . . .'

He indicated chairs, and we sat. The dark room looked right in October: imitation flames burnt imitation coals in the fireplace, giving the room a life that the sun of June hadn't achieved.

I hadn't seen Archie since then. I absorbed again the probably deliberate greyness of his general appearance, and I saw again the whole internet in the dark eyes.

He said casually, 'You've been having a bit of a rough time.'

'Does it show?'

'Yes.'

'Never mind,' I said. 'Will you answer some questions?'

'It depends what they are.'

I drank some of his undistinguished whisky and let my muscles relax into the ultimate of non-aggressive, non-combative postures.

'For a start, what do you do?' I said.

'I'm a civil servant.'

'That's not ... well ... specific.'

'Start at the other end,' he said.

I smiled. I said, 'It's a wise man who knows who's paying him.'

He paused with his own glass halfway to his lips.

'Go on,' he said.

'Then ... do you know Davis Tatum?'

After a pause he answered, 'Yes.'

It seemed to me he was growing wary; that he, as I did, had to sort through a minefield of facts one could not or should not reveal that one knew. The old dilemma – does he know I know he knows – sometimes seemed like child's play.

I said, 'How's Jonathan?'

He laughed. 'I hear you play chess,' he said. 'I hear you're a whiz at misdirection. Your opponents think they're winning, and then ... wham.'

I played chess only with Charles at Aynsford, and not very often.

'Do you know my father-in-law?' I asked. 'Ex-father-in-law, Charles Roland?'

231

With a glimmer he said, 'I've talked to him on the telephone.'

At least he hadn't lied to me, I thought; and, if he hadn't lied he'd given me a fairly firm path to follow. I asked about Jonathan, and about his sister, Betty Bracken.

'That wretched boy is still at Combe Bassett and now that the water ski-ing season is over he is driving everyone *mad*. You are the only person who sees any good in him.'

'Norman does.'

'Norman sees a talented water-skier with criminal tendencies.'

'Has Jonathan any money?'

Archie shook his head. 'Only the very little we gave him for toothpaste and so on. He's still on probation. He's a mess.' He paused. 'Betty has been paying for the water ski-ing. She's the only one in our family with real money. She married straight out of school. Bobby's thirty years older – he was rich when they married and he's richer than ever now. As you saw, she's still devoted to him. Always has been. They had no children; she couldn't. Very sad. If Jonathan had any sense he would be *nice* to Betty.'

'I don't think he's that devious. Or not yet, anyway.'

'Do you like him?' Archie asked curiously.

'Not much, but I hate to see people go to waste.'

'Stupid boy.'

'I checked on the colt,' I said. 'The foot stayed on.'

After a longish pause, I said, 'Do you know a man called Archibald Kirk?'

'No, I don't think so.'

'He says he talked to you on the telephone. It was months ago, I think. He's a civil servant and a magistrate. He lives near Hungerford, and I've come here from his house. Can you remember? Way back. I think he may have been asking you about *me*. Like sort of checking up, like a reference. You probably told him that I play chess.'

He thought about it, searching for the memory.

'I would always give you a good reference,' he said. 'Is there any reason why you'd prefer I didn't?'

'No, definitely not.'

'I've been asked several times about your character and ability. I always say if they're looking for an investigator they couldn't do better.'

'You're . . . very kind.'

'Kind, my foot. Why do you ask about this Archibald Church?'

'Kirk.'

'Kirk, then.'

I drank some brandy and said, 'Do you remember that day you came with me to the Jockey Club? The day we got the head of the Security section sacked?'

'I could hardly forget it, could I?'

'You didn't tell Archie Kirk about it, did you?'

'Of course not. I *never* talk about it. I gave you my word I wouldn't.'

'Someone has,' I said morosely.

'The Jockey Club didn't actually swear an oath of silence.'

'I know.' I thought a bit and asked, 'Do you know a barrister called Davis Tatum? He's the head of chambers of the prosecution counsel at Ellis's trial.'

'I know *of* him. Never met him.'

'You'd like him. You'd like Archie, too.' I paused, and went on, 'They both know about that day at the Jockey Club.'

'But Sid . . . does it really matter? I mean, you did the Jockey Club a tremendous favour, getting rid of their villain.'

'Davis Tatum and, I'm sure, Archie, have engaged me to find out who is moving behind the scenes to get the Quint trial quashed. And I'm not telling you that.'

He smiled. 'Client confidentiality?'

'Right. Well, Davis Tatum made a point of telling me that he knew all about the mandarins insisting I took off my shirt, and why. I think he and Archie are trying to reassure themselves that if they ask me to do something dangerous, I'll do it.'

He gave me a long slow look, his features still and expressionless.

Finally he said, 'And will you?'

I sighed, 'Probably.'

'What sort of danger?'

'I don't think they know. But realistically, if someone has an overwhelming reason for preventing Ellis's trial

236

from ever starting, who is the person standing chiefly in the way?'

'*Sid!*'

'Yes. So they're asking me to find out if anyone might be motivated enough to ensure my permanent removal from the scene. They want me to find out *if* and *who* and *why*.'

'God, Sid.'

From a man who never blasphemed, those were strong words.

'So . . .' I sighed. 'Davis Tatum gave me a name, Owen Yorkshire, and told me he owned a firm called Topline Foods. Now Topline Foods gave a sponsored lunch at Aintree on the day before the Grand National. Ellis Quint was guest of honour. Also among the guests was a man called Lord Tilepit, who is both on the Board of Topline Foods and the proprietor of *The Pump*, which has been busy mocking me for months.'

He sat as if frozen.

'So,' I said, 'I'll go and see what Owen Yorkshire and Lord Tilepit are up to, and if I don't come back you can kick up a stink.'

When he'd organised his breath, he said, 'Don't do it, Sid.'

'No . . . but if I don't, Ellis will walk out laughing, and my standing in the world will be down the tubes for ever, if you see what I mean.'

He saw.

After a while he said, 'I do vaguely remember talk-

237

ing to this Archie fellow. He asked about your *brains*. He said he knew about your physical resilience. Odd choice of words – I remember them. I told him you played a wily game of chess. And it's true, you do. But it was a long time ago. Before all this happened.'

I nodded. 'He already knew a lot about me when he got his sister to phone at five-thirty in the morning to tell me she had a colt with his foot off.'

'So that's who he is? Mrs Bracken's brother?'

'Yeah.' I drank brandy and said, 'If you're ever talking to Sir Thomas Ullaston, would you mind asking him – and don't make a drama of it – if he told Archie Kirk or Davis Tatum about that morning in the Jockey Club?'

Sir Thomas Ullaston had been Senior Steward at the time, and had conducted the proceedings which led to the removal of the head of the Security section who had arranged for Chico and me to be thoroughly deterred from investigating anything ever again. As far as I was concerned it was all past history, and I most emphatically wanted it to remain so.

Charles said he would ask Sir Thomas.

'Ask him not to let *The Pump* get hold of it.'

Charles contemplated that possibility with about as much horror as I did myself.

The bell of the side-door rang distantly, and Charles frowned at his watch.

'Who can that be? It's almost eight o'clock.'

We soon found out. An ultra-familiar voice called

238

'Daddy?' across the hall outside, and an ultra-familiar figure appeared in the doorway. Jenny ... Charles's younger daughter ... my sometime wife. My still-embittered wife, whose tongue had barbs.

Smothering piercing dismay I stood up, and Charles also.

'Jenny,' Charles said, advancing to greet her. 'What a lovely surprise.'

She turned her cheek coolly, as always, and said, 'We were passing. It seemed impossible not to call in.' She looked at me without much emotion and said, 'We didn't know *you* were here until I saw your car outside.'

I took the few steps between us and gave her the sort of cheek to cheek salutation she'd bestowed on Charles. She accepted the politeness, as always, as the civilised acknowledgement of adversaries after battle.

'You look thin,' she observed, not with concern but with criticism, from habit.

She, I thought, looked as beautiful as always, but there was nothing to be gained by saying so. I didn't want her to sneer at me. To begin with, it ruined the sweet curve of her mouth. She could hurt me with words whenever she tried, and she'd tried often. My only defence had been – and still was – silence.

Her handsome new husband had followed her into the room, shaking hands with Charles and apologising for having appeared without warning.

'My dear fellow, any time,' Charles assured him.

Anthony Wingham turned my way and with self-conscious affability said, 'Sid . . .' and held out his hand.

It was extraordinary, I thought, enduring his hearty embarrassed grasp, how often one regularly shook hands in the course of a day. I'd never really noticed it before.

Charles poured drinks and suggested dinner. Anthony Wingham waffled a grateful refusal. Jenny gave me a cool look and sat in the gold brocade chair.

Charles made small talk with Anthony until they'd exhausted the weather. I stood with them but looked at Jenny, and she at me. Into a sudden silence, she said, 'Well, Sid, I don't suppose you want me to say it, but you've got yourself into a proper mess this time.'

'No.'

'No what?'

'No, I don't want you to say it.'

'Ellis Quint! Biting off more than you can chew. And back in the summer the papers pestered me too. I suppose you know?'

I unwillingly nodded.

'That reporter from *The Pump*,' Jenny complained. 'India Cathcart, I couldn't get rid of her. She wanted to know all about you and about our divorce. Do you know what she wrote? She wrote that I'd told her that quite apart from being crippled, you weren't man enough for me.'

'I read it,' I said briefly.

'Did you? And did you like it? Did you like that, Sid?'

I didn't reply. It was Charles who fiercely protested. '*Jenny!* Don't.'

Her face suddenly softened, all the spite dissolving and revealing the gentle girl I'd married. The transformation happened in a flash, like prison bars falling away. Her liberation, I thought, had dramatically come at last.

'I didn't say that,' she told me, as if bewildered. 'I really didn't. She made it up.'

I swallowed. I found the re-emergence of the old Jenny harder to handle than her scorn.

'What *did* you say?' I said.

'Well . . . I . . . I . . .'

'*Jenny,*' Charles said again.

'I told her,' Jenny said to him, 'that I couldn't live in Sid's hard world. I told her that whatever she wrote she wouldn't smash him or disintegrate him because no one had ever managed it. I told her that he never showed his feelings and that steel was putty compared to him, and that I couldn't live with it.'

Charles and I had heard her say much the same thing before. It was Anthony who looked surprised. He inspected my harmless-looking self from his superior height and obviously thought she had got me wrong.

'India Cathcart didn't believe Jenny either,' I told him soothingly.

'*What?*'

'He reads minds, too,' Jenny said, putting down her glass and rising to her feet. 'Anthony, darling, we'll go now. OK?' To her father she said, 'Sorry it's such a short visit,' and to me, 'India Cathcart is a bitch.'

I kissed Jenny's cheek.

'I still love you,' I said.

She looked briefly into my eyes. 'I couldn't live with it. I told her the truth.'

'I know.'

'Don't let her break you.'

'No.'

'Well,' she said brightly, loudly, smiling. 'When birds fly out of cages they sing and rejoice. So . . . goodbye, Sid.'

She looked happy. She laughed. I ached for the days when we'd met, when she looked like that always; but one could never go back.

'Goodbye, Jenny,' I said.

Charles, uncomprehending, went with them to see them off and came back frowning.

'I simply don't understand my daughter,' he said. 'Do you?'

'Oh, yes.'

'She tears you to pieces. *I* can't stand it, even if you can. Why don't you ever fight back?'

'Look what I did to her.'

'She knew what she was marrying.'

'I don't think she did. It isn't always easy, being married to a jockey.'

242

'You forgive her too much! And then, do you know what she said just now, when she was leaving? I don't understand her. She gave me a hug – a hug – not a dutiful peck on the cheek, and she said, "Take care of Sid." '

I felt instantly liquefied inside: too close to tears.

'Sid . . .'

I shook my head, as much to retain composure as anything else.

'We've made our peace,' I said.

'When?'

'Just now. The old Jenny came back. She's free of me. She felt free quite suddenly . . . so she'll have no more need to . . . to tear me to pieces, as you put it. I think that all that destructive anger has finally gone. Like she said, she's flown out of the cage.'

He said, 'I hope so,' but looked unconvinced. 'I need a drink.'

I smiled and joined him, but I discovered, as we later ate companionably together, that even though his daughter might no longer despite or torment me, what I perversely felt wasn't relief, but loss.

CHAPTER TEN

Leaving Aynsford early I drove back to London on Thursday morning and left the car, as I normally did, in a large public underground car park near Pont Square. From there I walked to the laundry where I usually took my shirts and waited while they fed my strip of rag from Northampton twice through the dry-cleaning cycle.

What emerged was a stringy looking object, basically light turquoise in colour, with a non-geometric pattern on it of green, brown and salmon pink. There were also black irregular stains that had stayed obstinately in place.

I persuaded the cleaners to iron it, with the only result that I had a flat strip instead of a wrinkled one.

'What if I wash it with detergent and water?' I asked the burly half-interested dry cleaner.

'You couldn't exactly *harm* it,' he said sarcastically.

So I washed it and ironed it and ended as before: turquoise strip, wandering indeterminate pattern, stubborn black stain.

With the help of Yellow Pages I visited the wholesale showrooms of a well-known fabric designer. An infinitely polite old man there explained that my fabric pattern was *woven*, while theirs – the wholesaler's – was *printed*. Different market, he said. The wholesaler aimed at the upper end of the middle-class market. I, he said, needed to consult an interior decorator, and with kindness he wrote for me a short list of firms.

The first two saw no profit in answering questions. At the third address I happened on an underworked twenty-year-old who ran pale long fingers through clean shoulder-length curls while he looked with interest at my offering. He pulled out a turquoise thread and held it up to the light.

'This is silk,' he said.

'Real silk?'

'No possible doubt. This was expensive fabric. The pattern is woven in. See.' He turned the piece over to show me the back. 'This is remarkable. Where did you get it? It looks like a very old lampas. Beautiful. The colours are organic, not mineral.'

I looked at his obvious youth and asked if he could perhaps seek a second opinion.

'Because I'm straight out of design school?' he guessed without umbrage. 'But I studied *fabrics*. That's why they took me on here. I *know* them. The designers don't weave them, they use them.'

'Then tell me what I've got.'

He fingered the turquoise strip and held it to his lips

and his cheek and seemed to commune with it as if it were a crystal ball.

'It's a modern copy,' he said. 'It's very skilfully done. It is lampas, woven on a Jacquard loom. There isn't enough of it to be sure, but I think it's a copy of a silk hanging made by Philippe de Lasalle in about 1760. But the original hadn't a blue-green background, it was cream with this design of ropes and leaves in greens and red and gold.'

I was impressed. 'Are you sure?'

'I've just spent three years learning this sort of thing.'

'Well, who makes it now? Do I have to go to France?'

'You could try one or two English firms but, you know what—'

He was brusquely interrupted by a severe-looking woman in a black dress and huge Aztec-type necklace who swept in and came to rest by the counter on which lay the unprepossessing rag.

'What are you doing?' she asked. 'I asked you to catalogue the new shipment of *passementerie*.'

'Yes, Mrs Lane.'

'Then please get on with it. Run along now.'

'Yes, Mrs Lane.'

'Do you want help?' she asked me briskly.

'Only the names of some weavers.'

On his way to the *passementerie*, my source of knowledge spoke briefly over his shoulder. 'It looks like a solitary weaver, not a firm. Try Saul Marcus.'

'Where?' I called.

'London.'

'Thanks.'

He went out of sight. Under Mrs Lane's inhospitable gaze I picked up my rag, smiled placatingly and departed.

I found Saul Marcus first in the telephone directory and then in white-bearded person in an airy artist's studio near Chiswick in west London where he created fabric patterns.

He looked with interest at my rag but shook his head.

I urged him to search the far universe.

'It might be Patricia Huxford's work,' he said at length, dubiously. 'You could try her. She does – or did – work like this sometimes. I don't know of anyone else.'

'Where would I find her?'

'Surrey. Sussex. Somewhere like that.'

'Thank you very much.'

Returning to Pont Square I looked for Patricia Huxford in every phone book I possessed for Surrey and Sussex and, for good measure, the bordering southern counties of Hampshire and Kent. Of the few Huxfords listed, none turned out to be Patricia, a weaver.

I really *needed* an assistant, I thought, saying goodbye to Mrs Paul Huxford, wife of a double-glazing salesman. This sort of search could take hours. Damn Chico, and his dolly-bird protective missus.

With no easy success from the directories I started on directory enquiries, the central computerised number-finder. As always, to get a number one had to give an address, but the computer system contemptuously spat out Patricia Huxford, Surrey, as being altogether too vague.

I tried Patricia Huxford, Guildford (Guildford being Surrey's county town) but learned only of the two listed P. Huxfords that I'd already tried. Kingston, Surrey: same lack of results. I systematically tried all the other main areas: Sutton, Epsom, Leatherhead, Dorking ... Surrey might be a small county in square-mile size, but large in population. I drew a uniform blank.

Huxfords were fortunately rare. A good job she wasn't called Smith.

Sussex, then. There was East Sussex (county town Lewes) and West Sussex (Chichester). I flipped a mental coin and chose Chichester, and could hardly believe my lucky ears.

An impersonal voice told me that the number of Patricia Huxford was ex-directory and could only be accessed by the police, in an emergency. It was not even in the C.O. grade one class of ex-directory, where one could sweet-talk the operator into phoning the number on one's behalf (C.O. stood for Calls Offered). Patricia Huxford valued absolute grade two privacy and couldn't be reached that way.

In the highest, third grade, category, there were the numbers that weren't on any list at all, that the exchanges and operators might not know even existed; numbers for government affairs, the Royal Family and spies.

I yawned, stretched and ate cornflakes for lunch.

While I was still unenthusiastically thinking of driving to Chichester, roughly seventy more miles of armache, Charles phoned from Aynsford.

'So glad to catch you in,' he said. 'I've been talking to Thomas Ullaston, I thought you'd like to know.'

'Yes,' I agreed with interest. 'What did he say?'

'You know, of course, that he's no longer Senior Steward of the Jockey Club? His term of office ended.'

'Yes, I know.'

I also regretted it. The new Senior Steward was apt to think me a light-weight nuisance. I supposed he had a point, but it never helped to be discounted by the top man if I asked for anything at all from the department heads in current power. No one was any longer thanking me for ridding them of their villain: according to them, the whole embarrassing incident was best forgotten, and with that I agreed, but I wouldn't have minded residual warmth.

'Thomas was dumbfounded by your question,' Charles said. 'He protested that he'd meant you no harm.'

'Ah!' I said.

'Yes. He didn't deny that he'd told someone about that morning, but he assured me that it had been only *one* person, that that person was someone of utterly good standing, a man of the utmost probity. I asked if it was Archibald Kirk, and he *gasped*, Sid. He said it was early in the summer when Archie Kirk sought him out to ask about you. Archie Kirk told him he'd heard you were a good investigator and he wanted to know *how* good. It seems Archie Kirk's branch of the Civil Service occasionally likes to employ independent investigators quietly, but that it's hard to find good ones they can trust. Thomas Ullaston told him to trust *you*. Archie Kirk apparently asked more and more questions, until Thomas found himself telling about that chain and those awful marks ... I mean, sorry, Sid.'

'Yeah,' I said, 'go on.'

'Thomas told Archie Kirk that with your jockey constitution and physical resilience – he said physical resilience, Thomas did, so that's exactly where Kirk got that phrase from – with your natural inborn physical resilience you'd shaken off the whole thing as if it had never happened.'

'Yes,' I said, which wasn't entirely true. One couldn't ever forget. One could, however, ignore. And it was odd, I thought, that I never had nightmares about whippy chains.

Charles chuckled. 'Thomas said he wouldn't want young master Halley on his tail if he'd been a crook.'

Young master Halley found himself pleased.

Charles asked, 'Is there anything else I can do for you, Sid?'

'You've been great.'

'Be careful.'

I smiled as I assured him I would. Be careful was hopeless advice to a jockey, and at heart I was as much out to win as ever.

On my way to the car I bought some robust adhesive bandage and, with my right forearm firmly strapped and a sufficient application of ibuprofen, drove to Chichester in West Sussex, about seven miles inland from the coast.

It was a fine spirits-lifting afternoon. My milk-coffee Mercedes swooped over the rolling South Downs and sped the last flat mile to the cathedral city of Chichester, wheels satisfyingly fast but still not as fulfilling as a horse.

I sought out the public library and asked to see the electoral roll.

There was masses of it: all the names and addresses of registered voters in the county, divided into electoral districts.

Where was Chico, blast him?

Resigned to a long search that could take two or three hours, I found Patricia Huxford within a short fifteen minutes. A record. I hated electoral rolls: the small print made me squint.

Huxford, Patricia Helen, Bravo House, Lowell.

Hallelujah.

I followed my road map, and asked for directions in the village of Lowell, and found Bravo House, a small converted church with a herd of cars and vans outside.

It didn't look like the reclusive lair of an ex-directory hermit.

As people seemed to be walking in and out of the high heavy open west door, I walked in too. I had arrived, it was soon clear, towards the end of a photographic session for a glossy magazine.

I said to a young woman hugging a clipboard, 'Patricia Huxford?'

The young woman gave me a radiant smile. 'Isn't she *wonderful*?' she said.

I followed the direction of her gaze. A small woman in an astonishing dress was descending from a sort of throne that had been built on a platform situated where the old transepts crossed the nave. There were bright theatrical spotlights that began to be switched off, and there were photographers unscrewing and dismantling and wrapping cables into hanks. There were effusive thanks in the air and satisfied excitement and the overall glow of a job done well.

I waited, looking about me, discovering the changes from church to modern house. The window glass, high up, was clear, not coloured. The stone-flagged nave had rugs, no pews, comfortable modern sofas pushed back against the wall to accommodate the crowd, and a large-screen television set.

A white-painted partition behind the throne platform cut off the view of what had been the altar area, but nothing had been done to spoil the sweep of the

252

vaulted ceiling, built with soaring stone arches to the glory of God.

One would have to have a very secure personality, I thought, to choose to live in that place.

The media flock drifted down the nave and left with undiminished goodwill. Patricia Huxford waved to them and closed her heavy door and, turning, was surprised to find me still inside.

'So sorry,' she said, and began to open the door again.

'I'm not with the photographers,' I said. 'I came to ask you about something else.'

'I'm tired,' she said. 'I must ask you to go.'

'You look beautiful,' I told her, 'and it will only take a minute.' I brought my scrap of rag out and showed it to her. 'If you are Patricia Huxford, did you weave this?'

'Trish,' she said absently. 'I'm called Trish.'

She looked at the strip of silk and then at my face.

'What's your name?' she asked.

'John.'

'John what?'

'John Sidney.'

John Sidney were my real two first names, the ones my young mother had habitually used. 'John Sidney, give us a kiss.' 'John Sidney, wash your face.' 'John Sidney, have you been fighting again?'

I often used John Sidney in my job: whenever, in fact, I didn't want to be known to be Sid Halley. After the past months of all-too-public drubbing I wasn't sure that Sid Halley would get me anything anywhere but a swift heave-ho.

Trish Huxford, somewhere, I would have guessed, in the middle to late forties, was pretty, blonde (natural?), small-framed and cheerful. Bright observant eyes looked over my grey business suit, white shirt, unobtrusive tie, brown shoes, dark hair, dark eyes, unthreatening manner; my usual working confidence-inspiring exterior.

She was still on a high from the photo session. She needed someone to help her unwind, and I looked – and was – safe. Thankfully I saw her relax.

The amazing dress she had worn for the photographs was utterly simple in cut, hanging heavy and straight from her shoulders, floor length and sleeveless with a soft ruffled frill round her neck. It was the cloth of the dress that staggered: it was blue and red and silver and gold, and it *shimmered*.

'Did you weave your dress?' I asked.

'Of course.'

'I've never seen anything like it.'

'No, you wouldn't, not nowadays. Can I do anything for you? Where did you come from?'

'London. Saul Marcus suggested you might know who wove my strip of silk.'

'Saul! How is he?'

'He has a white beard,' I said. 'He seemed fine.'

'I haven't seen him for years. Will you make me some tea? I don't want marks on this dress.'

I smiled. 'I'm quite good at tea.'

She led the way past the throne and round the white-painted screen. There were choir stalls beyond, old and untouched, and an altar table covered by a cloth that brought me to a halt. It was of a brilliant royal blue with shining gold Greek motifs woven into its deep hem. On the table, in the place of religious altar furniture, stood an antique spinning wheel, good enough for Sleeping Beauty. Above the table, arched clear glass windows rose to the roof.

'This way,' Patricia Huxford commanded, and, leading me past the choir stalls, turned abruptly through a narrow doorway which opened onto what could only probably have been a vestry and was now a small modern kitchen with a bathroom beside it.

'My bed is in the south transept,' she told me, 'and my looms are in the north. You might expect us to be going to drink China tea with lemon out of a silver teapot, but in fact I don't have enough time for that sort of thing, so the tea bags and mugs are on that shelf.'

I half filled her electric kettle and plugged it in, and she spent the time walking around watching the miraculous colours move and mingle in her dress.

Intrigued, waiting for the water to boil, I asked, 'What is it made of?'

'What do you think?'

'Er, it looks like ... well ... gold.'

She laughed. 'Quite right. Gold, silver thread, and silk.'

I rather clumsily filled the mugs.

'Milk?' she suggested.

'No, thank you.'

'That's lucky. The crowd that's just left finished it off.' She gave me a brilliant smile, picked up a mug by its handle and returned to the throne, where she sat neatly on the vast red velvet chair and rested a thin arm delicately along gilt carving. The dress fell into sculptured folds over her slender thighs.

'The photographs,' she said, 'are for a magazine about a festival of the arts that Chichester is staging all next summer.'

I stood before her like some mediaeval page: stood chiefly because there was no chair nearby to sit on.

'I suppose,' she said, 'that you think me madly eccentric?'

'Not madly.'

She grinned happily. 'Normally I wear jeans and an old smock.' She drank some tea. 'Usually I work. Today is play-acting.'

'And magnificent.'

She nodded. 'No one, these days, makes cloth of gold.'

'The Field of the Cloth of Gold,' I exclaimed.

'That's right. What do you know of it?'

'Only that phrase.'

'The field was the meeting place at Guines, France,

in June 1520, of Henry VIII of England and Francis I of France. They were supposed to be making peace between England and France but they hated each other and tried to outdo each other in splendour. So all their courtiers wore cloth woven out of gold and they gave each other gifts you'd never see today. And I thought it would be historic to weave some cloth of gold for the festival . . . so I did. And this dress weighs a ton, I may tell you. Today is the only time I've worn it and I can't bear to take it off.'

'It's breathtaking,' I said.

She poured out her knowledge. 'In 1476 the Duke of Burgundy left behind a hundred and sixty gold cloths when he fled from battle against the Swiss. You make gold cloth – like I made this – by supporting the soft gold on threads of silk, and you can recover the gold by burning the cloth. So when I was making this dress, that's what I did with the pieces I cut out to make the neck and armholes. I burnt them and collected the melted gold.'

'Beautiful.'

'You know something?' she said. 'You're the only person who's seen this dress who hasn't asked how much it cost.'

'I did wonder.'

'And I'm not telling. Give me your strip of silk.'

I took her empty mug and tucked it under my left arm, and in my right hand held out the rag, which she took; and I found her looking with concentration at my left hand. She raised her eyes to meet my gaze.

'Is it . . .?' she said.

'Worth its weight in gold,' I said flippantly. 'Yes.'

I carried the mugs back to the kitchen and returned to find her standing and smoothing her fingers over the piece of rag.

'An interior decorator,' I said, 'told me it was probably a modern copy of a hanging made in 1760 by . . . um . . . I think Philippe de Lasalle.'

'How clever. Yes, it is. I made quite a lot of it at one time.' She paused, then said abruptly, 'Come along,' and dived off again, leaving me to follow.

We went this time through a door in another white-painted partition and found ourselves in the north transept, her workroom.

There were three looms of varying construction, all bearing work in progress. There was also a business section with filing cabinets and a good deal of office paraphernalia, and another area devoted to measuring, cutting and packing.

'I make fabrics you can't buy anywhere else,' she said. 'Most of it goes to the Middle East.' She walked towards the largest of the three looms, a monster that rose in steps to double our height.

'This is a Jacquard loom,' she said. 'I made your sample on this.'

'I was told this piece was . . . a lampas? What's a lampas?'

258

She nodded. 'A lampas is a compound weave with extra warps and wefts which put patterns and colours on the face of the fabric only, and are tucked into the back.' She showed me how the design of ropes and branches of leaves gleamed on one side of the turquoise silk but hardly showed on the reverse. 'It takes ages to set up,' she said. 'Nowadays almost no one outside the Middle East thinks the beauty is worth the expense, but once I used to sell quite a lot of it to castles and great houses in England, and all sorts of private people. I only make it to order.'

I said neutrally, 'Would you know who you made this piece for?'

'My dear man. No, I can't remember. But I probably still have the records. Why do you want to know? Is it important?'

'I don't know if it is important. I was given the strip and asked to find its origin.'

She shrugged. 'Let's find it then. You never know, I might get an order for some more.'

She opened cupboard doors to reveal many ranks of box files, and ran her fingers along the labels on the spines until she came to one that her expression announced as possible. She lifted the box file from the shelf and opened it on a table.

Inside were stiff pages with samples of fabric stapled to them, with full details of fibres, dates, amount made, names of purchasers and receipts.

She turned the stiff pages slowly, holding my strip

in one hand for comparison. She came to several versions of the same design, but all in the wrong colour.

'That's it!' she exclaimed suddenly. 'That's the one. I see I wove it almost thirty years ago. How time flies. I was so young then. It was a hanging for a four-poster bed. I see I supplied it with gold tassels made of gimp.'

I asked without much expectation, 'Who to?'

'It says here a Mrs Gordon Quint.'

I said, '... Er ...' meaninglessly, my breath literally taken away.

Ginnie? *Ginnie* had owned the material.

'I don't remember her or anything about it,' Trish Huxford said. 'But all the colours match. It must have been this one commission. I don't think I made these colours for anyone else.' She looked at the black stains disfiguring the strip I'd brought. 'What a pity! I think of my fabrics as going on for ever. They could easily last two hundred years. I love the idea of leaving something beautiful in the world. I expect you think I'm a sentimental old bag.'

'I think you're splendid,' I said truthfully, and asked, 'Why are you ex-directory, with a business to run?'

She laughed. 'I hate being interrupted when I'm setting up a design. It takes vast concentration. I have a mobile phone for friends – I can switch it off – and I have an agent in the Middle East who gets orders for me. Why am I telling you all this?'

'I'm interested.'

She closed the file and put it back on the shelf, asking, 'Does Mrs Quint want some more fabric to replace this damaged bit, do you think?'

Mrs Quint was sixteen floors dead.

'I don't know,' I said.

On the drive back to London I pulled off the road to phone Davis Tatum at the number he'd given me, his home.

He was in and, it seemed, glad to hear from me, wanting to know what I'd done for him so far.

'Tomorrow,' I said, 'I'll give Topline Foods a visit. Who did you get Owen Yorkshire's name from?'

He said, stalling, 'I beg your pardon?'

'Davis,' I said mildly, 'you want me to take a look at Owen Yorkshire and his company, so why? Why *him*?'

'I can't tell you.'

'Do you mean you promised not to, or you don't know?'

'I mean . . . just go and take a look.'

I said, 'Sir Thomas Ullaston, Senior Steward last year of the Jockey Club, told Archie Kirk about that little matter of the chains, and Archie Kirk told *you*. So did the name Owen Yorkshire come to you from Archie Kirk?'

'Hell,' he said.

'I like to know what I'm getting into.'

After a pause he said, 'Owen Yorkshire has been seen twice in the boardroom of *The Pump*. We don't know why.'

'Thank you,' I said.

'Is that enough?'

'To be going on with. Oh, and my mobile phone is now safe. No more leaks. See you later.'

I drove on to London, parked in the underground garage and walked along the alleyway between tall houses that led into the opposite side of the square from my flat.

I was going quietly and cautiously in any case, and came to a dead stop when I saw that the street light almost directly outside my window was not lit.

Boys sometimes threw stones at it to break the glass. Normally its darkness wouldn't have sent shudders up my spine and made my right arm remember Gordon Quint from fingers to neck. Normally I might have crossed the square figuratively whistling while intending to phone in the morning to get the light fixed.

Things were not normal.

There were two locked gates into the central garden, one opposite the path I was on, and one on the far side, opposite my house. Standing in shadow I sorted out the resident-allocated garden key, went quietly across the circling roadway and unlocked the near gate.

Nothing moved. I eased the gate open, slid through, and closed it behind me. No squeaks. I moved slowly from patch to patch of shaded cover, the half-lit tree branches moving in a light breeze, yellow leaves drifting down like ghosts.

Near the far side I stopped and waited.

There could be no one there. I was foolishly afraid over nothing.

The street light was out.

It had been out at other times . . .

I stood with my back to a tree, waiting for alarm to subside to the point where I would unlock the second gate and cross the road to my front steps. The sounds of the city were distant. No cars drove into the cul-de-sac square.

I couldn't stand there all night, I thought . . . *and then I saw him.*

He was in a car parked by one of the few meters. His head – unmistakably Gordon Quint's head – moved behind the window. He was looking straight ahead, waiting for me to arrive by road or pavement.

I stood immobile as if stuck to the tree. It had to be obsession with him, I thought. The burning fury of Monday had settled down not into grief but revenge. I hadn't been in my flat for about thirty hours. How long had he been sitting there waiting? I'd had a villain wait almost a week for me once, before I'd walked unsuspectingly into his trap.

Obsession – fixation – was the most frightening of enemies and the hardest to escape.

I retreated, frankly scared, expecting him to see my movement, but he hadn't thought of an approach by

263

garden. From tree to tree, round the patches of open grass, I regained the far gate, eased through it, crossed the road and drifted up the alleyway, cravenly expecting a bellow and a chase and, as he was a farmer, perhaps a shotgun.

Nothing happened. My shoes, soled and heeled for silence, made no sound. I walked back to my underground car and sat in it, not exactly trembling but nonetheless stirred up. So much, I thought, for Tatum's myth of a clever, unafraid investigator.

I kept always in the car an overnight bag containing the personality-change clothes I'd got Jonathan to wear; dark two-piece tracksuit (trousers and zip-up jacket) navy blue trainers, and a baseball cap. The bag also contained a long-sleeved open-necked shirt, two or three charged-up batteries for my arm, and a battery charger, to make sure. Habitually round my waist I wore a belt with a zipped pocket big enough for a credit card and money.

I had no weapons nor defences like mace. In America I might have carried both.

I sat in the car considering the matter of distance and ulnas. It was well over two hundred miles from my London home to Liverpool, city of my birth. Frodsham, the base of Topline Foods, wasn't quite as far as Liverpool, but still over two hundred miles. I had already, that day, steered a hundred and fifty – Chichester and back. I'd never missed Chico so much.

I considered trains. Too inflexible. Airline? Ditto.

TeleDrive? I lingered over the comfort of TeleDrive but decided against, and resignedly set off northwards.

It was an easy drive normally; a journey on wide fast motorways taking at most three hours. I drove for only one hour, then stopped at a motel to eat and sleep, and at seven o'clock in the morning wheeled on again, trying to ignore both the obstinately slow-mending fracture and India Cathcart's column that I'd bought from the motel's news stand.

Friday mornings had been a trial since June. Page fifteen in *The Pump* – trial by the long knives of journalism, the blades that ripped the gut.

She hadn't mentioned at all seeing Tatum and me in the Le Meridien bar. Perhaps she'd taken my advice and pretended we hadn't been there. What her column said about me was mostly factually true but spitefully wrong. I wondered how she could do it? Had she no sense of humanity?

Most of her page concerned yet another politician caught with his trousers at half-mast, but the far-right column said:

Sid Halley, illegitimate by-blow of a nineteen-year-old window cleaner and a packer in a biscuit factory, ran amok as a brat in the slums of Liverpool. Home was a roach-infested council flat. Nothing wrong with that! But this same Sid Halley now puts on airs of middle-class gentility. A flat in Chelsea? Sheraton furniture? Posh accent? Go back to your roots, lad.

No wonder Ellis Quint thinks you funny. Funny pathetic!

The slum background clearly explains the Halley envy. Halley's chip on the shoulder grows more obvious every day. Now we know why!

The Halley polish is all a sham, just like his pathetic left hand.

Christ, I thought, how much more? Why did it so bloody *hurt*?

My father had been killed in a fall eight months before my birth and a few days before he was due to marry my eighteen-year-old mother. She'd done her best as a single parent in hopeless surroundings. 'Give us a kiss, John Sidney...'

I hadn't ever run amok. I'd been a quiet child, mostly. 'Have you been fighting again, John Sidney...?' She hadn't liked me fighting, though one had to sometimes, or be bullied.

And when she knew she was dying she'd taken me to Newmarket, because I'd been short for my age, and had left me with the king of trainers to be made into a jockey, as I'd always wanted.

I couldn't possibly go back to Liverpool 'roots'. I had no sense of ever having grown any there.

I had never envied Ellis Quint. I'd always liked him. I'd been a better jockey than he, and we'd both known it. If anything, the envy had been the other way round. But it was useless to protest, as it had been all along.

Protests were used regularly to prove *The Pump*'s theories of my pitiable inadequacy.

My mobile phone buzzed. I answered it.

'Kevin Mills,' a familiar voice said. 'Where are you? I tried your flat. Have you seen today's *Pump* yet?'

'Yes.'

'India didn't write it,' he said. 'I gave her the info, but she wouldn't use it. She filled that space with some parts on sexual stress and her editor rubbed them out.'

Half of my muscles unknotted, and I hadn't realised they'd been tense. I forced unconcern into my voice even as I thought of hundreds of thousands of readers sniggering about me over their breakfast toast.

'Then you wrote it yourself,' I said. 'So who's a shit now? You're the only person on *The Pump* who's seen my Sheraton desk.'

'Blast you. Where are you?'

'Going back to Liverpool. Where else?'

'Sid, look, I'm sorry.'

'Policy?'

He didn't answer.

I asked, 'Why did you phone to tell me India didn't write today's bit of demolition?'

'I'm getting soft.'

'No one's listening to this phone any more. You can say what you like.'

'Jeez.' He laughed. 'That didn't take you long.' He paused. 'You might not believe it, but most of us on

267

The Pump don't any more like what we've been doing to you.'

'Rise up and rebel,' I suggested dryly.

'We have to eat. And you're a tough bugger. You can take it.'

You just try it, I thought.

'Listen,' he said, 'the paper's received a lot of letters from readers complaining that we're not giving you a fair deal.'

'How many is a lot?'

'Two hundred or so. Believe me, that's a *lot*. But we're not allowed to print any.'

I said with interest, 'Who says so?'

'That's just it. The Ed, Godbar himself, says so, and he doesn't like it either, but the policy is coming from the very top.'

'Tilepit?'

'Are you *sure* this phone's not bugged?'

'You're safe.'

'You've had a bloody raw mauling, and you don't deserve it. I know that. We all know it. I'm sorry for my part in it. I'm sorry I wrote today's venom, especially that bit about your hand. Yes, it's Tilepit. The proprietor himself.'

'Well . . . thanks.'

He said, 'Did Ellis Quint *really* cut off those feet?'

I smiled ruefully. 'The jury will decide.'

'Sid, look here,' he protested, 'you *owe* me!'

'Life's a bugger,' I said.

CHAPTER ELEVEN

Nine o'clock Friday morning I drove into the town of Frodsham and asked for Topline Foods.

Not far from the river, I was told. Near the river; the Mersey.

The historic docks of Liverpool's Mersey waterfront had long been silent, the armies of tall cranes dismantled, the warehouses converted or pulled down. Part of the city's heart has stopped beating. There had been by-pass surgery of sorts, but past muscle would never return. The city had a vast red-brick cathedral, but faith, as in much of Britain, had dimmed.

For years I'd been to Liverpool only to ride there on Aintree racecourse. The road I'd once lived in lay somewhere under a hyper-market. Liverpool was a place, but not home.

At Frodsham there was a 'Mersey View' vantage point with, away to the distant north, some still-working docks at Runcorn on the Manchester Ship Canal. One of those docks (I'd been told earlier by telephone from the dockmaster's office) was occupied by Topline

Foods. A ship lying alongside bearing the flag and insignia of Canada had been unloading Topline grain.

I'd stopped the car from where I could see the sweep of river with the seagulls swooping and the stiff breeze tautening flags at the horizontal. I stood in the cold open air, leaning on the car, smelling the salt and the mud, and hearing the drone of traffic on the road below.

Were these roots? I'd always loved wide skies, but it was the wide sky of Newmarket Heath that I thought of as home. When I'd been a boy there'd been no wide skies, only narrow streets, the walk to school, and rain. 'John Sidney, wash your face. Give us a kiss.'

The day after my mother died I'd ridden my first winner, and that evening I'd got drunk for the first and only time until the arrest of Ellis Quint.

Soberly, realistically, in the Mersey wind I looked at the man I had become: a jumble of self-doubt, ability, fear and difficult pride. I had grown as I was from the inside out. Liverpool and Newmarket weren't to blame.

Stirring and getting back into the car I wondered where to find all those tungsten nerves I was supposed to have.

I didn't know what I was getting into. I could still at that point retreat and leave the field to Ellis. I could – and I couldn't. I would have myself to live with, if I did.

I'd better simply get on with it, I thought.

I drove down from the vantage point, located the Topline Foods factory, and passed through its twelve foot high but hospitably open wire-mesh gates. There was a guard in a gatehouse who paid me no attention.

Inside there were many cars tidily parked in ranks. I added myself to the end of one row and decided on a clothing compromise of suit trousers, zipped up tracksuit top, white shirt, no tie, ordinary shoes. I neatly combed my hair forward into a young-looking style and looked no threat to anybody.

The factory, built round three sides of a big central area, consisted of loading bays, a vast main building and a new-looking office block. Loading and unloading took place under cover, with articulated lorries backing into the bays. In the one bay I could see into clearly, the cab section had been disconnected and removed; heavy sacks that looked as if they might contain grain were being unloaded from a long container by two large men who slung the sacks onto a moving conveyor belt of rollers.

The big building had a row of windows high up: there was no chance of looking in from outside.

I ambled across to the office building and shouldered open a heavy glass door that led into a large but mostly bare entrance hall, and found there the reason for the unguarded front gates. The security arrangements were all inside.

Behind a desk sat a purposeful-looking middle-aged woman in a green jumper. Flanking her were two men in navy blue security-guard suits with Topline Foods insignia on their breast pockets.

'Name, please,' said the green jumper. 'State your business. All parcels, carriers and handbags must be left here at the desk.'

She had a distinct Liverpool accent. With the same inflection in my own voice, I told her that, as she could see, I had no bag, carrier or handbag with me.

She took the accent for granted and unsmilingly asked again for my name.

'John Sidney.'

'Business?'

'Well,' I said as if perplexed by the reception I was getting. 'I was asked to come here to see if you made some horse-nuts.' I paused. 'Like,' I lamely finished, dredging up the idiom.

'Of course we make horse-nuts. It's our business.'

'Yes,' I told her earnestly, 'but this farmer, like, he asked me to come in, as I was passing this way, to see if it was you that made some horse-nuts that someone had given him, that were very good for his young horse, like, but he was given them loose and not in a bag and all he has is a list of what's in the nuts and he wanted to know if you made them, see?' I half pulled a sheet of paper from an inside pocket and pushed it back.

She was bored by the rigmarole.

'If I could just *talk* to someone,' I pleaded. 'See, I owe this farmer a favour and it wouldn't take no more than a minute, if I could talk to someone. Because this farmer, he'll be a big customer if these are the nuts he's looking for.'

She gave in, lifted a telephone, and repeated a shortened version of my improbable tale.

She inspected me from head to foot. 'Couldn't hurt a fly,' she reported.

I kept the suitably feeble half-anxious smile in place.

She put down the receiver. 'Miss Rowse will be down to help you. Raise your hands.'

'Eh?'

'Raise your hands . . . please.'

Surprised, I did as I was told. One of the security guards patted me all over in the classic way of their job, body and legs. He missed the false hand and the cracked bone. 'Keys and mobile phone,' he reported. 'Clean.'

Green jumper wrote 'John Sidney' onto a clip-on identity card and I clipped it dutifully on.

'Wait by the lift,' she said.

I waited.

The doors finally parted to reveal a teenage girl with wispy fair hair who said she was Miss Rowse. 'Mr Sidney? This way, please.'

I stepped into the lift with her, and rode to the third floor.

She smiled with bright inexperienced encouragement and led me down a newly carpeted passage to an office conspicuously labelled 'Customer Relations' on its open door.

'Come in,' Miss Rowse said proudly. 'Please sit down.'

I sat in a Scandinavian-inspired chair of blond wood with arms, simple lines, blue cushioning and considerable comfort.

'I'm afraid I didn't really understand your problem,' Miss Rowse said trustingly. 'If you'll explain again, I can get the right person to talk to you.'

I looked round her pleasant office, which showed almost no sign of work in progress.

'Have you been here long?' I asked. (Guileless Liverpool accent, just like hers.) 'Nice office. They must think a lot of you here.'

She was pleased, but still honest. 'I'm new this week. I started on Monday – and you're my second enquiry.'

No wonder, I thought, that she'd let me in.

I said, 'Are all the offices as plush as this?'

'Yes,' she said enthusiastically. 'Mr Yorkshire, he likes things nice.'

'Is he the boss?'

'The managing director,' she nodded. The words sounded stiff and unfamiliar, as if she'd only newly learned them.

'Nice to work for, is he?' I suggested.

She confessed, 'I haven't met him yet. I know what he looks like, of course, but ... I'm new here, like I said.'

I smiled sympathetically and asked what Owen Yorkshire looked like.

She was happy to tell me. 'He's ever so *big*. He's got a big head and a lovely lot of hair, wavy like.'

'Moustache?' I suggested. 'Beard?'

'No,' she giggled. 'And he's not *old*. Not a grandad. Everyone gets out of his way.'

Do they indeed, I thought.

She went on, 'I mean, Mrs Dove, she's my boss really, she's the office manager, she says not to make him angry, whatever I do. She says just to do my job. She has a lovely office. It used to be Mr Yorkshire's own, she says.'

Miss Rowse, shaped like a woman, chattered like a child.

'Topline Foods must be doing all right to have rich new offices like these,' I said admiringly.

'They've got the TV cameras coming tomorrow to set up for Monday. They brought dozens of potted plants round this morning. Ever so keen on publicity, Mrs Dove says, Mr Yorkshire is.'

'The plants do make it nice and homey,' I said. 'Which TV company, do you know?'

She shook her head. 'All the Liverpool big noises are coming to a huge reception on Monday. The TV cameras are going all over the factory. Of course, although they're going to have all the machines running, they won't really make any nuts on Monday. It will all be pretend.'

'Why's that?'

'Security. They have to be security mad, Mrs Dove says. Mr Yorkshire worries about people putting things in the feed, she says.'

'What things?'

'I don't know. Nails and safety-pins and such. Mrs Dove says all the searching at the entrance is Mr Yorkshire's idea.'

'Very sensible,' I said.

An older and more cautious woman came into the office, revealing herself to be the fount of wisdom, Mrs Dove. Middle-aged and personally secure, I thought. Status, ability and experience all combining in priceless efficiency.

'Can I help you?' she said to me civilly, and to the girl, 'Marsha dear, I thought we'd agreed you would always come to me for advice.'

'Miss Rowse has been really helpful,' I said. 'She's going to find someone to answer my question. Perhaps you could, yourself?'

Mrs Dove (grey hair pinned high under a flat black bow, high heels, customer-relations neat satin shirt, cinched waist and black tights) listened with slowly glazing eyes to my expanding tale of the nutty farmer.

'You need our Willy Parrot,' she said when she could insert a comment. 'Come with me.'

I waggled conspiratorial fingers at Marsha Rowse and followed Mrs Dove's busy backview along the expensive passage with little partitioned but mostly empty offices on each side. She continued through a thick fire-door at the end, to emerge on a gallery round an atrium in the main factory building, where the nuts came from.

276

Rising from the ground, level almost to the gallery, were huge mixing vats, all with paddles circulating, activated from machinery stretching down from above. The sounds were an amalgam of whirr, rattle and slurp: the air bore fine particles of cereal dust and it looked like a brewery, I thought. It smelled rather the same also, but without the fermentation.

Mrs Dove passed me thankfully on to a man in brown overalls who inspected my dark clothes and asked if I wanted to be covered in fall-out.

'Not particularly.'

He raised patient eyebrows and gestured to me to follow him, which I did, to find myself on an iron staircase descending one floor, along another gallery and ending in a much-used battered little cubby-hole of an office, with a sliding glass door that he closed behind us.

I commented on the contrast from the office building.

'Fancy fiddle-faddle,' he said. 'That's for the cameras. This is where the work is done.'

'I can see that,' I told him admiringly.

'Now, lad,' he said, looking me up and down, unimpressed, 'what is it you want?'

He wasn't going to be taken in very far by the farmer twaddle. I explained in a shorter version and produced the folded paper bearing the analysis of the nuts from the Combe Bassett and the Land-Rover, and asked if it was a Topline formula.

He read the list that by then I knew by heart.

Wheat, oatfeed, ryegrass, straw, barley, maize, molasses, salt, linseed.
Vitamins, selenium, copper, other substances and probably the antioxidant Ethoxyquin.

'Where did you get this?' he asked.

'From a farmer, like I told you.'

'This list isn't complete,' he said.

'No . . . but is it enough?'

'It doesn't give percentages. I can't possibly match it to any of our products.' He folded the paper and gave it back. 'Your cubes might be our supplement feed for horses out at grass. Do you know anything about horses?'

'A little.'

'Then the more oats you give them, the more energy they expend. Racehorses need more oats. I can't tell you for sure if these cubes were for racehorses in training unless I know the proportion of oats.'

'They weren't racehorses in training.'

'Then your farmer friend couldn't do better than our Sweetfield mix. They do contain everything on your list.'

'Are other people's cubes much different?'

'There aren't very many manufacturers. We're perhaps fourth on the league table but after this advertisement campaign we expect that to zoom up. The new management aims for the top.'

'But ... um ... do you have enough space?'

'Capacity?'

I nodded.

He smiled. 'Owen Yorkshire has plans. He talks to us man to man.' His face and voice were full of approval. 'He's brought the old place back to life.'

I said inoffensively, 'Mrs Dove seems in awe of his anger.'

Willy Parrott laughed and gave me a male chauvinist-type wink. 'He has a flaming temper, has our Owen Yorkshire. And the more a man for that.'

I looked vaguely at some charts taped to a wall. 'Where does he come from?' I asked.

'Haven't a clue,' Willy told me cheerfully. 'He knows bugger all about nutrition. He's a salesman, and *that's* what we needed. We have a couple of nerds in white coats working on what we put in all the vats.'

He was scornful of scientists as well as women. I turned back from the wall charts and thanked him for his time. Very interesting job, I told him. Obviously he ran the department that mattered most.

He took the compliment as his due and saved me the trouble of asking by offering to let me tag along with him while he went to his next task, which was to check a new shipment of wheat. I accepted with an enthusiasm that pleased him. A man good at his job often enjoyed an audience, and so did Willy Parrott.

He gave me a set of over-large brown overalls and told me to clip the identity card on the outside, like his own.

'Security is vital,' he said to me. 'Owen's stepped it all up. He lectures us on not letting strangers near the mixing vats. I can't let you any nearer than this. Our competitors wouldn't be above adding foreign substances that would put us out of business.'

'D'you mean it?' I said, looking avid.

'You have to be specially careful with horse feed,' he assured me, sliding open his door when I was ready. 'You can't mix cattle food in the same vats, for instance. You can put things in cattle feed that are prohibited for racehorses. You can get traces of prohibited substances in the horse-cubes just by using the same equipment, even if you think you've cleaned everything thoroughly.'

There had been a famous example in racing of a trainer getting into trouble by unknowingly giving his runners contaminated nuts.

'Fancy,' I said.

I thought I might have overdone the impressed look I gave him, but he accepted it easily.

'We do nothing else except horse-cubes here,' Willy said. 'Owen says when we expand we'll do cattle feed and chicken pellets, and all sorts of other muck, but I'll be staying here, Owen says, in charge of the equine branch.'

'A top job,' I said with admiration.

He nodded. 'The best.'

We walked along the gallery and came to another fire-door, which he lugged open.

'All these internal doors are locked at night now, and there's a watchman with a dog. Very thorough, is Owen.' He looked back to make sure I was following, then stopped at a place from which we could see bags marked with red maple leaves travelling upwards on an endless belt of bag-sized ledges, only to be tumbled off the top and be manhandled by two smoothly swinging muscular workers.

'I expect you saw those two security men in the entrance hall?' Willy Parrott said, the question of security not yet exhausted.

'They frisked me,' I grinned. 'Going a bit far, I thought.'

'They're Owen's private bodyguards,' Willy Parrott said with a mixture of awe and approval. 'They're real hard men from Liverpool. Owen says he needs them in case the competitors try to get rid of him the old-fashioned way.'

I frowned disbelievingly. 'Competitors don't kill people.'

'Owen says he's taking no risks because he definitely is trying to put other firms out of business, if you look at it that way.'

'So you think he's right to need bodyguards?'

Willy Parrott turned to me and said, 'It's not the

world I was brought up in, lad. But we have to live in this new one, Owen says.'

'I suppose so.'

'You won't get far with that attitude, lad.' He pointed to the rising bags. 'That's this year's wheat straight from the prairie. Only the best is good enough, Owen says, in trade wars.'

He led the way down some nearby concrete stairs and through another heavy door, and I realised we were on ground level just off the central atrium. With a smile of satisfaction he pushed through one more door and we found ourselves amid the vast mixing vats, pygmies surrounded by giants.

He enjoyed my expression.

'Awesome,' I said.

'You don't need to go back upstairs to get out,' he said. 'There's a door out to the yard just down here.'

I thanked him for his advice about the nuts for the farmer, and for showing me round. I'd been with him for half an hour and couldn't reasonably stretch it further, but while I was in mid-sentence he looked over my shoulder and his face changed completely from man-in-charge to subservient subject.

I turned to see what had caused this transformation and found it not to be a Royal Person but a large man in white overalls accompanied by several anxious blue-clad attendants who were practically walking backwards.

'Morning, Willy,' said the man in white. 'Everything going well?'

'Yes, Owen. Fine.'

'Good. Has the Canadian wheat come up from the docks?'

'They're unloading it now, Owen.'

'Good. We should have a talk about future plans. Come up to my new office at four this afternoon. You know where it is? Top floor, turn right from the lift, like my old office.'

'Yes, Owen.'

'Good.'

The eyes of the businessman glanced my way briefly and incuriously, and passed on. I was wearing brown overalls and an identity card, after all, and looked an employee. Not an employee of much worth, either, with my over-big overalls wrinkling around my ankles and drooping down my arms to the fingers. Willy didn't attempt to explain my presence, for which I was grateful. Willy was almost on his knees in reverence.

Owen Yorkshire was, without doubt, impressive. Easily over six foot tall, he was simply large, but not fat. There was a lot of heavy muscle in the shoulders, and a trim, sturdy belly. Luxuriant closely-waving hair spilled over the collar, with the beginnings of grey in the lacquered wings sweeping back from above his ears. It was a hairstyle that in its way made as emphatic a statement as Jonathan's. Owen Yorkshire intended not only to rule but to be remembered.

His accent was not quite Liverpool and not at all London, but powerful and positive. His voice was unmistakably an instrument of dominance. One could imagine that his rages might in fact shake the building. One could have sympathy with his yes-men.

Willy said, 'Yes, Owen,' several more times.

The man-to-man relationship that Willy Parrott prized so much extended, I thought, not much farther than the use of first names. True, Owen Yorkshire's manner to Willy was of the 'we're all in this together' type of management technique, and seemed to be drawing the best out of a good man; but I could imagine the boss also finding ways of getting rid of his Willy Parrott, if it pleased him, with sad shrugs and 'You know how it is these days, we no longer *need* a production manager just for horse-cubes; your job is computerised and phased out. Redundancy money? Of course. See my secretary. No hard feelings.'

I hoped it wouldn't happen to Willy.

Owen Yorkshire and his satellites swept onwards. Willy Parrott looked after him with pride tinged very faintly with anxiety.

'Do you work tomorrow?' I asked. 'Is the factory open on Saturdays?'

He reluctantly removed his gaze from the Yorkshire backview and began to think I'd been there too long.

'We're opening on Saturdays from next week,' he said. 'Tomorrow they're making more advertising films. There will be cameras all over the place, and on

Monday too. We won't get anything useful done until Tuesday.' He was full of disapproval, but he would repress all that, it was clear, for man-to-man Owen. 'Off you go then, lad. Go back to the entrance and leave the overalls and identity tag there.'

I thanked him again and this time went out into the central yard which, since my own arrival, had become clogged with vans and truckloads of television and advertising people. The television contingent were from Liverpool. The advertisement makers, according to the identification on their vans, were from Intramind Imaging (Manchester) Ltd.

One of the Intramind drivers, in the unthinking way of his kind, had braked and parked at an angle to all the other vehicles. I walked across to where he still sat in his cab and asked him to straighten up his van.

'Who says so?' he demanded belligerently.

'I just work here,' I said, still in the brown overalls that, in spite of Willy Parrott's instructions, I was not going to return. 'I was sent out to ask you. Big artics have to get in here.' I pointed to the unloading bays.

The driver grunted, started his engine, straightened his vehicle, switched off and jumped down to the ground beside me.

'Will that do?' he asked sarcastically.

'You must have an exciting job,' I said enviously. 'Do you see all those film stars?'

He sneered. 'We make *advertising* films, mate. Sure,

sometimes we get big names, but mostly they're endorsing things.'

'What sort of things?'

'Sports gear, often. Shoes, golf clubs.'

'And horse-cubes?'

He had time to waste while others unloaded equipment. He didn't mind a bit of showing off.

He said, 'They've got a lot of top jockeys lined up to endorse the horse-nuts.'

'Have they?' I asked interestedly. 'Why not trainers?'

'It's the jockeys the public know by their faces. That's what I'm told. I'm a football man myself.'

He didn't, I was grateful to observe, even begin to recognise my own face, that in years gone by had fairly taken up space on the nation's sports pages.

Someone in the team called him away and I walked off, sliding into my own car and making an uneventful exit through the tall unchecked outward gates. Odd, I thought, that the security-paranoid Owen Yorkshire didn't have a gate bristling with electronic barriers and ominous name-gatherers; and the only reason I could think of for such laxity was that he didn't always *want* name-takers to record everyone's visits.

Blind-eye country, I thought, like the private backstairs of the great before the India Cathcarts of the world floodlit the secretive comings and goings, and rewarded promiscuity with taint.

Perhaps Owen Yorkshire's backstairs was the lift to

the fifth floor. Perhaps Mrs Green Jumper and the bouncers in blue knew who to admit without searching.

Perhaps this, perhaps that. I'd seen the general layout and been near the power running the business, but basically I'd done little there but reconnoitre.

I stopped in a public car park, took off the brown overalls and decided to go to Manchester.

The journey was quite short, but it took me almost as long again to find Intramind Imaging (Manchester) Ltd which, although in a back street, proved to be a much bigger outfit than I'd pictured; I shed the tracksuit top and the Liverpool accent and approached the reception desk in suit, tie and business aura.

'I've come from Topline Foods,' I said. 'I'd like to talk to whoever is in charge of their account.'

Did I have an appointment?

No, it was a private matter.

If one pretended sufficient authority, I'd found doors got opened, and so it was at Intramind Imaging. A Mr Gross would see me. An electric door-latch buzzed and I walked from the entrance lobby into an inner hallway, where cream paint had been used sparingly and there was no carpet underfoot. Ostentation was out.

Mr Gross was 'third door on the left'. Mr Gross's door had his name and a message on it, 'Nick Gross. What the F do you want?'

Nick Gross looked me up and down. 'Who the hell

are *you*? You're not Topline Foods top brass, and you're over-dressed.'

He himself wore a black satin shirt, long hair and a gold earring. Forty-five disintegrating to fifty, I thought, and stuck in a time warp of departing youth. Forceful, though. Strong lines in his old-young face. Authority.

'You're making advertising films for Topline,' I said.

'So what? And if you're another of their whinging accountants sent to beg for better terms, the answer is up yours, mate. It isn't our fault you haven't been able to use those films you spent millions on. They're all brilliant stuff, the best. So you creep back to your Mr Owen effing Yorkshire and tell him there's no deal. Off you trot, then. If he wants his jockey series at the same price as before he has to send us a cheque every week. *Every week* or we yank the series, got it?'

I nodded.

Nick Gross said, 'And tell him not to forget that in ads the magic is the *cutting*, and the cutting comes *last*. No cheque, no cutting. No cutting, no magic. No magic, no message. No message, we might as well stop right now. Have you got it?'

I nodded again.

'Then you scurry right back to Topline and tell them no cheque, no cutting. And that means no campaign. Got it?'

'Yes.'

'Right. Bugger off.'

I meekly removed myself but, seeing no urgent

reason to leave altogether, I turned the wrong way out of his office and walked as if I belonged there down a passage between increasingly technical departments.

I came to an open door through which one could see a screen showing startlingly familiar pieces of an ad campaign currently collecting critical acclaim as well as phenomenally boosting sales. There were burst of pictures as short as three seconds followed by longer intervals of black. Three seconds of fast action. Ten of black.

I stopped, watching, and a man walked into my sight and saw me standing there.

'Yes?' he said. 'Do you want something?'

'Is that,' I said, nodding towards the screen, 'one of the mountain bike ads?'

'It will be when I cut it together.'

'Marvellous,' I said. I took half a step unthreateningly over his threshold. 'Can I watch you for a bit?'

'Who are you exactly?'

'From Topline Foods. I came to see Nick Gross.'

'Ah.' There was a world of comprehension in the monosyllable: comprehension that I immediately aimed to transfer from his brain to mine.

He was younger than Nick Gross and not so mock-rock-star in dress. His certainty shouted from the zany speed of his three-second flashes and the wit crackling in their juxtaposition: he had no need for earrings.

I said, quoting the bike campaign's slogan, 'Every kid under fifty wants a mountain bike for Christmas.'

He fiddled with reels of film and said cheerfully, 'There'll be hell to pay if they don't.'

'Did you work on the Topline ads?' I asked neutrally.

'No, thank Christ. A colleague did. Eight months of award-worthy brilliant work sitting idle in cans on the shelves. No prizes for us, and your top man's shitting himself, isn't he? All that cabbage spent and bugger all back. And all because some twisted little pipsqueak gets the star attraction arrested for something he didn't do.'

I held my breath, but he had no flicker of an idea what the pipsqueak looked like. I said I'd better be going and he nodded vaguely without looking up from his problems.

I persevered past his domain until I came to two big doors, one saying 'Sound Stage. Keep Out' and one, opening outwards with a push-bar, marked 'Backlot'. I pushed that door half open and saw outside in the open air a huge yellow crane dangling a red sports car by a rear axle. Film cameras and crews were busy round it. Work in progress.

I retreated. No one paid me any attention on the way out. This was not, after all, a bank vault, but a dream factory. No one could steal dreams.

The reception lobby, as I hadn't noticed on my way in, bore posters round the walls of past and current purse-openers, all prestigious prize-winning campaigns. Ad campaigns, I'd heard, were now considered an OK step on the career ladder for both directors and actors.

Sell cornflakes one day, play Hamlet the next. Intramind Imagining could speed you on your way.

I drove into the centre of Manchester and anonymously booked into a spacious restful room in the Crown Plaza Hotel. Davis Tatum might have a fit over the expense but if necessary I would pay for it myself. I wanted a shower, room-service and cosseting, and hang the price.

I phoned Tatum's home number and got an answering machine. I asked him to call back to my mobile number and repeated it, and then sat in an armchair watching racing on television – Flat racing at Ascot.

There was no sight of Ellis on the course. The commentator mentioned that his 'ludicrous' trial was due to resume in three days' time, on Monday. Sid Halley, he said, was sensibly keeping his head down as half Ellis's fan club was baying for his blood.

This little tit-bit came from a commentator who'd called me a wizard and a force for good not long ago. Times changed: did they ever. There were smiling close-ups of Ellis's face, and of mine, both helmetless but in racing colours, side by side. 'They used to be the closest of friends,' said the commentator sadly. 'Now they slash and gore each other like bulls.'

Sod him, I thought.

I also hoped that none of Mrs Green Jumper, Marsha Rowse, Mrs Dove, Willy Parrott, the Intramind van driver, Nick Gross and the film cutter had switched on to watch racing at Ascot. I didn't think Owen Yorkshire's sliding glance across my overalls would have left an imprint, but the others would remember me for a day or two. It was a familiar risk, sometimes lucky, sometimes not.

When the racing ended I phoned Intramind Imaging and asked a few general questions that I hadn't thought of in my brief career on the spot as a Topline Foods employee.

Were advertising campaigns originally recorded on film or on disks or on tape, I wanted to know, and could the public buy copies. I was answered helpfully: Intramind usually used film, especially for high-budget location-based ads and no, the public could *not* buy copies. The finished film would eventually be transferred onto Broadcast Quality video tape, known as BETACAM. These tapes then belonged to the clients, who paid television companies for air time. Intramind did not act as an agent.

'Thanks very much,' I said politely, grateful always for knowledge.

Davis Tatum phoned soon after.

'Sid,' he said, 'where are you?'

'Manchester, city of rain.'

It was sunny that day.

'Er . . .' Davis said. 'Any progress?'

'Some,' I said.

'And, er . . .' he hesitated again. 'Did you read India Cathcart this morning?'

292

'She didn't write that she'd seen us at Le Meridien,' I said.

'No. She took your excellent advice. But as to the rest . . .!'

I said, 'Kevin Mills phoned especially to tell me that she didn't write the rest. He did it himself. Policy. Pressure from above. Same old thing.'

'But wicked.'

'He apologised. Big advance.'

'You take it so lightly,' Davis said.

I didn't disillusion him. I said, 'Tomorrow evening – would you be able to go to Archie Kirk's house?'

'I should think so, if it's important. What time?'

'Could you arrange that with him? About six o'clock, I should think. I'll arrive there sometime myself. Don't know when.'

With a touch of complaint he said, 'It sounds a bit vague.'

I thought I'd better not tell him that with burglary, times tended to be approximate.

CHAPTER TWELVE

I phoned *The Pump*, asking for India Cathcart. Silly me.

Number one, she was never in the office on Fridays.

Number two, *The Pump* never gave private numbers to unknown callers.

'Tell her Sid Halley would like to talk to her,' I said, and gave the switchboard operator my mobile number, asking him to repeat it so I could make sure he had written it down right.

No promises, he said.

I sat for a good while thinking about what I'd seen and learned, and planning what I would do the next day. Such plans got altered by events as often as not, but I'd found that no plan at all invited nil results. If all else failed try Plan B. Plan B, in my battle strategy, was to escape with skin intact. Plan B had let me down a couple of times but disasters were like falls in racing; you never thought they'd happen until you were nose down to the turf.

I had some food sent up and thought some more, and at ten-fifteen my mobile buzzed.

'Sid?' India said nervously.

'Hello.'

'Don't say anything! I'll cry if you say anything.' After a pause she said, 'Sid! Are you there?'

'Yes. But I don't want you to cry so I'm not saying anything.'

'Oh, God.' It was half a choke, half a laugh. 'How can you be so . . . so *civilised*?'

'With enormous difficulty,' I said. 'Are you busy on Sunday evening? Your restaurant or mine?'

She said disbelievingly, 'Are you asking me out to dinner?'

'Well,' I said, 'it's not a proposal of marriage. And no knife through the ribs. Just food.'

'How can you *laugh*?'

'Why are you called India?' I asked.

'I was conceived there. What has that got to do with anything?'

'I just wondered,' I said.

'Are you *drunk*?'

'Unfortunately not. I'm sitting soberly in an armchair contemplating the state of the universe, which is C minus, or thereabouts.'

'Where? I mean, where is the armchair?'

'On the floor,' I said.

'You don't trust me!'

'No,' I sighed, 'I don't. But I do want to have dinner with you.'

'Sid,' she was almost pleading, 'be sensible.'

Rotten advice, I'd always thought. But then if I'd been sensible I would have two hands and fewer scars, and I reckoned one had to be *born* sensible, which didn't seem to have happened in my case.

I said, 'Your proprietor – Lord Tilepit – have you met him?'

'Yes.' She sounded a bit bewildered. 'He comes to the office party at Christmas. He shakes everyone's hand.'

'What's he like?'

'Do you mean to look at?'

'For a start.'

'He's fairly tall. Light-brown hair.'

'That's not much,' I said, when she stopped.

'He's not part of my day-to-day life.'

'Except that he burns saints,' I said.

A brief silence, then, 'Your restaurant, this time.'

I smiled. Her quick mind could reel in a tarpon where her red mouth couldn't. 'Does Lord Tilepit,' I asked, 'wear an obvious cloak of power? Are you aware of his power when you're in a room with him?'

'Actually . . . no.'

'Is anyone . . . *could* anyone be physically in awe of him?'

'No.' It was clear from her voice that she thought the idea laughable.

'So his leverage,' I said, 'is all economic?'

'I suppose so.'

'Is there anyone that *he* is in awe of?'

'I don't know. Why do you ask?'

'That man,' I said, 'has spent four months directing his newspaper to ... well ... ruin me. You must allow, I have an interest.'

'But you aren't ruined. You don't sound in the least ruined. And anyway, your ex-wife said it was impossible.'

'She said *what* was impossible?'

'To ... to ...'

'Say it.'

'To reduce you to rubble. To make you beg.'

She silenced me.

She said, 'Your ex-wife's still in love with you.'

'No, not any more.'

'I'm an expert on ex-wives,' India said. 'Wronged wives, dumped mistresses, women curdled with spite, women angling for money. Women wanting revenge, women breaking their hearts. I know the scenery. Your Jenny said she couldn't live in your purgatory, but when I suggested you were a selfish brute she defended you like a tigress.'

Oh *God*, I thought. After nearly six years apart the same old dagger could pierce us both.

'Sid?'

'Mm.'

'Do you still love *her*?'

I found a calm voice. 'We can't go back, and we don't want to,' I said. 'I regret a lot, but it's now finally over. She has a better husband, and she's happy.'

'I met her new man,' India said. 'He's sweet.'

'Yes.' I paused. 'What about your own ex?'

'I fell for his looks. It turned out he wanted an admiration machine in an apron. End of story.'

'Is his name Cathcart?'

'No,' she said. 'Patterson.'

Smiling to myself I said, 'Will you give me your phone number?'

She said, 'Yes,' and did so.

'Kensington Place restaurant. Eight o'clock.'

'I'll be there.'

When I was alone, which was usual nowadays, since Louise McInnes and I had parted, I took off my false arm at bedtime and replaced it after a shower in the morning. I couldn't wear it in showers, as water wrecked the works. Taking it off after a long day was often a pest, as it fitted tightly and tended to cling to my skin. Putting it on was a matter of talcum powder, getting the angle right and pushing hard.

The arm might be worth its weight in gold, as I'd told Trish Huxford, but even after three years, whatever lighthearted front I might now achieve in public, in private the management of amputation still took me a positive effort of the 'get on with it' ethos. I didn't know why I continued to feel vulnerable and sensitive. Too much pride, no doubt.

I'd charged up the two batteries in the charger overnight, so I started the new day, Saturday, with a fresh battery in the arm and a spare in my pocket.

It was by then five days since Gordon Quint had cracked my ulna, and the twinges had become less acute and less frequent. Partly it was because one naturally found the least painful way of performing any action, and partly because the ends of bone were beginning to knit. Soft tissue grew on the site of the break and on the eighth day it would normally begin hardening, the whole healing process being complete within the next week. Only splintered displaced ends caused serious trouble, which hadn't occurred in this case.

When I'd been a jockey the feel of a simple fracture had been an almost twice-yearly familiarity. One tended in jump racing to fall on one's shoulder, quite often at thirty miles an hour, and in my time I'd cracked my collar bones six times each side: only once had it been distinctly bad.

Some jockeys had stronger bones than others, but I didn't know anyone who'd completed a top career unscathed. Anyway, by Saturday morning, Monday's crack was no real problem.

Into my overnight bag I packed the battery charger, washing things, pyjamas, spare shirt, business suit and shoes. I wore both pieces of the tracksuit, white shirt, no tie and the dark trainers. In my belt I carried money

299

and a credit card, and in my pocket a bunch of six keys on a single ring, which bore also a miniature torch. Three of the keys were variously for my car and the entry doors of my flat. The other three, looking misleadingly simple, would between them open any ordinary lock, regardless of the wishes of the owners.

My old teacher had had me practise until I was quick at it. He'd shown me also how to open the simple combination locks on suitcases; the method used by airport thieves.

I checked out of the hotel and found the way back to Frodsham, parking by the kerb within sight of the Topline Foods' wire-mesh gates.

As before, the gates were wide open and, as before, no one going in and out was challenged by the gatekeeper. No one, in fact, seemed to have urgent business in either direction and there were far fewer cars in the central area than on the day before. It wasn't until nearly eleven o'clock that the promised film crews arrived in force.

When getting on for twenty assorted vans and private cars had come to a ragged halt all over the place, disgorging film cameras (Intramind Imaging), a television camera (local station) and dozens of people looking purposeful with heavy equipment and chest-hugged clipboards, I got out of my car and put on the ill-fitting brown overalls, complete with identity badge. Into the boot I locked my bag and also the mobile phone, first taking the SIM card out of it and stowing it in my belt.

'Get into the habit of removing the SIM card,' my supplier had advised. 'Then if someone steals your phone, too bad, they won't be able to use it.'

'Great,' I'd said.

I started the car, drove unhesitatingly through the gates, steered a course round the assorted vans and stopped just beyond them, nearest to the unloading bays. Saturday or not, a few other brown-overall hands were busy on the rollers and the shelf escalator, and I simply walked straight in past them, saying 'Morning' as if I belonged.

They didn't answer, didn't look up, took me for granted.

Inside, I walked up the stairs I'd come down with Willy Parrott and, when I reached the right level, ambled along the gallery until I came to his office.

The sliding glass door was closed and locked and there was no one inside.

The paddles were silent in the vats. None of the day before's hum and activity remained, and almost none of the smells. Instead, there were cameras being positioned below, with Owen Yorkshire himself directing the director, his authoritative voice telling the experts their job.

He was too busy to look up. I went on along the gallery, coming to the fire-door up the flight of metal stairs. The fire-doors were locked at night. Willy had said. By day, they were open. Thankful, I reached in the end the plush carpet of the offices.

301

There was a bunch of three media people in there, measuring angles and moving potted plants. Office work, I gathered, was due for immortality on Monday. Cursing internally at their presence, I walked on towards the lift, passing the open door of 'Customer Relations'. No Marsha Rowse.

To the right of the lift there was a door announcing 'Office Manager, A. Dove', fastened with businesslike locks.

Looking back, I saw the measuring group taking their damned time. I needed them out of there and they infuriatingly dawdled.

I didn't like to hover. I returned to the lift and, to fill in time, opened a nearby door which proved to enclose fire-stairs, as I'd hoped.

Down a floor, and through the fire-door there, I found an expanse of open space, unfurnished and undecorated, the same in area as the office suite above. Up two storeys, above the offices, there was similar quiet, undivided, clean-swept space. Owen Yorkshire had already built for expansion, I gathered.

Cautiously, I went on upwards to the fifth floor, lair of the boss.

Trusting that he was still down among the vats, I opened the fire-door enough to put my head through.

More camera people moved around. Veritable banks of potted plants blazed red and gold. To the left, open opulently-gleaming double doors led into an entertaining and boardroom area impressive enough for a major industry of self-importance. On the right, more double doors led to Yorkshire's own new office; not, from what I could see, a place of paperwork. Polished wood gleamed. Plants galore. A tray of bottles and glasses.

I retreated down the unvarnished nitty-gritty fire-stairs until I was back on the working-office floor, standing there indecisively, wondering if the measurers still barred my purpose.

I heard voices, growing louder and stopping on the other side of the door. I was prepared to go into a busy-employee routine, but it appeared they preferred the lift to the stairs. The lifting machinery whirred on the other side of the stairwell, the voices moved into the lift and diminished to zero. I couldn't tell whether they'd gone up or down, and I was concerned only that they'd *all* gone up and not left one behind.

There was no point in waiting. I opened the fire-door, stepped onto the carpet and looked left and right towards Mrs Dove's domain.

I had the whole office floor to myself.

Great.

Mrs Dove's door was locked twice: an old-looking mortise and a new knob with a keyhole in the centre. These were locks I liked. There could be no nasty surprises like bolts or chains or wedges on the inside: also the emphatic statement of *two* locks probably meant that there were things of worth to guard.

The mortise lock took a whole minute, with the ghost of my old master breathing disapprovingly down my neck. The modern lock took twenty seconds of delicate probing. One had to 'feel' one's way through. False fingers for that, as for much else, were useless.

Once inside Mrs Dove's office I spent time relocking the door so that anyone outside trying it for security would find it as it should be. If anyone came in with keys, I would have warning enough to hide.

Mrs Dove's cote was large and comfortable with a wide desk, several of the Scandinavian-design arm-chairs and grainy blow-up black and white photographs of racing horses round the walls. Along one side there were the routine office machines – fax, copier and large print-out calculator, and, on the desk, a computer, shrouded for the weekend in a fitted cover. There were multiple filing cabinets and a tall white-painted and – as I discovered – locked cupboard.

Mrs Dove had a window with louvred blinds and a distant view of the Mersey. Mrs Dove's office was managing director stuff.

I had only a vague idea of what I was looking for. The audited accounts I'd seen in Companies House seemed not to match the actual state of affairs at Frod-sham. The audit did, of course, refer to a year gone by, to the first with Owen Yorkshire in charge, but the fragile bottom-line profit, as shown, would not suggest or justify expensive publicity campaigns or televised receptions for the notables of Liverpool.

The old French adage 'look for the lady' was a century out of date, my old teacher had said. In modern times it should be 'look for the money'; and, shortly before he died, he had amended that to 'follow the paper'. Shady or doubtful transactions, he said, always left a paper trail. Even in the age of computers, he'd insisted that paper showed the way; and over and over again I'd proved him right.

The paper in Mrs Dove's office was all tidied away in the many filing cabinets, which were locked.

Most filing cabinets, like these, locked all drawers simultaneously with a notched vertical rod out of sight within the right-hand front corner, operated by a single key at the top. Turning the key raised the rod, allowing all the drawers to open. I wasn't bad at opening filing cabinets.

The trouble was that Topline Foods had little to hide, or at least not at first sight. Pounds of paper referred to orders and invoices for incoming supplies; pounds more to sales, pounds more to the expenses of running an industry, from insurance to wages, to electricity to general maintenance.

The filing cabinets took too long and were a waste of time. What they offered was the entirely respectable basis of next year's audit.

I locked them all again and, after investigating the desk drawers themselves, which held only stationery, took the cover off the computer and switched it on, pressing the buttons for 'List Files', and 'Enter'. Scrolls of file names appeared and I tried one at random: 'Aintree'.

Onto the screen came details of the lunch given the day before the Grand National, the guest list, the menu, a summary of the speeches and a list of the coverage given to the occasion in the press.

Nothing I could find seemed any more secret. I switched off, replaced the cover and turned my lock-pickers to the tall white cupboard.

The feeling of time running out, however irrational, shortened my breath and made me hurry. I always envied the supersleuths in films who put their hands on the right papers in the first ten seconds and, this time, I didn't know if the right paper even existed.

It turned out to be primarily not a paper but a second computer.

Inside the white cupboard, inside a drop-down desk arrangement in there, I came across a second keyboard and a second screen. I switched the computer on and nothing happened, which wasn't astounding as I found an electric lead lying alongside, disconnected. I plugged it into the computer and tried again, and with a grumble or two the machine became ready for business.

I pressed 'List Files' again, and this time found myself looking not at individual subjects, but at 'Directories', each of which contained file names such as 'Formula A'.

What I had come across were the more private records, the electronic files, some very secret, some not.

In quick succession I highlighted the 'Directories' and brought them to the screen until one baldly listed

'Quint': but no amount of button-pressing got me any further.

Think.

The reason I couldn't get the Quint information onto the screen must be because it wasn't in the computer.

OK? OK. So where was it?

On the shelf above the computer stood a row of box-files, numbers 1 to 9, but not one labelled Quint.

I lifted down Number 1 and looked inside. There were several letters filed in there, also a blue computer floppy disk in a clear cover. According to the letters, box-file No. 1 referred to loans made to Topline Foods, loans not repaid on the due date. There was also a mention of 'sweeteners' and 'quid pro quos'. I fed the floppy disk into the drive slot in the computer body and got no further than a single unhelpful word on the screen: PASSWORD?

Password? Heaven knew. I looked into the box-files one by one and came to 'Quint' in No. 6. There were three floppies in there, not one.

I fed in the first.

PASSWORD?

Second and third disks – PASSWORD?

Bugger, I thought.

Searching for anything helpful I lifted down a heavy white cardboard box, like a double-height shoebox, that filled the rest of the box-file shelf. In there was a row of big black high-impact plastic protective coverings. I picked out one and unlatched its fastening, and found inside it a video tape, but a tape of double the ordinary width. A label on the tape said 'Broadcast Quality Videotape'. Underneath that was the single word BETACAM. Under that was the legend 'Quint series. 15 × 30 secs.'

I closed the thick black case and tried another one. Same thing. Quint series. 15 × 30 secs. All of the cases held the same.

These double-size tapes needed a special tape player not available in Mrs Dove's office. To see what was on these expensive tapes meant taking one with me.

I could, of course, simply put one of them inside my tracksuit jacket and walk out with it. I could take all the 'PASSWORD' disks. If I did I was a) stealing, b) in danger of being found carrying the goods, and c) making it impossible for any information they held to be used in any later legal enquiry. I would steal the information itself, if I could, but not the hardware.

Think.

As I'd told Charles at Aynsford, I'd had to learn a good deal about computers just to keep a grip on the accelerating world, but the future became the present so fast that I could never get ahead.

Someone tried to open the door.

There was no time to restore the room to normal. I could only speed across the carpet and stand where I would be hidden by the door when it swung inwards. Plan B meant simply running – and I was wearing running shoes.

The knob turned again and rattled, but nothing else happened. Whoever was outside had presumably been either keyless or reassured: in either case it played havoc with my breathing.

Oddly, the pumping adrenalin brought me my computer answer which was, if I couldn't bring the contents of a floppy disk to the screen, I could transfer it whole to *another* computer, one that would give me all the time I needed to crack the password, or to get help from people who could.

Alongside the unconnected electric cable there had been a telephone cable, also unattached. I snapped it into the telephone socket on the computer, thereby connecting Mrs Dove's modem to the world-wide Internet.

It needed a false start or two while I desperately tried to remember half-learned techniques, but finally I was rewarded by the screen prompting: 'Enter telephone number.'

I tapped in my own home number in the flat in Pont Square, and pressed 'Enter', and the screen announced nonchalantly 'dialling in progress', then 'call accepted', then 'transfer', and finally 'transfer complete'.

Whatever was on the first guarded 'Quint' disk was now in my own computer in London. I transferred the other two 'Quint' floppies in the same way, and then the disk from box-file No. 1, and for good measure another from Box 3, identified as 'Tilepit'.

There was no way that I knew of transferring the

BETACAM tapes. Regretfully I left them alone. I looked through the paper pages in the 'Quint' box and make a photocopy of one page – a list of unusual racecourses – folding it and hiding it within the zipped pocket of my belt.

Finally I disconnected the electric and telephone cables again, closed the computer compartment, checked that the box-files and BETACAM tapes were as they should be, relocked the white cupboard, then unlocked and gently opened the door to the passage.

Silence.

Breathing out with relief I relocked Mrs Dove's door and walked along through the row of cubby-hole offices and came to the first setback: the fire-door leading to brown-overalls territory was not merely locked but had a red light shining above it.

Shining red lights often meant alarm systems switched on with depressingly loud sirens ready to screech.

I'd been too long in Mrs Dove's office. I retreated towards her door again and went down the fire-stairs beside the lift, emerging into the ground-floor entrance hall with its glass doors to the parking area beyond.

One step into the lobby proved to be one step too far. Something hit my head rather hard and one of the beefy body-guards in blue flung a sort of strap round my body and effectively pinned my upper arms to my sides.

I plunged about a bit and got another crack on the

head which left me unable to help myself and barely able to think. I was aware of being in the lift, but wasn't quite sure how I'd got there. I was aware of having my ankles strapped together and of being dragged ignominiously over some carpet and dropped in a chair.

Regulation Scandinavian chair with wooden arms, like all the others.

'Tie him up,' a voice said, and a third strap tightened across my chest, so that when the temporary mist cleared I woke to a state of near physical immobility and a mind full of curses.

The voice belonged to Owen Yorkshire. He said, 'Right. Good. Well done. Leave the wrench on the desk. Go back downstairs and don't let anyone up here.'

'Yes, sir.'

'Wait,' Yorkshire commanded, sounding uncertain. 'Are you sure you've got the right man?'

'Yes, sir. He's wearing the identity badge we issued to him yesterday. He was supposed to return it when he left, but he didn't.'

'All right. Thanks. Off you go.'

The door closed behind the bodyguards and Owen Yorkshire plucked the identity badge from my overalls, read the name and flung it down on his desk.

We were in his fifth-floor office. The chair I sat in was surrounded by carpet. Marooned on a desert island, feeling dim and stupid.

The man-to-man all-pals-together act was in abeyance. The Owen Yorkshire confronting me was very angry, disbelieving and, I would have said, *frightened*.

'What are you doing here?' he demanded, bellowing.

His voice echoed and reverberated in the quiet room. His big body loomed over me, his big head close to mine. All his features, I thought, were slightly oversized: big nose, big eyes, wide forehead, large flat cheeks, square jaw, big mouth. The collar-length black waving hair with its grey-touched wings seemed to vibrate with vigour. I would have put his age at forty; maybe a year or two younger.

'Answer,' he yelled. 'What are you doing here?'

I didn't reply. He snatched up from his desk a heavy fifteen-inch-long silvery wrench and made as if to hit my head with it. If that was what his boys-in-blue had used on me, and I gathered it was, then connecting it again with my skull was unlikely to produce any answer at all. The same thought seemed to occur to him, because he threw the wrench down disgustedly onto the desk again, where it bounced slightly under its own weight.

The straps round my chest and ankles were the sort of fawn close-woven webbing often used round suit-cases to prevent them from bursting open. There was no elasticity in them, no stretch. Several more lay on the desk.

I felt a ridiculous desire to chatter, a tendency I'd noticed in the past in mild concussion after racing falls, and sometimes on waking up from anaesthetics. I'd learned how to suppress the garrulous impulse, but it was still an effort, and in this case, essential.

Owen Yorkshire was wearing man-to-man togs; that is to say, no jacket, a man-made-fibre shirt (almost white with vertical stripes made of interlocking beige-coloured horseshoes), no tie, several buttons undone, unmissable view of manly hairy chest, gold chain and medallion.

I concentrated on the horseshoe stripes. If I could count the number of horseshoes from shoulder to waist I would not have any thoughts that might dribble out incautiously. The boss was talking. I blanked him out and counted horseshoes and managed to say nothing.

He went abruptly out of the room, leaving me sitting there looking foolish. When he returned he brought two people with him: they had been along in the reception area, it seemed, working out table placements for Monday's lunch.

They were a woman and a man; Mrs Dove and a stranger. Both exclaimed in surprise at the sight of my trussed self. I shrank into the chair and looked mostly at their waists.

'Do you know who this is?' Yorkshire demanded of them furiously.

The man shook his head, mystified. Mrs Dove, frowning, said to me, 'Weren't you here yesterday? Something about a farmer?'

'This,' Yorkshire said with scorn, 'is Sid Halley.'

The man's face stiffened, his mouth forming an O.

'*This*, Verney,' Yorkshire went on with biting sarcasm, 'is the feeble creature you've spent months thundering on about. *This!* And Ellis said he was dangerous! Just look at him! All those big guns to frighten a mouse.'

Verney *Tilepit*. I'd looked him up in *Burke's Peerage*. Verney Tilepit, 3rd Baron, aged forty-two, a director of Topline Foods, proprietor – by inheritance – of *The Pump*.

Verney Tilepit's grandfather, created a baron for devoted allegiance to the then prime minister, had been one of the old roistering, powerful opinion-makers who'd had governments dancing to their tune. The first Verney Tilepit had put his shoulder to history and given it a shove. The third had surfaced after years of quiescence, primarily, it seemed, to discredit a minor investigator. Policy! His bewildered grandfather would have been speechless.

He was fairly tall, as India had said, and he had brown hair. The flicking glance I gave him took in also a large expanse of face with small features bunched in the middle: small nose, small mouth, small sandy moustache, small eyes behind large, light-framed glasses. Nothing about him seemed physically threatening. Perhaps I felt the same disappointment in my adversary as he plainly did about me.

'How do you know he's Sid Halley?' Mrs Dove asked.

314

Owen Yorkshire said disgustedly, 'One of the TV crew knew him. He swore there was no mistake. He'd filmed him often. He *knows* him.'

Bugger, I thought.

Mrs Dove pulled up the long left sleeve of my brown overalls, and looked at my left hand. 'Yes. It must be Sid Halley. Not much of a champion now, is he?'

Owen Yorkshire picked up the telephone, pressed numbers, waited and forcefully spoke.

'Get over here quickly,' he said. 'We have a crisis. Come to my new office.' He listened briefly. 'No,' he said, 'just get over here.' He slammed down the receiver and stared at me balefully. 'What the sod are you doing here?'

The almost overwhelming urge to tell him got as far as my tongue and was only over-ridden by clamped-shut teeth. One could understand why people confessed. The itch to unburden outweighed the certainty of retribution.

'Answer,' yelled Yorkshire. He picked up the wrench again. 'Answer, you little cuss.'

I did manage an answer of sorts.

I spoke to Verney Tilepit directly in a weak, mock-respectful tone, 'I came to see you . . . sir.'

'My lord,' Yorkshire told me. 'Call him my lord.'

'My lord,' I said.

Tilepit said, 'What for?' and 'What made you think I would be here?'

'Someone told me you were a director of Topline

315

Foods, my lord, so I came here to ask you to stop and I don't know why I've been dragged up here and tied up like this.' The last twenty words just dribbled out. Be *careful*, I thought. *Shut up.*

'To stop *what*?' Tilepit demanded.

'To stop your paper telling lies about me.' Better.

Tilepit didn't know how to answer such naivety. Yorkshire properly considered it barely credible. He spoke to Mrs Dove, who was dressed for Saturday morning, not in office black and white, but in bright red with gold buttons.

'Go down and make sure he hasn't been in your office.'

'I locked it when I left last night, Owen.'

Mrs Dove's manner towards her boss was interestingly like Will Parrott's. All-equals-together; up to a point.

'Go and look,' he said. 'And check that cupboard.'

'No one's opened that cupboard since you moved offices up here this week. And you have the only key.'

'Go and check anyway,' he said.

She had no difficulty with obeying him. I remembered Marsha Rowse's ingenuous statement – 'Mrs Dove says never to make Mr Yorkshire angry.'

Mrs Dove, self-contained, confident, was taking her own advice. She was not, I saw, in love with the man, nor was she truly afraid of him. His temper, I would have thought, was to her more of a nuisance than life – or even job – threatening.

As things stood, or rather as I sat, I saw the wisdom of following Mrs Dove's example for as long as I could.

She was gone a fair time, during which I worried more and more anxiously that I'd left something slightly out of place in that office, that she would know by some sixth sense that someone had been in there, that I'd left some odour in the air despite never using after-shave, that I'd closed the filing cabinets incorrectly, that I'd left visible fingerprints on a shiny surface, that I'd done *anything* that she knew she hadn't.

I breathed slowly, trying not to sweat.

When she finally came back she said, 'The TV crews are leaving. Everything's ready for Monday. The florists are bringing the Lady Mayoress's bouquet at ten o'clock. The red-carpet people are downstairs now measuring the lobby. And, oh, the man from Intramind Imaging says they want a cheque.'

'What about the office?'

'The office? Oh, the office is all right.' She was unconcerned. 'It was all locked. Just as I left it.'

'And the cupboard?' Yorkshire insisted.

'Locked.' She thought he was over-reacting. I was concerned only to show no relief.

'What are you going to do with *him*?' she asked, indicating me. 'You can't keep him here, can you? The TV crew downstairs were talking about him being here. They want to interview him. What shall I say?'

Yorkshire with black humour said, 'Tell them he's all tied up.'

She wasn't amused. She said, 'I'll say he went out the back way. And I'll be off, too. I'll be here by eight, Monday morning.' She looked at me calmly and spoke to Yorkshire, 'Let him go,' she said unemotionally. 'What harm can he do? He's pathetic.'

Yorkshire, undecided, said, 'Pathetic? Why pathetic?'

She paused composedly halfway through the door, and dropped a pearl beyond price.

'It says so in *The Pump*.'

Neither of these two men, I thought, listening to them, was a full-blown criminal. Not yet. Yorkshire was too near the brink.

He still held the heavy adjustable wrench, slapping its head occasionally against his palm, as if it helped his thoughts.

'Please untie me,' I said. At last I found the fatal loquaciousness had abated. I no longer wanted to gabble, but just to talk my way out.

Tilepit himself might have done it. He clearly was unused to – and disturbed by – even this level of violence. His power base was his grandfather's name. His muscle was his hire-and-fire clout. There were only so many top editorships in the British Press and George Godbar, editor of *The Pump*, wasn't going to lose his hide to save mine. Matters of principle were all too often an unaffordable luxury, and I didn't believe that in George Godbar's place, or even in Kevin Mills' or India's, I would have done differently.

Yorkshire said, 'We wait.'

He opened a drawer in his desk and drew out what looked bizarrely like a jar of gherkins. Dumping the wrench temporarily, he unscrewed the lid, put the jar on the desk, pulled out a green finger and bit it, crunching it with large white teeth.

'Gherkin?' he offered Tilepit.

The third baron averted his nose.

Yorkshire, shrugging, chewed uninhibitedly and went back to slapping his palm with the wrench.

'I'll be missed,' I said mildly, 'if you keep me much longer.'

'Let him go,' Tilepit said with a touch of impatience. 'He's right, we can't keep him here indefinitely.'

'We wait,' Yorkshire said heavily, fishing out another gherkin and, to the accompaniment of noisy munching, we waited.

I could smell the vinegar.

The door opened finally behind me and both Yorkshire and Tilepit looked welcoming and relieved.

I didn't. The newcomer, who came round in front of me blankly, was Ellis Quint.

Ellis, in open-necked white shirt; Ellis, handsome, macho, vibrating with showmanship; Ellis, the nation's darling, farcically accused. I hadn't seen him since Ascot races, and none of his radiance had waned.

319

'What's *Halley* doing here?' he demanded, sounding alarmed. 'What has he learned?'

'He was wandering about,' Yorkshire said, pointing a gherkin at me. 'I had him brought up here. He can't have learned a thing.'

Tilepit announced, 'Halley says he came to ask me to stop *The Pump*'s campaign against him.'

Ellis said positively, 'He wouldn't have done that.'

'Why not?' Yorkshire asked. 'Look at him. He's a wimp.'

'A *wimp*!'

Despite my precarious position I smiled involuntarily at the depth of incredulity in his voice. I even grinned at him sideways from below half-lowered eyelids, and saw the same private smile on his face: the acknowledgment of brotherhood, of secrecy, of shared esoteric experience, of cold winter afternoons, perils embraced, disappointments and injuries taken lightly, of indescribable triumphs. We had hugged each other standing in our stirrups, ecstatic after winning posts. We had trusted, bonded, and twinned.

Whatever we were now, we had once been more than brothers. The past – our past – remained. The intense and mutual memories could not be erased.

The smiles died. Ellis said, 'This *wimp* comes up on your inside and beats you in the last stride. This wimp could ruin us all if we neglect our inside rail. This wimp was champion jockey for five or six years and might have been still, and we'd be fools to forget it.'

320

He put his face close to mine. 'Still the same old Sid, aren't you? Cunning. Nerveless. Win at all costs.'

There was nothing to say.

Yorkshire bit into a gherkin. 'What do we do with him, then?'

'First we find out why he's here.'

Tilepit said, 'He came to get *The Pump* to stop—'

'Balls,' Ellis interrupted. 'He's lying.'

'How can you tell?' Tilepit protested.

'I know him.' He said it with authority, and it was true.

'What, then?' Yorkshire asked.

Ellis said to me, 'You'll not get me into court, Sid. Not Monday. Not ever. You haven't been able to break my Shropshire alibi, and my lawyers say that without that the prosecution won't have a chance. They'll withdraw the charge. Understand? I know you *do* understand. You'll have destroyed your own reputation, not mine. What's more, my father's going to kill you.'

Yorkshire and Tilepit showed, respectively, pleasure and shock.

'Before Monday?' I asked.

The flippancy fell like lead. Ellis strode round behind me and yanked back the right front of my brown overalls, and the tracksuit beneath. He tore a couple of buttons off my shirt, pulling that back after, then he pressed down strongly with his fingers.

'Gordon says he broke your collar-bone,' he said.

'Well, he didn't.'

Ellis would see the remains of bruising and he could feel the bumps of callus formed by earlier breaks, but it was obvious to him that his father had been wrong.

'My father will kill you,' he repeated. 'Don't you care?'

Another unanswerable question.

It seemed to me as if the cruel hidden side of Ellis suddenly took over, banishing the friend and becoming the threatened star who had everything to lose. He roughly threw my clothes together and continued round behind me until he stood on my left side.

'You won't defeat me,' he said. 'You've cost me half a million. You've cost me lawyers. You've cost me *sleep*.'

He might insist that I couldn't defeat him, but we both knew I would in the end, if I tried, because he was guilty.

'You'll pay for it,' he said.

He put his hands on the hard shell of my left forearm and raised it until my elbow formed a right angle. The tight strap round my upper arms and chest prevented me from doing anything to stop him. Whatever strength that remained in my upper left arm (and it was, in fact, quite a lot) was held in uselessness by that strap.

Ellis peeled back the brown sleeve, and the blue one underneath. He tore open my shirt cuff and pulled that sleeve back also. He looked at the plastic skin underneath.

'I know something about that arm,' he said. 'I got a

brochure on purpose. That skin is a sort of glove, and it comes off.'

He felt up my arm until, by the elbow, he came to the top of the glove. He rolled it down as far as the wrist and then, with concentration, pulled it off finger by finger, exposing the mechanics in all their detail.

The close-fitting textured glove gave the hand an appearance of life, with knuckles, veins and shapes like finger nails. The works inside were gears, springs and wiring. The bared forearm was bright pink, hard and shiny.

Ellis smiled.

He put his own strong right hand on my electrical left and pressed and twisted with knowledge and then, when the works clicked free, unscrewed the hand round several turns until it came right off.

Ellis looked into my eyes as at a feast. 'Well?' he said.

'You *shit*.'

He smiled. He opened his fingers and let the unscrewed hand fall onto the carpet.

CHAPTER THIRTEEN

Tilepit looked shocked enough to vomit, but not York-shire: in fact, he laughed.

Ellis said to him sharply, 'This man is not funny. Everything that has gone wrong is because of *him*, and don't you forget it. It's this Sid Halley that's going to ruin you, and if you think he doesn't care about what I've just done' – he put his toe against the fallen hand and moved it a few inches – 'if you think it's something to laugh at, I'll tell you that for *him* it's almost unbearable ... but *not* unbearable, is it, Sid?' He turned to ask me, and told Yorkshire at the same time. 'No one yet has invented anything you've found actu-ally unbearable, have they, Sid?'

I didn't answer.

Yorkshire protested, 'But he's only—'

'Don't say *only*,' Ellis interrupted, his voice hard and loud. 'Don't you understand it yet? What do you think he's doing here? How did he get here? What does he know? He's not going to tell you. His nickname's tung-sten carbide – that's the hardest of all metals and it

324

saws through steel. I *know* him. I've almost loved him. You have no idea what you're dealing with, and we've got to decide what to do with him. How many people know he's here?'

'My bodyguards,' Yorkshire said. 'They brought him up.'

It was Lord Tilepit who gave him the real bad news. 'It was a TV crew who told Owen that Sid Halley was in the building.'

'*A TV crew!*'

'They wanted to interview him. Mrs Dove said she would tell them he'd gone.'

'*Mrs Dove!*'

If Ellis had met Mrs Dove he would know, as I did, that she wouldn't lie for Yorkshire. Mrs Dove had seen me, and she would say so.

Ellis asked furiously, 'Did Mrs Dove see him tied in that chair?'

'Yes,' Tilepit said faintly.

'You *stupid* . . .' Words failed Ellis, but for only a few short seconds. 'Then,' he said flatly, 'you can't kill him here.'

'*Kill* him?' Tilepit couldn't believe what he'd heard. His whole large face blushed pink. 'I'm not . . . are you talking about *murder*?'

'Oh yes, my lord,' I said dryly, 'they are. They're thinking of putting your lordship behind bars as an accessory. You'll love it in the slammer.'

I'd meant only to get Tilepit to see the enormity of

what Ellis was proposing. but in doing so I'd made the mistake of unleashing Yorkshire's rage.

He took two paces and kicked my unscrewed hand with such force that it flew across the room and crashed against the wall. Then he realised the wrench was still in his hand and swung it at my head.

I saw the blow coming but couldn't get my head back far enough to avoid it altogether. The wrench's heavy screw connected with my moving cheekbone and tore the skin, but didn't this time knock me silly.

In Owen Yorkshire, the half-slipping brakes came wholly off. Perhaps the very sight of me, left-handless and bleeding and unable to retaliate, was all it took. He raised his arm and the wrench again, and I saw the spite in his face and the implacably murderous intention and I thought of nothing much at all, which afterwards seemed odd.

It was Ellis who stopped him. Ellis caught the descending arm and yanked Owen Yorkshire round sideways, so that although the heavy weapon swept on downwards, it missed me altogether.

'You're *brainless*,' Ellis shouted. 'I said *not in here*. You're a raving lunatic. Too many people know he came here. Do you want to splatter his blood and brains all over your new carpet? You might as well go and shout from the rooftops. Get a grip on that frigging temper and find a tissue.'

'A what?'

'Something to stop him bleeding. Are you terminally

insane? When he doesn't turn up wherever he's expected, you're going to get the police in here looking for him. TV crew! Mrs Dove! The whole frigging country! You get one drop of his blood on anything in here, you're looking at twenty-five years.'

Yorkshire, bewildered by Ellis's attack and turning sullen, said there weren't any tissues. Verney Tilepit tentatively produced a handkerchief; white, clean and embroidered with a coronet. Ellis snatched it from him and slapped it on my cheek, and I wondered if ever, in any circumstances, I could, to save myself, deliberately kill *him*, and didn't think so.

Ellis took the handkerchief away briefly, looked at the scarlet staining the white, and put it back, pressing.

Yorkshire strode about, waving the wrench as if jerked by strings. Tilepit looked extremely unhappy. I considered my probable future with gloom and Ellis, taking the handkerchief away again and watching my cheek critically, declared that the worst of the bleeding had stopped.

He gave the handkerchief back to Tilepit, who put it squeamishly in his pocket, and he snatched the wrench away from Yorkshire and told him to cool down and *plan*.

Planning took them both out of the office, the door closing behind them. Verney Tilepit didn't in the least appreciate being left alone with me and went to look out of the window, to look anywhere except at me.

'Untie me,' I said with force.

327

No chance. He didn't even show he'd heard.

I asked, 'How did you get yourself into this mess?'

No answer.

I tried again. I said, 'If I walk out of here free, I'll forget I ever saw you.'

He turned round, but he had his back to the light and I couldn't see his eyes clearly behind the spectacles.

'You really are in deep trouble,' I said.

'Nothing will happen.'

I wished I believed him. I said, 'It must have seemed pretty harmless to you, just to use your paper to ridicule someone week after week. What did Yorkshire tell you? To save Ellis at all costs. Well, it *is* going to cost you.'

'You don't understand. Ellis is blameless.'

'I understand that you're up to your noble neck in shit.'

'I can't do anything.' He was worried, unhappy and congenitally helpless.

'Untie me,' I said again, with urgency.

'It wouldn't help. I couldn't get you out.'

'Untie me,' I said. 'I'll do the rest.'

He dithered. If he had been capable of reasoned decisions he wouldn't have let himself be used by Yorkshire, but he wasn't the first or last rich man to stumble blindly into a quagmire. He couldn't make up his mind to attempt saving himself by letting me free and, inevitably, the opportunity passed.

328

Ellis and Yorkshire came back, and neither of them would meet my eyes.

Bad sign.

Ellis, looking at his watch, said, 'We wait.'

'What for?' Tilepit asked uncertainly.

Yorkshire answered, to Ellis's irritation, 'The TV people are on the point of leaving. Everyone will be gone in fifteen minutes.'

Tilepit looked at me, his anxieties showing plainly. 'Let Halley go,' he begged.

Ellis said comfortingly, 'Sure, in a while.'

Yorkshire smiled. His anger was preferable, on the whole.

Verney Tilepit wanted desperately to be reassured, but even he could see that if freeing me was the intention, why did we have to wait.

Ellis still held the wrench. He wouldn't get it wrong, I thought. He wouldn't spill my blood. I would probably not know much about it. I might not consciously learn the reciprocal answer to my self-searching question: could *he* personally kill *me*, to save himself? How deep did friendship go? Did it ever have absolute taboos? Had I already, by accusing him of evil, melted his innermost restraints? He wanted to get even. He would wound me any way he could. But *kill* . . . I didn't know.

He walked round behind me.

Time, in a way, stood still. It was a moment in which to plead, but I couldn't. The decision, whatever I said, would be *his*.

He came eventually round to my right-hand side and murmured, 'Tungsten,' under his breath.

Water, I thought, I had water in my veins.

He reached down suddenly and clamped his hand round my right wrist, pulling fiercely upwards.

I jerked my wrist out of his grasp and without warning he bashed the wrench across my knuckles. In the moment of utter numbness that resulted he slid the open jaws of the wrench onto my wrist and tightened the screw. Tightened it further, until the jaws grasped immovably, until they squeezed the upper and lower sides of my wrist together, compressing blood vessels, nerves and ligaments, bearing down on the bones inside.

The wrench was heavy. He balanced its handle on the arm of the chair I was sitting in and held it steady so that my wrist was up at the same level. He had two strong hands. He persevered with the screw.

I said, 'Ellis,' in protest, not from anger or even fear, but in disbelief that he could do what he was doing: in a lament for the old Ellis, in a sort of passionate sorrow.

For the few seconds that he looked into my face, his expression was flooded with awareness . . . and shame. Then the feelings passed, and he returned in deep concentration to an atrocious pleasure.

It was extraordinary. He seemed to go into a kind of trance, as if the office and Yorkshire and Tilepit didn't exist, as if there were only one reality, which was

330

the clench of forged steel jaws on a wrist and the extent to which he could intensify it.

I thought: if the wrench had been lopping shears, if its jaws had been knives instead of flat steel, the whole devastating nightmare would have come true. I shut my mind to it: made it cold. Sweated, all the same.

I thought: what I see in his face is the full-blown addiction; not the cruel satisfaction he could get from unscrewing a false hand, but the sinful fulfilment of cutting off a live hoof.

I glanced very briefly at Yorkshire and Tilepit and saw their frozen bottomless astonishment, and I realised that until that moment of revelation they hadn't wholly believed in Ellis's guilt.

My wrist hurt. Somewhere up my arm the ulna grumbled.

I said, '*Ellis*,' sharply, to wake him up.

He got the screw to tighten another notch.

I yelled at him, '*Ellis*,' and again, '*Ellis*.'

He straightened, looking vaguely down at fifteen inches of heavy stainless steel wrench incongruously sticking out sideways from its task. He tied it to the arm of the chair with another strap from the desk and went over to the window, not speaking, but not rational either.

I tried to dislodge myself from the wrench but my hand was too numb and the grip too tight. I found it difficult to think. My hand was pale blue and grey. Thought was a crushed wrist and an abysmal shattering fear that if the damage went on too long, it would be permanent. Hands could be lost.

Both hands . . . Oh God. Oh *God*.

'Ellis,' I said yet again, but in a lower voice this time: a plea for him to return to the old self, that was there all the time, somewhere.

I waited. Acute discomfort and the terrible anxiety continued. Ellis's thoughts seemed far out in space. Tilepit cleared his throat in embarrassment and Yorkshire, as if in unconscious humour, crunched a gherkin.

Minutes passed.

I said, 'Ellis . . .'

I closed my eyes. Opened them again. More or less prayed.

Time and nightmare fused. One became the other. The future was a void.

Ellis left the window and crossed with bouncing steps to the chair where I sat. He looked into my face and enjoyed what he could undoubtedly see there. Then he unscrewed and untied the wrench with violent jerks and dropped the abominable ratchet from a height onto the desk.

No one said anything. Ellis seemed euphoric, high, full of good spirits, striding round the room as if unable to contain his exhilaration.

I got stabbing pins and needles in my fingers, and thanked the fates for it. My hand felt dreadful but turned slowly yellowish pink.

Thought came back from outer space and lodged again earthily in my brain.

Ellis, coming down very slightly, looked at his watch. He plucked from the desk the cosmetic glove from my false arm, came to my right side, shoved the glove inside my shirt against my chest and, with a theatrical flourish, zipped up the front of my blue tracksuit to keep his gift from falling out.

He looked at his watch again. Then he went across the room, picked up the unscrewed hand, returned to my side, and slapped the dead mechanism into my living palm. There was a powerful impression all round that he was busy making sure no trace of Sid Halley remained in the room.

He went round behind me and undid the strap fastening me into the chair. Then he undid the second strap that held my upper arms against my body.

'Screw the hand back on,' he instructed.

Perhaps because they had bent from being kicked around, or perhaps because my real hand was eighty per cent useless, the screw threads wouldn't mesh smoothly, and after three half turns they stuck. The hand looked re-attached, but wouldn't work.

'Stand up,' Ellis said.

I stood, swaying, my ankles still tied together.

'You're letting him go,' Tilepit exclaimed, with grateful relief.

'Of course,' Ellis said.

Yorkshire was smiling.

333

'Put your hands behind your back,' Ellis told me.

I did so, and he strapped my wrists tight together.

Last, he undid my ankles.

'This way.' He pulled me by the arm over to the door and through into the passage. My feet walked like automatons.

Looking back, I saw Yorkshire put his hand on the telephone. Beyond him, Tilepit was happy with foolish faith.

Ellis pressed the call button for the lift, and the door opened immediately.

'Get in,' he said.

I looked briefly at his now unsmiling face. Expressionless. That made two of us, I thought, two of us thinking the same thing and not saying it.

I stepped into the lift and he leaned in quickly and pressed the button for the ground floor, then jumped back. The door closed between us. The lift began its short journey down.

To tie together the wrists of a man who could unscrew one of them was an exercise in futility. All the same, the crossed threads and my fumbling fingers gave me trouble and some severe moments of panic before the hand slipped free. The lift had already reached its destination by the time I'd shed the tying strap, leaving no chance to emerge from the opening door with everything anywhere near normal.

I put the mechanical hand deep into my right-hand tracksuit trousers pocket. Surreal, I grimly thought. The long sleeve of brown overall covered the void where it belonged.

Ellis had given me a chance. Not much of one, probably, but at least I did have the answer to my question, which was no, he wouldn't personally kill me. Yorkshire definitely would.

The two blue-clad bodyguards were missing from the lobby.

The telephone on the desk was ringing, but the bodyguards were outside, busily positioning a Topline Foods van. One guard was descending from the driver's seat. The other was opening the rear doors.

A van, I understood, for abduction. For a journey to an unmarked grave. A bog job, the Irish called it. How much, I wondered, were they being paid.

Ellis's timing had given me thirty seconds. He'd sent me down too soon. In the lobby I had no future. Out in the open air . . . some.

Taking a couple of deep breaths, I shot out through the doors as fast as I could, and sprinted: and I ran out to the right towards my own car, but veered left round the van toward the open gates.

There was a shout from one of the blue figures, a yell from the second and I thought for a moment that I could avoid them, but to my dismay the gatekeeper himself came to unwelcome life, emerging from his kiosk and barring my exit. Big man in another blue uniform, over-confident.

I ran straight at him. He stood solidly, legs apart, his

weight evenly balanced. He wasn't prepared for or expecting my left foot to knock aside the inside of his knee or for my back to bend and curl like a cannon ball into his stomach: he fell over backwards and I was on my way before he struggled to his knees. The other two, though, had gained ground.

The sort of judo Chico had taught me was in part the stylised advances and throws of a regulated sport and in part an individual style for a one-handed victim. For a start, I never wore, in my private sessions with him, the loose white judogi uniform. I never fought in bare feet but always in ordinary shoes or trainers. The judo I'd learned was how to save my life, not how to earn a black belt.

Ordinary judo needed two hands. Myoelectric hands had a slow response time, a measurable pause between instruction and action. Chico and I had scrapped all grappling techniques for that hand and substituted clubbing; and I used all his lessons at Frodsham as if they were as familiar as walking.

We hadn't exactly envisaged no useful hands at all, but it was amazing what one could do if one wanted to live. It was the same as it had been in races: win now, pay later.

My opponents were straight muscle men with none of the subtlety of the Japanese understanding of lift and leverage and speed. Chico could throw me every time, but Yorkshire's watch-dogs couldn't.

The names of the movements clicked like a litany in

336

my brain – shintai, randori, tai-sabaki. Fighting literally to live, I stretched every technique I knew and adapted others, using falling feints that involved my twice lying on the ground and sticking a foot into a belly to fly its owner over my head. It ended with one blue uniform lying dazed on its back, one complaining I'd broken his nose, and one haring off to the office building with the bad news.

I stumbled out onto the road, feeling that if I went back for my car the two men I'd left on the ground would think of getting up again and closing the gates.

In one direction lay houses, so I staggered that way. Better cover. I needed cover before anyone chased me in the Topline Foods van.

The houses, when I reached them, were too regular, the gardens too tidy and small. I chose one house with no life showing, walked unsteadily up the garden path, kept on going, found myself in the back garden with another row of houses over the back fence.

The fence was too high to jump or vault, but there was an empty crate lying there, a gift from the gods.

No one came out of any of the houses to ask me what I thought I was doing. I emerged into the next street and began to think about where I was going and what I looked like.

Brown overalls. Yorkshire would be looking for brown overalls.

I took them off and dumped them in one of the houses' brown-looking beech hedges.

Taking off the overalls revealed the non-existence of a left hand.

Damn it, I thought astringently. Things are never easy, so *cope.*

I put the pink exposed end of arm, with its bare electrical contacts, into my left-hand jacket pocket, and walked, not ran, up the street. I wanted to run, but hadn't the strength. Weak ... Stamina, a memory: a laugh.

There was a boy in the distance roller-blading, coming towards me and wearing not the ubiquitous baseball cap but a striped woollen hat. That would do, I thought. I fumbled some money out of the zip pocket in my belt and stood in his way.

He tried to avoid me, swerved, overbalanced and called me filthy names until his gaze fell on the money in my hand.

'Sell me your hat,' I suggested.

'Yer wha?'

'Your hat,' I said, 'for the money.'

'You've got blood on your face,' he said.

He snatched the money and aimed to roller-blade away. I stuck out a foot and knocked him off his skates. He gave me a bitter look, and a choice of swear words, but also the hat, sweeping it off and throwing it at me.

It was warm from his head and I put it on hoping he didn't have lice. I wiped my face gingerly on my sleeve and slouched along towards the road with traffic that crossed the end of the residential street ... and saw the Topline Foods van roll past.

Whatever they were looking for, it didn't seem to be a navy tracksuit with a striped woollen hat.

Plan B – run away. OK.

Plan C – where to?

I reached the end of the houses and turned left into what might once have been a shopping street, but which now seemed to offer only estate agents, building societies and banks. Marooned in this unhelpful landscape were only two possible refuges – a betting shop and a place selling ice-cream.

I chose the ice-cream. I was barely through the door when outside the window my own Mercedes went past.

Ellis was driving.

I still had its keys in my pocket. Jonathan, it seemed, wasn't alone in his car-stealing skill.

'What do you want?' a female voice said behind me.

She was asking about ice-cream: a thin young woman, bored.

'Er ... that one,' I said, pointing at random.

'Tub or cone? Large or small?'

'Cone. Small.' I felt disoriented, far from reality. I paid for the ice-cream and licked it, and it tasted of almonds.

'You've cut your face,' she said.

'I ran into a tree.'

There were four or five tables with people sitting at them, mostly adolescent groups. I sat at a table away from the window and within ten minutes saw the Top-line van pass twice more and my own car, once.

Tremors ran in my muscles. Fear, or over-exertion, or both.

There was a door marked Gents at the back of the shop. I went in there when I'd finished the ice-cream and looked at my reflection in the small mirror over the wash basin.

The cut along my left cheekbone had congealed into a blackening line, thick and all too visible. Dampening a paper towel I dabbed gently at the mess, trying to remove the clotted blood without starting new bleeding, but making only a partial improvement.

Locked in a cubicle I had another try at screwing my wandering hand into place, and this time at length got it properly aligned and fastened, but it still wouldn't work. Wretchedly depressed, I fished out the long covering glove and with difficulty, because of no talcum powder and an enfeebled right hand, pulled that too into the semblance of reality.

Damn Ellis, I thought mordantly. He'd been right about some things being near to unbearable.

Never mind. Get on with it.

I emerged from the cubicle and tried my cheek again with another paper towel, making the cut paler, fading it into skin colour.

Not too bad.

The face below the unfamiliar woollen hat looked strained. Hardly a surprise.

I went out through the ice-cream shop and walked along the street. The Topline Foods van rolled past quite slowly, driven by one of the blue guards, who was intently scanning the other side of the road. That bodyguard meant, I thought, that Yorkshire himself might be out looking for me in a car I couldn't recognise.

Perhaps all I had to do was go up to some sensible-looking motorist and say, 'Excuse me, some people are trying to kill me. Please will you drive me to the police station?' And then, 'Who are these people?' 'The managing director of Topline Foods, and Ellis Quint.' 'Oh yes?? And you are . . .??'

I did go as far as asking someone the way to the police station – 'Round there, straight on, turn left – about a mile' – and for want of anything better I started walking that way; but what I came to first was a bus shelter with several people standing in a queue, waiting. I added myself to the patient half dozen and stood with my back to the road, and a woman with two children soon came up behind me, hiding me well.

Five long minutes later my Mercedes pulled up on the far side of the road with a white Rolls Royce behind it. Ellis stepped out of my car and Yorkshire out of the Rolls. They conferred together, furiously stabbing the air, pointing up and down the street while I bent my head down to the children and prayed to remain unspotted.

The bus came while the cars were still there.

Four people got off. The waiting queue, me included, surged on. I resisted the temptation to look out of the

341

window until the bus was travelling again, and then saw with relief that the two men were still talking.

I had no idea where the bus was going.

Who cared? Distance was all I needed. I'd paid to go to the end of the line, wherever that was.

Peaceful Frodsham in Cheshire, sometime Saturday, people going shopping in the afternoon. I felt disconnected from that sort of life; and I didn't know what the time was, as the elastic metal bracelet watch I normally wore on my left wrist had come off in Yorkshire's office and was still there, I supposed.

The bus slowly filled at subsequent stops. Shopping baskets. Chatter. Where was I going?

The end of the line proved to be the railway station in Runcorn, halfway to Liverpool, going north when I needed to go south.

I got off the bus and went to the station. There was no Mercedes, no Rolls Royce, no Topline Foods van in sight, which didn't mean they wouldn't think of buses and trains eventually. Runcorn railway station didn't feel safe. There was a train to Liverpool due in four minutes, I learned, so I bought a ticket and caught it.

The feeling of unreality continued, also the familiar aversion to asking for help from the local police. They didn't approve of outside investigators. If I ever got into messes, besides, I considered it my own responsibility to get myself out. Norman Pictons were rare. In Liverpool, moreover, I was probably counted a local boy who'd been disloyal to his 'roots'.

At Liverpool station I read the well-displayed time-table for trains going south.

An express to London, I thought; then backtrack to Reading and get a taxi to Shelley Green, Archie Kirk's house.

No express for hours. What else, then?

The incredible words took a time to penetrate: Liverpool to Bournemouth, departing at 3.10 pm. A slow train, meandering southwards across England, right down to the Channel, with many stops on the way . . . and one of the stops was *Reading*.

I sprinted, using the last shreds of strength. It was already, according to the big station clock, ticking away at 3.07. Whistles were blowing when I stumbled into the last carriage in the long train. A guard helped thrust me in and close the door. The wheels rolled. I had no ticket and little breath, but a marvellous feeling of escape. That feeling lasted only until the first of the many stops, which I discovered with horror to be Runcorn.

Square one: where I'd started. All fear came flooding back. I sat stiff and immobile, as if movement itself would give me away.

Nothing happened. The train quietly rolled onwards. Out on the platform a blue-clad Topline Foods security guard was speaking into a hand-held telephone and shaking his head.

*

343

Crewe, Stafford, Wolverhampton, Birmingham, Coventry, Leamington Spa, Banbury, Oxford, Didcot, Reading.

It took four hours. Slowly, in that time, the screwed-tight wires of tension slackened to manageable if not to ease. At every stop, however illogical I might tell myself it was, dread resurfaced. Oversize wrenches could kill when one wasn't looking ... Don't be a fool, I thought. I'd bought a ticket from the train conductor between Runcorn and Crewe, but every subsequent appearance of his dark uniform as he checked his customers bumped my heart muscles.

It grew dark. The train clanked and swayed into realms of night. Life felt suspended.

There were prosaically plenty of taxis at Reading. I travelled safely to Shelley Green and rang Archie Kirk's bell.

He came himself to open the door.

'Hello,' I said.

He stood there staring, then said awkwardly, 'We'd almost given you up.' He led the way into his sitting-room. 'He's here,' he said.

There were four of them. Davis Tatum, Norman Picton, Archie himself, and Charles.

I paused inside the doorway. I had no idea what I looked like, but what I saw on their faces was shock.

'Sid,' Charles said, recovering first and standing up. 'Good. Great. Come and sit down.'

The extent of his solicitude always measured the

depth of his alarm. He insisted I take his place in a comfortable chair and himself perched on a hard one. He asked Archie if he had any brandy and secured for me a half-tumblerful of a raw-tasting own-brand from a supermarket.

'Drink it,' he commanded, holding out the glass.

'Charles . . .'

'Drink it. Talk after.'

I gave in, drank a couple of mouthfuls and put the glass on a table beside me. He was a firm believer in the life-restoring properties of distilled wine and I'd proved him right oftener than enough.

I remembered that I still wore the soft stripey hat, and took it off; and its removal seemed to make my appearance more normal to them, and less disturbing.

'I went to Topline Foods,' I said.

I thought: I don't feel well; what's wrong with me?

'You've cut your face,' Norman Picton said.

I also ached more or less all over from the desperate exertions of the judo. My head felt heavy and my hand was swollen and sore from Ellis's idea of entertainment. On the bright side, I was alive and home, safe . . . and reaction was all very well but I was *not* at this point going to faint.

'Sid!' Charles said sharply, putting out a hand.

'Oh . . . yes. Well, I went to Topline Foods.'

I drank some brandy. The weak feeling of sickness abated a bit. I shifted in my chair and took a grip on things.

345

Archie said, 'Take your time,' but sounded as if he didn't mean it.

I smiled. I said, 'Owen Yorkshire was there. So was Lord Tilepit. So was Ellis Quint.'

'Quint!' Davis Tatum exclaimed.

'Mm. Well... you asked me to find out if there was a heavyweight lumbering about behind the Quint business, and the answer is yes, but it is Ellis Quint himself.'

'But he's a playboy,' Davis Tatum protested. 'What about the big man, Yorkshire?' Tatum's own bulk quivered. 'He's getting known. One hears his name.'

I nodded. 'Owen Cliff Yorkshire is a heavyweight in the making.'

'What do you mean?'

I ached. I hadn't really noticed the wear and tear until then. Win now, pay later.

'Megalomania,' I said. 'Yorkshire's on the edge. He has a violent unpredictable temper and an uncontrolled desire to be a tycoon. I'd call it incipient megalomania because he's spending far beyond sanity on self-aggrandisement. He's built an office block fit for a major industry – and it's mostly empty – before building the industry first. He's publicity mad – he's holding a reception for half of Liverpool on Monday. He has plans – a *desire* – to take over the whole horse-feed nuts industry. He employs at least two bodyguards who will murder to order because he fears his competitors will assassinate him... which is paranoia.'

I paused, then said, 'It's difficult to describe the impression he gives. Half the time he sounds reasonable, and half the time you can see that he will simply get rid of anyone who stands in his way. And he is desperate ... *desperate* ... to save Ellis Quint's reputation.'

Archie asked 'Why?' slowly.

'Because,' I said, 'he has spent a colossal amount of money on an advertising campaign featuring Ellis, and if Ellis is found guilty of cutting off a horse's foot, that campaign can't be shown.'

'But a few advertisements can't have cost that much,' Archie objected.

'With megalomania,' I said, 'you don't just make a few economically priced advertisements. You really go to town. You engage an expensive highly prestigious firm – in this case, Intramind Imaging of Manchester – and you travel the world.'

With clumsy fingers I took from my belt the folded copy of the paper in the Quint box-file in Mrs Dove's office.

'This is a list of racecourses,' I said. 'These racecourses are where they filmed the commercials. A thirty-second commercial gleaned from each place. The expense is phenomenal.'

Archie scanned the list uncomprehendingly and passed it to Charles, who read it aloud.

'Flemington, Germiston, Sha Tin, Churchill Downs, Woodbine, Longchamps, K.L., Fuchu ...'

There were fifteen altogether. Archie looked lost.

'Flemington,' I said, 'is where they run the Melbourne Cup in Australia. Germiston is outside Johannesburg. Sha Tin is in Hong Kong. Churchill Downs is where they hold the Kentucky Derby. K.L. is Kuala Lumpur in Malaysia, Woodbine is in Canada, Longchamps is in Paris, Fuchu is where the Japan Cup is run in Tokyo.'

They all understood.

'Those commercials are reported to be brilliant,' I said, 'and Ellis himself wants them shown as much as Yorkshire does.'

'Have you seen them?' Davis asked.

I explained about the box of BETACAM tapes. 'Making those special Broadcasting Quality tapes themselves must have been fearfully expensive – and they need special playing equipment which I didn't find at Topline Foods, so no, I haven't seen them.'

Norman Picton, with his policeman's mind, asked, 'Where did you see the tapes? Where did you get that list of racecourses?'

I said without emotion, 'In an office at Topline Foods.'

He gave me a narrow inspection.

'My car,' I told him, 'is still somewhere in Frodsham. Could you get your pals up there to look out for it?' I gave him its registration number, which he wrote down.

'Why did you leave it?' he asked.

'Er . . . I was running away at the time.' For all that I tried to say it lightly, the grim reality reached them.

'Well,' I sighed, 'I'd invaded Yorkshire's territory. He found me there. It gave him the opportunity to get rid of the person most likely to send Ellis to jail. I accepted that possibility when I went there but, like you, I wanted to know what was causing terrible trouble behind the scenes. And it is the millions spent on those ads.' I paused, and went on, 'Yorkshire and Ellis set out originally, months ago, not to kill me but to discredit me so that nothing I said would get Ellis convicted. They used a figurehead, Topline Foods director Lord Tilepit, because he owned *The Pump*. They persuaded Tilepit that Ellis was innocent and that I was all that *The Pump* has maintained. I don't think Tilepit believed Ellis guilty until today. I don't think *The Pump* will say a word against me from now on.' I smiled briefly. 'Lord Tilepit was duped by Ellis, and so, also, to some extent, was Owen Yorkshire himself.'

'How, Sid?' Davis asked.

'I think Yorkshire too believed in Ellis. Ellis dazzles people. Knowing Ellis, to Yorkshire, was a step up the ladder. Today they planned together to . . . er . . . wipe me out of the way. Yorkshire would have done it himself in reckless anger. Ellis stopped him, but left it to chance that the bodyguards might do it . . . but I escaped them. Yorkshire now knows Ellis is guilty, but he doesn't care. He cares only to be able to show that brilliant ad campaign, and make himself king of the horse-nuts. And, of course, it's not just horse-nuts that it's all about. They're a stepping stone. It's about being the Big Man with the power to bring mayors to his doorstep. If Yorkshire isn't stopped you'll find him manipulating more than *The Pump*. He's the sort of man you get in the kitchens of political clout.'

After a moment, Archie asked, 'So how do we stop him?'

I shifted wearily in the chair and drank some brandy, and said, 'I can, possibly, give you the tools.'

'What tools?'

'His secret files. His financial manoeuvrings. His debts. Details of bribes, I'd guess. Bargains struck. You scratch my back, I'll scratch yours. Evidence of leverage. Details of all his dealings with Ellis, and all his dealings with Tilepit. I'll give you the files. You can take it from there.'

'But,' Archie said blankly, 'where are these files?'

'In my computer in London.'

I explained the Internet transfer and the need for password cracking. I couldn't decide whether they were gladdened or horrified by what I'd done. A bit of both, I thought.

Charles looked the most shocked, Archie the least.

Archie said, 'If I ask you, will you work for me another time?'

I looked into the knowing eyes, and smiled, and nodded.

'Good,' he said.

CHAPTER FOURTEEN

I went home to Aynsford with Charles.

It had been a long evening in Archie's house. Archie, Davis, Norman and Charles had all wanted details, which I found as intolerable to describe as to live through. I skipped a lot.

I didn't tell them about Ellis's games with my hands. I didn't know how to explain to them that, for a jockey, his hands were at the heart of his existence ... of his skill. One knew a horse by the feel of the bit on the reins, one listened to the messages, one interpreted the vibrations, one *talked* to a horse through one's hands. Ellis understood more than most people what the loss of a hand had meant to me, and that day he'd been busy punishing me in the severest way he could think of for trying to strip him of what he himself now valued most, his universal acclaim.

I didn't know how to make them understand that to Ellis the severing of a horse's foot had become a drug more addictive than any substance invented, that the risk and the power were intoxicating; that I'd been lucky he'd had only a wrench to use on me.

I didn't know how near he had come in his own mind to irrevocably destroying the right hand. I only knew that to me it had seemed possible that he would. I couldn't tell them that I'd intensely lived my own nightmare and still shook from fear inside.

I told them only that an adjustable wrench in Yorkshire's hands had cut my face.

I told them a little about the escape by judo, and all about the boy on roller-blades and the ice-cream cone and catching the bus within sight of Yorkshire and Ellis. I made it sound almost funny.

Archie understood that there was a lot I hadn't said, but he didn't press it. Charles, puzzled, asked, 'But did they *hurt* you, Sid?' and I half laughed and told him part of the truth. 'They scared me witless.'

Davis asked about Ellis's Shropshire alibi. His colleague, the Crown Prosecutor, was increasingly concerned, he said, that Ellis's powerful lawyers would prevent the trial from resuming.

I explained that I hadn't had time to find out at what hour Ellis had arrived at the dance.

'Someone must know,' I said. 'It's a matter of asking the local people, the people who helped to park the cars.' I looked at Norman. 'Any chance of the police doing it?'

'Not much,' he said.

'Round the pubs,' I suggested.

Norman shook his head.

'There isn't much time,' Davis pointed out. 'Sid, couldn't you do it tomorrow?'

Tomorrow, Sunday. On Monday, the trial.

Archie said firmly, 'No, Sid can't. There's a limit . . . I'll try and find someone else.'

'Chico would have done it,' Charles said.

Chico had undisputedly saved my pathetic skin that day. One could hardly ask more.

Archie's wife, before she'd driven over to spend the evening with her sister-in-law Betty Bracken, had, it appeared, made a mound of sandwiches. Archie offered them diffidently. I found the tastes of cheese and of chicken strange, as if I'd come upon them new from another world. It was weird the difference that danger and the perception of mortality made to familiar things. Unreality persisted even as I accepted a paper napkin to wipe my fingers.

Archie's doorbell rang. Archie went again to the summons and came back with a pinched displeased expression, and he was followed by a boy that I saw with surprise to be Jonathan.

The rebel wings of hair were much shorter. The yellow streaks had all but grown out. There were no shaven areas of scalp.

'Hi,' he said, looking round the room and fastening his attention on my face. 'I came over to see you. The aunts said you were here. Hey, man, you look different.'

'Three months older,' I nodded, 'so do you.'

Jonathan helped himself to a sandwich, disregarding Archie's disapproval.

'Hi,' he said nonchalantly to Norman. 'How's the boat?'

'Laid up for winter storage.'

Jonathan chewed and told me, 'They won't take me on an oil-rig until I'm eighteen. They won't take me in the navy. I've got good pecs. What do I do with them?'

'Pecs?' Charles asked, mystified.

'Pectoral muscles,' Norman explained. 'He's strong from weeks of water ski-ing.'

'Oh.'

I said to Jonathan, 'How did you get here from Combe Bassett?'

'Ran.'

He'd walked into Archie's house not in the least out of breath.

'Can you ride a motor-bike,' I asked, 'now that you're sixteen?'

'Do me a favour!'

'He hasn't got one,' Archie said.

'He can hire one.'

'But . . . what for?'

'To go to Shropshire,' I said.

I was predictably drowned by protests. I explained to Jonathan what was needed. 'Find someone – anyone – who saw Ellis Quint arrive at the dance. Find the people who parked the cars.'

'He can't go round the pubs,' Norman insisted. 'He's under age.'

Jonathan gave me a dark look which I steadfastly returned. At fifteen he'd bought gin for a truck-driver's wife.

'Hey,' he said. 'Where do I go?'

I told him in detail. His uncle and everyone else disapproved. I took all the money I had left out of my belt and gave it to him. 'I want receipts,' I said. 'Bring me paper. A signed statement from a witness. It's all got to be solid.'

'Is this,' he asked slowly, 'some sort of test?'

'Yes.'

'OK.'

'Don't stay longer than a day,' I said. 'Don't forget, you may be asked to give evidence this week at the trial.'

'As if I could forget.'

He took a bunch of sandwiches, gave me a wide smile, and without more words departed.

'You *can't*,' Archie said to me emphatically.

'What do *you* propose to do with him?'

'But ... he's ...'

'He's bright,' I said. 'He's observant. He's athletic. Let's see how he does in Shropshire.'

'He's only *sixteen*.'

'I need a new Chico.'

'But Jonathan steals cars.'

'He hasn't stolen one all summer, has he?'

'That doesn't mean . . .'

'An ability to steal cars,' I said with humour, 'is in my eyes an asset. Let's see how he does tomorrow, with this alibi.'

Archie, still looking affronted, gave in.

'Too much depends on it,' Davis said heavily, shaking his head.

I said, 'If Jonathan learns nothing, I'll go myself on Monday.'

'That will be too late,' Davis said.

'Not if you get your colleague to ask for one more day's adjournment. Invent flu or something.'

David said doubtfully, 'Are you totally committed to this trial? *The Pump* – or Ellis Quint – they haven't got to you in any way, have they? I mean . . . the hate campaign . . . do you want to back out?'

Charles was offended on my behalf. 'Of course he doesn't,' he said.

Such faith! I said plainly to Davis, 'Don't let your colleague back down. That's the real danger. Tell him to insist on prosecuting, alibi or no alibi. Tell the prosecution service to dredge up some guts.'

'Sid!' He was taken aback. 'They're realists.'

'They're shit-scared of Ellis's lawyers. Well, I'm not. Ellis took the foot off Betty Bracken's colt. I wish like hell that he hadn't, but he did. He has no alibi for that night. You get your colleague to tell Ellis's lawyers that the Northampton colt was a copycat crime. If we can't break Ellis's alibi, copycat is our story and we're sticking to it, and if you have any influence over your colleague the prosecutor, you make sure he gives me a chance in court to say so.'

Davis said faintly, 'I must not instruct him to do anything like that.'

'Just manage to get it dripped into his mind.'

'So there you are, Davis,' Archie said dryly, 'our boy shows no sign of the hate campaign having been successful. Rather the opposite, wouldn't you say?'

'Our boy' stood up, feeling a shade fragile. It seemed to have been a long day. Archie came out into the hall with Charles and me and offered his hand in farewell. Charles shook it warmly. Archie lifted my wrist and looked at the swelling and the deep bruising that was already crimson and black.

He said, 'You've had difficulty holding your glass all evening.'

I shrugged a fraction, long resigned to occupational damage. My hand was still a hand, and that was all that mattered.

'No explanation?' Archie asked.

I shook my head.

'Stone walls tell more,' Charles informed him calmly.

Archie, releasing my wrist, said to me, 'The British Horseracing Board wants you to double-check some of their own members for loyalty. Ultra-secret digging.'

'They wouldn't ask *me*.' I shook my head. 'I'm not the new people's idea of reliable.'

'They asked *me*,' he said, the eyes blazing with amusement. 'I said it would be you or nobody.'

'Nobody,' I said.

He laughed. 'You start as soon as the Quint thing is over.'

The trouble, I thought, as I sat quietly beside Charles as he drove to Aynsford, was that for me the Quint thing would never be over. Ellis might or might not go to jail ... but that wouldn't be the end for either of us. Gordon's obsession might deepen. Ellis might maim more than horses. In both of them lay a compulsive disregard of natural law.

No one could ever be comprehensively protected from obsession. One simply had to live as best one could and disregard the feral threat lying in wait: and I would somehow have to shake Gordon loose from staking out my Pont Square door.

Charles said, 'Do you consider that transferring Yorkshire's secret files to your own computer was at all immoral? Was it ... theft?'

He spoke without censure, but censure was implied. I remembered a discussion we'd had once along the lines of what was honourable and what was not. He'd said I had a vision of honour that made my life a purgatory and I'd said he was wrong, and that purgatory was abandoning your vision of honour and knowing you'd done it. 'Only for you, Sid,' he'd said. 'The rest of the world has no difficulty at all.'

It seemed he was applying to me my own rash judgement. Was stealing knowledge ever justified, or was it not?

I said without self-excuse, 'It was theft, and dishonourable, and I would do it again.'

'And purgatory can wait?'

I said with amusement, 'Have you read *The Pump*?'

After about five miles he said, 'That's specious.'

'Mm.'

'*The Pump*'s a different story of purgatory.'

I nodded and said idly, 'The anteroom to hell.'

He frowned, glancing across in distaste. 'Has hell arrived, then?' He hated excess emotion. I cooled it.

I said, 'No. Sorry. It's been a long day.'

He drove another mile, then asked, 'How *did* you hurt your hand?'

I sighed. 'I don't want a fuss. Don't *fuss*, Charles, if I tell you.'

'No. All right. No fuss.'

'Then . . . Ellis had a go at it.'

'*Ellis?*'

'Mm. Lord Tilepit and Owen Yorkshire watched Ellis enjoy it. That's how they now know he's guilty as charged with the colts. If Ellis had had shears instead of a wrench to use on my wrist, I would now have no hands – and for God's sake, Charles, keep your eyes on the road.'

'But *Sid* . . .'

'No fuss. You promised. There'll be no lasting harm.' I paused. 'If he'd wanted to kill me today, he could

359

have done it, but instead he gave me a chance to escape. He wanted ...' I swallowed, 'he wanted to make me pay for defeating him ... and he did make me pay ... and on Monday in court I'll try to disgrace him for ever ... and I *loathe* it.'

He drove to Aynsford in a silence I understood to be at least empty of condemnation. Braking outside the door he said regretfully, 'If you and Ellis hadn't been such good friends ... no wonder poor Ginnie couldn't stand it.'

Charles saw the muscles stiffen in my face.

'What is it, Sid?' he asked.

'I ... I may have made a wrong assumption.'

'What assumption?'

'Mm?' I said vaguely. 'Have to think.'

'Then think in bed,' he said lightly. 'It's late.'

I thought for half the night. Ellis's revenge brutally throbbed in my fingers. Ellis had tied my wrists and given me thirty seconds ... I would be dead, I thought, if we hadn't been friends.

At Aynsford I kept duplicates of all the things I'd lost in my car – battery charger, razor, clothes and so on – all except the mobile phone. I did have the SIM card, but nothing to use it in.

The no-car situation was solved again by TeleDrive who came to pick me up on Sunday morning.

To Charles's restrained suggestion that I pass the

day resting with him – 'A game of chess, perhaps?' – I replied that I was going to see Rachel Ferns. Charles nodded.

'Come back,' he said, 'if you need to.'

'Always.'

'Take care of yourself, Sid.'

Rachel, Linda told me on the telephone, was home from the hospital for the day.

'Oh, do come,' she begged. 'Rachel *needs* you.'

I went empty-handed with no fish or wigs, but it didn't seem to matter.

Rachel herself looked bloodless, a white wisp of a child in the foothills of a far country. In the five days since I'd seen her, the bluish shadows under her eyes had deepened, and she had lost weight so that the round cheeks of the steroids under the bald head and the big shadowed eyes gave her the look of an exotic little bird, unlike life.

Linda hugged me and cried on my shoulder in the kitchen.

'It's good news, really,' she said, sobbing. 'They've found a donor.'

'But that's *marvellous*.' Like a sunburst of hope, I thought, but Linda still wept.

'He's a Swiss,' she said. 'He's coming from Switzerland. He's coming on Wednesday. Joe is paying his air fare and the hotel bills. Joe says money's no object for his little girl.'

'Then stop crying.'

'Yes . . . but it may not work.'

'And it *may*,' I said positively. 'Where's the gin?'

She laughed shakily. She poured two glasses. I still didn't much care for gin but it was all she liked. We clinked to the future and she began talking about paella for lunch.

Rachel was half sitting, half lying, on a small sofa that had been repositioned in the sitting-room so that she could look straight and closely into the fish tank. I sat beside her and asked how she felt.

'Did my mum tell you about the transplant?' she said.

'Terrific news.'

'I might be able to run again.'

Running, it was clear from her pervading lassitude, must have seemed at that point as distant as the moon.

Rachel said, 'I begged to come home to see the fishes. I have to go back tonight, though. I hoped you would come. I begged God.'

'You knew I would come.'

'I meant *today*, while I'm home.'

'I've been busy since I saw you on Tuesday.'

'I know, Mummy said so. The nurses tell me when you phone every day.'

Pegotty was crawling all round the floor, growing in

362

size and agility and putting everything unsuitable in his mouth; making his sister laugh.

'He's so *funny*,' she said. 'They won't let him come to the hospital. I begged to see him and the fishes. They told me the transplant is going to make me feel sick, so I wanted to come home first.'

'Yes,' I said.

Linda produced steamy rice with bits of chicken and shrimps in, which we all ate with spoons.

'What's wrong with your hand?' Linda asked. 'In places it's almost black.'

'It's only a bruise. It got a bit squashed.'

'You've got sausage fingers,' Rachel said.

'They'll be all right tomorrow.'

Linda returned to the only important subject. 'The Swiss donor,' she said, 'is older than I am! He has three children of his own. He's a school teacher . . . he sounds a nice man, and they say he's so pleased to be going to give Rachel some of his bone marrow.'

Rachel said, 'I wish it had been Sid's bone marrow.'

I'd had myself tested, right at the beginning, but I'd been about as far from a match as one could get. Neither Linda nor Joe had been more than fifty per cent compatible.

'They say he's a ninety per cent match,' Linda said. 'You never get a hundred per cent, even from siblings. Ninety per cent is great.'

She was trying hard to be positive. I didn't know

enough to put a bet on ninety per cent. It sounded fine to me; and no one was going to kill Rachel's own defective bone marrow if they didn't believe they could replace it.

'They're going to put me into a bubble,' Rachel said. 'It's a sort of plastic tent over my bed. I won't be able to touch the Swiss man, except through the plastic. And he doesn't speak English, even. He speaks German. *Danke schön.* I've learned that, to say to him. Thank you very much.'

'He's a lucky man,' I said.

Linda, clearing the plates and offering ice-cream for pudding, asked if I would stay with Rachel while she took Pegotty out for a short walk in fresh air.

'Of course.'

'I won't be long.'

When she'd gone, Rachel and I sat on the sofa and watched the fish.

'You see that one?' Rachel pointed. 'That's the one you brought on Tuesday. Look how fast he swims! He's faster than all the others.'

The black and silver angel fish flashed through the tank, fins waving with vigour.

'He's you,' Rachel said. 'He's Sid.'

I teased her, 'I thought half of them were Sid.'

'Sid is always the fastest one. That's Sid,' she pointed. 'The others aren't Sid any more.'

'Poor fellows.'

She giggled. 'I wish I could have the fishes in the hospital. Mummy asked, but they said no.'

'Pity.'

She sat loosely cuddled by my right arm but held my other hand, the plastic one, pulling it across towards her. That hand still wasn't working properly, though a fresh battery and a bit of tinkering had restored it to half-life.

After a long silent pause, she said, 'Are you afraid of dying?'

Another pause. 'Sometimes,' I said.

Her voice was quiet, almost murmuring. It was a conversation all in a low key, without haste.

She said, 'Daddy says when you were a jockey you were never afraid of anything.'

'Are you afraid?' I asked.

'Yes, but I can't tell Mummy. I don't like her crying.'

'Are you afraid of the transplant?'

Rachel nodded.

'You will die without it,' I said matter-of-factly. 'I know you know that.'

'What's dying like?'

'I don't know. No one knows. Like going to sleep, I should think.' If you were lucky, of course.

'It's funny to think of not being here,' Rachel said. 'I mean, to think of being a *space*.'

'The transplant will work.'

'Everyone says so.'

'Then believe it. You'll be running by Christmas.'

365

She smoothed her fingers over my hand. I could feel the faint vibrations distantly in my forearm. Nothing, I thought, was ever entirely lost.

She said, 'Do you know what I'll be thinking, lying there in the bubble feeling awfully sick?'

'What?'

'Life's a bugger.'

I hugged her, but gently. 'You'll do fine.'

'Yes, but tell me.'

'Tell you what?'

'How to be brave.'

What a question, I thought. I said, 'When you're feeling awfully sick, think about something you like doing. You won't feel as bad if you don't think about how bad you feel.'

She thought it over. 'Is that all?'

'It's quite a lot. Think about fishes. Think about Pegotty pulling off his socks and putting them in his mouth. Think about things you've enjoyed.'

'Is that what *you* do?'

'It's what I do if something hurts, yes. It does work.'

'What if nothing hurts yet, but you're going into something scary!'

'Well . . . it's all right to be frightened. No one can help it. You just don't have to let being frightened stop you.'

'Are you ever frightened?' she asked.

'Yes.' Too often, I thought.

She said lazily, but with certainty, 'I bet you've never

366

been so frightened you didn't do something. I bet you're always brave.'

I was startled. 'No ... I'm not.'

'But Daddy said ...'

'I wasn't afraid of riding in races,' I agreed. 'Try me in a pit full of snakes, though, and I wouldn't be so sure.'

'What about a bubble?'

'I'd go in there promising myself I'd come out running.'

She smoothed my hand. 'Will you come and see me?'

'In the bubble?' I asked. 'Yes, if you like.'

'You'll make me brave.'

I shook my head. 'It will come from inside you. You'll see.'

We went on watching the fish. My namesake flashed his fins and seemed to have endless stamina.

'I'm going into the bubble tomorrow,' Rachel murmured. 'I don't want to cry when they put me in there.'

'Courage is lonely,' I said.

She looked up into my face. 'What does that mean?'

It was too strong a concept, I saw, for someone of nine. I tried to make things simpler.

'You'll be alone in the bubble,' I said. 'So make it your own palace. The bubble is to keep you safe from infection – safe from dragons. You won't cry.'

She snuggled against me; happier, I hoped. I loved

her incredibly. The transplant had a fifty-fifty chance of success. Rachel would run again. She *had* to.

Linda and Pegotty came back laughing from their walk and Linda built towers of bright plastic building blocks for Pegotty to knock down, a game of endless enjoyment for the baby. Rachel and I sat on the floor, playing draughts.

'You always let me be white,' Rachel complained, 'and then you sneak up with the black counters when I'm not looking.'

'You can play black, then.'

'It's disgusting,' she said, five minutes later. 'You're cheating.'

Linda looked up and said, astounded, 'Are you two *quarrelling*?'

'He always wins,' Rachel objected.

'Then don't play with him,' Linda said reasonably.

Rachel set up the white pieces as her own. I neglected to take one of them halfway through the game and with glee she huffed me, and won.

'Did you *let* me win?' she demanded.

'Winning's more fun.'

'I hate you.' She swept all the pieces petulantly from the board and Pegotty put two of them in his mouth.

Rachel, laughing, picked them out again and dried them and set up the board again, with herself again as white, and peacefully we achieved a couple of close finishes until, suddenly as usual, she tired.

Linda produced tiny chocolate cakes for tea and

talked happily of the Swiss donor and how everything was going to be *all right*. Rachel was convinced, I was convinced, Pegotty smeared chocolate all over his face. Whatever the next week might bring to all of us, I thought, that afternoon of hope and ordinariness was an anchor in reality, an affirmation that small lives mattered.

It wasn't until after she'd fastened both children into the back of her car to drive to the hospital that Linda mentioned Ellis Quint.

'That trial is on again tomorrow, isn't it?' she asked.

We stood in the chilly air a few paces from her car. I nodded. 'Don't let Rachel know.'

'She doesn't. It hasn't been hard to keep it all away from her. She never talks about Silverboy any more. Being so ill . ... she hasn't much interest in anything else.'

'She's terrific.'

'Will Ellis Quint go to prison?'

How could I say 'I hope so'? And *did* I hope so? Yet I had to stop him, to goad him, to make him fundamentally wake up.

I said, dodging it, 'It will be for the judge to decide.'

Linda hugged me. No tears. 'Come and see Rachel in her bubble?'

'You couldn't keep me away.'

'God . . . I hope . . .'

'She'll be all right,' I said. 'So will you.'

*

Patient TeleDrive took me back to London and, because of the fixed hour of Linda's departure to the hospital, I again had time to spare before meeting India for dinner.

I again ducked being dropped in Pont Square in the dark evening, and damned Gordon for his vigilance. He had to sleep *sometime* ... but when?

The restaurant called Kensington Place was near the northern end of Church Street, the famous road of endless antique shops, stretching from Kensington High Street in the south, up to Notting Hill Gate, north. Teledrive left me and my overnight bag on the north-west corner of Church Street where I dawdled a while looking in the brightly lit windows of Waterstone's bookshop, wondering if Rachel would be able to hear the store's advertised children's audio tapes in her bubble. She enjoyed the subversive *Just William* stories. Pegotty, she thought, would grow up to be like him.

A large number of young Japanese people were milling around on the corner, all armed with cameras, taking flash pictures of each other. I paid not much attention beyond noticing that they all had straight black hair, short padded jackets, and jeans. As far as one could tell, they were happy. They also surged between me and Waterstone's windows.

They bowed to me politely, I bowed unenthusiastically in return.

They seemed to be waiting, as I was, for some pre-arranged event to occur. I gradually realised from their quiet chatter, of which I understood not a word, that half of them were men, and half young women.

We all waited. They bowed some more. At length, one of the young women shyly produced a photograph that she held out to me. I took it politely and found I was looking at a wedding. At a mass wedding of about ten happy couples wearing formal suits and western wedding dresses. Raising my head from the photo I was met by twenty smiles.

I smiled back. The shy young woman retrieved her photo, nodded her head towards her companions and clearly told me that they were all on their honeymoon. More smiles all round. More bows. One of the men held out his camera to me and asked – I gathered – if I would photograph them all as a group.

I took the camera and put my bag at my feet, and they arranged themselves in pairs neatly, as if they were used to it.

Click. Flash. The film wound on, quietly whirring.

All the newly-weds beamed.

I was presented, one by one, with nine more cameras. Nine more bows. I took nine more photos. Flash. Flash. Group euphoria.

What was it about me, I wondered, that encouraged such trust? Even without language there seemed to be no doubt on their part of my willingness to give pleasure. I mentally shrugged. I had the time, so what the hell. I took their pictures and bowed, and waited for eight o'clock.

I left the happy couples on Waterstone's corner and, carrying my bag, walked fifty yards down Church Street towards the restaurant. There was a narrow side street beside it, and opposite, on the other side of Church Street, one of those quirks of London life, a small recessed area of pavement with a patch of scrubby grass and a park bench, installed by philanthropists for the comfort of footsore shoppers and other vagrants. I would sit there, I decided, and watch for India. The restaurant doors were straight opposite the bench. A green-painted bench made of horizontal slats.

I crossed Church Street to reach it. The traffic on Sunday evening was sporadic to non-existent. I could see a brass plate on the back of the bench: the name of the benefactor who'd paid for it.

I was turning to sit when at the same time I heard a bang and felt a searing flash of pain across my back and into my right upper arm. The impact knocked me over and round so that I ended sprawling on the bench, half lying, half sitting, facing the road.

I thought incredulously, I've been *shot*.

I'd been shot once before. I couldn't mistake the *thud*. Also I couldn't mistake the shudder of outrage that my invaded body produced. Also ... there was a great deal of blood.

I'd been shot by Gordon Quint.

He walked out of the shadows of the side street opposite and came towards me across Church Street. He carried a hand-gun with its black round mouth pointing my way. He was coming inexorably to finish what he'd started, and he appeared not to care if anyone saw him.

I didn't seem to have the strength to get up and run away.

There was nowhere to run to.

Gordon looked like a farmer from Berkshire, not an obsessed murderer. He wore a checked shirt and a tie and a tweed jacket. He was a middle-aged pillar of the community, a judge and jury and a hangman ... a raw, primitive walking act of revenge.

There was none of the screaming out-of-control obscenity with which he'd attacked me the previous Monday. This killer was cold and determined and *reckless*.

He stopped in front of me and aimed at my chest.

'This is for Ginnie,' he said.

I don't know what he expected. He seemed to be waiting for something. For me to protest, perhaps. To plead.

His voice was hoarse.

'For Ginnie,' he repeated.

I was silent. I wanted to stand. Couldn't manage it.

'Say something!' He shouted in sudden fury. The gun wavered in his hand, but he was too close to miss. 'Don't you *understand*?'

I looked not at his gun but at his eyes. Not the best view, I thought inconsequentially, for my last on earth.

Gordon's purpose didn't waver. I might deny him

any enjoyment of my fear, but that wasn't going to stop him. He stared at my face. He didn't blink. No hesitancy there. No withdrawal or doubt. None.

Now, I thought frozenly. It's going to be *now*.

A voice was shouting in the road, urgent, frantic, coming nearer, far too late.

The voice shouted one despairing word.

'*Dad.*'

Ellis ... *Ellis* ... Running across the road waving a five-foot piece of black angled iron fencing and shouting in frenzy at his father, '*Dad* ... Dad ... Don't ... Don't do it.'

I could see him running. Nothing seemed very clear. Gordon could hear Ellis shouting but it wasn't going to stop him. The demented hatred simply hardened in his face. His arm straightened until his gun was a bare yard from my chest.

Perhaps I won't feel it, I thought.

Ellis swung the iron fencing post with two hands and all his strength and *hit his father on the side of the head*.

The gun went off. The bullet hissed past my ear and slammed into a shop window behind me. There were razor splinters of glass and flashes of light and shouting and confusion everywhere.

Gordon fell silently unconscious face down on the scrubby patch of grass, his right hand with the gun underneath him. My blood ran into a scarlet and widening pool below the slats of the bench. Ellis stood for an eternity of seconds holding the fencing post and staring at my eyes as if he could see into my soul, as if he would show me his.

For an unmeasurable hiatus blink of time it seemed there was between us a fusing of psyche, an insight of total understanding. It could have been a hallucination, a result of too much stress, but it was unmistakably the same for him.

Then he dropped the fencing post beside his father, and turned, and went away at a slow run, across Church Street and down the side road, loping, not sprinting, until he was swallowed by shadow.

I was suddenly surrounded by Japanese faces all asking unintelligible questions. They had worried eyes. They watched me bleed.

The gunshots brought more people, but cautiously. Gordon's attack, that to me had seemed to happen in slow motion, had in reality passed to others with bewildering speed. No one had tried to stop Ellis. People thought he was going to bring help.

I lost further account of time. A police car arrived busily, lights flashing, the first manifestation of all that I most detested – questions, hospitals, forms, noise, bright lights in my eyes, clanging and banging and being shoved around. There wasn't a hope of being quietly stitched up and left alone.

I told a policeman that Gordon, though unconscious at present, was lying over a loaded gun.

He wanted to know if Gordon had fired the shots in self-defence.

I couldn't be bothered to answer.

The crowd grew bigger and an ambulance made an entrance.

A young woman pushed the uniforms aside, yelling that she was from the Press. India . . . India . . . come to dinner.

'Sorry,' I said.

'*Sid* . . .' Horror in her voice and a sort of despair.

'Tell Kevin Mills . . .' I said. My mouth was dry from loss of blood. I tried again. She bent her head down to mine to hear above the hubbub.

With humour I said, 'Those Japanese people took a load of photos . . . I saw the flashes . . . so tell Kevin to get moving. Get those photos . . . and he can have . . . his exclusive.'

CHAPTER FIFTEEN

India wasn't a newspaperwoman for nothing. The front page of Monday's *Pump* bore the moderately accurate headline '*Shot in the Back*', with, underneath, a picture taken of Gordon Quint aiming his gun unequivocally at my heart.

Gordon's half-backview was slightly out of focus. My own face was sharp and clear with an expression that looked rather like polite interest, not the fatalistic terror I'd actually felt.

Kevin and *The Pump* had gone to town. *The Pump* acknowledged that its long campaign of denigration of Sid Halley had been a mistake.

Policy, I saw cynically, had done a one-eighty U-turn. Lord Tilepit had come to such senses as he possessed and was putting what distance he could between himself and Ellis Quint.

There had been twenty eyewitnesses to the shooting of J. S. Halley. Kevin, arming himself with a Japanese interpreter, had listened intently, sorted out what he'd been told, and got it right. Throughout his piece there was an undercurrent of awe that no one was going to be able to dispute the facts. He hadn't once said 'It is *alleged.*'

Gordon Quint, though still unconscious, would in due course be 'helping the police with their enquiries'. Kevin observed that Ellis Quint's whereabouts were unknown.

Inside the paper there were more pictures. One showed Ellis Quint, arms and fence post raised, on the point of striking his father. The Japanese collectively, and that one photographer in particular, had not known who Ellis Quint was. Ellis didn't appear on the TV screens in Japan.

Why had there been so much photo coverage? Because Mr Halley, Kevin said, had been kind to the honeymooners, and many of them had been watching him as he walked away down Church Street.

I read *The Pump* while sitting upright in a high bed in a small white side-room in Hammersmith Hospital, thankfully alone except for a constant stream of doctors, nurses, policemen and people with clipboards.

The surgeon who'd dealt with my punctures came to see me at nine in the morning, before he went off duty for the day. He looked a lot worse for wear by then than I did, I thought.

'How are you doing?' he asked, coming in wearily in a sweat-stained green gown.

'As you see ... fine, thanks to you.'

He looked at the newspaper lying on the bed. 'Your

bullet,' he said, 'ploughed along a rib and in and out of your arm. It tore a hole in the brachial artery, which is why you bled so much. We repaired that and transfused you with three units of blood and saline, though you may need more later. We'll see how you go. There's some muscle damage but with physiotherapy you should be almost as good as new. You seem to have been sideways on, when he shot you.'

'I was turning. I was lucky.'

'You could put it like that,' he said dryly. 'I suppose you do know you've also got a half-mended fracture of the forearm? And some fairly deep trauma to the wrist?'

I nodded.

'And we've put a few stitches in your face.'

'Great.'

'I watched you race,' he said. 'I know how fast jockeys heal. Ex-jockeys too, no doubt. You can leave here when you feel ready.'

I said, 'Thanks,' sincerely, and he smiled exhaustedly and went away.

I could definitely move the fingers of my right hand, even though only marginally at present. There had been a private moment of sheer cowardice in the night when I'd woken gradually from anaesthesia and been unable to feel anything in my arm from the shoulder down. I didn't care to confess or remember the abject dread in which I'd forced myself to *look*. I'd awoken once before to a stump. This time the recurrent nightmare of help-

379

lessness and humiliation and no hands had drifted hor-
rifyingly in and out, but when I did finally look, there
was no spirit-pulverising void but a long white-wrapped
bundle that discernibly ended in fingernails. Even so,
they didn't seem to be connected to me. I had lain for
a grim while trying to consider paralysis, and when at
length pain had roared back it had been an enormous
relief: only whole healthy nerves felt that like. I had an
arm . . . and a hand . . . and a life.

Given those, nothing else mattered.

In the afternoon Archie Kirk and Norman Picton
argued themselves past the NO VISITORS sign on the door
and sat in a couple of chairs bringing good news and
bad.

'The Frodsham police found your car,' Norman said,
'but I'm afraid it's been stripped. It's up on bricks – no
wheels.'

'Contents?' I asked resignedly.

'No. Nothing.'

'Engine?'

'Most of it's there. No battery, of course. Everything
movable's missing.'

Poor old car. It had been insured though, for a
fortune.

Archie said, 'Charles sends his regards.'

'Tell him thanks.'

'He said you would be looking as though nothing
much had happened. I didn't believe him. Why aren't
you lying down?'

'It's more comfortable sitting up.'

Archie frowned.

I amplified mildly. 'There's a bullet burn across somewhere below my shoulder blade.'

Archie said, 'Oh.'

They both looked at the tall contraption standing beside the bed with a tube leading from a high bag to my elbow. I explained that too.

'It's one of those "painkiller on demand" things,' I said. 'If I get a twinge I press a button, and bingo, it goes away.'

Archie picked up the copy of *The Pump*. 'All of a sudden,' he commented, 'you're Saint Sid who can do no wrong.'

I said, 'It's enough to make Ellis's lawyers weep.'

'But you don't think, do you,' Archie said doubtfully, 'that Ellis's lawyers *connived* at the hate-Halley campaign?'

'Because they are ethical people?' I asked.

'Yes.'

I shrugged and left it.

'Is there any news of Ellis?' I asked. 'Or of Gordon?'

'Gordon Quint,' Norman said in a policeman's voice, 'was, as of an hour ago, still unconscious in a secure police facility and suffering from a depressed skull fracture. He is to have an operation to relieve the pressure on his brain. No one is predicting when he'll wake up or what mental state he'll be in, but as soon as he can understand, he'll be formally charged with attempted murder. As you know, there's a whole flock of eye-witnesses.'

'And Ellis?' I asked.

Archie said, 'No one knows where he is.'

'It's very difficult,' I said, 'for him to go anywhere without being recognised.'

Norman nodded. 'Someone may be sheltering him. But we'll find him, don't worry.'

'What happened this morning,' I asked, 'about the trial?'

'Adjourned. Ellis Quint's bail is rescinded as he didn't turn up, and also he'll be charged with grievous bodily harm to his father. A warrant for his arrest has been issued.'

'He wanted to prevent his father from murdering,' I said. 'He can't have meant to hurt him seriously.'

Archie nodded. 'It's a tangle.'

'And Jonathan,' I asked, 'did he go to Shropshire?'

Both of them looked depressed.

'Well,' I said, 'didn't he go?'

'Oh yes, he went,' Norman said heavily. 'And he found the car-parkers.'

'Good boy,' I said.

'It's *not* so good.' Archie, like a proper civil servant, had brought with him a briefcase, from which he now produced a paper that he brought over to the bed. I pinned it down with the weight of my still-sluggish left hand and took in its general meaning.

The car-parkers had signed a statement saying that

382

Ellis Quint had dined with media colleagues and had brought several of them with him to the dance at about eleven-thirty. The parkers remembered him – of course – not only because of who he was (there had been plenty of other well-known people at the party, starting with members of the Royal Family) but chiefly because he had given them a tip and offered them his autograph. They knew it was before midnight, because their employment as car-parkers had ended then. People who arrived later had found only one car-parker – a friend of those who'd gone off duty.

Media colleagues! Damn it, I thought. I hadn't checked those with the duchess.

'It's an unbreakably solid alibi,' Norman observed gloomily. 'He was in Shropshire when the yearling was attacked.'

'Mm.'

'You don't seem disappointed, Sid,' Archie said, puzzled.

'No.'

'But why not?'

'I think,' I said, 'that you should phone Davis Tatum. Will he be in his office right now?'

'He might be. What do you want him for?'

'I want him to make sure the prosecutors don't give up on the trial.'

'You told him that on Saturday.' He was humouring me, I thought.

'I'm not light-headed from bullets, Archie, if that's

383

what you think. Since Saturday I've worked a few things out, and they are not as they may seem.'

'What things?'

'Ellis's alibi, for one.'

'But Sid—'

'Listen,' I said. 'This isn't all that easy to say, so don't look at me, look at your hands or something.' They showed no sign of doing so, so I looked at my own instead. I said, 'I have to explain that *I* am not as I seem. When people in general look at me they see a harmless person, youngish, not big, not tall, no threat to anyone. Self-effacing. I'm not complaining about that. In fact, I choose to be like that because people then *talk* to me, which is necessary in my job. They tend to think I'm cosy, as your sister Betty told me, Archie. Owen Yorkshire considers me a wimp. He said so. Only . . . I'm not really like that.'

'A *wimp*!' Archie exclaimed.

'I can look it, that's the point. But Ellis knows me better. Ellis calls me cunning and ruthless, and I probably am. It was he who years ago gave me the nickname of tungsten carbide because I wasn't easy to . . . er . . . intimidate. He thinks I can't be terrified, either, though he's wrong about that. But I don't mind him thinking it. Anyway, unlikely though it may seem, all this past summer, Ellis has been afraid of me. That's why he made jokes about me on television and got Tilepit to set his paper onto me. He wanted to defeat me by ridicule.'

384

I paused. Neither of them said a word.

I went on. 'Ellis is not what he seems, either. Davis Tatum thinks him a playboy. Ellis is tall, good-looking, outgoing, charming and *loved*. Everyone thinks him a delightful entertainer with a knack for television. But he's not only that. He's a strong, purposeful and power-ful man with enormous skills of manipulation. People underestimate both of us for various and different reasons – I look weak and he looks frivolous – but we don't underestimate each other. On the surface, the easy surface, we've been friends for years. But in our time we rode dozens of races against each other, and racing, believe me, strips your soul bare. Ellis and I know each other's minds on a deep level that has nothing to do with afternoon banter or chit-chat. We've been friends on that level too. You and Davis can't believe that it is Ellis himself who is the heavyweight, not Yorkshire, but Ellis and I both know it. Ellis has manipulated everyone – Yorkshire, Tilepit, *The Pump*, public opinion, and also those so-smart lawyers of his who think they're dictating the pace.'

'And you, Sid?' Norman asked. 'Has he pulled your strings too?'

I smiled ruefully, not looking at him. 'He's had a go.'

'I'd think it was impossible,' Archie said. 'He would have to put you underground to stop you.'

'You've learned a lot more about me, Archie,' I said lazily. 'I do like to win.'

He said, 'So why aren't you disappointed that Ellis's Shropshire alibi can't be broken?'

'Because Ellis set it up that way.'

'How do you mean?'

'Ever since the Northampton yearling was attacked, Ellis's lawyers have been putting it about that if Ellis had an unbreakable alibi for that night, which I bet he assured them he had, it would invalidate the whole Combe Bassett case. They put pressure on the Crown Prosecution Service to withdraw, which they've been tottering on the brink of doing. Never mind that the two attacks were separate, the strong supposition arose that if Ellis couldn't have done one, then he hadn't done the other.'

'Of course,' Norman said.

'No,' I contradicted. 'He made for himself a positively unbreakable alibi in Shropshire, and he got someone else to go to Northampton.'

'But no one *would*.'

'One person would. And did.'

'But *who*, Sid?' Archie asked.

'Gordon. His father.'

Archie and Norman both stiffened as if turned to pillars of salt.

The nerves in my right arm woke up. I pressed the magic button and they went slowly back to sleep. Brilliant. A lot better than in days gone by.

'He *couldn't* have done,' Archie said in revulsion.

'He did.'

'You're just *guessing*. And you're *wrong*.'

'No.'

'But *Sid* . . .'

'I know,' I sighed. 'You, Charles and I have all been guests in his house. But he shot me last night. See it in *The Pump*.'

Archie said weakly, 'But that doesn't mean . . .'

'I'll explain,' I said. 'Give me a moment.'

My skin was sweating. It came and went a bit, now and then. An affronted body, letting me know.

'A moment?'

'I'm not made of iron.'

Archie breathed on a smile. 'I thought it was tungsten?'

'Mm.'

They waited. I said, 'Gordon and Ginnie Quint gloried in their wonderful son, their only child. I accused him of a crime that revolted them. Ginnie steadfastly believed in his innocence; an act of faith. Gordon, however reluctantly, faced with all the evidence we gathered from his Land-Rover, must have come to acknowledge to himself that the unthinkable was true.'

Archie nodded.

I went on, 'Ellis's wretched persecution of me didn't really work. Sure, I hated it, but I was still *there*, and meanwhile the time of the trial was drawing nearer and nearer. Whatever odium I drew onto myself by doing it, I was going to describe in court, with all the Press and public listening, just how Ellis could have cut off the foot of Betty's colt. The outcome of the trial – whether or not the jury found Ellis guilty, and whether or not the judge sent him to jail – that wasn't the prime point. The trial itself, and all that evidence, would have convinced enough of the population of his guilt to destroy for ever the shining-knight persona. Topline Foods couldn't have – and, in fact, won't be able to – use those diamond-plated round-the-world ads.'

I took a deep couple of lungfuls of air. I was talking too much. Not enough oxygen, not enough blood.

I said, 'The idea of the Shropshire alibi probably came about gradually, and heaven knows to which of them first. Ellis received an invitation to the dance. The plan must have started from that. They saw it as the one effective way to stop the trial from taking place.'

Hell, I thought, I don't feel well. I'm getting old.

I said, 'You have to remember that Gordon is a farmer. He's used to the idea of the death of animals being profitable. I dare say that the death of one insignificant yearling was as nothing to him when set beside the saving of his son. And he knew where to find such a victim. He would have to have long replaced the shears taken by the police. It must have seemed quite easy, and in fact he carried out the plan without difficulty.'

Archie and Norman listened as if not breathing.

I started again. 'Ellis is many things, but he's not a murderer. If he had been, perhaps he would have been a serial killer of humans, not horses. That urge to do evil – I don't understand it, but it *happens*. Wings off butterflies and so on.' I swallowed. 'Ellis has given me a hard time, but in spite of several opportunities he hasn't let me be killed. He stopped Yorkshire doing it. He stopped his father last night.'

'People can hate until they make themselves ill,' Archie nodded. 'Very few actually murder.'

'Gordon Quint tried it,' Norman pointed out, 'and all but succeeded.'

'Yes,' I agreed, 'but that wasn't to help Ellis.'

'What was it, then?'

'Have to go back a bit.'

I'm too tired, I thought, but I'd better finish it.

I said to Norman, 'You remember that piece of rag you gave me?'

'Yes. Did you do anything with it?'

I nodded.

'What rag?' Archie asked.

Norman outlined for him the discovery at Northampton of the lopping shears wrapped in dirty material.

'The local police found the shears hidden in a hedge,' I said, 'and they brought them into the stud farm's office while I was there. The stud farm's owners, Miss Richardson and Mrs Bethany, were there, and so was Ginnie Quint, who was a friend of theirs and who had gone there to comfort them and sympathise. Ginnie forcibly said how much she despised me for falsely accusing her paragon of a son. For accusing my *friend*. She more or less called me Judas.'

'Sid!'

'Well, that's how it seemed. Then she watched the policeman unwrap the shears that had cut off the yearling's foot and, quite slowly, she went white ... and fainted.'

'The sight of the shears,' Norman said, nodding.

'It was much more than that. It was the sight of the *material*.'

'How do you mean?'

'I spent a whole day ... last Thursday, it seems a lifetime away ... I chased all over London with that little piece of cloth, and I finished up in a village near Chichester.'

'Why Chichester?' Archie asked.

'Because that filthy old cloth had once been part of some bed hangings. They were woven as a special order by a Mrs Patricia Huxford, who's a doll of the first rank. She has looms in Lowell, near Chichester. She looked up her records and found that that fabric had been made nearly thirty years ago especially – and exclusively – for a Mrs Gordon Quint.'

Archie and Norman both stared.

'Ginnie recognised the material,' I said. 'She'd just been giving me the most frightful tongue-lashing for believing Ellis capable of maiming horses, and she suddenly saw, because that material was wrapped round shears, that I'd been right. Not only that, she knew that Ellis had been in Shropshire the night Miss Richardson's colt was done. She knew the importance of his alibi . . . and she saw – she understood – that the only other person who could or would have wrapped lopping shears in that unique fabric was Gordon. Gordon wouldn't have thought twice about snatching up any old rag to wrap his shears in – and I'd guess he decided to dump them because we might have checked Quint shears again for horse DNA if he'd taken them home. Ginnie saw that *Gordon* had maimed the yearling. It was too big a shock . . . and she fainted.'

Archie and Norman, too, looked shocked.

I sighed. 'I didn't understand that then, of course. I didn't understand it until the night before last, when everything sort of *clicked*. But now . . . I think it wasn't just because of Ellis's terrible guilt that Ginnie killed herself last Monday, but because it was Gordon's guilt and reputation as well . . . and then the trial was starting in spite of everything . . . and it was all too much . . . too much to bear.'

I paused briefly and went on, 'Ginnie's suicide sent Gordon berserk. He'd set out to help his son. He'd caused his wife's death. He blamed me for it, for having destroyed his family. He tried to smash my brains in, the morning she'd died. He lay in wait for me outside my flat . . . he was screaming that I'd killed her. Then, last night, in the actual moment that the picture in *The Pump* was taken, he was telling me the bullets were for Ginnie . . . it was my life for hers. He meant . . . he meant to do it.'

I stopped talking.

The white room was silent.

Later in the day I phoned the hospital in Canterbury and spoke to the ward sister.

'How is Rachel?' I asked.

'Mr Halley! But I thought . . . I mean, we've all read *The Pump*.'

'But you didn't tell Rachel, did you?' I asked anxiously.

'No . . . Linda – Mrs Ferns – said not to.'

'Good.'

'But are you—'

'I'm absolutely OK,' I assured her. 'I'm in Hammersmith Hospital. Du Cane Road.'

'The best!' she exclaimed.

'I won't argue. How's Rachel?'

'You know that she's a very sick little girl, but we're all hopeful of the transplant.'

'Did she go into the bubble?'

'Yes, very bravely. She says it's her palace and she's its queen.'

'Give her my love.'

'How soon . . . oh dear, I shouldn't ask.'

'I'll make it by Thursday.'

'I'll tell her.'

*

Kevin Mills and India came to visit before ten o'clock the following morning, on their way to work.

I was again sitting up in the high bed but by then felt much healthier. In spite of my protests my shot and mending arm was still held immobile in a swaddle of splint and bandages. Give it another day's rest, I'd been told, and just practise wiggling your fingers: which was all very well, except that the nurses had been too busy with an emergency that morning to reunite me with my left hand, which lay on the locker beside me. For all that it didn't work properly, I felt naked without it, and could do nothing for myself, not even scratch my nose.

Kevin and India both came in looking embarrassed by life in general and said far too brightly how glad they were to see me awake and recovering.

I smiled at their feelings. 'My dear children,' I said, 'I'm not a complete fool.'

'Look, mate . . .' Kevin's voice faded. He wouldn't meet my eyes.

I said, 'Who told Gordon Quint where to find me?'

Neither of them answered.

'India,' I pointed out, 'you were the only person who knew I would turn up at Kensington Place at eight o'clock on Sunday evening.'

'Sid!' She was anguished, as she had been in Church Street when she'd found me shot; and she wouldn't look at my face, either.

Kevin smoothed his moustache. 'It wasn't her fault.'

'Yours, then?'

'You're right about your not being a fool,' Kevin said. 'You've guessed what happened, otherwise you'd be flinging us out of here right now.'

'Correct.'

'The turmoil started Saturday evening,' Kevin said, feeling secure enough to sit down. 'Of course, as there's no daily *Pump* on Sundays there was hardly anyone in the office. George Godbar wasn't. No one was. Saturday is our night off. The shit really hit the fan on Sunday morning at the editorial meeting. You know editorial meetings ... well, perhaps you don't. All the department editors – news, sport, gossip, features, whatever, and the senior reporters – meet to decide what stories will be run in the next day's paper, and there was George Godbar in a positive *lather* about reversing policy on S. Halley. I mean, Sid mate, you should've heard him swear. I never knew so many orifices and sphincters existed.'

'The boss had leaned on him?'

'*Leaned!* There was a panic. Our lord the proprietor wanted you *bought off.*'

'How nice,' I said.

'He'd suggested ten thousand smackers, George said. Try ten million, I said. George called for copies for everyone of the complete file of everything *The Pump* has published about you since June, nearly all of it in India's column on Fridays. I suppose you've kept all those pieces?'

394

I hadn't. I didn't say so.

'Such *poison*,' Kevin said. 'Seeing it all together like that. I mean, it silenced the whole meeting, and it takes a lot to do that.'

'I wasn't there,' India said. 'I don't go to those meetings.'

'Be fair to India,' Kevin told me, 'she didn't write most of it. I wrote some. You know I did. Six different people wrote it.'

India still wouldn't meet my eyes and still wouldn't sit in the one empty chair. I knew about 'policy' and being burned at the stake and all that, yet week after week I'd dreaded her by-line. Try as I would, I still felt sore from that savaging.

'Sit down,' I said mildly.

She perched uneasily.

'If we make another dinner date,' I said, 'don't tell anyone.'

'Oh, Sid.'

'She didn't mean to get you *shot*, for Chrissakes,' Kevin protested. 'The Tilepit wanted you found. Wanted! He was shitting himself, George said. *The Pump*'s lawyer had passed each piece week by week as being just on the safe side of actionable, but at the meeting, when he read the whole file at once, he was *sweating*, Sid. He says *The Pump* should settle out of court for whatever you ask.'

'And I suppose you're not supposed to be telling me that?'

'No,' Kevin confessed, 'but you did give me the exclusive of the decade.'

'How did Gordon Quint find me?' I asked again.

'George said our noble lord was babbling on about you promising not to send him to jail if you walked out free from somewhere or other, and you *had* walked out free, and he wanted to keep you to your promise. George didn't know what he was talking about, but Tilepit made it crystal that George's job depended on finding you within the next five minutes, if not sooner. So George begged us all to find you, to say *The Pump* would confer sainthood immediately and fatten your bank balance, and I phoned India on the off-chance, and she said not to worry, she would tell you herself... and I asked her how... and where. There didn't seem to be any harm in it.'

'And you told George Godbar?' I said.

Kevin nodded.

'And he,' I said, 'told Lord Tilepit? And *he* told Ellis, I suppose... because Ellis turned up too.'

'George Godbar phoned Ellis's father's house, looking for Ellis. He got an answering machine telling him to try a mobile number, and he reached Gordon Quint in a car somewhere... and he told Gordon where you would be, if Ellis wanted to find you.'

Round and round in circles, and the bullets come out *here*.

I sighed again. I was lucky to be alive. I would settle for that. I also wondered how much I would screw out of *The Pump*. Only enough, I decided, to keep his lordship grateful.

Kevin, the confession over, got restlessly to his feet and walked round the room, stopping when he reached the locker on my left side.

He looked a little blankly at the prosthesis lying there and, after a moment, picked it up. I wished he wouldn't.

He said, surprised, 'It's bigger than I pictured. And heavier. And *hard*.'

'All the better to club you with,' I said.

'Really?' he asked interestedly. 'Straight up?'

'It's been known,' I said, and after a moment he put the arm down.

'It's true what they say of you, isn't it? You may not look it, but you're one tough bugger, Sid, mate, like I told you before.'

I said, 'Not many people look the way they are inside.'

India said, 'I'll write a piece about that.'

'There you are then, Sid.' Kevin was ready to go. 'I've got a rape waiting. Thanks for those Japs. Makes us even, right?'

'Even,' I nodded.

India stood up as if to follow him. 'Stay a bit,' I suggested.

She hesitated. Kevin said, 'Stay and hold his bloody hand. Oh shit. Well ... sorry, mate. *Sorry.*'

'Get out of here,' I said.

India watched him go.

'I'm really sorry,' she said helplessly, 'about getting you shot.'

'I'm alive,' I pointed out, 'so forget it.'

Her face looked softer. At that hour in the morning she hadn't yet put on the sharply outlined lipstick nor the matt porcelain make-up. Her eyebrows were as dark and positive, and her eyes as light blue and clear, but this was the essential India I was seeing, not the worldly package. How different, I wondered, was the inner spirit from the cutting brain of her column.

She too, as if compelled, came over to my left side and looked at the plastic arm.

'How does it work?' she asked.

I explained about the electrodes, as I had for Rachel.

She picked up the arm and put her fingers inside, touching the electrodes. Nothing happened. No movement in the thumb.

I swallowed. I said, 'It probably needs a fresh battery.'

'Battery?'

'It clips into the side. That box-like thing...' I nodded towards the locker. '... that's a battery charger. There's a recharged battery in there. Change them over.'

She did so, but slowly, because of the unfamiliarity. When she touched the electrodes again, the hand obeyed the signals.

'Oh,' she said.

She put the hand down and looked at me.

'Do you,' she said, 'have a steel rod up your backbone? I've never seen anyone more tense. And your forehead's sweating.'

She picked up the box of tissues lying beside the battery charger and offered it to me.

I shook my head. She looked at the immobilised right arm and at the left one on the locker, and a wave of understanding seemed to leave her without breath.

I said nothing. She pulled a tissue out of the box and jerkily dabbed at a dribble of sweat that ran down my temple.

'Why don't you put this arm on?' she demanded. 'You'd be better with it on, obviously.'

'A nurse will do it.' I explained about the emergency. 'She'll come when she can.'

'Let *me* do it,' India said.

'No.'

'Why not?'

'Because.'

'Because you're too bloody *proud*.'

Because it's too private, I thought.

I was wearing one of those dreadful hospital gowns like a barber's smock that fastened at the back of the neck and shapelessly covered the body. A white flap covered my left shoulder, upper arm, elbow, and what remained below. Tentatively India lifted and turned back the flap so that we both could see my elbow and the short piece of forearm.

'You hate it, don't you?' India said.

'Yes.'

'I would hate it, too.'

I can't bear this, I thought. I can bear Ellis unscrewing my hand and mocking me. I can't bear love.

India picked up the electric arm.

'What do I do?' she asked.

I said with difficulty, nodding again at the locker, 'Talcum powder.'

'Oh.' She picked up the prosaic white tinful of comfort for babies. 'In the arm, or on you?'

'On me.'

She sprinkled powder on my forearm. 'Is this right? More?'

'Mm.'

She smoothed the powder all over my skin. Her touch sent a shiver right down to my toes.

'And now?'

'Now hold it so that I can put my arm into it.'

She concentrated. I put my forearm into the socket, but the angle was wrong.

'What do I do?' she asked anxiously.

'Turn the thumb towards you a bit. Not too far. That's right. Now push up while I push down. That top bit will slide over my elbow and grip – and keep the hand on.'

'Like that?' She was trembling.

'Like that,' I said. The arm gripped where it was designed to.

I sent the messages. We both watched the hand open and close.

India abruptly left my side and walked over to where she'd left her handbag, picking it up and crossing to the door.

'Don't go,' I said.

'If I don't go, I'll cry.'

I thought that might make two of us. The touch of her fingers on the skin of my forearm had been a caress more intimate than any act of sex. I felt shaky. I felt more moved than ever in my life.

'Come back,' I said.

'I'm supposed to be in the office.'

'India,' I said, 'please . . .' Why was it always so impossible to plead? 'Please . . .' I looked down at my left hand. 'Please don't *write* about this.'

'Don't *write* about it?'

'No.'

'Well, I won't, but why not?'

'Because I don't like pity.'

She came halfway back to my side with tears in her eyes.

'Your Jenny,' she said, 'told me that you were so afraid of being pitied that you would never ask for help.'

'She told you too much.'

'Pity,' India said, coming a step nearer, 'is actually about as far from what I feel for you as it's possible to get.'

I stretched out my left arm and fastened the hand on her wrist.

She looked at it. I tugged, and she took the last step to my side.

'You're strong,' she said, surprised.

'Usually.'

I pulled her nearer. She saw quite clearly what I intended, and bent her head and put her mouth on mine as if it were not the first time, as if it were natural.

A pact, I thought.

A beginning.

Time drifted when she'd gone.

Time drifted to the midday news.

A nurse burst into my quiet room. 'Don't you have your television on? You're on it.'

She switched on knobs, and there was my face on the screen, with a newsreader's unemotional voice saying, 'Sid Halley is recovering in hospital.' There was a widening picture of me looking young and in racing colours: a piece of old film taken years ago of me weighing-in after winning the Grand National. I was holding my saddle in two hands and my eyes were full of the mystical wonder of having been presented with the equivalent of the Holy Grail.

The news slid to drought and intractable famine.

The nurse said 'Wait,' and twiddled more knobs,

and another channel opened with the news item and covered the story in its entirety.

A woman announcer whose lugubrious voice I had long disliked put on her portentous-solemn face and intoned:

'Police today found the body of Ellis Quint in his car deep in the New Forest in Hampshire...'

Frozen, I heard her saying, as if from a distance, 'Foul play is not suspected. It is understood that the popular broadcaster left a note for his father, still unconscious after an accidental blow to the head on Sunday night. Now over to our reporter in Hampshire, Buddy Bowes.'

Buddy Bowes, microphone in hand, filled the foreground of the screen with, slightly out of focus in the distance behind him, woodland and activity and a rear view of a white car.

'This is a sad ending,' Buddy Bowes said, appearing at least to show genuine regret, 'to a fairytale life. Ellis Quint, thirty-eight, who gave pleasure to millions with his appearances on television, will also be remembered as the dashing champion amateur steeplechase jockey whose courage and gallantry inspired a whole generation to get out there and *achieve*. In recent months he has been troubled by accusations of cruelty to animals from his longtime colleague and supposed friend, Sid Halley, ex-professional top jockey. Quint was due to appear in court yesterday to refute those charges...'

There was a montage of Ellis winning races, striding

403

about in macho riding boots, wowing a chat-show audience, looking glowingly alive and handsome.

'Ellis will be mourned by millions,' Buddy Bowes finished. 'And now back to the studio . . .'

The nurse indignantly switched off the set. 'They didn't say anything about you being shot.'

'Never mind.'

She went away crossly. The reputation Ellis had manufactured for me couldn't be reversed in a night, whatever *The Pump* might now say. Slowly perhaps. Perhaps never.

Ellis was dead.

I sat in the quiet white room.

Ellis was *dead*.

An hour later a hospital porter brought me a letter that he said had been left by hand on the counter of the hospital's main reception desk and overlooked until now.

'Overlooked since when?'

Since yesterday, he thought.

When he'd gone I held the envelope in the pincer fingers and tore it open with my teeth.

The two-page letter was from Ellis, his handwriting strong with life.

It said:

Sid, I know where you are. I followed the ambulance. If you are reading this, you are alive and I am dead. I didn't think you would catch me. I should have known you would.

If you're wondering why I cut off those feet, don't *you* ever want to break out? I was tired of goody goody. I wanted the dark side. I wanted to smash. To explode. To mutilate. I wanted to laugh at the fools who fawned on me. I hugged myself. I mocked the proles.

And that *scrunch*.

I did that old pony to make a good programme. The kid had leukaemia. Sob-stuff story, terrific. I needed a good one. My ratings were slipping.

Then I lusted to do it again. The danger. The risk, the difficulty. And that *scrunch*. I can't describe it. It gives me an ecstasy like nothing else. Cocaine is for kids. Sex is nothing. I've had every woman I ever wanted. The scrunch of bones is a million-volt orgasm.

And then there's you. The only one I've ever envied. I wanted to corrupt you too. No one should be unbendable.

I know all you fear is helplessness. I know you. I wanted to make you helpless in Owen Yorkshire's office but all you did was sit there watching your hand turn blue. I could feel you willing me to be my real self but my real self wanted to hear your wrist bones *crunch* to dust. I wanted to prove that

405

no one was good. I wanted you to crumble. To be like me.

And then, you'll think I'm crazy, I was suddenly glad you weren't sobbing and whining and I was proud of you that you really were how you are, and I felt happy and higher than a kite. And I didn't want you to die, not like that, not for anything. Not because of me.

I see now what I've done. What infinite damage.

My father did that last colt. I talked him into it.

It's cost my mother's life. If my father lives they'll lock him up for trying to kill you. They should have let me hang, back in June, when I tried with my tie.

They say people want to be caught. They go on and on sinning until someone stops them.

The letter ended there except for three words much lower down the page:

You win, Sid.

The two sheets of paper lay on the white bedclothes. No one else would see them, I thought.

I remembered Rachel saying how odd it would be to be dead. To be a *space*.

The whole white room was space.

Good and evil, he had been my friend. An enemy: but finally a friend.

The sour, cruel, underside of him receded.

I had the win, but there was no one standing in the stirrups to share it with.

Regret, loss, acceptance and relief; I felt them all.

I grieved for Ellis Quint.